The

BEACHSIDE

Flower Stall

KAREN CLARKE

The
BEACHSIDE
Flower Stall

bookouture

Published by Bookouture
An imprint of StoryFire Ltd.
23 Sussex Road, Ickenham, UB10 8PN
United Kingdom
www.bookouture.com

ISBN: 978-1-78681-157-8
eBook ISBN: 978-1-78681-156-1

For my family, with all my love

Chapter 1

Tonight was the night. It was Tom's twenty-first, and his parents were throwing a big party. It seemed like the perfect time to tell him I loved him.

'Carrie? Why are you muttering?' Megan whispered, as we were ushered out of the cold into the chandeliered hallway of Hudson Grange, and divested of our coats by a uniformed doorman.

'I'm not,' I said, a flush rising up my throat. In truth, I was rehearsing my opening lines in my head.

'Tom, we've been friends for nearly a year now, but the thing is, I'm in love with you…'

'Tom, I feel as if I've known you forever, and even though you're three years older than me…' Why would I mention my age?

'Tom, I love you, and I think that, maybe, you have feelings for me too.'

'Tom, last night I dreamt we were in bed, listening to a thunderstorm, and you kissed the side of my neck…'

'Tom, I love you.'

'Carrie!' Megan finger-snapped me back to the present, where the air was alive with food smells and the sound of chatter and music. 'You've got a weird look on your face,' she said, tugging some strands of hair from my backcombed heap, and arranging them around my cheeks. Tom liked redheads. His mentioning it a few weeks ago had seemed significant.

'I'm fine,' I lied.

Megan gave me a despairing look. 'We're not gatecrashing, we've been invited,' she reminded me, which wasn't completely true. I'd been invited, and Megan had leapt at the opportunity to come as my 'plus one'. She'd been angling to set foot in Hudson Grange since the moment I told her about Tom. Probably because his father owned a string of hotels, and was rich and well-connected. Things like that mattered to Megan. Tom didn't even live at Hudson Grange. He'd only agreed to the party to please his mother.

'I feel a bit sick,' I confessed, smoothing my hands over the chiffon dress Megan had helped me choose, which flattered my curves without being clingy. Silver peep-toe heels had elevated me above my usual five feet two, but I hadn't quite mastered walking in them without looking as if I'd sprained my ankles.

'You've nothing to feel sick about, you look great,' Megan said, plucking a designer brand lipstick from her clutch, and dabbing at my puckered lips. 'Stop chewing your mouth.'

'I'd have been better drawing on some whiskers,' I said, when she'd finished. 'At least it would make him laugh.'

'Whiskers?' She aimed a dazzling smile at an expensively clad couple, seeming perfectly at home in such grand surroundings, reminding me how very different our backgrounds were; that her parents had paid for her education at Royal Bedworth Girls' School, while I'd been there on a scholarship, and that her mother was descended from royalty. 'Why are you talking about whiskers?'

'It was a joke, because Tom's training to be a vet,' I said, adding, 'he's never seen my legs.'

'You've got a pair, what else does he need to know?' An air of suppressed excitement was making her wide grey eyes look extra shiny. 'Why are you fretting?'

'I'm not,' I mumbled, wondering if I should just come clean about my true feelings for Tom. But they were precious, and Megan was withering on the topic of love because of her parents' divorce, and I knew she'd probably tease me and spoil things.

'Would you like a drink?' A passing waiter stopped and offered his silver tray, eyes fixed on Megan's stretch-knit dress, which had a cut-out panel that displayed her cleavage. As usual, she looked like she'd stepped off a catwalk, with her swishy black hair framing cheekbones you could cut yourself on.

'Thanks.' She helped herself to a flute of champagne, then stiffened. 'Is that him?' Her gaze moved past me and narrowed. 'You didn't tell me he was gorgeous.'

Heart exploding, I spun around to see Tom descending the sweeping staircase, hands in his trouser pockets.

'Carrie!' Brightening, he jumped the last few steps. 'Thanks for coming.' He tugged at his bow tie as though it was strangling him. 'I wasn't sure you would.'

Really? 'Hi,' I said, feeling shy. Seeing him in such different surroundings, scrubbed up and clean-shaven, his dark hair neater than usual, was disconcerting. He was wearing aftershave and the scent ignited my senses.

'You look like nice,' he said, his Marmite-coloured eyes grazing my hair, which immediately felt too bouffy. 'I like the dress.'

Resisting an impulse to cover myself with my hands, I muttered, 'Thanks.' Feeling more was required, I added, 'You too. Nice, you look.' Now I sounded like Yoda.

I handed over a card and a gift-wrapped picture of his dog, which I'd had framed. Hovis – so-called because he resembled a small, brown loaf – was the three-legged terrier I'd rescued from the side of the road the year before, on my way to college, and had driven to the nearest vet's – the one where Tom was working as part of his veterinary training.

'Happy Birthday,' I said, trying and failing to screw up the courage to kiss him. I'd never done it before and worried we might end up bumping noses.

'That's nice of you.' His face relaxed into his familiar crinkly-eyed smile. 'I hope you won't be bored,' he said. 'Most of the guests are people my father knows, and relatives I haven't seen for years.'

''Course not,' I said, in lieu of a witty comeback. Normally we chatted easily, but normally we'd be at the pub, or watching a film with his house-share friends, or walking Hovis on the beach, not standing in a hall that could have passed as a hotel lobby.

Aware of Megan's barely concealed impatience, I said, 'I hope it was okay to bring a friend.' He turned his head, as if he'd only just noticed I wasn't alone. 'This is Megan Ford.'

'Hi, Megan.' He nodded politely.

'Hello, birthday boy.' Why was she using her flirty voice? 'I've heard a lot about you,' she said, dancing her fingernails up his arm as she tilted her cheek for a kiss.

'All good I hope?'

A small gasp escaped me, as Tom's lips briefly touched her skin. *Why* hadn't I kissed him? Now Megan had been more intimate with him than I had.

'Carrie's always going on about your little walks with that adorable dog you adopted,' she said, though I knew for a fact she hated dogs, and had pulled a horrible face when I showed her a picture of Hovis.

'Unlike me, she loves being outdoors.' She threw me an 'aren't you adorable?' look, reducing my status to that of annoying sister. 'When she hasn't got her head buried in a maths book.'

She made it sound as though studying accounts was missing the point of life, but before I could defend myself, she prised my unopened card and gift from Tom's hand, passed them back to me, and slipped her slender arm through his.

'Your home is amazing, you *have* to give me a tour,' she said. 'Then maybe you can introduce me to your parents. I'd love to pick your father's brain.'

Tom threw me a comical look over his shoulder, but let her propel him towards a set of double doors, which were open to reveal a high-ceilinged room, strung with bunting and silver balloons, and filled with people in evening dress, talking over each other.

I dumped his gift and card on a curvy console table and scuttled after them, stiff-legged in my heels, accepting a drink from the waiter's tray on the way. When I looked up, I saw Megan laughing – inappropriately loudly – at something Tom had said, and was hit by a wave of jealousy.

'What are you doing?' I said half an hour later, dragging her into a side room, away from the blaring jazz and over-dressed press of gym-honed bodies.

'What do you mean?' Megan wrenched from my grasp, a frown marring her face. 'I was trying to get Tom to dance.'

'He hates dancing,' I said peevishly.

'He won't when I've finished with him.' Megan grinned, and adjusted her dress with a sexy wiggle.

'He likes the Red Hot Chilli Peppers, not music with trumpets,' I said, with the logic of a grumpy toddler.

'Well, maybe he fancies a change as it's his special birthday.' Megan double-checked her breasts were where they should be. 'Where are his friends, anyway?'

'They didn't want to come,' I said. 'It's not that sort of party.'

Her eyes expanded. 'It sounds like his father is right and he's been hanging out with the wrong people,' she said.

I'd seen her chatting at length with Mr Hudson – an older, more polished version of Tom, with the same, thick dark hair – who'd seemed enchanted by her, and no wonder. She was the sort of girlfriend he'd think perfect for his only son. Tom had been standing stiffly to one side, clutching a bottle of beer, eyes scoping the room (for me, I liked to think). I knew he didn't get on with his father, who was always on at him to join the company, so seizing the opportunity I'd darted over and tried to join in, but they were discussing something political I couldn't grasp. I'd gone to the buffet and Tom had hastily followed. He tried to introduce me to his mother, an elegant woman in a shimmering navy dress, but she was immediately distracted by a woman choking on an olive, then Megan dragged him away.

'His friends are nice,' I said, too loudly now, and a middle-aged man looked over at me as though I'd puked on the carpet. 'They don't fit in here and neither do I.'

'Oh, Bagsy, stop being such a killjoy.' I wished she wouldn't use that silly nickname; a shortened version of Carrier-bag, which was hardly any better. 'Hey, I've seen the way Tom's cousin was looking at you.' Her smile danced back and she grabbed my hands. 'I think he fancies you.'

'Ed?' I said, pulling my chin in. 'The fat one, with the hair?'

'Sshh!' Megan giggled. 'He's cute. I bet he wouldn't mind dirty-dancing with you.'

'I don't dance dirtily, I want to talk to Tom, but you're monopol... mompelising... keeping him to yourself.' I'd had a couple more drinks to steady my nerves, while Megan had worked the room, clutching Tom's arm. I couldn't avoid noticing how perfect they looked together – both tall and good-looking, and easy in a room of people who earned more in a month than my family earned in a year.

'Come on, silly.' Megan backed away, shimmying her shoulders. 'I'll tell Tom you're feeling lonely and send him over.'

'No, don't tell him that!' I stumbled after her, but she was quickly absorbed by a mass of people, including Tom, listening to a member of the band playing a trumpet solo. Tom caught my eye and pretended to stifle a yawn, which made me smile. I made to go over, but Megan whispered something in his ear, and he avoided looking at me after that.

The next hour or so passed in a blur of one-sided conversation with Cousin Ed, who turned out to be an expert on cricket, and loved to talk about it.

'I'm so glad you invited me!' Megan gushed at one point, clutching my hand in passing and planting a kiss on my cheek. 'I think I'm in love!'

My heart lurched. 'Look, about Tom,' I said, keeping hold of her fingers. 'I know I've not said anything before, but—'

'Ooh, somebody wants that dirty dance!' She spun me around to face Ed, before diving out of earshot, and I found myself drawn into an uncoordinated jive.

Afterwards, panting and queasy, I managed a chorus of 'Happy Birthday' when the band struck up, and cheered along when an embarrassed-looking Tom blew his candles out, because I didn't want him to see me looking miserable. All the time, a knot was tightening in my chest. I couldn't even get him alone, never mind pour out my feelings. In desperation, I drank some more champagne. It was now or never.

Rebuffing Ed's request for my phone number, I scanned the room, and caught sight of Megan, ushering Tom through a set of French doors, onto a patio lit with fairy lights.

I followed, as fast as my high heels would allow, with no idea of what I was going to say, but words deserted me when I saw Megan's arms snaking around Tom's neck, and his hands resting on her hips. Time seemed to slow, then speed up again, as she crushed her lips to his.

Turning, I fled through the crowded room and into the hallway, where I fumbled out my phone. 'Dad, can you come and get me?'

Then I sank down on the stairs and burst into tears. Why had Tom been avoiding me? Maybe he was ashamed to be seen with me in front of his family.

'Everything OK?'

My head whipped up. It was Mr Hudson, looking more impatient than concerned, as if I was a wet leaf that had blown in and got stuck to his shoe.

'Fine,' I muttered, my false eyelashes dropping in my lap like a pair of caterpillars. 'Too much to drink, that's all.'

He gave a disdainful smile that was nothing like Tom's, before striding away without another word.

I scrubbed at my face with a tissue, located my coat and headed outside, catching my reflection in an ornate wall mirror on the way. It looked like someone had rubbed coal in my eyes, and my backcombed hair had collapsed like a soufflé.

'Carrie?'

Out on the steps, I turned to see Tom, and backed into the shadows so he couldn't see my tear-ravaged face.

'I have to go,' I said, pretend-rummaging in my purse.

'Already?' Backlit as he was by the twinkling chandelier in the hallway, I couldn't make out his expression. 'I really wanted to talk to you, but...'

'You don't have to,' I said. I couldn't bear for him to know I'd seen him with Megan, or to hear his excuses. 'I've an early start tomorrow, anyway.'

'Oh.' Was that disappointment or relief? 'Megan said you were—'

'She's so lovely, isn't she?' I blurted.

'She seems nice.' He sounded cautious. 'My father certainly likes her. He said he might have a job for her.'

My heart plunged into my hideously uncomfortable shoes. 'I knew she'd be perfect for you.' I sniffed surreptitiously. 'That's why I invited her.' *What the hell?* 'She really likes you, I can tell.'

'Carrie...' He seemed about to say more, when Megan appeared like a heat-seeking missile and rested a proprietorial hand on his shoulder.

'Are you going?' she said, sounding surprised. 'It's only eleven o'clock.'

Tom didn't move, as though her touch had turned him to ice.

'I've an early start,' I said, injecting my voice with a brightness I was far from feeling. 'I'm going to Manchester, to see Sarah.'

'Oh, yes, your sister's at uni there.' Megan gave Tom a meaningful look. 'Another little brain-box, and engaged to her boyfriend already.'

'You didn't mention you were going,' Tom said, coming to life again.

'You have fun, Carrie, I can make my own way home.' Megan spoke at the same time, her eyes glittering as though full of stars. 'Looks like your ride's here.'

I turned to see Dad's car sweeping up the drive. The headlights captured Tom and Megan posed in the doorway, like a perfect couple in a lifestyle magazine, and I wondered how I'd ever thought that Tom would look at me as anything more than a friend.

''Bye, then,' I said, pulling on a smile, feeling as if my heart had snapped in two. 'See you!'

As I stumbled and tripped down the rest of the steps, landing in a knicker-revealing heap, I had no idea it would be ten long years before I would see either of them again.

Chapter 2

'I'd like a bouquet for my girlfriend's birthday, please.'

Nine words I'd hoped not to hear. They weren't unreasonable, considering the man was standing at a flower stall, but I'd only been there an hour.

'A bouquet,' I echoed, trying to radiate confidence. Luckily, he was staring at his phone with a lobotomised expression, while I cast my eyes around for inspiration. An array of colours from the abundance of flowers arranged in silver buckets, bounced off my retinas, and their mingled perfume, combined with the tang of the sea, made my nostrils tingle.

'Roses?' I prompted, my gaze settling on a cluster of silky white petals.

'Christ, no.' He looked at me as if I'd offered him arsenic. 'We're not at that lovey-dovey stage.'

'They don't have to be red,' I said. 'White is for... friendship?' I was certain he had no more idea than I had. It was years since I'd helped my aunt on the stall, and even then I'd only been in charge of handing out change.

'No roses,' he said, adding helpfully, 'she likes pink.'

'Pink, pink, pink,' I murmured. I'd assumed that arranging a bouquet would be a doddle, after a YouTube tutorial, undertaken one wine-fuelled evening with my friend and lodger, Jasmine. We hadn't even used flowers, but had improvised with cutlery, using newspaper for wrapping, finding ourselves hilarious.

'Why me?' I'd said, when Mum had phoned to tell me Dad's sister was in 'one of her funks' and would I mind helping out on her flower stall by the sea in Dorset. 'I'm an accountant, not a florist.'

'An out-of-work accountant,' she kindly reminded me. The car rental company I worked for had recently gone bust. 'And you *have* worked there before.'

'A few weekends for pocket money one summer doesn't count. And anyway, I hardly know Aunt Ruby. I haven't spoken to her once since leaving Dorset.'

'She had a soft spot for you,' Mum said, clearly desperate to get me to agree.

'Why can't you do it?'

'Because Sarah might need me.' Although that might have been true – my sister's five-year-old twins would give Supernanny a run for her money – the real reason was that Mum didn't get on with her sister-in-law, and Dad wasn't much better.

'Doesn't Ruby have anyone else who could help?'

But it turned out her part-time assistant, Jane, had called Dad as a 'last resort', because she'd booked a holiday she couldn't cancel and there was no one else to ask.

'Can't she just shut the stall down?'

'Of course not, it's her livelihood. And it'll only be for a few weeks, until she's pulled herself together.' Mum's voice had turned rather acid. She was probably recalling the time she and Dad had paid Ruby a visit, just after she opened her stall. Apparently, it had been super-awkward, with Dad going into technical mode, asking how it fitted together, and Mum declaring it must be a faff, and Ruby giving her a pitying look as if, 'Despite running an engineering business with your dad for thirty years, I know nothing!'

Then Dad started advising Ruby about money, and she told him she'd managed without him all these years and to 'do one'.

'Anyway, we're off to Kazakhstan next weekend,' Mum had said, when I continued to protest. After Sarah had had the twins, our parents had sold their business in Dorset and moved up to Manchester to be closer to us all, and she and Dad had developed a thing for visiting far-flung countries.

'Well, our water pipe burst,' I'd parried. 'Workmen are coming next week.'

'It's the summer holidays, so Jasmine will be there,' Mum shot back.

Jasmine was a science teacher, and in the enviable position of having six weeks off work. The cutlery arranging had been her bright idea.

'Go,' she'd urged, when I told her about the flower stall. 'I'll be here until the last week of the hols, and you could do with a break.'

'I have to find a new job.'

'You can do that when you get back. I know you've got savings.' She gave me a sly look. 'Anyway, wasn't that bloke you were in love with from Dorset?'

She'd got me tipsy one night and I'd spilled the whole Tom saga, telling her how Megan had called the next day, to say she'd spent the night with him, and that was when I'd decided to stay in Manchester and finish my accountancy course at the university there.

'Didn't you call him, or anything?'

'Yes, but I kept getting his voicemail. He couldn't face me, even on the phone,' I'd wailed, over-dramatic on three and a half vodka-tonics, and I made her promise never to mention him again.

But in the end, the thought of a summer break in Dorset was what had swung it. That, and a surreptitious Google search, which unexpectedly revealed that Tom now owned a veterinary practice in – of all places – Shipley, where Ruby had her flower stall.

But now I was there, things were turning out to be anything but simple. Jane, who'd promised to run me through everything before going on holiday, had been taken ill after erecting the stall with the help of her strapping son, Calum, who'd driven her home in the van, while she muttered about a stomach bug.

'Listen, I haven't got all day.' The man's voice dragged me back to the moment, where I was dithering by a bucket of dusky-pink... I squinted at the wooden label... dahlias.

'These look nice.' I grabbed some, then plucked out a mass of green stuff speckled with white bits, water dripping on my feet.

With hindsight, it probably hadn't been a good idea to wear my work clothes. I looked like I was going for an interview at a bank, as Jane had pointed out, eyeing my elephant-grey trousers before her face had turned a similar shade of grey.

'You could put some fuchsias in too, for contrast,' said a voice.

With a start, I saw a lady standing in front of me, with neatly bobbed hair in a shade my mum would call ash-blonde. She looked about seventy, but well preserved, in a figure-flattering dress and sensible sandals, and was pointing to one of the buckets.

'Thanks,' I said, diving for a handful.

'Doris Day,' she said, rather confusingly. 'Where's Ruby?'

'She's, um, having a little break.' An image of my aunt's ashen face flashed into my head. I'd been shocked by how unhappy she'd looked, peering at me from the cocoon of her duvet, when I'd arrived the night before. 'I'm Carrie, her niece.' I waited.

'I just told you,' she said, a crease between her eyebrows. 'Doris Day.'

'Oh! Right. I'm sorry.'

'And Jane?'

'Ill,' I said.

'Oh dear.' Doris Day looked concerned. 'She's my neighbour. We live on Maple Hill, on the other side of the parade,' she elaborated.

'Can we move this along?' The man tucked his phone away and pushed back his floppy fringe. 'I haven't got all day.'

I glanced at the sea – a twinkling ribbon of silver in the August sunshine – and wished I was in it.

'Use the brown paper.' Doris moved closer to oversee proceedings, shifting her wicker basket from the crook of one elbow to the other. 'I've seen how it's done, my dear. I've been coming by for years.'

Aware of the man's scrutiny, I moved to the workbench, which was covered with a daisy-patterned oilskin cloth, and scrunched a wad of brown paper around the flower stems, careful not to crush them.

'Now use Sellotape.' Doris indicated one of several plastic trays.

'Ribbon?' I asked. Doris, not the customer.

She turned to him. 'Ribbon?'

He shrugged and scratched his chin. 'S'pose.'

'In there.' She flicked her gaze to a different tray, filled with colourful spools. I located some scissors and snipped off a length of pink ribbon, and tied it around the paper with fingers that felt fatter than usual.

'Use the blade to make it go curly.'

'I was going to.' I wasn't, but I did my best, and managed not to slice my finger off.

Doris gave the result an appraising look. 'Hmmm,' she said. 'Not bad.'

'It's a bit pink,' said the man.

Make your mind up. I remembered something I'd skim-read in one of Jasmine's interior magazines. 'Block colours are in at the moment.'

'Really?'

'Really?' said Doris, less sarcastically than the man.

'Really.' I could feel my hair sliding out of its clip, and knew my face was as pink and shiny as the flower petals, but not as attractive. 'I'm sure she'll love it.'

'Of course she will,' agreed Doris, in a tone that brooked no argument.

Looking resigned, the man dug around in his pocket. 'How much?'

Doris gestured at the price list pegged to one of the poles supporting the green-and-cream canopy overhead. 'Twelve pounds.'

'Five,' I corrected. Charging more for my amateurish attempt would have felt like daylight robbery.

Evidently impressed, the man handed over a note, which I fumbled into the money-belt Jane had insisted I wear, pretending not to hear Doris's sharp intake of breath.

The man strode away without a goodbye, and one of the flowers slid out of the wrapping and landed on the pavement.

Luckily, neither he nor Doris noticed.

'You should have charged him double, rude little bugger,' she said tartly. 'Tell Ruby I'll pop in some time.'

Before I could respond, she was walking away, basket swinging, one hand fluttering a wave.

A little shaky, I reached for my bag and pulled out my phone.

Jasmine had texted: Remember to relax and breathe. USE YOUR APP!! She was a fan of relaxation apps, and had insisted I download one, but this was hardly the time for whale music. Instead, I called Ruby's number. She picked up on the eleventh ring.

'Carrie? Is everything OK?'

She sounded so fearful I didn't dare tell her that Jane had gone home.

'All good!' I said. 'Just checking in. It's so lovely down here!'

That much was true. The stall overlooked the beach, from a cobbled square between a parade of shops and Main Street, where Ruby lived above the bakery. There was a standpipe close by, perfect for watering the flowers, and the stall itself was eye-catching, surrounded by buckets of flowers, and trays of plants stacked on wooden pallets. A wooden wheelbarrow planted with wildflowers doubled as a sign, with *Ruby's Blooms* painted in white on the side. It weighed a ton, so was a permanent fixture, according to Jane, and normally the van stayed too. It was kept in her garage overnight because there was no lock-up at Ruby's.

As if on cue, it drew up at its spot behind the stall, and Calum stepped out, grinning broadly. 'Alright?' he said, as I quickly trilled a goodbye to Ruby and hung up. 'Mum said I should hang about. She can't get off the bog.'

Charming. 'Shouldn't you be at work?' I said, eyeing his oil-splattered overalls. Jane had mentioned he was doing a marine engineering apprenticeship down by the harbour.

'I've told them I won't be in today, it's cool,' he said. 'I'll get us a coffee from Cooper's, yeah?' He thumbed the café on the corner, and I nodded gratefully.

'Thanks.'

I doubted he'd be much help, and wasn't keen on the idea of him keeping an eye on me. I was used to working under my own steam. I wondered whether to send him to get some shopping for Ruby when he came back.

Shielding my eyes from the sun's glare, I found myself scanning the sunlit square, hoping for a glimpse of Tom. Mum had informed me, about six months after I left, that he and Megan must have broken up. She knew someone who knew someone who worked at Hudson Grange, and although Megan apparently worked for Mr Hudson now, Tom had moved to Scotland. Alone.

'You can come home,' she'd said. I'd had to tell her the real reason for moving to Manchester, because she'd been so upset that both her daughters had 'deserted' the family home and rarely visited. 'If you're worried about bumping into that little... that so-called friend of yours, I doubt she'd have the nerve to get in touch.'

'It's fine, Mum,' I'd said, though my heart had tripped over. 'I've a job here and friends. I'm happy.'

A voice crashed into my thoughts. 'Could I have a hand-tied posy, please?'

I turned to see a twinkly-eyed woman, dressed for the office in a light-coloured skirt suit, a laptop bag on her shoulder, and felt a pang for my old office at Cars 4 U. 'Posy?'

'Hand-tied,' she repeated, with a helpful smile. 'It's for a colleague's birthday. Nothing too formal.'

'A hand-tied posy.' I really should stop repeating things, in the hope they'd make more sense. As I stared at the different flowers, hoping a selection might jump out, a shadow fell across the cobbled ground.

'Garden ones are best.' It was Calum, filling the space with his broad frame. He put down the coffees and crouched by the buckets, his dark blond hair falling forward. 'Daisies and cornflowers, lavender for contrast – and 'cos it smells nice – and a couple of hydrangeas.' He handed me several stems of each. 'I sometimes helped out in the holidays when I was a kid,' he said in his broad Dorset accent, by way of an explanation. 'Strip the leaves off, or they'll be too bulky.' I stared at the bunch in my hand. 'Wrap a bit of florist's tape round, it's in the tray, and some string over the top.'

'String?'

'It's fancy string, 'specially for flowers, it looks...' he waggled his fingers, searching for the right word. 'Natural, like.'

'Right.' I sloped across to the workbench and did as instructed, cheeks buzzing with colour. Maybe Jane should have put Doris and Calum in charge. Both seemed to know what they were doing.

'Don't try and arrange them too much, see? They's meant to look like you 'aven't really tried.'

'Fine,' I said, shoving my hair back with my wrist.

It took a few goes to get the stems to stay together, and I could feel Calum itching to take over. At one point, even the customer leaned over and said, 'Would you like me to put my finger on that, while you tie the knot?'

'I'm OK, thanks.' My voice was more shrill than usual.

The result looked a little battered, and the customer studied it for a nerve-shredding moment, before saying on a sigh, 'It'll have to do, I suppose.'

She brightened when I told her there was no charge, but as she left, Calum hissed air through his teeth.

'Not cool, mate,' he said, 'Things aren't exactly cooking as it is.'

'You mean, financially?'

He shrugged and picked up his coffee. 'From what I've heard, like.' His ears were blushing, as though he regretted speaking.

'How old are you, Calum?'

'Eighteen.' He eyed me suspiciously. 'And a half.'

I remembered myself at that age, and, once again, Tom sprang into my head. It was as if a catch had been sprung, and after years of mostly not thinking about him, now I couldn't stop. 'Well, I appreciate your help, Calum, but I have a lot of financial experience, and I'll do what I think's best right now.'

'Whatever,' he said, drinking his coffee in one go.

He didn't seem inclined to speak much after that, but took his role as 'watcher' very seriously, his grey-green eyes scanning my every move.

'You seem a bit tense, like,' he said eventually, picking up on the rigid set of my shoulders after I'd struggled to wrangle two potted plants into a plastic bag for a customer, without spilling soil everywhere. 'You probably shouldn't have any more coffee.'

At lunchtime, he nipped across to the café and came back with two glasses of ice-cold orange juice and a couple of bananas 'for energy and magnesium'.

Later still, when I pricked my thumb on a rose thorn, and dripped blood all over the wrapping, he redid the bouquet for me, before fetching a plaster from a first-aid box in the van.

'Thanks, Calum,' I mumbled, readjusting my opinion. He was a lot more mature than most eighteen-and-a-half-year-olds I'd met.

By five o'clock I was boiling hot, starving, and tetchy with exhaustion, but at least there hadn't been any more catastrophes.

As Calum deftly dismantled the stall, I noticed my first customer of the day, hurrying across the square.

'Thanks for that,' he said, red in the face, a suit jacket flung over his shoulder.

'Er, you're welcome?'

'She's dumped me,' he blasted, passing a palm over his sweating face. 'She said she's allergic to flowers, and that if I cared about her I'd have known.'

'Not really my fault—'

'And even if she wasn't allergic, she said it was the most pathetic bouquet of flowers she'd ever set eyes on.'

'Ah.'

His eyes bulged in the manner of someone being throttled. 'Is that all you have to say?'

I was aware people were craning their necks, perhaps hoping to see a fight, and that Calum was trying not to laugh.

Squashing the urge to ask for the girlfriend's number, so I could tell her she'd had a lucky escape, I said, 'I suppose you want your fiver back.'

Chapter 3

'I'm sorry I left you in the lurch, Carrie. I meant to come back, but... well, let's just say, it wasn't pretty.'

I was back at Ruby's, and on the other end of the phone Jane's voice was small and weak. 'Dennis and Calum went down with it last week, but I thought I'd escaped,' she added. I presumed that Dennis was her husband.

'Don't worry, I was fine,' I said. 'Calum was really helpful.'

'Did you have any calls?'

'There's a phone?'

'I left it on the workbench.'

'Oh, that.' I'd popped it in my bag, thinking it was Jane's and she'd left it by mistake. 'Not that I know of.'

'That's a shame.' She sounded deflated.

'Well, if it rang I didn't hear it,' I said, keeping my voice down in case Ruby could overhear. Though, unless she'd rolled out of bed and pressed a glass to the wall, it seemed unlikely. When I'd checked on her she was asleep again, wearing a velvet eye mask and foam plugs in her ears.

'It's a pity.' Jane gave a heavy sigh that I suspected was about more than her upset stomach. 'Business is a bit slow at the moment.'

'I suppose Aunt Ruby being... ill doesn't help,' I said, stumbling over the word. 'Has she been like it for long?'

'It tends to come out of the blue,' Jane said indiscreetly. 'She'll seem fine then *wham!* I jumped. 'One morning, she can't get out of bed.'

'And you don't know why?'

'I suppose it's that depression.' Jane said it with the baffled air of someone who'd never felt miserable in her life – stomach bug notwithstanding. 'It seems to fit, but she won't see a doctor or take anything for it. She says it'll pass, and it does.'

'How often does it happen?' I wished my parents had been more forthcoming about Ruby's condition, if that's what it was. Mum had made it sound as if Ruby was a bit pissed off, and Dad clearly hadn't a clue.

'It's usually about this time every year,' Jane said, then made a horrible noise like a cat coughing up a fur ball. 'Gotta go,' she croaked, and there was the sound of the phone being clattered down, followed by silence.

I hung up and glanced around, heart sinking. When I'd arrived the previous night, hot and tired from the drive, and from trying to squeeze my Golf into the allocated space at the back of the bakery, Jane had let me in – a small, bird-like woman, with a mass of frizzy brown hair – and shown me round, before pressing the spare key into my hand, and telling me to meet her at the stall at 7 a.m. sharp.

I hadn't really taken in how small the flat was – much smaller than I remembered. Spread over several rooms, with an open-plan living room and kitchen, it could have been spacious, but instead looked like it had been burgled, with drawers hanging open, clothes heaped about, and dirty dishes and mugs on all the surfaces.

The room I'd slept in wasn't much better. It had a workshop vibe, with boxes everywhere, and only a narrow bed and a clothes rail hung with hangers, to indicate it could double as a bedroom.

'Sorry,' Jane had said, with a wince. 'I thought she might have tidied up for you.'

In fact, apart from a whispered, 'Thank you for coming, Carrie,' when I poked my head around her bedroom door to say hello, I hadn't seen Ruby. She'd still been sleeping when I crept out into the unfamiliar morning.

Sighing, I crossed from the living room, through the narrow passageway, where a lurid painting of sunflowers hung over a cupboard with shoes spilling out, and into Ruby's bedroom, where I stood in the gloom, watching the bulk underneath the duvet move in time with her snores.

Despite the sizzling weather, the curtains were pulled across. The smell in the room reminded me of the hamster I'd had when I was eight. I was forever forgetting to clean his cage, leading Mum to ban us from having any more pets.

'Aunt Ruby,' I said in a stage whisper, feeling completely helpless. When there was no response, I approached the bed like a bomb-disposal expert and gently shook her shoulder.

'AAAARRGGGGHHHH!'

The strength and volume of Ruby's scream sent me reeling. I stumbled on the edge of the rug and toppled against the dressing table, sending the items on top crashing to the floor.

'Jesus,' I said, my heart pounding. 'It's only me, Ruby.'

She pushed her eye mask into her thatch of straw-coloured hair, and goggled as if she'd encountered an extra from *The Walking Dead.*

'Carrie!' she cried, taking a minute to adjust to the sight of me; enough time for me to see that her strappy top had twisted round, and one of her boobs had popped out. 'You scared me half to death,' she said, removing her earplugs and dropping them in a mug of half-drunk tea on the bedside cabinet. 'Why were you creeping around?'

'I wasn't,' I said, as my pulse returned to normal, hurt by her slightly hostile tone. 'I was checking you were OK.'

'I was sleeping,' she said, rubbing her eye with her fist in a childlike gesture. 'Was I snoring?'

'What? No,' I fibbed, bending to pick up the knick-knacks scattered across the carpet, which looked like it hadn't seen a vacuum cleaner for weeks.

'Leave it!' she ordered, when I reached for a wooden box with a mess of papers and photos spilling out.

'It's no trouble,' I said, but I switched my attention to a velvety red jewellery case instead. Luckily it had stayed shut, and I replaced it carefully on the dust-layered dressing table, next to a wood-framed photo of a younger Ruby, in a beaded dress, holding the arm of a heavyset man with twinkling eyes. Presumably Henry, the man she'd lived in Hong Kong with, who'd died and left her enough money to return to Dorset and set up her flower stall.

I reached over to open the flimsy curtains, and a sliver of apricot sunlight slanted into the room. The bakery was opposite an old-fashioned picture-framing shop, and I noticed a couple in the window above, kissing like a Hollywood couple. His hands cupped her face, while their lips locked together, and I felt a flutter of envy. I'd never been kissed like that. The last man who'd tried had thrust his tongue into my mouth so hard, I accidentally gagged.

Dragging my gaze away, I opened the window, and turned to see Ruby cowering from the brightness like a vampire, her forearm over her eyes.

'What's that smell?' she said, wrinkling her nose.

'It's the sea.' I inhaled for effect, drawing in a lungful of dust particles. 'And fresh air,' I spluttered, when I'd finished coughing.

'Oh, that.' She crashed back on her pillows, her fingers laced over her chest.

Moving closer I studied her face, remembering how she'd possessed an otherworldly glamour when she was younger, from a photo I'd seen of her standing next to Dad in their back garden. Seven years older, he'd looked more like her father than her brother, in his sensible tank-top and slacks combo, his auburn hair neatly parted. Ruby had had a white-blonde crop and her lips had been painted red. Harlot-red, their mother had called it, according to Dad. Their parents had been strict and very religious. The worst kind of religious, I heard Mum say once to her mother on the phone. 'The sort that doesn't tolerate anyone different. I'm amazed Ken turned out to be normal, but I can't say I'm surprised his sister left home the minute she turned sixteen.'

Even bare-faced, with her dark roots showing, Ruby looked younger than her fifty-six years. It just was a shame her blue eyes were dull, as if they needed a polish. She appeared nothing like the cheery woman I remembered from my weekends on the stall; a woman who'd had the ability to make people smile, and walk away with a bunch of flowers they hadn't intended to buy.

'Why are you looking at me?' Ruby's gaze shifted downwards, and for a surreal moment I thought she was talking to her breast as she nudged it back into her top.

'Tell me what's wrong,' I said impulsively, perching on the side of the bed. 'Maybe I can help.'

'You're already helping, love.' She focused her eyes on me with obvious difficulty. 'Your mum said you're between jobs, that's why you offered to come.'

Offered? Typical of Mum. 'I am.'

'I'm sorry,' Ruby said.

'It's OK.' My fingers plucked at the duvet cover. It wasn't so much that I missed Cars 4 U, where the atmosphere had been reminiscent of *The Office* rather than *Suits*, but I'd enjoyed the structure the job had given my days. I was also proud of having worked my way up, from junior assistant to accounts manager, through sheer determination and hard work. It had been hard to adjust to not being there. By week two of my unemployment, Jasmine claimed the house could pass an army inspection – apart from her room, which looked like she was permanently clearing out her wardrobe.

'I'm sure I'll find something else soon,' I said to Ruby. 'In the meantime, it's lovely to see you.' I squeezed her hand, surprised to find it was true. 'It's been ages.'

'Too long,' she said unexpectedly, returning the pressure of my fingers. 'I always enjoyed visiting when you were toddlers, but…' she paused. 'I wasn't too good around young children.'

I was surprised to see her eyelashes were damp. 'Oh, Ruby, that's not true,' I said, reaching to pass her a tissue. In my few memories of her flying visits to Dorchester she was always smiling, her face alight with life. I couldn't reconcile that image with the woman slumped in bed, blinking back tears.

'I didn't realise things were so bad,' I said, patting her upper arm, which was patched with freckles. 'I don't think Mum and Dad do either.'

Ruby made a sound, between a laugh and a sob. 'I always liked your mother,' she said, still blinking. 'She's good for Kenneth, always seemed so sure of herself. Still is, I suppose.' She swallowed. 'That's what comes of having a loving family behind her.'

I felt a twinge of guilt as I thought of Grandma and Grandpa Perkins, who'd been like a story-book couple, and had spoilt Sarah and me rotten whenever we'd stayed at their cosy farmhouse in Bridport.

Dad's parents, much older, had died when I was six and my memories of them were vague. I remembered Granny Dashwood berating Mum for not re-using her tea-bags, which she considered a 'terrible waste' and that Grandfather – as we were urged to call him – was an older, meaner-looking version of Dad, with hair sprouting from his ears.

'Your parents even moved to be near you and your sister, when they'd lived in Dorset all their lives,' Ruby said. 'That's true devotion.'

I couldn't argue with that, though sometimes wished they'd discussed it first, instead of springing it on me and Sarah once they'd sold the house.

'It was partly because my grandparents had passed away, and I think Mum felt there was nothing left for her here.'

'They've always supported you, though, and in turn you'll support your own children, because that's how it works.'

All this talk of children was making me nervous. Although I adored my niece and nephew, I hadn't yet located my biological clock, and was starting to wonder whether I even had one. 'I've always found work a good distraction,' I said, hoping to invigorate her, remembering how I'd immersed myself in my job at Cars 4 U, keen to shake off the Carrie who'd fled her home with a broken heart. 'Maybe you should get back to it.'

'It's not that simple, Carrie.' There was a mild rebuke in Ruby's voice, and I immediately felt ashamed. Of course it wasn't, or she wouldn't be swaddled in her duvet with a tear-stained face, prepared to let a niece she hadn't seen for years loose on her flower stall.

'Do you enjoy your job, usually I mean?' I said, changing tactic, slightly fearful of her response. I wasn't experienced at dealing with difficult feelings – even my own.

'I love my stall, but it was always a means to an end,' Ruby said, scouring her eyes with the tissue. 'I worked in a florists' a long time ago and learned a lot there.' I vaguely remembered her telling me that once, but I'd been too busy wondering how soon I could get to the beach and go for a paddle. 'I'm not much good at anything else, not like your father. He was the brainy one.'

I wished she'd stop comparing herself. 'You've been running a business for years, so you must be clever,' I said.

'I enjoy the creative side more, the flower arranging.' She showed a spark of animation for the first time. 'Although my father would have preferred me to become a nun.'

Not sure how to respond to that, I said, 'Sarah's started making candles, since leaving banking when she had the twins. She's not very good at it though.' I was thinking of the set she'd presented me with at Christmas, which had given off so much smoke, and smelt so strongly of paraffin, I'd had to report back that they were a health hazard.

'How was your first day?' Ruby made an obvious effort to look interested.

I decided to be honest. 'I didn't really know what I was doing and had to give someone a refund.'

'WHAT?' She erupted from the duvet like a deep-sea diver, almost tipping me over. 'Where was Jane?'

'She had a tummy bug,' I said, alarmed. 'But it's fine, her son helped out. She'll be back tomorrow, and it'll be fine, I'm sure it'll be fine.' I was repeating myself, and pressing the air with my hands like a politician.

'But your mum told Jane that when you knew you were coming, you did a refresher course in flower arranging.'

What? 'That's… right,' I said carefully. I knew I shouldn't have mentioned the YouTube tutorial to Mum. 'I was just a bit thrown by Jane going off, and it being my first day.' Switching topic, I said, 'Doris Day said she'd pop by.'

Confusion crossed Ruby's face.

'Do you know her?' I said, tentatively.

Her expression cleared. 'Yes,' she said, deflating like a pricked balloon. 'She's got her nose into everything, that woman. You didn't tell her anything, did you?'

'Only that you were on holiday. Shouldn't I have?'

'Oh, it doesn't matter.' Ruby was burrowing back beneath the bedding, as if our exchange had drained her. 'None of it matters, really.'

'I'll do better tomorrow,' I promised rashly. 'Now, would you like something to eat?'

Her eyes appeared over the covers. 'Maybe an omelette with cheese,' she said limply. 'And there should be some ham in the fridge.'

'OK.' I felt cheered. Things couldn't be too bad if she felt like eating, could they? 'Should I tidy up a bit in here?' I cast my gaze around the room, catching sight of a jumble of clothes through the half-open doors of her wardrobe.

'Don't bother,' she said, bashing her pillows into shape underneath her head. 'I don't mind a bit of mess.'

One of Mum's favourite sayings – 'a messy house reflects a messy mind' – sprang up as I stepped around the detritus on the floor. If the chaos was a reflection of the inside of Ruby's head, it was worse than any of us knew.

At the door, I stooped to pick up a photo, and one of the letters that had landed there when I knocked the box off the dressing table. Not wanting to disturb Ruby again, I slipped them into my pocket as I left, and closed the door behind me.

In the living room, I switched on the television for company, then rummaged in the kitchen for a clean pan and omelette ingredients.

But by the time I'd made it and taken it through to the bedroom, Ruby was snoring again and I didn't have the heart to wake her.

I ate it myself, after clearing a space on the table under the living-room window, then looked through the teetering pile of paperwork and wished I hadn't.

There were several bills that hadn't been paid, and according to her latest bank statement, Ruby was overdrawn and practically broke. Whatever money she'd had was gone. I did some quick calculations. In order to cover Jane's salary, her rent, the cost of buying flowers from… I checked the last delivery note… All Seasons Nursery, she needed to be taking double what was coming in now. More, if she wanted to make a profit.

After shuffling the papers back together, so Ruby couldn't tell I'd been snooping, I wondered whether I should discuss her finances with her, but after fetching my iPad and googling 'depression', I decided it wasn't a good idea. The reality might push her over the edge.

Sighing, I found a florist on YouTube, and watched her wrapping flowers in a way a toddler could have managed. I eyed a bunch of lilies in a vase, and considered practising, but decided against it. They were past their best anyway, shedding petals all over the table.

A wave of loneliness engulfed me. Normally, at this time, Jasmine and I would be catching up over dinner – usually a stir-fry, or a ready-meal if we couldn't be bothered to cook – and if Jasmine didn't have homework to mark, or a party to go to, and she hadn't set me up on a blind date, we'd go to the pub, or she'd show me some yoga moves to help my tension, which usually ended with us collapsed and laughing on the floor.

I thought about phoning Mum, then remembered the five hour time difference meant she and Dad would be asleep, and there was no point calling Sarah as she'd be wrestling the twins into bed.

On impulse, I looked up the number of Tom's veterinary practice, and as if in a trance, I pressed the numbers into my phone.

'Hello?'

I froze. It was nearly eight thirty. I hadn't expected anyone to answer, least of all Tom. There was no mistaking his voice; the warm pitch of it was imprinted on my heart.

'Hello?' he repeated, sounding a little wary. 'Mrs Finch? Don't worry, Tabitha's fine, she's sleeping off the anaesthetic.'

My vocal cords felt squeezed, and for a second I considered hanging up.

'Hi, Tom,' I squeaked at last. 'It's me! Carrie. Carrie Dashwood.'

Shock pulsed down the line. '*Carrie?*'

A nervous giggle escaped. 'I know! It's been so *long*.'

'I thought you were Tabitha's owner.' He sounded dazed.

'Tabitha?'

'A cat, she brought her in earlier. She's had an operation, and I was keeping an eye on her. The cat, I mean.'

I felt as if my bones were melting. 'How are you?' I said, my voice still an octave too high.

'I'm fine,' he said quickly. 'Carrie, I can't believe it's you.'

'It is me, and I've got my driving licence to prove it!'

Silence swelled, and memories came hurtling back; Dad driving me away from Hudson Grange, while I tried to hide my tears; leaving for Manchester the following morning, not knowing I wouldn't be back.

Megan's call later that day, to tell me she'd spent the night with Tom. *'I know you two were friends, but it's not as if he ever liked you that way.'*

'How did you get this number?'

I started. 'I looked you up,' I confessed, my ears burning. 'I'm in Shipley for a couple of weeks—'

'You're here?' His voice sharpened. 'Not Dorchester?'

'My parents don't live there any more,' I said, bringing my voice down a notch. 'My aunt has a flower stall here, and I'm helping out for a bit. She's not well.' My heart was racing, and my breathing was shallow.

'I'm sorry,' he said, reflexively.

I tried to picture him again, but could only see his shadowy outline in the doorway that night with Megan, and realised that what I wanted, more than anything, was to pull him back into the light.

'I thought while I was here it might be nice to meet up,' I managed, twining a length of hair around my fingers until it pulled tight. 'I'd really like to explain a few things about the night of your twenty-first, and why I left so suddenly—'

'Megan told me.'

I stiffened. 'Told you what?'

'She said you'd been planning to move to Manchester, to be with your sister, and that you'd only stayed because you wanted to come to my twenty-first and see inside the house.' He hesitated. 'I wish you'd told me you were thinking of leaving.'

My mouth had fallen open. 'Tom, that's not true...' I began.

'She was really hurt that you dropped her,' he went on. 'She thought you were her best friend.'

What?

But even as my mind was spinning at the roaring injustice, I wasn't as shocked as I could have been. Looking back, I could see that Megan had always been capable of twisting things to suit her own ends, and I could imagine how she'd made me look to Tom.

'I thought something was a bit off with you that night,' he was saying, as if it was coming back to him in dribs and drabs. 'I wanted to come and talk to you, but Megan said you were in a funny mood and that we should leave you alone.'

I remembered her whispering to him, and wondered whether to tell him I'd been in a funny mood because she'd laid claim to Tom, as if it was her right, and seeing them together had made me doubt myself. 'We *were* friends,' I said, instead, deciding to take the high road. 'But she…' *stole you.* Hardly. You can't *steal* a person. *Made me feel that you were out of my league.* No. That was my lack of self-confidence. 'Once I saw you and Megan together, I…' *couldn't stand it?*

I needed to stop completing sentences in my head, but felt certain whatever I said would come out wrong. 'We're very different people, that's all,' I managed, lamely.

'You were certainly keen to pair us off,' he said. 'Remember? You said she was perfect for me.'

Why, oh why, had I said that? More importantly, why had he believed me?

'And suddenly you'd gone for good.' A loaded pause. 'Hovis missed you.'

Tears leapt to my eyes at the thought of the little dog. I'd missed him badly, too; had treasured the copy of the photo I'd given to Tom, which I wasn't sure he'd even opened that night, along with a picture of Tom I'd taken, of him holding a lop-eared rabbit with a bandaged foot. 'I tried phoning a few times, but you never picked up.'

'Did you?' He sounded sceptical.

Yes, I bloody did. 'Anyway, it's all in the past now.' I switched my tone to one I hoped sounded cheerleader perky and not – as I suspected – dangerously unstable. 'Would you *like* to meet up while I'm here?'

'Carrie, I—' He was interrupted by the tortured yowl of an animal in the background.

'Look, forget I called,' I said, unable to bear it any longer. He was obviously thinking of a polite way to let me down, and it struck me that I knew nothing about his circumstances. He could be married with five kids, for all I knew. 'Nice to speak to you,' I chirruped. ''Bye!'

I rang off, then opened the line so he would get the engaged tone should he be tempted to call back and reiterate that he wasn't interested.

'That went well,' I said out loud, cringing as I replayed every word of the call in my head. What had I been expecting? This was real life, not a romantic movie about former sweethearts reuniting. Not that we'd ever been sweethearts.

I felt sick, imagining how I must have come across.

From the passageway came the sonorous sound of Ruby snoring, and suddenly I wanted nothing more than the oblivion of sleep.

I switched off the television and went through to the spare room, where I set my phone alarm to wake me at seven, before peeling off my clothes. Then I crawled under the duvet in my single bed, without bothering to brush my teeth.

Chapter 4

I woke to a yeasty aroma from the bakery below. It made such a nice change from the usual whiff of petrol fumes outside my house in Manchester that, for a few blissful seconds, I was glad to be in Shipley – until I remembered my conversation with Tom.

Groaning, I buried my face in the pillow. I should never have called. All I'd done was remind him what a complete idiot I was.

My phone burst into life, and I sat up in fright. I thought I'd set the alarm to wake me with a wind-chime sound, but had obviously pressed the drum 'n' bass one instead.

I switched it off and dropped back on my pillow. Jane would be there to set up the stall with Calum, so there was no need to get out of bed just yet.

But what if her tummy was still playing up?

Reluctantly, I forced myself out of bed and into the tiny bathroom, where I had a lukewarm shower, and decided I missed my house after all. At least I could turn around there without bashing into something.

I still hadn't unpacked properly, so pulled on the trousers I'd worn the day before, with a fresh top that was only a little bit crumpled, and dragged my hair off my cheeks into a crocodile clip. I'd normally spend at least ten minutes grooming, but couldn't see the point if I was going to be outdoors all day. I made do with a slick of lip balm, before making myself a mug of instant coffee and a slice of toast in the kitchen.

Hefty snores were barrelling out of Ruby's room, but I took her a mug of coffee in anyway and left it by her bed. The window was shut and the curtains drawn and I fretted about whether I should try to persuade her to get up. In the end, I left a note, to call if she needed anything.

'She'll get up when she's good and ready,' Jane said, when I arrived at the stall five minutes later and blurted out my worries. 'Ruby's her own woman, and won't be told.' She was a little pale, but otherwise seemed recovered, though her hair was flattened on one side as though she'd run out of energy halfway through brushing it. Her outfit – navy boiler suit tucked into green wellies (despite the sun already warming the air) – spoke of someone whose priorities weren't exactly fashion focused.

'I just feel a bit useless,' I said.

'It means a lot to Ruby that you came, even if she doesn't show it.'

'She wouldn't...' I hesitated, while Jane picked up a floral cup and poured in some coffee from a Thermos. 'She wouldn't do anything stupid?'

'Try to kill herself you mean?' Jane shook her head. 'Never has before,' she said, matter-of-factly. 'I don't think she'd do that,' she added. 'It's more like she's waiting for something that never happens, but I don't know what it is. I'm not sure she does either.'

Unrequited love? I wondered. Maybe her heart had been broken around this time of year. Or could it be the anniversary of when Henry had died? Although, according to Mum, he'd been more of a father figure for Ruby than a passionate lover. Still, she must miss him.

'And she's like this every summer?'

'Never this bad.' Jane put down her cup and bent to pick up a cream-coloured rose petal. 'Last year it was just a few days. She watched daytime telly and ate a lot of pastry.'

'So, how did you come to work with her?'

Jane scrunched up her freckled nose. 'I've always loved growing flowers, you should see my garden,' she said. 'I used to work in a nursery – the garden sort – when Calum was growing up, but it was miles away and I wanted something closer to home, so I approached your aunt one day and asked if she'd like an assistant.' She shrugged. 'I've got a flair for it,' she said, immodestly. 'Self-trained with my flower arranging, and your aunt's taught me a lot.' She thrust the petal under my nose. 'Smell that.'

I inhaled, my senses flooding with the delicate perfume. I wondered whether there was a process to describing its scent, like wine-tasting. Should I be able to smell berries, and windswept moors, with a top-note of angel's wings?

'It's… nice?'

Jane nodded, encouragingly. 'Patience.'

I thought some more, struggling for appropriate words. 'I'm sure I can smell vanilla,' I began, and Jane gave a stuttering laugh.

'No, silly, the rose is called Patience.' Her eyes – the colour of stone-washed denim – were mischievous behind her round glasses. 'Most wholesale roses look similar and don't have much scent, but I grow this variety at home.'

Trying to hide a blush, I looked around. 'I've worked for a car rental company for years, doing the accounts. No flowers involved.'

'Now don't be modest.' Jane wagged a finger. 'Your mum told me that you can turn your hand to practically anything. She said you'd done—'

'An online tutorial in flower arranging,' I said flatly. *Bloody Mum.*

'I'm impressed.' Jane passed a hand over her hair, which immediately sprang back to its original height. 'It's good to know the stall will be in good hands while I'm away.'

Feeling my blush take hold, I made a show of straightening the buckets into a regimental line and straightening the flowers.

The sun was gathering strength, and people were filtering through the square on their way to work, or towards the beach for a run.

'I usually make up a few bouquets first thing.' Jane began moving briskly, transferring flowers to the workbench, and I wondered how she knew what went with what, but didn't want to give away my ignorance by asking.

'Here,' I said, handing her the scissors for snipping stems.

'It seems a shame to be doing accounts, if you've inherited your aunt's creative streak,' she said.

I returned her smile through gritted teeth. Mum obviously hadn't mentioned the picture I'd once drawn for Ruby. It was of a miniature Shetland pony, but Ruby mistook it for a pair of dancing Mexicans, and I could still remember the way she'd swallowed her laughter, not wanting to upset me. 'Accounting is creative, in its own way,' I said. 'Not that I do anything illegal,' I added, hastily.

'Well, as you know, flower arranging is all about colour and design, and knowing what looks right.'

'U-huh,' I said, agreeably. After moving into my house, I'd kept the walls magnolia, and had chosen minimalist furniture, scared of getting it wrong, but since then, the twins had decorated the walls with fingerprints, and Jasmine had introduced bright throws to 'break up the beige'.

'Look!' Jane was artistically arranging the flowers she'd gathered, in a process that took a matter of seconds.

'That's lovely,' I said, as she secured the wrapping with a much smaller strip of Sellotape than I'd used the day before.

She plopped the bouquet in a bucket. 'Why don't you make up a couple, while I refill my flask with some coffee at Cooper's?'

Relieved she wasn't about to watch, I attempted to emulate her movements, but by the time I'd finished it looked like a bird had started building a nest, and got bored halfway through.

'Oh dear,' said Jane when she returned, placing her flask beside my mangled arrangement. 'I don't think Shipley's ready for something so...' she tipped her head. 'Modern?'

'That's OK, I'll tone it down,' I said, trying to sound casual. A couple of passers-by stopped to look at some plants, bristling with bright green leaves, and I was relieved when Jane shot over to talk to them.

I slipped my bird's-nest affair beneath the bench, my mind switching back to Tom. I wondered if I'd blown my chances of ever seeing him again.

'So where is it you're going?' I asked Jane, after she'd persuaded the couple to buy another plant, made up of violently purple flowers.

'Look, I know it's not the best time to book a break,' she said, as if she'd read some judgement in my face. 'But it's important to me. My marriage is depending on it.'

'Oh?'

'Things aren't good in the bedroom,' she said, as if discussing the state of the economy. 'Now Calum's a grown man, it's time for Dennis and me to get back some intimacy.'

'Ri-i-i-ight.'

'It's not going to happen at home,' she persisted, seeming unaware of my growing discomfort. 'Not with family photos looking on.'

'I see.' I grabbed one of the cups she'd filled with coffee, and took a reviving swig.

'It's since I read *Fifty Shades*, you see.' Jane's gaze went somewhere else, and a menopausal flush travelled up her throat. 'It made me realise how stale things had become between us,' she said. 'Do you know what I mean?'

I nodded, armpits prickling. What was I supposed to say? Jasmine had dragged me to see *Fifty Shades* and I'd come away feeling grimy. The only dominant trait I was comfortable with in a man was if he ordered pizza on my behalf. I was hopeless at choosing toppings.

'Dennis isn't sure about it yet,' Jane continued. 'He won't so much as kill a fly, bless him, so the idea of taking a hairbrush to my backside...'

'I think someone needs help,' I said, keen to stop her surge of words, but the man who'd been eyeing a pail of carnations took fright and scurried away.

'Ooh, I've made you blush!' Jane gave me a playful shove and I staggered backwards, slopping coffee down my top. She was surprisingly strong for someone with such a small frame. 'So, you can see why I need a holiday,' she added. 'If we don't get away, I dread to think what will happen.'

I dreaded to think what would happen if they *did* get away, and wondered if Ruby knew the nature of Jane's holiday. Perhaps I would ask her later; it might make her smile.

'Don't worry, I'll take care of things,' I said, rubbing at the spreading stain on my top. 'Do you know where the vet's is, by the way?'

I hadn't meant to say it, and wasn't sure why I had.

Jane frowned. 'You're not planning to have your aunt put down, are you?' Her face cleared. 'Only teasing,' she said. 'Here's the lady you want to ask.' She waved over a woman with a walking stick and a

Labrador, approaching from the parade. 'One of my neighbours,' she said. 'She does puppy-training sessions there.'

'Are you talking about me?' said the woman, flourishing her stick. She had on a fluorescent green maxi-dress with blindingly white trainers, and a pair of giant sunglasses nestled in her fluffy grey hair. 'Celia Appleton,' she said to me, not waiting for a reply. The Labrador wagged his tail and I patted his head. 'Where's Ruby? I haven't see her for a few days.'

'Having a little break,' Jane said, loyally. 'This is Carrie, her niece, and she'd like to know where the vet's is.'

If Celia thought it strange, she didn't comment. 'It's a five-minute drive from here, Nightingale Lane, near the primary school. Nice chap, the vet,' she added, giving me a piercing look. My heart lurched, as if the reference to Tom might conjure him up. 'Nothing like his father, thank goodness, though my boyfriend, Paddy, says he's mellowed a bit since his wife died. He works for Mr Hudson, you see.'

Tom's mother was dead?

I felt a pinch of sadness. Tom had loved her, even though she hadn't always stood up for him when his dad was on his back to join the business.

'Thanks,' I said, but Celia was already striding away, her Labrador sashaying at her heels.

'Nice woman,' Jane said, watching her go. 'There's not much she doesn't know about dogs.' She turned, and nodded at my top. 'Mop yourself up, and I'll run through the payment process with you,' she said, flipping back into business mode. 'Hopefully, there'll be plenty of customers to practise on.'

I'd just grabbed a sheet of industrial towel roll from the back of the van and started dabbing at the stain, which was pointless because it had already dried, when I heard a blast of tinny music from the work mobile, still in my bag from the day before.

Glancing back, I saw Jane in conversation with a woman holding up a baby to be admired.

I took out the phone. 'Hello, Cars 4 U,' I said. 'I mean, the flower stall, um, Ruby's Blooms.'

'I thought I'd got the wrong number for a minute,' said a fretful female voice at the other end. 'I take it you're not' – there was a pause, as if she was looking up the name – 'Ruby Dashwood?'

'No,' I said, still scrubbing at my top, wondering if I should nip back to the flat and get changed. Apart from anything, it was already too warm for long sleeves. 'Can I help?'

'I hope so.' The voice sounded vaguely familiar, and for some reason my scalp began to tingle. 'My daughter's getting married the weekend after next, and the florist we'd booked has rather let us down.' I made an appropriate murmur. 'We're having trouble finding someone who isn't fully booked, and wondered if you might be able to step in?'

Jane was holding the baby now, who was squealing with delight, and reaching out to clutch her hair. I moved to the workbench, and scrabbled for a notepad and pen among the clutter. 'If you'd like to give me some details, I'll see what we can do.'

'The wedding's on the 28th, a Saturday, at Hudson Grange.' My heart flipped. *Hudson Grange?* So, they were doing weddings there now.

'You've probably heard of it,' the woman said, pride trickling into her voice, and suddenly – shockingly – I knew exactly who she was.

'My daughter is marrying Tom Hudson there,' she went on, openly bragging now. 'Her name's—'

'Megan Ford,' I finished, feeling as if someone had opened a valve and drained all the blood from my body.

Tom and Megan were not only back together, they were getting married.

Chapter 5

'Who was that?' Jane balanced the baby on her hip and looked at me with concern. 'Bad news?'

'No, nothing like that.' I forced a smile as I put the phone down, but my heart gave a juddering wallop. Tom was *marrying Megan*?

I thought again of my phone call the night before, and had to bite my lip to stop a groan of mortification escaping.

But didn't they break up? Unless the grapevine had got it wrong, all those years ago.

Not that I still had romantic feelings for Tom.

But, *Megan*?

Still, it was none of my business, and the sooner I pushed the pair of them out of my head, the better. I'd managed it (mostly) for the last ten years, and if I'd never quite got closure, then maybe it was because I didn't deserve it. After all, as Tom had reminded me, I'd practically pushed them together.

'Carrie?'

I jumped, and realised Jane was waiting for an explanation.

'Sorry, I answered the call,' I said, meaning it literally.

'It's OK, that's what you're here for, silly.' She unhooked the baby's chubby fingers from her hair and handed her back. 'So, who was it?'

'A possible wedding booking,' I said, marvelling that I'd managed to take down the details, when my hand had been shaking so badly I could barely hold the pen. 'At Hudson Grange.' I cleared my throat. 'Their florist has let them down, and they'd like us to do the flowers.'

'WHAT?' Jane's hands flew to her cheeks. 'Hudson *Grange?*' she repeated, as though I'd said Buckingham Palace. '*The* Hudson Grange, in Moreton?'

I nodded, knowing I'd enjoy her reaction a lot more if I wasn't still in shock. 'Tom Hudson is getting married.' It felt as if I was coughing up a fur ball, but Jane seemed too enraptured to notice my strangled tone.

'Oh my days!' Her face split into a grin, revealing crooked teeth in need of a polish. 'Why us?'

'Every other florist in the area's booked.' When the spark went out of her eyes, I wished I hadn't said it.

'Oh.' Her hands dropped to her sides. 'I thought maybe someone had recommended us,' she said. 'We did the flowers for Ellen Partridge's daughter's wedding, last year.' She said it as though I should know who Ellen Partridge's daughter was. 'Ellen's a good friend of mine,' she elaborated. She darted to the van, returning with an old-fashioned portfolio. 'Her daughter teaches yoga classes in the community centre. They're very popular,' she said. 'I went a couple of times, but all that bending and stretching released a lot of gas, and in the end I couldn't hold it in.' Her cheeks blotched with colour as she flicked through the few pages inside. 'Here,' she said.

I found myself examining an array of shots of a bridal bouquet in delicate shades of lilac and cream, and a high-ceilinged reception hall, where each table was decorated with a daintily elaborate centrepiece.

'They're lovely,' I said, trying to focus.

Tom and Megan are getting married, Tom and Megan are getting married. The words pranced around my head, like show ponies.

'Your aunt let me help.' Jane inflated again, studying the pictures fondly over my shoulder. 'It was our first wedding, and we're hoping to do more but… well, she turned down a few bookings when she started to feel unwell.'

I remembered the paperwork I'd looked at. A few weddings were exactly what Ruby's Blooms needed.

'The arrangements are great,' I said, recoiling from a photo of the bride, grinning maniacally and gripping her bouquet like a gun. I wondered what had possessed her to cram her curves into a plunging white sheath, split to the crotch at the front. With her tanned flesh spilling out at both ends, she looked like a sausage baguette.

'I think all eyes were on the flowers,' said Jane, though I was certain they wouldn't have been.

'And Ruby decorated the church.' Jane turned the page, and I admired bunches of ethereal flowers tied to the pews with long, trailing ribbons, lit by coloured sunlight streaming through a stained-glass window.

'She's good,' I murmured, shoving away an image of Tom and Megan at the altar, gazing into each other's eyes. 'Weddings wouldn't be the same without flowers, would they?'

'When you think about it, flowers are associated with the saddest and happiest times in people's lives,' Jane said, simply. 'And we florists play a big part in what those memories look like.'

'No pressure then.' A thought struck me. Megan's mother had booked an appointment, which meant… *Megan would be coming to the stall.* My heart picked up speed.

Had Tom told her about my call? I wondered. Did she know I was in Shipley?

I can't see her. I had to get out of it. 'Do you think Ruby will want to meet the bride-to-be?' I couldn't even vocalise Megan's name.

'It's worth mentioning,' Jane said, slamming the portfolio so a puff of dust flew out. 'It could be just what she needs, a high-profile booking like this.'

'High-profile?'

'The Hudson son and heir getting married.' Jane's eyes went dreamy. 'I wouldn't be surprised if *Hello!* magazine got involved, what with his dad owning all those hotels,' she gushed. 'Didn't Leonardo DiCaprio stay in one, when he was filming that zombie movie in Cornwall?'

'I've no idea,' I said, the mention of Tom's dad sending a tremor through me. He was probably over the moon that Tom was finally marrying Megan; someone whose family – although dysfunctional – had credentials.

I switched my mind away, glad to see a customer waiting to speak to Jane.

'Can you do me a bouquet?' she said with a friendly smile. 'It's my mother-in-law's birthday and she loves fresh flowers. Anything apart from tiger lilies, which make her sneeze.'

Jane sprang into action, selecting a colourful arrangement, and although I pretended to watch, my thoughts kept catapulting off. Long-buried feelings were rising to the surface like mud off a riverbed, and I didn't like it one bit.

'Carrie?'

Jane's voice forced me back and I smiled, as if I'd been present all along. 'That was a lovely bouquet,' I said automatically, watching the customer walk off with it cradled in her arms.

Jane's brow furrowed. 'I was saying, did you write down the time of the appointment?'

'What? Oh! Yes.' I kept my smile intact. 'Ten o'clock tomorrow, if that's OK.' I should have said we were fully booked. *Why* hadn't I said that?

'Do you want to tell Ruby?' Jane rubbed her hands together as if trying to start a fire. 'I bet you anything she'll be out of that bed in a flash.'

'I could go and tell her now, if you like,' I said, desperate to escape.

'Why don't you ring her?' Jane jutted her chin at the phone.

I shook my head. 'I'd rather tell her in person.'

Jane lowered her eyebrows. 'We *have* to make a good impression,' she said. 'This booking could bring in more business.'

'I know, I get it,' I said, cheeks aching with the effort of smiling. 'It'll be good for business.' It *would* be good for business, there was no doubt about that.

If only it wasn't Tom and Megan's wedding.

'Now.' Jane glanced around in a businesslike way. 'How about you tell me the names of the flowers without looking at the labels?' she suggested. 'They all have meanings, you know.' Her glasses slipped down to the end of her nose 'Orange blossom for virginity, camellias for faithfulness, dahlias for dignity and elegance, and daffodils for unrequited love.'

I wondered why anyone would send daffodils to someone they weren't in love with? Surely *not* sending daffodils would get the message across more successfully.

'There aren't any daffodils,' I said, glancing about.

'They're not in season yet.'

'Ah.'

'What are those?' Jane nodded at a pail of pom-pom-like flowers, but my focus had slipped again.

'Maybe I could go and get us something to eat?' I said. 'I feel a bit peckish.'

Disappointment flashed over Jane's face, which was as expressive as a retriever's. 'I'm still off my food,' she said, twiddling her plain gold wedding band around her finger. 'But you go and get something.'

'I won't be long.'

Cooper's Café looked busy, so I sped off in the direction of the bakery, past dawdling holidaymakers in swimsuits and sarongs, their sandy feet in flip-flops. The sun baked the back of my neck, and I paused to gaze at the swathe of sea, sparkling like blue-green silk. I wished I'd never heard of Tom Hudson or Megan Ford.

Waiting in the queue in the bakery, half-heartedly eyeing the display of generously filled sandwiches, I felt in the back pocket of my trousers for the ten-pound note I kept for emergencies. My fingers closed over the photo and letter I'd picked up off Ruby's floor the day before. I pulled them out and looked at the small Polaroid, its colours badly faded.

As the woman in front of me ordered two prawn sandwiches, four flapjacks and three jam doughnuts – 'not all for me!' she blustered, unconvincingly – I studied the photograph and recognised Ruby by her crest of bright blonde hair. She looked about sixteen, and was sitting on a bed, holding a tiny baby. A boy baby, judging by the pale blue shawl he was parcelled in. His face had the crumpled look of a newborn, and his hair was a feather-soft swirl of brown.

My pulse quickened. As far as I knew, Ruby had been living abroad when Sarah and I were born, so who did the baby belong to?

I turned the photo over and saw the name *Donny* written on the back in spidery black ink. I recognised Ruby's handwriting from Christmas and birthday cards, and for the second time in twenty-four hours felt as if I was falling down a lift-shaft.

'Can I help you?' The assistant's chirpy voice was like an alarm.

'I haven't decided yet.' I turned to a man behind me, who smelt faintly of mackerel. 'You go ahead,' I told him.

As he sidled past, I unfolded the letter, which was soft with handling. As I read the neatly handwritten paragraphs, my heart crashed about in my chest.

When I'd finished, I had to bite my lip to stop myself crying.

How had Ruby kept a secret like this for so many years?

And more importantly, why?

Chapter 6

'What would you like, madam?'

The assistant's voice snapped me into action.

'Nothing,' I said, and ducked behind the counter. Ignoring her cry, I shot through the kitchen, registering the astonished face of a ruddy-cheeked man in a baker's hat, who was expertly plaiting a loaf. I took the stairs to the flat two at a time, unlocked the door, and flung myself into Ruby's bedroom, panting as though I'd escaped a serial killer. 'You had a baby!'

Ruby remained motionless beneath the duvet, only a wad of hair visible in the patchy light leaking through the curtains. The air smelt of bins, and cake wrappers were scattered on the rug, alongside a half-eaten Scotch egg. A fly hovered over an open ketchup bottle, tipped on its side, the scene reminiscent of a Tate Modern art installation.

'I know you can hear me,' I said, in a trembling voice. 'You gave him up, then found him, but he doesn't want to know, and he threatened to get a restraining order if you contacted his family again.' I was fighting to get air in my lungs. 'That's why you're feeling like this, why you get down every year. It's the anniversary of when he was adopted.'

There was the tiniest movement in the bed.

'Oh, Ruby, *why* haven't you told anyone?' I cried. 'What happened? Why did you give him away?'

The duvet was shaking in earnest now, and a strange sound erupted, like a weasel having an asthma attack.

'Talk to me,' I pleaded, sinking onto the bed as my jelly-like legs gave way.

The duvet moved to reveal my aunt's tear-mottled face. 'I don't know what to say.' The words were a ragged whisper.

'I can't believe you kept something like this a secret,' I said, lifting my fingers to her cheek to brush away a tear. 'I'm assuming it *is* a secret?'

'How did you find out?' she managed, her face contorting as a fresh bout of crying took hold.

'I found some stuff when I was in here yesterday,' I confessed, showing her the photo still clutched in my other hand. 'There was a letter from him, from Donny, though he's called Peter now.' I glanced at the scribbled signature at the bottom of the grimly worded letter. 'I didn't mean to snoop, but—'

'It's not your fault,' Ruby hiccupped. 'I normally keep them in my knicker drawer, but was going through some things the other day and stuffed them in that box.'

I looked at it, still tipped over on the floor. There was a wristband lying beside it that I hadn't noticed before; the sort you get in hospital. It was the size of a baby's ankle.

'Oh, Ruby,' I said again. I picked it up and read the faded letters, my brain fumbling with meaning. *Dashwood 5/8/76.* 'Do Mum and Dad know?' I knew it was unlikely. Mum wouldn't have been able to resist mentioning it, and I doubted Dad would have kept it from her if he'd known. They were very vocal about honesty being crucial in a marriage – apart from the true price of clothes, which Mum said men didn't understand. Especially Dad, who bought his clothes at Tesco's.

'Of course they don't know,' Ruby said, as though the idea was unthinkable. She peered at me through swollen eyelids. 'It wasn't something I could talk about.'

'But it was the seventies,' I said, tentatively. 'Things like that were more acceptable, weren't they?'

'I was sixteen when I got pregnant, and my parents were about as Catholic as you could get.' She ground the heels of her hands into her eyes. 'So, no, they weren't acceptable, not in our house.'

I rewound to myself at sixteen. The closest I'd come to romance was a tingling feeling in the pit of my stomach whenever I saw a boy called Digger, from the boys' school nearby. Megan ended up going out with him for a while, but what if it had been me and I'd become pregnant? It was impossible to imagine. I hadn't even been kissed at sixteen.

'What about the father?' I asked Ruby.

'He was killed in a car crash a few months later.'

I clapped a hand to my mouth. 'Ruby, I'm so sorry.'

'It's all in the past,' she said, voice cracking. 'He was just a boy I didn't even know that well.'

'And you definitely couldn't keep the baby?'

She looked at me with soaking wet eyes. 'If you'd got to know my parents, you'd have understood.' She spoke with such sadness my throat tightened. 'Your dad was older, he'd left home by then, and they didn't want to be saddled with a grandchild to help bring up, so they sent me to stay with my grandmother until the baby was born.'

'That's so sad.' I tried to imagine my parents' reaction, if Sarah or I had been in that situation. It wouldn't have been what they wanted, but I was certain they'd have stood by us.

Ruby sniffed. 'Anyway, he was adopted by a local family, which I knew was best for him, and I stupidly thought that one day I'd find him and explain. I had this fantasy about us reuniting.' She looked at me through her fingers. 'When I came back from Hong Kong after Henry died, I was in my forties, and decided it was time to look Donny up, but he practically slammed the door in my face. Said he was happy with his life, and didn't need a mother who'd abandoned him.' More tears pulsed down her cheeks. 'He was married and had a little girl,' she wailed, grinding her eyes with her fists. 'I have a granddaughter, Carrie, and I'll never know her, just as I never knew my son, and it serves me right.'

She was sobbing so hard I felt frightened.

'Don't cry.' I crawled around on the duvet so I was kneeling in front of her. 'Come here,' I said, hauling her up by her shoulders and wrapping my arms around her as far as they would go.

I felt her muscles soften as she leaned into me and wept. 'He's called Peter Robson, h-h-how boring is that?' she cried, body heaving. 'Peter Robson! Not my Donny Dashwood any more. But he's still my son!'

A sob wavered at the back of my throat. 'Of course he is.' I kissed her hair, which smelt faintly of straw and chocolate. 'He'll always be your son.'

She pulled away, making a visible effort to pull herself together. 'I'm sorry,' she croaked, blotting her nose on the back of her hand. 'I always think I've got it out of my system, but around this time it hits me all over again.' She gulped. 'He turned forty this year, I think that's why it's worse. Another milestone I've missed.'

'Here,' I murmured, pulling a tissue from a box on the bedside cabinet and handing it to her. 'I wish we'd known.'

She trumpeted into the tissue, scrunched it in her palm, and sucked in a shaky breath. 'There was nothing anyone could do.' Her voice had become sing-song, as if to deny the terrible weight of her words. 'I kept hoping he'd change his mind one day, but he moved a few years ago and I don't even know where he is. I had another go at contacting him, you see.'

I realised my own cheeks were damp, and wiped them with my fingers. 'I wish I could help.'

She summoned a smile. 'It's enough that you're here, love, while Jane has a little break. I just can't be on the stall while I'm feeling like this.'

'But, Ruby—'

'I mean it, Carrie.' She sounded resolute. 'I'm really sorry to have dumped all this on you, but I don't want to discuss it any more.'

I stared at the littered carpet. If my parents had any idea they'd be there for her, I knew they would. Dad would probably be gutted that she'd never told him.

'Don't you even think about telling your parents,' Ruby said, as if my teeming thoughts had flashed up in neon lights. 'Please, Carrie. It's my secret to bear and I intend to carry on doing it.'

'OK,' I said, reluctantly. I knew it was none of my business, really. I'd only been back in Ruby's life a couple of days, and it wasn't up to me to start dictating how I thought she should live her life. But still…

A son. A cousin I'd never meet. With a child. My… second cousin? Cousin-in-law?

'Anyway, shouldn't you be at the stall?' Ruby folded her pillow beneath her head, revealing a glittering cluster of Quality Street wrappers that brought fresh tears to my eyes.

'I was going to get something to eat,' I said, reminded of the real reason I'd wanted to escape from the stall, before Ruby's bombshell had pushed all thoughts of Tom and Megan from my mind.

I got up jerkily, placed the baby photo and wristband on Ruby's dressing table, and folded the letter beside it. Ruby's eyes were as tightly shut as the curtains, as if to block me out, and I was swept with a feeling of helplessness. I suddenly longed for my old job, where my biggest concern had been what to wear on dress-down Fridays, which had grown increasingly silly, with staff turning up in onesies or superhero costumes.

'Ruby, we've a possible wedding booking,' I said, dragging the words out with an effort. 'It's at Hudson Grange, on the 28th.'

One of her eyelids peeled back. 'Oh?'

'Tom Hudson's getting married.' I hated the tiny quiver in my voice. 'His fiancée's mother has made an appointment tomorrow at ten, if you'd like to be there.'

'Where?' Her other eye pinged open.

'At the stall.'

'Why me?' Her voice was sticky from crying.

'I thought you might want to be there.' I remembered what Jane had said. 'As it's, you know, a high-profile wedding.' No response. 'It'll be good for business.'

Ruby tightened the duvet around her, as though under threat from some unseen force.

'Can't Jane take care of it?' She looked at me through damp lashes. 'I'm sure they won't care, as long as someone's there.'

'But they'll want to talk to the owner,' I said, desperation creeping in.

'You're family.' She was starting to sound sleepy. 'You can represent me.'

My stomach tipped. 'But…'

'You don't mind, do you, Carrie?' She stifled a yawn. 'I know it's a lot to ask, and I promise I'll help with the actual flowers, but I can't face talking to anyone at the moment.' She dipped her chin to her chest, appearing to notice the state of her food-stained top. 'Not like this.'

I nearly suggested that a shower and a change of clothes would do wonders for her appearance, and maybe her state of mind, but sensed it would be pointless. 'OK,' I said, bending to pick a plate off the floor, and a mould-encrusted mug off the bedside cabinet. 'I'll do it.'

'Sure?' Her eyebrows pleaded with me to say yes.

I nodded, hoping my smile projected reassurance. 'I'm sure,' I said. 'I want to help.'

'Thank you, sweetheart.' She subsided, with a sigh that sounded like air being let out of a tyre. 'I'm so glad you're here, Carrie.'

I paused for a moment, letting her words wrap around me. 'I'd better get back,' I said quietly. 'And don't worry, your secret's safe with me.'

I let myself out of the room and collided with a woman on the landing. A scream flew out of my mouth.

'What is it?' Ruby called, in a way that suggested getting up to save her niece from the clutches of a madman was more than she could face.

Luckily, it wasn't a madman. It was Doris Day, holding a feather duster, a look of excited shock on her lightly furrowed face.

'Just me, Ruby!' she called, round the side of her hand. 'Remember I said I'd pop in and give this place a clean as you're not well?'

'Did you?' Now Ruby sounded half asleep again. 'Thanks, Doll.'

'She always calls me that,' Doris whispered to me, seeming not to notice that I was rigid with shock, my heart clattering my ribs. She sounded pleased, as if having a nickname meant she and Ruby were best friends, but that wasn't the impression I'd had from Ruby. 'She's a funny one, your aunt,' Doris went on, smoothing a rubber-gloved hand over her immaculate hair. Hadn't I told her Ruby was having a break, not that she was unwell? 'I've always wanted to get to the bottom of her, but she plays her cards close to her chest.'

Doris was clearly Shipley's resident busybody, and I regretted letting her help me the day before. I was about to ask how she'd gained access to Ruby's flat, but she'd started speaking again.

'Your aunt hasn't been well before, around this time of year, you see.' She assessed me with shrewd blue eyes, before cupping her hand around my elbow and leading me into the kitchen. 'Leave that, I'll clear it up,' she said, when I craned my neck to look at the plate and mug I'd dropped. 'Good job the floor's carpeted, or they'd have smashed to smithereens,' she went on. 'Anyway, as I was saying, I called round this time last year, after Jane told me your aunt wasn't well, to ask if there was anything I could do, and she could barely take her eyes off that television screen.' Doris shook her head, looking slightly scandalised. 'She just said, "whatever" but I insisted, so she said I could get her some shopping, told me where she keeps the spare key and to let myself in. I popped by every day until she was back on her stall, and I'm happy to do the same again.'

'That's nice of you,' I said, trying to work out if it was, or whether Doris was using the opportunity to have a snoop. 'So… you came in without knocking?'

'Your aunt didn't like being disturbed the last time she was feeling poorly,' Doris said. 'I just came in to have a tidy up, sometimes made a cake, and cleaned the windows and watered her window boxes, and maybe touched up the paintwork if I had time, then made her a cup of tea before I left.'

A thought struck. I hadn't noticed Doris when I came bursting in, but I'd been so intent on confronting Ruby I probably wouldn't have noticed if there'd been a herd of goats roaming around.

'Have you been here long?' I said casually, watching her swipe at a delicate cobweb on the kitchen ceiling. She was wearing a polka-dot apron over her skirt and top, and I wondered whether she carried it around, ready to start cleaning whenever the urge took hold.

'About half an hour.' She darted me a meaningful look. 'Long enough to understand why your aunt can't get out of bed.'

Chapter 7

'You shouldn't have been eavesdropping.' I dropped my voice to a whisper, appalled that this stranger knew a secret my own family didn't.

'You shot into her bedroom and yelled, "You had a baby",' Doris countered, with infuriating calm. 'I'd have overheard if I'd been wearing earmuffs.'

'You should have made yourself known.' I began pacing the kitchen, but it was too small. I bashed into the sink and stopped. 'You could have coughed, or something.'

'Then your aunt would have known I'd overheard.'

Fair point. I pushed my hair back into its clip and tried to think.

'Like I said, I try not to disturb her if she's sleeping,' Doris said. Lowering her voice, she added, 'I think it's clear no one knows your aunt as well as they think.'

I stared. 'You won't tell anyone, will you?'

Doris drew her shoulders back. 'I'm very good at keeping secrets.' She tapped the side of her nose with a neatly manicured fingertip. 'But I know someone who might be able to help.'

'What do you mean?' I couldn't believe we were having this conversation. Just hours ago, I was fretting about my phone call to Tom, and worried about creating bouquets that didn't look like they'd been assembled by baboons, and now I was discussing my aunt's secret son, and trying to pretend I wouldn't soon be face to face with my once-best-friend, discussing flowers for her marriage to a man I had unresolved feelings for.

'I'm just saying, I know someone who might be able to find Donny, so you can talk to him for your aunt.' She said his name, as though they were old acquaintances. 'I've a friend who does a bit of detective work on the side.'

'Oh, for god's sake!' I brought my voice down. 'This isn't an episode of...' I tried to think of a TV drama I could equate our situation to.

'*Murder She Wrote*?' Doris cocked an eyebrow.

'What? No! Nobody's died.'

'*Without a Trace*?' Seeing my blank look, she elaborated. 'It's an American show, where a group of detectives track down people who've gone missing. It stars a lovely actor called Anthony LaPaglia, who's rather fit as my Eric would say.' Her face softened. 'He's gay you know. My Eric, not Anthony LaPaglia.' She chuckled. 'He and his partner Lance have just had a baby girl, so I'm a grandmother now.' Her gaze locked with mine. 'I suppose I've got babies on the mind at the moment, and I'm guessing your aunt has too. That's all I'm saying.'

It clearly wasn't *all* she was saying. Even the way she was standing – upright and alert, like a particularly perky meerkat – was speaking volumes.

'Look, I know this is my fault,' I said, deploying the soothing tone I'd sometimes used with clients at Cars 4 U. 'But I'd really appreciate it if you could forget what you just heard.' I looked around, to check Ruby hadn't materialised. 'My aunt would be horrified if we interfered.'

Doris gave me a challenging stare, so I made my eyes go big and round, and tried to project my thoughts like a hypnotist until she looked away.

'Fine,' she said mildly. 'But if you change your mind...'

'I won't,' I said, glancing at my watch. I'd been away from the stall for ages. 'And while I'm staying with my aunt, there's no need for you to be here.'

'As you wish.' Doris seemed unperturbed. 'I'll just finish up and I'll be off,' she said, bending to sweep up a trail of crumbs with brisk efficiency. 'You get yourself back to work.'

I stared at the top of her smooth hair for several seconds, but couldn't think of a reply.

❀

Jane seemed more anxious than angry when I returned to the stall in a state of sweaty dishevelment, and without my lunch.

'I guessed you'd gone to check on Ruby,' she said, her hair spiralling in different directions as though reacting to her emotions. 'Is everything OK?' She plucked a yellow rose from a bucket, and handed it to a man with a Zorro moustache without taking her eyes off me.

'She's fine,' I fibbed. 'I told her about the appointment tomorrow, but she doesn't want to be here.'

'That's a shame.'

I tried to interpret Jane's expression. Did she know Ruby's secret? Was she wondering whether *I* knew? But she didn't seem the sort to dissemble. And even if she did know, there was no point bringing it up. Ruby had made her position on the subject clear. It was to remain our secret.

Thankfully, I didn't have much time to think about Ruby, or anything else, as Jane began running through the day-to-day basics of managing the stall. Determined to focus this time, I realised it wasn't that complicated after all. It was clear I wouldn't be creating any award-winning floral pieces, but I felt confident that I could cope.

'Just take in the delivery from Jools, from All Seasons Nursery, each morning, write down any bookings, sell some flowers, and anything else can wait until I return.'

'You will be here tomorrow morning?' Maybe I could persuade Jane to deal with Megan. The thought of seeing her again was making my stomach cramp. Perhaps I could invent an upset stomach; imply I'd caught Jane's bug.

'I'll be here,' Jane promised. 'Providing Dennis doesn't leave me handcuffed to the bed.' She gave a lusty cackle that startled a seagull assaulting a dropped ice-cream cone. 'We've been having a little practice,' she said, with a horribly lewd wink.

'Listen, about this appointment…'

'Don't worry, I won't cramp your style. I'll let you handle it,' Jane said.

Panic shuttled through me. 'But you're more experienced at this than me.'

She shook her head. 'You look the part,' she said, frankly. 'She won't want to deal with some frizzy-haired troll in a boiler suit.'

'You could always wear something smarter. Not that you are a troll, or frizzy-haired.' My cheeks went hot. 'I just meant…'

'I know what you meant.' She gave a rueful smile and shrug. 'But what if Mr Hudson turns up with his daughter-in-law-to-be?' I hadn't even thought of that. 'He's quite the silver fox, you know, like that man from *The Great British Bake Off*.' That wasn't at all how I remembered Mr Hudson. 'He's been in the news once or twice, and I have to admit I sometimes fantasise about him—'

I coughed loudly to stop her, not wanting an image of a frolicking Jane and Mr Hudson infiltrating my brain. 'It's OK, I'll do it,' I said. It looked like the past was going to find me whether I liked it or not. I might as well face it head on. 'I'll be fine.'

'Of course you will,' Jane said. 'And if you run into any problems while I'm away, Ruby won't leave you to struggle on your own.'

'I'm not sure Ruby cares. You've seen what she's like.'

'Nonsense.' Jane passed me a long-handled broom. 'I've known her for years, and it's never got to the stage where I thought she'd give up the stall.'

I didn't argue as I began sweeping petals and leaves into a neat little pile. Jane didn't know the truth. She didn't know Ruby's heart was broken and that, in comparison, the stall didn't matter to her.

Over the next few hours I dealt with several customers under Jane's watchful eye, and managed not to drop or ruin anything. Admittedly, they'd been easy sales; a potted gerbera to a thin-lipped woman who complained about the price; a couple of bouquets that Jane had already made up, and I gathered and wrapped some sweet-smelling stocks for a woman who explained that the scent reminded her of her mother.

'Smell's so evocative,' Jane said, as the woman walked away, sniffing the flowers. 'When my mother had Alzheimer's, the only thing that made her smile was the scent of sweet peas, which my father gave her every birthday.' She sighed. 'She remembered, you see.'

I recalled my grandparents' garden, where sweet peas had curled like butterflies around bamboo tepees, and tried to remember whether Dad had ever bought Mum flowers. He wasn't romantic in the traditional sense, but neither was she. Last year, he'd bought her some ugly sandals that doubled as metal-detectors for her birthday. She'd loved them.

'No one's ever bought me flowers,' I said. By 'no one', I meant a man. Not that anyone else had bought me them, either.

'You could always buy them for yourself.' Jane deftly wrapped a bunch of freesias and thrust them at me. 'That'll be eight pounds, please.'

'Oh.' I looked for my bag, unsure whether I had enough cash.

'Your face!' Jane exploded into laughter. 'I'm joking,' she said, patting my arm. 'You can have them for a fiver.'

When I finally got back to the flat, with aching feet, my head reeling from all the new information crammed inside, I was stopped on the landing by a voice floating up the stairs.

'How's Ruby?'

It was the ruddy-faced man I'd spotted on my sprint through the bakery kitchen earlier.

'She's fine,' I said, moving to the top of the stairs and peering down. 'And you are?'

'Her landlord, Bob the baker.'

'Shouldn't that be builder?'

It was a lame attempt at a joke but he smiled gamely, as if he'd never heard it before.

'I thought she might like these.' He started to come up, holding out a bag. 'There were some teacakes left over and I thought... well, she always said it was the smell of my buns that got her up in the mornings.'

'That's kind of you,' I said, meeting him halfway. Stuffing the freesias under my arm I grasped hold of the bag, as if we were secret agents. 'She's, ah, not too well at the moment.'

'I gathered that.' He pushed his hands in the pockets of his baggy trousers and peered at me more closely. I was poised in a shaft of sunshine from the skylight window, and felt like an X-Factor contestant, awaiting the judges' verdict. 'You're quite a lot like her,' he said.

'I'm her niece.'

'Ah.' He nodded, as though it made sense, and I realised I didn't mind being told I resembled Ruby. Sarah was the spitting image of Mum, but in spite of us both inheriting her red hair, that's where the resemblance ended. 'Something about the eyes,' he added, approvingly.

Without his white apron and hat, Bob looked more like a trawlerman than a baker, with his wild dark hair, sea-green eyes, and weather-beaten skin. There was matted chest-hair where his shirt was unbuttoned, and I could almost see him standing at the helm of a boat.

'She comes sailing with me sometimes,' he said, and I wondered whether my thoughts were coming out of my head in a bubble. 'We get on.' It came out gruffly, and I realised what he was trying to tell me.

'You're her boyfriend?'

'Oh, no, I wouldn't say that.' Looking alarmed, as if I'd accused him of gross misconduct, he began backing down the stairs. 'I mean, I admire your aunt greatly and we talk a lot, but no, no, I wouldn't say I was her boyfriend, though I'd like to be, obviously, she's a fine-looking woman.' He passed a broad hand over his face. 'Give her my regards…'

'Carrie,' I supplied, half amused by his insistence that he and my aunt were just friends, when it was clearly more than that – at least on his part.

'Well, give her my regards, Carrie, and tell her I'd love to see her when she's up and about.'

'I will,' I promised, deciding I liked Bob. There was something solid and reassuring about him. He seemed like the sort of man Ruby could rely on – if she ever decided to open up and be honest about her past. 'I'll tell her now.'

Inside the flat, I sagged against the door. Even after the busiest day at Cars 4 U, I'd rarely felt this drained. I wasn't used to moving about so much, for a start. Sitting at a desk all day hadn't required much effort.

Casting my weary eyes around, I noted that Doris had worked some sort of magic in the flat. Bathed in an early-evening glow, the living room was spotless, the surfaces polished to a gleam. There were even some grapes in a bowl on the table, glowing like rubies, and the sofa had been cleared of clutter, and its blueberry-coloured cushions freshly plumped. I longed to sink into them and have someone fetch me dinner.

'It's Carrie, I'm home!' I called brightly. Doris had thrown away the wilting lilies, and after filling the vase with water at the kitchen sink, I dropped the freesias in and put it on the windowsill.

My stomach rumbled and I dug my hand in the bag of buns and pulled one out. I bit into it and groaned with pleasure. It was filled with plump, juicy raisins, and the dough was soft, and fragrant with cinnamon.

'I've just met Bob the baker,' I said, as I entered Ruby's bedroom. 'He seems nice.' I put the bag of buns on the dressing table before leaning over to open the curtains, still convinced some natural light would make Ruby feel better. 'He said to give you his regards, and to tell you he'd love to see you.' I turned, unnerved by her silence. 'I didn't know you liked sailing.'

She stirred, and wrapped a hand over her eyes as if I was shining a torch in them.

'Could you close the curtains, please?' she murmured. 'I really need to sleep.'

Chapter 8

'You're early,' said Jane the following morning, though she'd still arrived before me and had already finished setting up the stall. Sunshine glinted off the framework and silver buckets, which were brimming with fresh flowers, the explosion of colour competing with the duck-egg sky, and the fudge-coloured stretch of beach, opposite.

'I wanted to get stuck in,' I said, helping her to arrange the buckets on their respective pallets, before jabbing in the wooden labels.

I was already starting to know my aster (*a talisman of love and a symbol of patience*) from my iris (*associated with royalty*), with the help of a dictionary of flowers I'd found on Ruby's bookshelf.

Unable to settle, once Ruby had made it clear she wasn't in the mood for chatting the previous evening, I'd heated a pizza from the freezer, then took it into my bedroom and phoned Mum for a chat. I'd completely forgotten they were five hours ahead in Kazakhstan, but she'd been happy to burble on about how clean the metro system was, and how spacious their Airbnb apartment.

'Honestly, Carrie, it's a bit *too* smart, if anything. We were hoping for something more—'

'Authentic?' I'd said, soothed by the familiarity of her voice. 'Something nomadic?'

'Exactly,' she said. 'Though we had some local food last night that we had to eat with our fingers. Your dad was a bit put out when he realised the sausage was made of horsemeat, so we had to find a McDonald's.'

'No bridges?' I said. They had a thing about bridges, finding them 'magical' and would take about a thousand photos to show Sarah and me. We had to look interested, or Dad would get huffy.

'Ooh, yes, we went to look at the Arch Bridge in Astana yesterday, but some silly boys had climbed on top to take a selfie, and the police were there, so it wasn't really an—'

'Authentic experience?'

'Are you taking the mickey?'

I assured her I was, and she chuckled.

'How are things there?'

'Not great,' I began, then stopped myself. I longed to tell her the truth about Ruby, but knew my aunt would never forgive me if I did. I couldn't face explaining about Tom and Megan either, so instead made her laugh about my first day on the flower stall.

'It sounds more fun than that place where you used to work,' she said. 'And it'll do you good, being out in the fresh air.'

'It's certainly authentic,' I said, and she tutted and put me on to Dad, who informed me sleepily that Kazakhs believed that whistling a song inside a building would make you poor for the rest of your life, and every time he set foot in one he couldn't resist whistling.

'It's weird, because I've never been a whistler,' he said, and a huge surge of love had welled up inside me, and I'd had to pretend that Ruby was calling me.

'Give her my best,' he'd said, before hanging up.

I still hadn't been able to settle, and the birdsong on my relaxation app had only added an annoying soundtrack to my churning thoughts.

I'd eventually got up, checking Ruby was snoring peacefully, before creeping through to the living room to browse her bookshelves.

She was a fantasy fan, judging by most of the covers, but I wasn't in the mood for shape-shifters, so settled on *The A–Z of Flowers and Their Meanings*, which soon had my eyelids drooping.

'You look tired,' Jane observed now, taking in my hastily scraped-back hair and make-up free face, complete with pink-rimmed eyes. 'Coffee?'

'Please,' I said, having forgotten to make one earlier. 'You seem much better.'

'Right as rain,' she said, patting her stomach. She was wearing khaki dungarees tucked into turquoise wellies. 'I managed some kippers for breakfast.'

After updating her about Ruby, which didn't take long, she set about fashioning a funeral wreath, using a circle of green foam, which she skilfully entwined with lilies, white roses and greenery, and secured with wire. 'A Mr Johnson will collect this later,' she said.

'Do you do deliveries?'

'No, though it's something we've been thinking of looking into since Poll 'n' Nate at the top of Main Street closed last year. No competition, you see.'

'Pollinate?'

'Clever, isn't it?' she said with a grin. 'The owners were called Polly and Nathan.'

'That was handy.'

'All ready for your appointment?' she said half an hour later, as I checked the pails of flowers for water. My heart gave a massive thud. Mesmerised by the routine, and soothed by the seaside sounds I'd forgotten since living in Manchester, Megan and Tom had slipped to the back of my mind.

'I suppose so,' I said, wondering if it was too late to invent a medical emergency. Then again, there was an outside chance Megan might not recognise me out of context. I doubted she'd given me a second thought in the past ten years, having apparently wiped our so-called friendship from her mind the minute she'd hooked up with Tom.

I'd resisted any urges to look her up on social media, telling myself there was no point torturing myself. I still didn't have a Facebook or Twitter account, which Jasmine said made me a 'throwback' but rather adorable.

'I'll take care of any customers when she turns up,' Jane went on, stabbing in a final rose stem, and doing something complicated with a length of ribbon. 'Don't forget to show them—'

'Them?' I almost dropped my coffee.

'Brides-to-be usually bring their mothers,' she said, tweaking a petal into place.

My shoulders sagged. For a horrible moment, I'd thought she'd meant Tom. Unbidden, images of him gatecrashed my brain; his crinkly-eyed smile; the way he rubbed his eyebrow when he was tired; his pretend tough-guy face the time Hovis wee'd indoors. It had been pouring with rain one Saturday afternoon, and we'd run from the beach, back to the house he shared, where he'd let me choose a couple of CDs, while he mopped up Hovis's puddle. I still had them, tucked away in a box in my wardrobe at home.

'It might be an idea to take them to Cooper's Café.' Jane's voice yanked me back up memory lane. 'That way, you can talk in peace.'

'But I won't know what to say.' And I couldn't imagine Megan sipping a latte with me. In truth, I couldn't imagine her at all. In my head, she was still eighteen, her head thrown back and a glass in her hand. I'd never seen her drink anything but Diet Coke or champagne.

'They'll do most of the talking,' Jane was saying. 'You just show them our portfolio and make sure you write everything down.'

'I think I'd be better off staying here—'

'Now, why don't you write out a card for this wreath?' Jane butted in. 'The message is in the book under tomorrow's date, and there's a selection of cards in the top tray.'

'Right,' I said, glad to at least have something to occupy my mind.

Job done, I gave the card to Jane and she slipped it among the flowers, distracted by a teenage boy asking if he could buy half a bouquet for his mum's birthday, as he couldn't afford a whole one.

It was almost ten o'clock.

I moved from under the shade of the canopy into a patch of sunlight, and stood for a moment, inflating my belly with air. I wanted to be calm when I saw Megan; cool and in control. If she recognised me I would try not to visibly react. I would say something like: *'Oh, Megan, hi, it is you. I thought the name rang a bell,'* and perhaps give an enigmatic smile. *'I suppose there wouldn't be another Megan Ford, marrying a Tom Hudson in Dorset.'* I would glance at my watch to indicate how busy I was. *'Shall we get on?'* No, that sounded cold. She'd know I was trying to hide my real feelings. *'Let's grab a coffee and you can tell me what kind of flowers you'd like in your bouquet.'* Better.

I conjured an image of us in the café, our heads bent (was her hair still long and liquorice black?), browsing photos, but it quickly disintegrated into me tipping a cappuccino over her head and kicking her in the shins.

Maybe I should confront her about the way she'd behaved back then. It wasn't just Tom, I'd had time to realise in the months after I left; she'd been pretty mean at school sometimes, too.

But if I did, she'd think it still bothered me, and even if it did, I didn't want her to know that.

I decided to aim for sophistication. After all, I was the one who'd moved away and made a new life for myself, while she'd remained in Dorset.

If only my hair wasn't the same untameable beast it had always been.

Stop it. It didn't matter what Megan thought. All that mattered was persuading her to let Ruby's Blooms supply the flowers for her wedding. I wouldn't even think about Tom's part in it.

I inhaled again and breathed out slowly. The day was getting busier, people pausing to browse the shops on their way to the beach. There was a newsagent's across the square called Flannery's, and a man was polishing the windows to a sparkle. I glimpsed my reflection, outlined by the flower stall behind me, and noticed my hands were balled into fists.

I stretched them out and wiggled my fingers, wishing my nerves would stop twanging. I was calm, I was Zen. I knew how to change a car tyre and manage a burst water pipe—

A hand landed on my shoulder and I jumped about a foot in the air. As I wheeled around, I stumbled over my own feet, and let out a strangled yelp as I fell over backwards.

Chapter 9

'Oh my god, I'm so *sorry*!'

As I lay on my back, blinking at the cloudless sky, I had a sense of déjà vu. I barely needed to look at the face looming over me to know it was her; my body had reacted of its own accord by leaping away from her touch.

Megan looked the same, yet subtly different. Her lips looked slightly plumper, but her hair was the same shade of liquorice-black, cascading over her shoulders, her sculpted face tanned an olive shade that enhanced her silver-grey eyes.

'Are you OK?' The same slight drawl, overlaying her well-bred accent.

'I'm fine.' Gathering my wits, I rolled onto my side, pretending not to notice her outstretched hand, tipped with blood-red nails.

Jane's wellington-booted feet appeared in my line of vision. 'Carrie, what on earth are you doing?' she said, as if I'd thrown myself down in a tantrum. 'Has she fainted?' she asked Megan, who'd dropped to her haunches, her blush-pink skinny-jeaned knees touching her chin as she inspected me more closely.

'Oh. My. *God.*' She clapped her hands to her cheekbones. 'It's you, isn't it?' she shrieked. 'It's Bagsy!'

I winced. It was ten years since I'd heard that horrible nickname. '*Is* it you?' She craned forward, eyes narrowed like a professor working out a tricky calculation. 'It's *got* to be, with that hair.'

I scrabbled to my feet, blisteringly aware that I must look deeply uncool – in both senses of the word – in crumpled trousers and short-sleeved shirt, while Megan looked effortlessly stylish in the sort of white vest-top that would have made me look like a young offender.

'Yes, it's me,' I said, ungraciously. Tom couldn't have mentioned my phone call the other night. 'Hi.'

She straightened and clasped me to her, as if I'd returned from being missing, presumed dead.

'I can't *believe* it!' She let me go and stood back, shaking her head so her hair rippled and glinted in the sunshine. She was still taller than me, even in sparkly flat sandals.

'We knew each other at school,' she said in a confiding tone to Jane, who was darting looks from Megan's flawless face to my perspiring one, as if she couldn't comprehend that such a creature could be connected to me. 'I'm Megan Ford,' she elaborated. 'You do remember me, don't you?' She returned her gaze to my stunned-deer one, her eyes clouding with doubt. 'It *was* a long time ago.'

Was she joking? 'Of *course* I remember.'

Megan gave a swirl of laughter. 'Phew,' she said, swiping the back of her hand across her forehead. 'I thought for a minute I was losing it.'

I couldn't seem to breathe properly, taking sips of air. It was obvious she'd had no idea I was in Shipley, but was going to make a meal of it now she'd found me.

'We lost touch when she moved away,' she said to Jane, sticking her bottom lip out and making her eyes go sad. 'Doncaster, wasn't it?'

'Manchester, and it wasn't really like that,' I said, realising when Jane's eyebrows flew up that it sounded too intense.

'Oh?' Megan hoisted her slouchy, tan-leather bag onto her shoulder, her smooth expanse of forehead crinkling slightly. 'I remember you couldn't wait to leave Tom's party that night...' She stopped, and for a split second I thought she was being diplomatic, but then she shot out a hand to grasp my wrist. 'You'll never guess what?' she said, eyes glinting. 'I'm marrying him next weekend, can you *believe* it?'

I really couldn't.

She thrust her hand under my nose, and I briefly glimpsed an engagement ring with a gem the size of a Fox's Glacier Mint. 'Gorgeous, isn't it?' she said, standing back as if to get a better view of my reaction. 'He was going to give me something that belonged to his grandmother, but I went out and chose this instead, it's much more me.' Her eyebrows gathered in a frown. 'Tom Hudson!' she clarified, as I continued to gawp in stupefied silence. 'Don't tell me you've forgotten him too?' She flicked her hair back and I caught a whiff of coconut-scented shampoo. 'You introduced us, remember?'

'Of course I haven't forgotten him,' I managed. 'We were friends, *remember?*'

'That's right! You used to walk that funny little dog of his.'

Did she truly believe that was all Tom had been to me? A dog-walking companion? 'His name was *Hovis*,' I said forcefully.

Jane fidgeted, clearly growing impatient with this rather loaded exchange.

As if sensing it too, Megan glanced at a bangle-style watch on her wrist.

'Listen, we *must* have a proper catch-up while you're in Dorset,' she said, as though she'd always hoped to run into me one day.

'What I was going to ask, before you fell over, was whether you could tell me where Ruby's Blooms is?' She glanced around the crowded square, somehow missing the wheelbarrow with the name on. 'I had an appointment five minutes ago, but I'm rarely in Shipley unless Tom wants to meet for lunch, so I don't know it very well. We tend to go to The Anchor—'

'I know about the wedding,' I burst out, unable to keep up the charade. 'Your mother phoned to ask if we could do the flowers.'

Megan clutched her chest as if she'd been shot. '*You're* the florist I was supposed to meet?' Her eyes enlarged. 'Oh, Carrie, what a *coincidence!*' she cried. 'I didn't know you were a florist, I thought you'd be doing some office job "oop north, tha knows."' Her accent was offensive. Had she always been this… *awful?* 'Where was it again? Macclesfield?'

'Manchester,' I said, through gritted teeth.

'And you've moved back?' Something new had entered her too-bright tone. 'For good?'

'I'm helping my aunt out for a bit,' I said shortly. 'This is Ruby's Blooms.' I took a step back and brandished my arm at the stall.

Her gaze moved past me and widened further. 'You work *here?*'

'Temporarily,' I said, rattled by her tone.

'And this is your aunt?' She looked at Jane, taking in the dungarees and wellies. 'I thought she lived in Wales.'

So, she *had* remembered something about my life. Despite mostly talking about herself, she'd occasionally shown an interest in my family, seeming to find us vaguely amusing, as if we were circus performers. 'That's my mum's sister, Barbara,' I said. 'Ruby's my aunt on my dad's side, and this is her, erm… business partner, Jane.'

Jane bobbed her head, and for a horrible minute I thought she was going to curtsy.

'Carrie can take down the details of what you're looking for,' she said demurely, but Megan was shaking her head.

'Listen, my mother panicked and probably didn't realise this wasn't a legitimate business,' she said, in a rather condescending way. She'd never got on with her mother.

'It's totally legitimate,' I argued, and when Jane stiffened, tried to lighten my tone. 'My aunt's not well at the moment, but I can assure you—'

'Oh, poor thing.' Megan pressed a hand to her heart. 'I'm sorry to hear that, but it's just that I've been let down by Jay Simmons.' She paused, and I had the sense we were supposed to know who she was talking about. 'He's won lots of awards, and designed a wedding bouquet in the shape of a handbag for a supermodel,' she continued. 'We were lucky to get him in the first place, but my father's an old friend of his father and pulled some strings.'

I still had no idea who he was. 'You're back in touch with your father then,' I couldn't resist saying.

Her smile dimmed. 'Well, he's still in Canada, still married to that woman half his age, and they're having another *baby*, would you believe?' She said 'baby' the way most people said Rottweiler, and I remembered how upset she'd been when she'd heard her father's new girlfriend had given birth to twin girls, and another baby girl a year later. 'But he's doing what he can from over there, and he's going to try to be here on the day, pregnancy permitting.' She inhaled and shook back her hair, as if throwing off thoughts of them. 'Anyway, Jay has this cute little shop in Shoreditch, but he was arrested last week for smuggling cocaine into the country, which has left us rather in the lurch. I decided to go local instead but, no offence' – her voice grew kind – 'it wouldn't be fair to expect you to compete with that level of expertise.'

Nicely put, Megan. She'd always had a talent for cutting people down to size in the friendliest possible way. 'The smiling assassin' my sister once called her, but I hadn't seen it back then, too caught up in our shiny friendship.

Catching a desperate grimace from Jane, I remembered I was supposed to secure this booking, but couldn't bring myself to respond politely to Megan's patronising comment, and gave a little shake of my head.

Jane adjusted her face into a smile. 'We can't promise a bouquet in the shape of a handbag, but give us a chance to show you what we *can* do,' she said.

Megan was scrutinising me. 'You don't seem too well yourself, Carrie,' she said smoothly. 'You were never very good in the sun, with that hair and skin.'

'I'm fine,' I said, a hand shooting to my cheek. Was she remembering the time I got badly burnt, trying to attain a tan like hers during the summer holidays? All I'd got was peeling shoulders, and a skin-cancer lecture from Mum.

'Why don't you pop to Cooper's Cafe, and Carrie will show you our portfolio?' Jane said anxiously.

Megan eyed the stall doubtfully, as if it might be about to collapse. 'We-e-ell,' she said, tapping her chin with her fingers. 'Jay was doing the flowers at a discount as a favour to my father. He was only charging a couple of thousand, so maybe if you could match that?'

A couple of thousand, and that was a *discount*?

'I'll get the portfolio,' Jane squeaked, and scurried off.

The sun pulsed down, and I felt an answering throb in my temples.

Megan cast her eyes over the range of flowers and seemed to make up her mind.

'Hey, look, why not?' she said with a magnanimous shrug. 'I obviously bumped into you for a reason, after all this time, so why not help each other out?' She gave a sugary smile, and I refrained from reminding her that she'd bumped into me by appointment, rather than chance. 'My mother wanted to be with me, to approve,' she added, glancing over her shoulder. 'I don't know where she's got to. I left her parking the car.'

Should I ask her why she'd told Tom I'd been planning to move to Manchester? No. Too tragic. Plus, she'd know I'd spoken to him.

Instead, I tried to form an open and friendly expression. 'My aunt's the best in the business—'

'There's something else you'll never guess!' Megan gripped my arm as a grin spread over her face. 'I'm having a baby!'

I swayed slightly, as my eyes slid to her stomach.

A baby.

Tom's baby.

There was no sign of a baby. Her stomach was ironing-board flat.

Megan was still speaking. 'It's very early days, but I wanted to get married before I started to show.' Her smile grew to epic proportions, lifting the blades of her cheekbones.

'A baby,' I echoed, as if she'd spoken in code and it might mean something else.

'That's right.' Her head bobbed. 'Michael's hoping it'll be a boy.' It took a second to realise she meant Tom's father. 'Ooh, did you know I've been working for him for years?'

Mum might have mentioned it in passing. 'No,' I said weakly.

'Of course not, why would you?' She slapped a hand to her cheek, and hunched her shoulders. 'Well, not long after the party, Michael offered me a job in HR, overseeing the hiring and firing of staff at

all the hotels, which I have to say I'm very good at, but I also think
he wanted to keep me close. He always hoped Tom and I would get
married one day,' she prattled on, while my spinning mind tried to
process it all. 'I've really helped build his hotel brand into what it is
today.' She flapped a hand, as if waving away congratulations, though
I hadn't uttered a word. 'Anyway, Tom's mum got ill earlier this year,
and Tom was really moved by how I'd helped to take care of her and,'
she waggled her fingers, 'voila!' Her eyes were as sparkly as her ring.
'He popped the question!'

My brain was a seething mass of confusion. According to Mum's
source, Tom had moved to Scotland, alone. So he and Megan had
broken up, then got back together nearly ten years later? But why had
they broken up in the first place?

Then it hit me. Tom had *needed* to go, in order to find himself away
from family pressures, but Megan wouldn't have wanted to – not with
her shiny new role at Hudson Country Hotels. And Tom wouldn't have
liked that – her choosing the job over him. But then his mum got ill
and, when he came back, he realised he still loved Megan.

And what about her? Had she waited, knowing he'd return?

I tuned back into her voice, feeling sick.

'Between you and me, we're hoping Tom will give up this vet
thing and take his father's place as head of the company,' she was
saying. 'Michael's hoping to retire, you see, which we never thought
would happen, but he's got this urge to travel since Fiona died,
and he won't go until Tom's at the helm.' She gave a theatrical sigh,
and I remembered how she'd loved drama at school, performing in
the end-of-year plays to rave reviews. I'd been her biggest fan. 'It's
always been his dream to have his son take over, and I think we'll
be a perfect team...'

I zoned out again, feeling as if I'd done some strenuous exercise – climbed a mountain, perhaps, or cycled to Cornwall and back on a penny-farthing. I really needed to sit down.

'Though, obviously, I would say that.'

'Sorry?' I blinked.

Megan paused, and for the briefest second I caught a gleam of malice in her smoky eyes. 'I was saying, I think Tom will be a wonderful father, don't you?'

Chapter 10

Before I could respond, Megan dug her hand in her bag and pulled out her phone.

'Mum,' she said, after pressing in a number, 'I've seen the florist already, so I'll meet you back at the car.' She waited while her mother presumably protested. 'I know you did, but I can manage on my own, I'm not two years old.' Megan rolled her eyes at me, and a memory of Mrs Ford wormed through the static in my head; a tall, bony blonde, with a permanently anxious air. She couldn't have looked more different to Megan, who took after her father, a handsome physician who specialised in skin disorders.

I'd only visited their house a couple of times, because Mrs Ford didn't approve of her daughter bringing home 'unsuitable' friends. By 'unsuitable' she meant poorer than them, which ruled out nearly everyone. They lived in the poshest part of Dorchester, in a Georgian-style house on an elegant crescent, behind wrought-iron gates. In comparison, my home, though perfectly adequate, was the size of a shed.

'What do your parents do?' Mrs Ford had asked on my first visit, and an unusually rebellious impulse had prompted me to say 'they're porn stars', eliciting a delighted hoot of laughter from Megan. The colour had drained so rapidly from her mother's face that I'd thought she was going to faint.

'She didn't think there would be girls like you at Bedworth,' Megan had said afterwards. 'She thought scholarships went out in the fifties.'

It was the first time I'd felt ashamed to be there on merit, rather than because my parents could afford it.

'I wish she would find something else to focus on,' Megan said now, abruptly ending the call. 'She's been unbearable about the wedding.'

Megan's pregnant, Tom's the father kept dancing around my brain. An image zapped into my head, of an angel-faced boy with slicked-down hair, wearing a buttoned-up shirt. I swiped it aside, aware of Megan's scrutiny, relieved when Jane finally returned, her hair flattened under a straw hat.

'Here we are!' She flapped open the portfolio, and held it under Megan's nose.

'Actually, I don't have time for this,' Megan said, glancing again at her watch. 'I've a dress fitting in an hour.' Her luminous gaze met mine. 'I'll email you the details of what I want instead.' She was all smiles again – lady bountiful, blessing the peasants. 'If there are any problems get back to me asap. Time is of the essence.'

'We won't let you down,' Jane said, keenly. 'You can rely on us.'

'You do have an email address?' Megan looked dubious suddenly, as if running a flower stall was such a Dickensian concept she suspected we didn't even have electricity.

Did we have electricity?

'Of course.' Jane fished a business card out of her dungarees. 'Always carry a few with me,' she said, handing it over.

There was humour in Megan's smile as she caught my eye, and for a pinprick of time I felt myself being pulled in – remembered what fun she could be.

I tore my gaze away. 'We'll be in touch,' I said, noticing a toddler pick a flower out of one of the buckets and pull its head off. Jane hurried over as his fingers shot out to grasp another. 'Congratulations on your wedding, and the baby,' I felt compelled to add.

'Thanks,' said Megan, loftily. 'You know, I'd invite you but the invitations have gone out.'

'Oh god, no, that's fine, I couldn't have come anyway, I'm…' I racked my brain for an excuse. 'My boyfriend's up next weekend,' I said, my scalp prickling with sweat. 'He's been overseeing our house repair… renovations, and there's some paperwork to go over.' I groaned inwardly. If I was going to invent a boyfriend, I could have at least made him sound exciting. 'He's just stopping off for a couple of days before he goes back to – to Budapest.'

Megan was agog. 'Budapest?'

'He's a journalist… a war correspondent,' I said, gripped by an urge to prove I'd moved on, and wasn't remotely bothered that she was pregnant and marrying Tom.

'I didn't realise there was a war in Budapest.'

'Ah, yes, well,' I stuttered. I remembered how Megan's disdainful attitude to education had hidden an intelligence she'd never bothered to foster, preferring to party while I swotted for A levels.

'There isn't,' I said, cheeks stinging with tell-tale colour. Hopefully, she'd think it was sunburn. 'He's reporting on something else,' I improvised. 'I can't talk about it.'

'Sounds exciting,' she said in a conspiratorial way, and I wanted to kick myself. It now sounded as if I was trying to revive our friendship, which couldn't have been further from the truth. 'We should make up a foursome, go out for dinner before the wedding.' Her face lit up. 'I know Tom would love to see you.'

I nearly laughed, the idea was so preposterous. I couldn't imagine him agreeing to come anywhere near me, let alone sit through a meal with me and my fake boyfriend.

'What's he called?' she said.

'Sorry?'

'Your chap. I'll look for a date in my diary and pop you in.'

'Oh, um,' I cast my eyes around and spotted the sign in the shape of a coffee cup, outside Cooper's.

'Cooper,' I said quickly. 'Bradley.'

'Bradley Cooper?' She gave a wicked grin. 'Like the actor?'

'No, er, Cooper Bradley.' *Oh god.*

Her laugh was like the shriek of a saw on metal. 'That's *so* typical of you, Bagsy!'

'I don't know what you mean,' I said. But I did. She'd wangled her way into the Hudson family and was finally marrying Tom, while I was dating a man with a silly name, whose job I couldn't describe. *And he wasn't even real.*

'Do say you'll come,' she pleaded, pressing her palms together. 'It'll be like old times.'

That's exactly what I was afraid of.

'I think he'll want us to spend some time alone together.' I was going to trip up if she asked me any more questions about my fictitious boyfriend. 'We haven't seen each other in a while.'

Megan gave a filthy smile. 'I get it.' She winked. 'Although if your aunt's not well, she might not want to hear you two at it in the next room. I take it you're staying at her place?'

My nod was accompanied by a surge of nausea. The exchange felt way too intimate.

'Listen, I should get on,' I said, looking at the queue building up. Jane was dipping and darting like a robin, her glasses at the end of her nose. 'I'll be in touch.'

'Look forward to it.'

My muscles were clenched with the effort of willing her to go away.

'I have a lot to thank you for,' she said, without warning. 'I'd probably never have met Tom, or his father, if it wasn't for you.' Swooping in, she squashed her lips to my cheek, and I remembered briefly how special it had felt to be friends with Megan Ford. 'It's good to see you again.'

I watched her stride away, drawing eyes with her sassy strut, and wished I could time-travel back to the previous week.

I should never have come to Shipley.

Chapter 11

I entered Ruby's bedroom and yanked the curtains back.

'Could we check your emails?' I said. 'It's about that wedding I mentioned. I can't access your account and Jane's on holiday now.'

She'd driven off with a cheery, 'See you next week!' once we'd closed the stall, and I'd decided my best plan of attack was to get Ruby involved in the wedding. I simply couldn't face liaising with Megan again.

'Ruby?'

A stillness in the room alerted me to the fact that she wasn't there, and I spun around to stare at the bed. In the rosy evening sunshine, it looked rather magnificent with its thrown-back duvet, rumpled sheets and heaped-up pillows; as if it had staged a passionate encounter, rather than harbouring an unhappy woman with a growing food addiction. 'Ruby?'

It was the first time I'd seen the bed empty. I scanned the room as if she might be hiding, but saw only the usual chaos, which looked even worse with the curtains drawn back – as if someone had been abducted in the middle of a decluttering session.

'Ruby?'

A splashing sound reached me from across the landing. My shoulders unclenched. She was in the bath. Surely a good sign.

Then another sound emerged: distressed and high-pitched, like a tiny bird being strangled.

My blood froze.

Heart thumping, I raced from the bedroom and slammed my fist on the bathroom door. 'Ruby, are you OK? Aunt Ruby, answer me! RUBY!'

Nothing, apart from those odd little noises.

I turned the handle, heaving my shoulder against the door. It flew open, propelling me into the steam-fogged room, and I almost toppled headlong into the bath, where Ruby was reclining, up to her neck in bubbles. Her eyes were closed, and she was wearing a set of headphones, singing off-key snatches of an Adele song.

As I gripped the side of the bath, the lavender-scented air flew up my nostrils, prompting a sneeze.

Ruby's eyes flew open.

'AAAAAAARRRRRRRGGGGHHHHHHHHHH!' she screamed, rising from the water like a hippo. She yanked her headphones off and whacked me round the head.

'Ruby, it's me!' I said, grabbing hold of them.

'Are you trying to kill me?' She slid back down, so only her face was visible above the water. 'I'm just the right age to have a stress-induced heart attack.'

'I thought you'd tried to kill yourself,' I said, a sob blocking my throat. 'You weren't in bed and I heard a funny noise…'

Ruby reared up again. 'Oh, Carrie, I'm sorry,' she said. Resting a soapy hand on my arm, she leaned forward to kiss my fingers. 'I had an urge to get clean, that's all, and I like listening to music in the bath.' She nodded to her MP3 player on the side. 'I was singing along.'

'It didn't sound like it.' A tear plopped into the water. It was suddenly too much on top of seeing Megan, and the news about the baby, and Jane swanning off on her sex-break. 'I'd forgotten you can't hold a tune.'

'Oi, I'll have you know I sing in a choir, young lady.' There was the tiniest twinkle in her eyes.

'Do you?' Dad had mentioned once that Ruby was always singing into a hairbrush in front of the mirror when she was young, and had got into trouble for applying to go on a talent show called *Opportunity Knocks*.

Ruby nodded. 'We meet up once a week. At least I used to go, until…' She paused. 'I'll get back to it,' she said. 'It's a soft-rock choir, and belting out a bit of Bon Jovi is a pretty good outlet.' Her clinging wet hair gave her the appearance of a shipwreck survivor, but she suddenly seemed more present – as if the water had washed away some of her sorrow. 'You should try it some time.'

'I'm tone-deaf,' I admitted.

'I know,' Ruby said gravely. 'I came to see you in a school assembly when you were little, and thought there was an injured cat behind the radiator.' Her smile was like a burst of sunshine through a rain cloud.

'I don't remember that.'

'I was on a flying visit to the UK,' she said. 'It was only the second time I'd seen you since you were born.' I wondered if visiting had been too painful, after giving up her own child. 'You were a cute little thing.'

'Sarah was the pretty one.'

'So were you,' she said. 'The water's going cold.' She clamped her arm cross her chest. 'Can you pass me a towel?'

I stood up and handed her one off the back of the door.

'I thought we could order fish and chips for dinner,' she said, wrapping herself up.

'I don't mind cooking,' I lied. I'd never felt less like cooking, and the thought of battered cod and chunky chips, doused in salt and vinegar, made my mouth water. I hadn't eaten all day, my appetite non-existent after Megan's visit.

'No need,' said Ruby. 'It's my treat.'

'Well, if you're sure, I could pick some up while you get dressed. Which chippy is it?'

'There's only one.' Ruby stepped daintily out of the bath. She was short, like me, and cuddly, but light on her feet. It was oddly disconcerting to see her upright for once – like seeing a teddy bear come to life. 'Kerrigan's,' she said, glancing over her shoulder. 'It's at the bottom of the road, before the parade of shops.'

'What shall I get?'

'Cod and chips twice.' She wiped a hand over the steamy mirror of the bathroom cabinet and pushed her face to the glass. 'God, I look old.'

'You look lovely,' I said, truthfully. 'You suit not wearing make-up.'

'So do you.' She turned to study me, scrunching her china-blue eyes. 'You're very pretty, Carrie,' she said. 'That lovely red hair of yours. You should let it down more often.'

A blush swept over my face. I'd never known how to accept a compliment.

'Your birthday's May, isn't it?'

I nodded, puzzled.

'Your birth flower is lily of the valley, which symbolises humility and sweetness.' She touched my cheek. 'Very appropriate.'

My blush intensified. 'What's yours?'

'I'm October,' she said. 'Marigold.' Her hand fell away. 'It means sorrow.'

'Ah.' The mood had started to sour. 'I think I'll have haddock, instead of cod,' I said, to divert her.

Her eyebrows rose. 'The cod and chips twice was for me.'

✿

Ruby polished off her double portion in the time it took me to plough through half of mine.

'I eat my feelings,' she said, licking her fingers, perhaps seeing something in my expression. 'I always have, even when I was young.' She didn't seem too bothered. 'A healthy appetite, my grandfather used to say.' I wondered whether he'd been religious too, but her tone was affectionate. 'Your dad was the fussy one, I remember,' she said. 'Everything on his plate had to be eaten separately, and vegetables made him gag.'

'All vegetables?' I put my plate on the floor and collapsed back on the sofa. Ruby was sitting beside me, swaddled in her fleecy blue dressing gown, her bare feet up on the coffee table. She'd changed her bedding while I was out, and I was so relieved she hadn't climbed back beneath it that I wanted to keep her talking. 'Dad wouldn't let us leave the table until we'd eaten our veggies.'

'That's typical of Ken.' Ruby shook her head. Her hair had dried soft and fluffy, and stuck up here and there, like feathers. 'Do as I say, not as I do.' She wagged her finger in a parody of Dad that made me smile.

'What was he like as a boy?' I asked. 'In photographs, he always looked so serious.'

Ruby's face seemed to fold in on itself. 'There wasn't much smiling in our house.' She pulled a tissue from her dressing gown pocket and wiped her fingers. 'But your dad was lovely, always had a kind word for people, and loved playing the banjo. I really looked up to him.'

'Dad played the banjo?' I giggled. 'I can't imagine it.'

'"When I'm Cleaning Windows" was his party piece.'

'No wonder he never mentioned it.'

A companionable silence fell, broken by Ruby's stomach gurgling. She leaned her head back and closed her eyes. 'I always knew he'd be a good father.'

'He is,' I said, smiling. 'Although he's terrible at telling jokes. He always gets the punchline wrong.'

'I think I'd have been a good mother.' Ruby's words came out of the blue, and I held my breath as she began shredding the tissue in her lap. 'I didn't think I deserved to be one after giving Donny away, so I never tried again.'

I twisted round and watched a tear drop from her chin. 'You shouldn't think like that—'

'How did you get on at the stall?' She rubbed at her eyes with a scrap of the greasy tissue, and I knew the topic was closed.

I stifled a sigh. I didn't want to think about the stall. 'It was fine,' I said, remembering my original intention on returning to the flat. 'Would it be OK to take a quick look at your emails?' I untucked my legs and stood up. It was gone eight o'clock. With any luck, Megan would be miffed that I hadn't got back to her, and decided to try her luck with a different florist.

We have to make a good impression. Jane's voice in my head again.

Then I remembered Ruby's bank statement.

'It's about the wedding I mentioned,' I said, when she didn't respond. She was staring at her empty fish-and-chip wrapping, as if willing more food to appear. 'The one at Hudson Grange.'

'Hmm?' She glanced up with a slightly dazed air.

'Megan Ford is marrying Tom Hudson on the 28th, and would like us to do the flowers.' The words left a sour taste. Or maybe it was the battered haddock. 'She said she was going to email the details over.'

'Oh, right.' Still Ruby didn't move, but her gaze sidled in the direction of the bookshelf. 'My laptop's over there,' she said, flapping her hand. 'It's been plugged in, so should be charged.'

'I'll get it,' I said, though it was the last thing I wanted to do.

'Jane promised to deal with my messages until I'm back on my feet.' Ruby's voice was plaintive. 'Can't she do it?'

'She's gone away, remember?'

'Oh, yes.' Ruby subsided. 'I'm not used to her not being around,' she said. 'You can normally set your clock by her routines, especially in the evenings.'

'Really?' I found the laptop and carried it over to the table.

'Dennis cooks dinner, usually something with carrots, then they watch television until bedtime.' Her brow furrowed. 'They were working their way through *The Wire*, the last I heard.'

I couldn't imagine Jane watching *The Wire*. *Countryfile* seemed more her thing.

'She's got the hots for Dominic West.' Ruby's chest heaved in a throaty chuckle. 'Her menopause has brought on something of an awakening,' she added. 'She asked me the other week if I knew where the G-spot was.'

'Oh god,' I said, feeling a flush rise. I kept my gaze on the laptop as I sat down and fired it up. 'What did you say?'

'I said it was off the M40, just outside Oxford.'

Even as I laughed, I was trying to remember the last time I'd got physical with a man. It was nearly a year ago, with a colleague of Jasmine's – an IT teacher, who'd turned up looking like Ace Ventura in a Hawaiian shirt, with an oversized black quiff. All that was missing was a capuchin monkey on his shoulder. He'd talked non-stop about his ex, and after walking me back to my car had lunged at me, one hand squeezing my breast like a stress ball.

Thinking back, it was as if it had happened to someone else, and I realised a lot of my memories of Manchester were like that; a sepia show-reel of driving to work, reconciling columns of numbers, driving home, eating dinner with Jasmine, or Sarah (or Mum and Dad, after they moved from Dorset), and going on dates with interchangeable men. But whenever I thought of my life before, it always appeared in vivid Technicolor.

I didn't dare to think too closely about what that meant, and focused on the laptop.

'Do you have a boyfriend?' Ruby asked, as if it had just occurred to her.

'No,' I said shortly, cringing as I recalled my conversation with Megan. *Cooper Bradley.* What an idiot. 'What's your email address?'

'<u>rubysblooms@aol.com,</u>' she said on a heavy sigh, as if it was all too much trouble. 'Password, petalz with a z.'

I typed it in, and felt a squeeze of alarm when Megan's name appeared at the top of Ruby's inbox. 'Would you like to read it?' I said, without much hope. Ruby was in her default position; eyes shut, hands folded across her chest.

'Not really,' she said through a yawn. 'You do it.'

Playing for time, I glanced through the window instead. The sky had darkened to indigo, and there was a sliver of moon like a fingernail above the rooftops. I looked through the lamp-lit window above the picture-framing shop, and saw that the Hollywood couple were at opposite sides of a table, re-enacting *Lady and the Tramp* with a string of spaghetti, gazing into each other's eyes. Candlelight glinted off a wine bottle, and a black-and-white cat jumped onto the windowsill and began to wash its paws.

'For god's sake,' I muttered, turning back to open Megan's email.

My eyes widened as I read the long list of requirements. 'What are boutonnières, when they're at home?'

'Buttonholes,' said Ruby automatically.

'She could have just put that.' Apart from those, and the bridal bouquet, which was to comprise roses, peonies, and lily of the valley, there were two bridesmaids' bouquets, a basket of petals for the flower girl, thank-you bouquets for the maid of honour and her mother, corsages for ushers and assorted male relatives, flowers for a garden archway – preferably roses – a large urn arrangement of scented stock, foliage and seasonal flowers, and posy vases for twelve reception tables.

I swallowed. It sounded like an awful lot of work. 'Have you catered for a big wedding before?' I asked.

'Mmm,' murmured Ruby, sounding on the verge of sleep. 'Ellen Partridge's daughter spent five hundred pounds on her flowers last year. I even had to do the church,' she said. 'And she wanted a floral crown, which was a bit of a challenge.'

'Oh?'

'She's got an unusually large head,' said Ruby. Her eyes were still closed. 'I got the measurements wrong at first, and you could hardly see it when she tried it on.'

'Well, the budget for this one is two thousand pounds,' I said.

Ruby's eyes snapped open. 'Two *thousand*?'

I nodded, gratified by her response.

'Pounds?'

'Well… yes,' I said with a smile.

'Wowsers.' She was quiet for a moment. In the flickering light from the television, which was turned on with the sound down, I watched a range of emotions cross her face.

Finally, all traces of enthusiasm drained away. 'I honestly don't think I'm up to it,' she said, wearily. 'Perhaps you could email back and say it's too short notice.'

'OK,' I said, feeling as if someone had loosened a corset I hadn't realised I was wearing. At least I'd tried.

But as I prepared to type a response, my fingers faltered. Jane probably wouldn't get paid this month, and Ruby's overdraft was at its limit. As much as I hated it, a commission from Hudson Grange would probably secure more bookings in the future. Ruby's future.

The invisible corset tightened once more as I dithered.

Ruby heaved herself off the sofa and brushed a trail of salt from the front of her dressing gown. 'I'm bushed,' she said. 'I think I'll go to bed.'

And without another word she left the room.

Chapter 12

'Sure you can manage?' Calum's face was concerned. It was a boyish face, at odds with his stocky build. I'd attempted to help him erect the stall, but ended up getting in his way, so had opted to buy him a coffee from Cooper's instead. 'I could hang around, again.'

'I'll be fine,' I said, wondering what he would say if I begged him to stay. It was obvious he was more capable than I was.

'I'll see you later, then.' He downed his coffee in one long gulp and crumpled the cardboard cup. 'I promised Mum I'd knock off early while she's away, to help you pack up.'

'That's kind, but you really don't have to,' I said. 'I'm stronger than I look.'

He cast a doubtful look at my under-exercised arms. 'You sure?' he said, his friendly grin like his mum's, but with nicer teeth. 'No offence, but you don't look like you're used to physical work.'

'Is it that obvious?' Back home, as part of a New Year's resolution to get fit, Jasmine and I had started going to a climbing wall, which was basically a windowless room in a back street, with club music pumping from a sound system, but it wasn't the same as being outdoors and I'd dropped out after two sessions.

'I'm more used to sitting behind a desk,' I confessed, thinking longingly of my old computer, and the neat lines of figures I'd been used to dealing with.

'Just remember, you're giving people what they ask for,' he said, like a kindly uncle, despite being ten years younger than me.

'Sounds easy when you put it like that.' I smiled properly, but watching him stride away with a bit of a swagger, like a pop star greeting his fans, I remembered the upcoming wedding and my doubts came racing back.

I'd been certain Ruby was feigning sleep as I crept out of the flat, earlier. There'd been something forced about the snores coming from her room, and they'd stopped altogether when I'd approached her bed with a mug of coffee. I'd whispered her name, but she didn't stir, so I'd headed into the golden morning, trying to ignore the fact that I still hadn't responded to Megan's email.

As I checked the flowers, making sure no stems were broken, and removing any stray thorns, I thought about how the stall hadn't taken much money over the last two days – mostly thanks to me.

Money was no object for Megan's family, if her father was paying for the wedding, and it definitely wasn't an issue if the Hudsons were footing the bill. If the cocaine-smuggling florist had been doing the flowers at a discount, could they afford to pay even more?

The square was still quiet, apart from a trickle of customers in and out of the newsagent's, and some runners on the beach, making the most of a light breeze coming off the sea. I took out my phone and tapped 'Jay Simmons Florist' into Google, hoping to find some prices on his website. None were listed.

Contact me for a private consultation, and to discuss your theme.

On a whim, I pressed in the shop number. As it rang, I realised it was barely eight thirty, but reminded myself that a florist's day – not that I was calling myself one – started early. That's if Jay Simmons's business was still going, after his arrest. There was probably a manager in charge—

'Hello?' The voice was male, snappy, and ever-so-slightly camp. 'Jay Simmons, florist to the stars,' it added, as an afterthought.

My heart gave a thump. Like Tom the other night, I hadn't expected the man himself to pick up. 'Hello.'

'Hell*ooo*.' I'd never heard a word imbued with such sarcasm. 'What do you want?'

'There's no need to be rude,' I said, stung out of my usual politeness. 'I could be a potential client.'

'Are you?' The voice remained frosty. 'A potential client?'

'Well, I was hoping you could quote me for some wedding flowers, so yes,' I said, heart racing. I hadn't thought it through, but could hardly say I was pumping him for information. I tried to remember the list of things in Megan's email. 'I need an urn arrangement, some posies in vases, corsages... that kind of thing.'

'I know what wedding flowers are,' he said, still leaning heavily on the sarcasm. 'Is it for you, or your daughter?' I frowned. Did I sound like somebody's mother? 'Who are you, anyway?'

I fleetingly toyed with the idea of making up a character. Fifi La-Belle, reality star? Or an actress in an upcoming film. Ashley... Maddox?

'I haven't got all bloody day,' said Jay, interrupting my swarming thoughts.

Got a court appearance to go to by any chance? I jibed. In my head. 'My name's Carrie Dashwood,' I said. 'I'm nobody important.'

'Then I doubt you can afford my services.'

'A... friend recommended you. I was looking for a quote, that's all.'

'Friend?' His voice sharpened into suspicion. 'What friend?'

Shit.

'Name please, or I'm hanging up.'

'Megan Fox,' I blurted.

There was a stunned pause. 'You know Megan Fox?' His voice rose with excitement. 'The actress? Oh my *god*!'

Shit, shit. 'Sorry, I meant Megan Ford.'

'WHAT?'

Startled, I let out a short, sharp scream.

'The Megan Ford who's marrying Tom Hudson?' His voice dipped, hovering around glacial. 'The one who ditched me?'

Why, oh why, had I blabbed her name? 'She said you'd let her down.'

'Oh, did she now?'

I nodded, forgetting he couldn't see me.

'Hello?'

'I'm here,' I whispered.

'Why would Megan recommend my services when *she* ditched *me*?' He sounded furious.

'It was because of the cocaine,' I blabbed. 'She said you'd been arrested.'

'It was all a misunder*standing*,' Jay said, through heavily gritted teeth. 'I would have explained if that mother of hers had given me a chance.'

'I'm sorry,' I said, miserably. *Sorry?* What was I talking about?

'Who are you really?'

'What?'

'You're not looking for a quote,' he said, his voice hardening. 'Are you a reporter?'

'No, no,' I said. *Hang up, for Christ's sake.* 'I just wanted to know how much you normally charge for a wedding of that scale.'

'It depends,' he said, snarkily. 'On what you want and how famous you are.'

'I'm not famous at all.' As if that wasn't obvious. 'And I want the usual, I suppose.'

'I doubt you could afford me, sweetheart,' he sniped. 'Unless you've got five grand. London prices, sweetie.'

Five grand? 'OK, thanks,' I said, about to hang up.

'You're not a client, or a reporter, you're a florist,' he said silkily. 'She's asked you to do her wedding flowers, hasn't she?'

My shoulders slumped. Even as a child I'd been rubbish at lying, confessing immediately when confronted by an empty biscuit tin.

My silence said it all.

'You're going to have a fight on your hands, Carrie Dashwood,' Jay Simmons said. 'My reputation's been tarnished, thanks to a gross miscarriage of justice, and I need all the business I can get.'

'Well, we need it too.' An instinctive urge to fight had reared its head. Going against Ruby's advice from the night before, I said, 'And we've as good as got the job already.' The words 'so there' dangled in the air.

'Not in writing, I hope.' Jay Simmons had a grating 'that's hilarious' sort of laugh that set my teeth on edge. 'I'm used to charming my way out of difficult situations,' he said. 'I'm going to call Megan now, and I can guarantee you by the end of the day she'll be my client again.'

He rang off, and I stood for a moment, wondering what had just happened. Had I talked myself out of the biggest job Ruby's Blooms had ever been offered?

I imagined telling Jane, and bashed my head with my phone. '*Idiot.*'

A passing jogger swerved to avoid me.

'Hello?'

I turned to see a woman with an armful of gerberas and pastel-pink gladioli (*honour and remembrance*), and hastened over to serve her.

'I could have walked off with these,' she scolded, as I wrapped them up while she berated me for not putting the customer first. 'I'm sick to death of people constantly playing with their phones, instead of interacting with people,' she finished, counting out the right money in the palm of her hand. 'What did we ever do before they existed?'

I was saved from answering by the sound of big-band music erupting from her bag. Flushing, she fished out her phone and hurried away, talking in a hushed voice.

'Good morning, dear!' It was Doris Day, looking catalogue perfect in a red linen skirt and short-sleeved blouse, a bulging canvas bag hooked over her shoulder. 'Just off to the library,' she said, slowing her pace to a saunter and fingering a purple dahlia (*dignity and elegance*). 'How's your aunt?'

'Fine,' I said, distracted.

Megan had included her mobile number in her email. I could easily call her myself. *And say what? 'We'll do the flowers, but it'll cost you another thousand.'?*... That had been my half-baked plan, before giving myself away to Jay Simmons. Now, I'd probably have to undercut whatever he was planning to charge her.

Another thought struck. What if he offered to supply her wedding flowers for free, in exchange for an endorsement from the mighty Michael Hudson? Jay could be calling her right now.

I crunched my bottom lip between my teeth. Maybe I should leave it to fate. If Megan reinstated Jay, I couldn't deny it would be a massive reprieve. Yet the terrier instinct that had risen on Ruby's behalf hadn't quite subsided.

'Have you thought any more about what I said?'

'Sorry?' I refocused.

Doris was treating me to an arrow-eyed stare. 'If you were to let me have some details for Ruby's son I could set the ball rolling,' she said. 'I just need a name and date of birth, and anything else you know.'

I glared. 'I've already told you to forget it,' I said, heat rushing to my face. On the street where I lived, the only person I'd said more than hello to was my neighbour, Vinnie, to apologise, after Jasmine loudly speculated about the size of his manhood one Sunday morning, during a sunbathing session in the garden (she hadn't realised he was behind the hedge – or so she'd said), while the closest I'd got to anyone knowing my business was the postman, glancing through the window one winter's morning, and catching me on the sofa, watching *Star Trek* in a Slanket, eating a bowl of Frosties.

In Shipley, it seemed, privacy was a dirty word.

'No offence intended,' said Doris, digging a hand in her bag. 'Would you like to see a photograph of my granddaughter?' Before I could answer she'd whipped one out and thrust it in front of my eyes. 'I knitted that matinee jacket for my Eric, when he was a baby,' she said, as I shielded the picture from the sun with my hand and looked at a picture of a cute little girl with a riot of blonde curls, swamped in a pink woolly affair. 'It's a bit big on her now, but she'll grow into it,' she said, fondly.

'You knitted a pink coat for your son?'

'I was convinced he was going to be a girl,' said Doris. 'Now, isn't she adorable?'

I narrowed my eyes. 'I know what you're doing,' I said.

Doris's face was a picture of innocence. 'Erica will know her surrogate mummy as she grows up,' she said, tucking the photo away. 'It's all well and good having two daddies, but a child needs her mother too.'

'Erica?' was all I could think to say.

Doris's smile was proud. 'Named after her daddy, though I rather fancied Samantha,' she said. 'Still, I got my own way when Eric was born. Roger wanted to call him Columbo after his favourite TV show.'

She glanced at her man-sized watch. 'Anyway, must dash before this sunshine sets off my heat rash,' she said. 'Say hello to Ruby for me.'

I watched as she crossed to the newsagent's, her bright hair gleaming in the sunshine. She did a little side-step, to avoid a man coming out, and something about the sight of him stopped my breath. He had a dog with him. A three-legged, loaf-brown terrier, wagging its tail, casting him little looks of treacle-eyed devotion.

It couldn't be.

But the fireworks going off in my stomach, and the blood thundering around my head, told me it was.

Tom Hudson was crossing the square, heading straight for the stall.

Again, my body reacted instinctively, this time throwing me down to my hands and knees. Ignoring the startled gaze of an elderly man eating an ice-cream on a bench, I did the only thing I could.

I crawled beneath the workbench and prayed for invisibility.

Chapter 13

'Are you playing hide-and-seek?'

I opened my eyes to see a small blonde girl peering at me with the frankness of the very young. I nodded and pressed a finger to my lips.

A delighted smile crossed her impish face. 'Can I play?' It was clearly a rhetorical question as she scooched beneath the workbench and crouched beside me.

'Are you on holiday?' I whispered.

She nodded, solemnly. 'We come early to play on the beach before smelly toerists are get there.' She had a surprisingly husky voice for such a small child. 'That's what my daddy says.' She screwed up her face, in what I presumed was an imitation of a grumpy father. 'Want to go to the sweet shop,' she added, plopping down on her bottom and folding her chubby arms. 'Mummy says no 'cos I brushed my teeth, so I have to wait.' She stuck her lower lip out. 'Mummy's a poo-poo head.'

Hugging my knees, I said, 'I'm sure your mummy's very nice.' I remembered how much I'd adored lemon sherbets as a child, loving the way the sherbet fizzed on my tongue. 'You should go and find her now.'

'Don't WANT to,' she said, with alarming ferocity. 'I HATE my mummy!'

'Please don't shout,' I whispered, aware it was completely the wrong thing to say. I had to get her out and back to her parents, before they realised she was missing and called the police.

'Is your mummy looking for you?' she enquired when I failed to move, tilting her head so her hair flopped over one eye.

'No,' I said, deciding to change tack. 'Actually, I'm not really hiding, I'm looking for something.'

'Is it a flower?'

'What?'

'Have you dropped your *flower*?' she persisted, like a teacher exercising patience with a difficult pupil. 'Mummy dropped hers once,' she went on, wriggling on the cobbled ground. 'Daddy broughted them home, and Mummy said Daddy had got a glittery conscious and throwed them away.'

I found myself oddly riveted by this slice of family strife. 'What happened?' I said.

She cupped her chin in her hand. 'Well, they did some kisses 'cos Daddy was very sorry, and then he helped Mummy get the flowers off the floor, but they'd gone squashed.'

Despite myself, I hid a small smile. At least Mummy and Daddy had made up, and his guilty conscience had got the better of him.

'Can I help you to look 'cos I'm very helpful?' she said, dipping her head and widening her eyes at the ground to demonstrate. 'I can see anything, even up to the moon.'

'That's brilliant,' I said, 'but I think you need to find your mummy and daddy now, before —'

'Oh, it's a DOGGY!' she cried, clapping her hands as a bundle of soft brown fur pushed under the oilskin cloth, his ears cocked.

'Hovis,' I whispered, as his moist brown eyes met mine. His whole body wagged violently, as he launched himself at me and licked my face, whimpering with unrestrained joy.

'I can't believe you remember me.' I was half crying as I held him at arm's length, loving the familiar feel of his solid little body in my hands. 'I've missed you so much, little fellow.' Realising the truth of my words, I brought him close and pressed my face into his fur, transported back to running along the beach, throwing his favourite ball, and panicking when he ran into the sea and got caught by a giant wave.

'Why hasn't he got enough legs?' The little girl was examining Hovis, a groove between her eyebrows.

'He only had three when I met him,' I said, putting him down, my face damp with tears and dog saliva.

'Couldn't he find the other one?'

'No,' I said with a sniff, unable to stop petting his ears. 'But he walks very well without it, don't you think?'

She nodded and scratched his head, her face lit with wonder when he nuzzled her under the chin. 'I want a doggy, but Mummy says no 'cos she has to pick up poos in her hands.' Her chin wobbled.

'Maybe she'll change her mind,' I said recklessly, overcome at seeing Hovis so very much alive – though he must be at least eleven by now.

'I'm gonna tell her to get one,' said the girl, as a voice, shrill with panic, began shrieking, 'Ellie, where *are* you? Please come out, sweetheart, you can have some sweeties now.'

As suddenly as she'd appeared, the girl had gone, closely followed by Hovis, and the space they'd left seemed vast.

Reality flew in. Tom was close by, Hovis had recognised me, and any minute now I'd be spotted, and would have to explain what I was doing.

'Is there anyone serving at this bloody stall?' A male voice, tetchy and disgruntled, reached my burning ears. 'I'm not asking for the moon, I just a want a bunch of these yellow things for the wife.'

'I'm sure the owner isn't too far away,' someone said, and recognition quivered through me. *Tom.*

Furious with myself for reacting like a lovesick teenager, I scrambled out and stood up too quickly, knocking over a potted azalea.

Black spots danced in front of my eyes. I blinked them away, and saw a man with dreadlocks bunched into a ponytail, clutching some yellow roses. His gaze was hidden behind round sunglasses, but his mouth was turned down at the corners. 'About time,' he said, sourly.

'That'll be six pounds fifty.' My voice shook. I grabbed the roses and wrapped them with fumbling hands, fighting the urge to look for Tom.

'I suppose they'll have to do,' the man said, snatching them off me and taking out a credit card. 'The service here is rubbish,' he grumbled, as I found the chip-and-pin device and held it up so he could stab in his number. 'I'll go to the supermarket next time.'

'Please don't.' I offered a wobbly smile. 'We do appreciate your custom.' I daren't move my head in case I caught sight of Tom, and it must have looked like I'd cricked my neck, because the man's frown deepened. 'You should get that looked at,' he said, before stalking away.

Over on the beach, I could see Ellie with her parents, who were as dark-haired as she was blonde. She appeared to be arguing furiously, making pouncing gestures, and holding up her hands like paws. To my relief her mother was laughing, and her father hoisted her onto his shoulders and led a charge to the sea.

How lovely it would be, to be a child again.

Smoothing a strand of hair back into my hastily assembled bun, I shifted my gaze left and right without moving my head, like a ventriloquist's dummy. I couldn't pick out a familiar face, and there was no sign of Hovis anywhere.

I puffed out a lungful of air.

Tom must have gone. Perhaps he hadn't come to see me after all, and it was a complete coincidence that he'd appeared two days after I called him, and the day after his fiancée had visited the stall to place an order for their wedding flowers.

'Hello, Carrie.'

I spun around, my stomach capsizing. 'Tom!' I was aiming for vague surprise, but it emerged as a ragged whisper.

'That's me.' He lifted his arms from his sides in an awkward little gesture I remembered. He'd always seemed more at ease around animals. 'How are you?'

'Good, good.'

We moved forward at the same time, and awkwardly bumped cheeks, and his hand briefly brushed my arm. It was the most we'd touched outside my daydreams, and every cell in my body came alive.

As he stepped back I drank in all the changes; new lines around his eyes, and a thinner, more grown-up face. His hair was shorter, and the three-day stubble he used to wear had gone. So had the jeans, sneakers, and hooded tops he'd favoured, replaced by smart, putty-coloured trousers, and a khaki shirt with the sleeves rolled up, revealing lightly tanned forearms.

He was both familiar and strange, like a well-loved song I hadn't heard for years, but on hearing it again, remembered every single note. It was as if he'd always been there, part of the bones of me.

So much for being over him.

I felt sick and dizzy, as if I was coming down with something, and wished I wasn't wearing old combat trousers, and had ironed my stripy shirt, or worn something that didn't make me look six months… pregnant. *Shit. He's with Megan now, he's with Megan now—*

'Listen, I wanted to apologise about the other night on the phone,' he said, when the breath-holding silence had stretched to breaking point.

'It's OK,' I lied, my heart flapping about like a trapped bird. 'I shouldn't have called you like that, out of the blue.'

'I meant to tell you about me and Megan, but—'

'It's fine,' I said, waving his words away, my stomach a melting pot of jealousy – even after all this time – at the words 'me and Megan'. 'Just forget it.'

'I felt really bad afterwards.'

'Well, you shouldn't.' *You should.*

He was looking at me now in that interested way I remembered, almost as if he couldn't help it. 'You look… well,' he said, then winced, as if realising how it sounded. 'I mean… good. You look good.'

'Thanks.' My face felt in danger of combusting, and was probably clashing horribly with my hair. 'I'm so glad you still have Hovis,' I blurted. He'd stationed himself by my feet, panting gently. 'I really missed him.'

'He obviously remembers you.' Tom's gaze steadied, as though he'd fixed me in his mind now. 'Why were you hiding under that table?'

'It's a workbench,' I said stupidly, a fresh tide of heat sweeping up my neck. 'I was helping a little girl to look for something.' I couldn't seem to tear my eyes from his. 'Something she'd lost. Under the table. Bench.'

'Ah.' He nodded sagely, and I caught another glimpse of the old Tom, who'd sometimes teased me when he thought I was being too precise. 'I thought it must be something like that.'

Hovis began barking at a seagull strolling by, and Tom bent to scoop him up. 'Do you remember when he ate an avocado?' he said, as if he was keen to dispel the tension between us.

I laughed, in spite of myself. 'We thought he'd developed a refined palate,' I said. 'Until we caught him eating leftovers out of the bin.'

Hovis's eyes flicked from Tom to me, as if he couldn't believe his two favourite people were face to face once more. I could hardly believe it myself. If it wasn't for the tiny matter of Tom's impending fatherhood and marriage, I could almost have imagined us picking up where we'd left off before his party.

As if he was following a similar train of thought, Tom said suddenly, 'I still can't believe you're here after all this time.'

'I can't believe you're marrying Megan Ford.' The words exploded out of me before I could stop them, and I wanted to kick myself.

Tom's smile withered. He set Hovis down, and when he straightened it was as if a shutter had come down. 'She told me she spoke to you yesterday.'

I fought an urge to say something uncharacteristically bitchy, like *How wonderful that she tells you everything.* 'That's right,' I said instead, trying to imagine the spirit in which Megan had told him. Had she been faux-sympathetic about poor little Bagsy returning to help her aunt? Implied she was doing me a favour by letting Ruby provide their wedding flowers? Or had I just imagined she was being disingenuous?

'You didn't tell her I'd called you.'

He shook his head, his face suddenly impenetrable. Maybe it had slipped his mind. He'd been busy with a sick cat, after all.

'She explained about the flowers,' he said, rather stiffly. 'She said she was going to email you the details.'

I wanted to grab his arms and shake him and say, *Isn't it ridiculous that we're talking about your wedding flowers? How can this be happening?* Instead, I said quickly, 'I meant to call to confirm this morning. I just needed to check out a few things, like, erm… suppliers and so on.'

'I can tell her if you like, save you the bother.' He bent to attach Hovis's lead so I couldn't read his face. 'I'm glad she's going with someone local, instead of that idiot in London.'

My mouth dried, as I recalled my conversation with Jay Simmons.

'You went to Scotland,' I said, not intending to.

He straightened and shook his head slightly. 'How—?'

'Megan told me.' I didn't mention I'd already heard it from Mum, and plucked nervously at my money belt. 'She… told me a few things.'

He nodded, as if it made sense. 'I went there after I graduated,' he said. 'One of my mates moved there and bought a farm—'

'My friend Jasmine's from Scotland,' I said, as if it was a tiny village and he might have bumped into her, even though she'd lived in Manchester since she was twelve. 'Where was the farm?'

'Near Inverness,' he obliged, and I nodded, as though I knew it well. 'I stayed with him for a bit and worked at an equine veterinary centre. I needed to get away, and ended up staying for years.'

'Wow.' So, we'd both left Dorset to build new lives, but while Tom's return appeared to be permanent, mine was only fleeting.

I pictured him with wind-ruffled hair and a rubber-gloved hand, helping a mare give birth. I wondered if he'd had girlfriends there. Of course he had. *Look at him.* With his brooding air, and love of animals, he must have been fighting them off.

And yet, no one had won his heart. Only Megan.

'I'm sorry about your mum,' I said, with a vague recollection of her being distracted at Tom's party by a woman choking on an olive. 'I had no idea.'

'Why would you?' A shadow passed over his face. 'She'd grown close to Megan while I was gone, especially after she became ill,' he said. 'She was really keen for Megan and me to tie the knot.'

It almost sounded as if he was defending his decision to rekindle their relationship.

'And now you're going to be a dad!' I seemed to be having trouble censoring myself.

'She told you that too, eh?' His eyes met mine, and there was something troubled in their depths. Maybe he hadn't wanted everyone knowing before the wedding.

'Congratulations!'

'Thanks,' he said, his gaze flickering to the side. 'Let's hope I make a better job of it than mine did.'

'Still annoyed you're not giving orders at Hudson Country Hotels?'

'Or HCH, as it's called these days. Megan's idea.' A faint smile lifted his mouth. 'Weirdly, he's not so bad since Mum died.'

I wondered if he knew of his father's plan to retire once Megan had persuaded Tom to come on board. 'Well, that's good,' I said.

He shrugged. 'Too little, too late.'

'But he approves of Megan.'

Something flared in his eyes, then quickly vanished. 'She seemed excited to have bumped into you,' he said quietly. 'I think she's hoping you two can be friends again.'

When hell freezes over.

'I won't be here much longer,' I said. 'In Shipley, I mean, not... you know... Dead.' I cringed. 'Sorry.'

His expression softened. Relieved there'd be no risk of bumping into me after he was married, probably. 'I expect you've a lot of catching up to do.'

Nope. I've said all I ever want to, to Megan Ford.

He didn't seem in any hurry to leave, and I tried not to read anything into it as I pulled forward a bucket of powder-blue delphiniums to hide a surge of misery. Their scent was overpowering – or maybe it was Tom's closeness.

'So, what do you do, when you're not selling flowers?' he said, when it became obvious my words had dried up. 'Did you become a high-flying accountant?'

'Something like that,' I said, lightening my tone to match his. 'Not very glamorous, but I liked it.'

'Liked?'

'The company I worked for went bust.'

'I'm sorry.' He sounded as if he meant it.

'I'll find another job soon.'

'And you're happy in Manchester?'

'It has a great Christmas market,' I said. *Brilliant.* 'And I've got my own house.' Hardly likely to impress, when his father owned a bunch of hotels. 'My parents live there too now,' I blathered on. 'And my sister had twins, so I'm an auntie.'

He gave a slow nod of approval. 'I never did thank you for my birthday gift,' he said, unexpectedly. 'The photo of Hovis. It was really thoughtful.'

I glanced at the dog, now lying with his head resting on his paws.

'Oh, you know,' I said, fiddling with my money belt. 'It was silly really, you don't need a photo to remind you of him.'

'No, but it was a nice memento of our walks together.'

Our eyes became glued together, and the air around us felt suddenly fraught with danger.

Tom looked away first. 'So, Megan mentioned that you're seeing someone.'

I bet she did.

'Yes!' I said, injecting my voice with enthusiasm. 'He's coming to visit soon.'

'She suggested we all go for a drink, or something to eat, while you're here.'

NO!

'Lovely!' I made a mental note to come down with gastric flu.

Tom glanced at his watch. 'I'd better get back to the surgery.' As if he understood, Hovis rose and shook himself, staggering a little. 'It was really good to see you, Carrie.'

As he started to walk away, I suddenly couldn't bear it. 'Tom, wait!'

He turned, eyebrows raised, and I recalled him wearing that same expression at the pub where we used to congregate, when I called him back from the bar once, to ask for a packet of crisps. 'What is it?'

My eyes darted about and landed on a bucket of pink and blue asters (*a talisman of love and a symbol of patience*). I plucked out a bunch and crumpled some paper around them. 'These are for you,' I said, almost tripping over a bucket of foliage in my hurry to get to him.

'Thanks.' He took them, and shot me a grin that made a rocket go off in my stomach. 'They'll look nice in the cottage.'

'Cottage?'

'Attached to the surgery,' he said, sniffing the flowers. 'I mostly live there, to be honest.'

Not sure what to make of that, I shielded my eyes with my hand. 'Listen, Tom, about that night,' I said, pausing as Hovis did his three-legged squat and weed against the foot of the bench where the elderly man was eating another ice-cream. Or maybe it was the same one.

'I hope that's all he does,' Tom said, frisking his pockets with his free hand. 'I haven't got any poo bags with me.' He looked at me. 'Sorry, you were saying?'

'Oh, nothing.' I crouched to pat Hovis's head. 'It was good to see you both, too.'

Chapter 14

'I don't get why it's a big deal.' My sister's voice reached me through a crackle of bad signal. 'When you came to Manchester, you said you never wanted to see either of them again.'

'I know, but —'

'It was ten years ago, Carrie.' Sarah emphasised the ten. 'What they're up to now is none of your business,' she continued, her voice dying out. Either the reception was fading or she was multitasking; sending an email, or spiralising courgettes for dinner. There was never an idle moment in my sister's life. 'You're there to do a job, and a pretty good one by the sound of it.'

'But of all the weddings in all the world...'

'You're not over him then?' Her voice filled my ear again. 'I knew it,' she said, with a hint of sisterly triumph.

'Of course I am, it's just weird, that's all. I could probably accept him marrying someone else,' I lied. 'It's just that they were supposed to have broken up.'

'Well, people reunite all the time,' said Sarah, as if she hadn't married her very first boyfriend, Phil, straight after university, and not looked at another man since. 'It sounds like it was an emotional time, with his mum dying. It must have made him realise he still had feelings for Megatron.' I almost smiled at the old nickname, from *The Transformers*: 'the viciously powerful leader of the Decepticons'.

'Maybe she planned it that way.'

'If that's what you want to think.'

For a second, I wished I hadn't called my sister, but I'd needed to talk to someone who'd known how things were back then.

'She's playing games with me, I'm sure of it,' I said. 'It might have been a coincidence, her mum phoning about the flowers, but she's going to make the most of it.'

'I'd have thought she wouldn't want you anywhere near Tom, knowing you two used to be friends.'

'Oh, she's not that insecure,' I said. 'She'll want to rub it in, how well she's done for herself, and to show me they're "in love".' The words were like splinters in my mouth.

'Or, you've massively misinterpreted the situation and she's pleased to see you.' Sarah let her words hang for a second. '*Do* you still have feelings for Tom?'

'No!' I remembered the way my pulse had misfired when I heard his voice; the way my heart had seemed to leap towards him. 'Do you know, the night of his party she told Tom I'd been planning to move to Manchester, and had only stayed for his twenty-first, implying I wanted to snoop around his fancy house.'

'And he believed her?'

'Apparently I'd been acting funny, so it kind of made sense.'

'But didn't you say you thought he had feelings for you?'

I wished I hadn't said that now. I'd rewound and replayed our friendship so many times, those first few weeks I'd stayed at Sarah's. Practically since the day I'd returned to the vets to see how Hovis was doing, and Tom had suggested I stop by the house if I was passing, and we'd fallen so easily into friendship, I'd hoped he might see me as more than a friend one day. I'd gradually become convinced his feelings were changing; that his eyes had started to linger on mine when we said goodbye, and he was always quick to suggest another meeting. And then he'd made the comment about loving red hair, which I'd clearly read too much into.

'I obviously got that wrong,' I said.

'Well, Megan Ford always was a massive bitch.' Sarah had swung the other way now. 'And if Tom couldn't see it, he wasn't right for you.'

'You never even met him,' I pointed out.

'And you never found out what he was like to live with. You didn't even sleep with him, so you don't know if he's crap in bed, or leaves his dirty undercrackers on the floor, or wears them for three days in a row, or forgets your birthday—'

'You're talking about Phil,' I said.

'Well, yes, but you know what I mean. He exists in this bubble in your head, all lovely and perfect, but I bet if you'd married him, you'd be divorced by now.'

Maybe she was right.

'If he thinks Megan's the one for him, then good luck to him,' Sarah added.

'But they're so different.' Maybe that was the point. Our likes and dislikes had been too similar, and he preferred a challenge.

'So were you and Megan,' Sarah said drily.

'She used to be nice sometimes.' I wasn't sure why I was bothering. Megan and I only became friends during our second-to-last year at school, after I found her sobbing in the toilets one day and asked her what was wrong. Normally I wouldn't have bothered, because the scholarship girls tended to avoid the posh girls, who were mostly into clothes, bitching, boys and horse-riding, but Megan – normally so poised – had looked so wretched, I couldn't walk away.

It was a sign of how upset she'd been that she confessed to me – of all people – that her father had just left her mother, and she'd wanted to go too, but he'd refused to let her, and now she blamed her mother. She'd begged me not to tell anyone, and I'd promised I wouldn't, and after that we'd stuck together.

I knew my friends made fun of us, but I didn't care. Everything seemed brighter and more fun in Megan's company, and on her own she could be funny and kind, giving me make-up and horse-riding lessons, and inviting me to parties – though I rarely went, because someone always ended up with alcohol poisoning. And though she could be a bit cruel, inventing my nickname to amuse her cronies, and joining in when they laughed, there'd been something magnetic about her that was hard to pull away from.

'She didn't always have it easy at home,' I said, 'with her dad leaving and having more babies…'

'Blah, blah, blah,' Sarah interjected. 'We all have our problems, but it doesn't mean you make a move on the man your best friend's in love with.'

'To be fair, she thought we were just friends—'

'Oh, I bet she didn't,' Sarah said. 'You'd have been giving off all sorts of signs, believe me.'

'Well, he didn't have to respond,' I pointed out. 'Anyway, his father probably had a hand in things. I bet the minute Megan told him her mother was related to royalty, he saw it as some kind of merger.'

'Look, if you don't want to be involved in this wedding, it's simple,' said Sarah, losing a bit of patience. 'Let Ruby deal with it.'

'It's not that simple at all,' I said. 'She's not in a fit state for a start.' I thought for a moment. 'Do you remember much about her from when we were kids?'

'Jesus Christ!'

'What?' I said, startled.

'There's a hair growing out of my chin.' Sarah made a sound of despair. 'I'm turning into an old hag,' she said. 'I need to get a strimmer to my thigh-brows as it is, before I take the children swimming.'

I winced at the mental image. It was rubbish anyway. Sarah was tall and striking, and always turned heads with her piercing blue eyes, and her hair was a deeper russet than my flaming red.

'Aunt Ruby?' I prompted, watching a group of teenagers playing volleyball on the beach. It was lunchtime, and the sand was packed with bodies. The tide was out and the sun was high and hot. I was hungry and thirsty, and still hadn't contacted Megan.

'We never saw much of her, did we?' Sarah said, finally responding to my question. 'Didn't she live with some chap in China for years?'

'Henry, yes, and it was Hong Kong. She was nice when we did see her though, wasn't she?'

'I don't really remember, to be honest.' I sensed Sarah's attention slipping back to one of the many things that made up her busy days. 'What's it like, staying with her?'

'She's really down,' I said, knowing I couldn't tell Sarah the truth. Being a mother, she might not understand how Ruby could have given up a baby – and she might tell Mum and Dad.

'I'm sure she'll get over it,' Sarah said. 'She probably just wants someone to wait on her hand and foot.'

After ringing off, and not feeling much better than I had before our conversation, I took a swig from a bottle of lukewarm water I'd stuffed in my bag, then topped up the water in the flower buckets, before pulling up Ruby's emails on my phone. Making up my mind, I pressed in Megan's number.

'Hello?' She sounded harassed and slightly breathless.

'Megan,' I said, in the most businesslike tone I could muster. 'It's Carrie from Ruby's Blooms.'

'Hi, Carrie!' Her voice warmed up. 'I'm just on my way to a cake-tasting session,' she said. 'My mother wanted to make the wedding cake, but even the birds won't touch her baking.' I couldn't think of a single thing to say to that. 'She did a course last year,' Megan continued. 'She's still terrible, though. She's doing Italian lessons now, god help them. The Italians, I mean.'

Determined not to become distracted, I said, 'We're happy to provide your wedding flowers, but need to agree on a price.'

'The money doesn't matter, but do go on.' She sounded amused. In the background, I heard the bleep of a car door unlocking. Something sporty, no doubt, like the car her father bought her when she passed her test first time, transferring the money from Canada, as if it could make up for his absence.

'We thought three thousand, five hundred,' I said, adding the five hundred on the spur of the moment. How wonderful to be able to say that money didn't matter, when to most people, it mattered a great deal.

Megan didn't miss a beat. 'I had a call earlier from Jay Simmons,' she said breezily. 'Apparently, his arrest was the result of a misunderstanding and he's keen to get back to work.'

My heart plummeted. 'I see.' If I hadn't called him he probably wouldn't have contacted her. This was all my fault. 'Well, I'm sure we can match his price.'

'Actually, he's charging more,' she said. 'He's miffed that I gave him the elbow, says he'd already ordered the flowers.'

'Right.' So that was that.

'I'll tell you what.' Megan raised her voice above the sound of a car engine revving. 'Why don't you bring an arrangement to Hudson Grange this Sunday and I'll make a decision then.'

'Hudson Grange?'

'I practically live here now,' she said, as though it made perfect sense. 'Though sometimes I spend the night with Tom at the little cottage at the surgery, if he's on call. It's so cosy there, the two of us snuggled in the attic room.' I remembered how she'd hated animals, apart from horses. Maybe she'd had a change of heart.

'Why do I need to bring an arrangement?' I said.

'It's only fair, don't you think?' I didn't. 'I know that Jay's got a solid reputation, at least in the floristry world, but I don't know if your aunt's any good. I mean,' she went on, before I could speak, 'it would be silly not to have a sample, like with the cakes.'

'But you have to taste cake to know what you want,' I pointed out. 'Flowers are visual. You can look at a photo and know whether they're good.'

'It doesn't tell me much about the quality of the flowers though, does it?' She was obviously enjoying herself. 'Just a simple, good quality arrangement shouldn't be too much to ask,' she added. 'I'll get Jay to do the same, and Tom and I will choose.'

God Almighty. 'Fine,' I said, keeping my voice even. 'What time?'

'Let's say eleven o' clock.' I heard the crunch of gravel beneath tyres. 'You'll have to excuse me, I'm due at the tasting in half an hour, and I have to pick up Tom.'

She rang off without saying goodbye, leaving me feeling marooned. And also confused. Was she hoping I'd make a fool of myself in front of Tom? Or did she just want me to see them together, presenting a united front?

My stomach gurgled with hunger, and I backed across the square to the newsagent's, eyes trained on the stall, ready to run back if a customer materialised.

Inside, the shop felt blissfully cool. I was tempted to loiter, but grabbed a carton of orange juice from the fridge and a couple of bags of crisps.

'Business not very brisk,' said the man behind the counter as I approached. It sounded more like a statement than a question.

'I'm just helping out for a bit,' I said politely. He was pale, with darting eyes and coal-black hair, and was wearing a cable-knit jumper as though it was winter. 'I don't know what business is like normally.'

'People like Ruby,' he said. 'She's good with them.' He sounded slightly puzzled, as if he couldn't quite grasp the concept. 'Mr Flannery,' he said, and it took me a second to realise he was introducing himself.

'I'm her niece, Carrie.' I wished he'd just take my money.

'I like her, because she's not competition.' His mouth bent into an approximation of a smile.

'What do you mean?'

'I mean, that since the sweet shop along the parade won an award a couple of months ago, hardly anyone buys their sweets from me.' He sounded as sour as a lemon, and I suspected it wasn't just the competition that had put people off.

I reached for a Mars bar and laid it on the counter. 'I'll take that too,' I said, mustering some sympathy. One of the reasons Cars 4 U had gone under was relentless competition from a rival. It was hard in the cut-throat world of business. 'Nice to meet you,' I added.

'Looks like your takings are going to be down even more today.' Mr Flannery was looking beyond me, a baleful gleam in his eyes.

I spun around to look through the open door, in time to see two teenage boys hurrying away from the stall with masses of flowers pressed to their chests, heads twisting to check they hadn't been spotted.

'Oi!' I cried, rushing out and giving chase, but there were too many people around and the boys were quickly swallowed by the crowd.

'I think they went that way,' said a man at a table outside Cooper's Café, pointing to a side street. 'Want me to go after them?'

'No, don't worry,' I said, close to tears. 'They're only flowers.'

I trudged back to the stall and stared at several empty buckets, with just an inch of water left in each.

Now what?

Figuring it was better than the truth, I told potential customers that everything had sold out, and it seemed an age until Calum returned to help me pack up what was left.

Thoroughly fed up by the time we'd finished, I came to a decision.

I would tell Ruby that things weren't working out, and I was needed back in Manchester. She would have to either summon Jane back, or close the stall until she returned. I would email Megan and tell her to give the job to Jay Simmons, and head back to Manchester, and everyone could get on with their lives.

Including me.

Chapter 15

Bob the baker was at the foot of the stairs as I stepped through the door behind the bakery.

'I've just taken some pastries up to your aunt,' he said, easing past me in the small space. 'I thought it might perk her up.'

'Did it work?' I said. If Ruby was up and about it would be much easier to break the news that I was leaving. After walking back from the stall, I'd sat in my car for ten minutes, rehearsing a speech I'd prepared in my head, but couldn't get past the image of her sad, pale face, poking from under her duvet the evening I arrived.

'I'm not sure,' he said, brow furrowed. His hair was dusted white with flour at the front, giving him a distinguished air. 'She seemed a bit distracted.'

That didn't bode well. 'Is she in bed?'

His face grew even ruddier. 'We weren't... we haven't, I mean, I wouldn't...' He seemed lost for words. 'I respect your aunt too much to take advantage of her,' he managed, pulling himself a little taller. 'I hope she considers me a gentleman.' He inclined his head next door. 'And anyway, I'm still at work.'

I realised too late the direction his mind had taken. 'Oh god, no, I didn't mean that. I wasn't implying you'd' – I couldn't say 'had sex' – 'been intimate,' I said, like a prissy great-grandmother. 'She's been sleeping a lot lately, that's all, and I just wondered whether she was up.'

The tension visibly left Bob's sturdy body. 'She is,' he said, with more than a little reserve.

'That's... good?' I started climbing the stairs.

'She wasn't dressed.'

I stopped and turned. 'Not dressed?'

'I don't mean she had nothing on,' he said, eyes wide with alarm, as if worried I might think he was imagining Ruby naked. 'What I mean is...'

I took pity on him. 'It's OK, Bob. I know what you meant.'

'Oh, and tell her she can keep the calculator.'

'Calculator?'

But he'd already vanished, back to the safety of his loaves.

I let myself into the flat rather gingerly, unsure what to expect. I'd got so used to Ruby being in her bedroom that it was a surprise to see her sitting at the table under the window, a delicious smell of cooking in the air.

'I thought I'd make a casserole,' she said, looking up from a pile of papers. 'I don't think you've eaten a proper meal since you arrived.'

'It smells great,' I said, my mouth watering. 'You didn't have to.'

'I forget sometimes that cooking makes me feel better.' Her eyes returned to whatever she'd been reading when I came in. 'I've made a lemon cake, a fruit cake, some fairy cakes, a banana loaf and some chocolate Rice Krispie cakes, so there's plenty of choice for dessert, and Bob's just dropped off some pastries, if you fancy something while the potatoes are boiling.'

'You have been busy,' I said. There was a slightly manic air about her, as if once she'd started doing things she couldn't stop. She was still swaddled in her dressing gown like a pupa, and her face looked inflamed.

'Smells great,' I said, unfastening my money belt and dropping it on the sofa. I crossed to the kitchen and turned down the gas beneath a bubbling pan of potatoes. The worktops were strewn with debris from her baking spree, and there were enough cakes cooling on racks to fill a bakery of her own.

The weather was really too warm for a casserole, but Ruby was right; I hadn't been eating properly, and I knew I needed my strength for the conversation that lay ahead.

I washed my hands at the sink, and decided not to mention the stolen flowers.

'I wondered if we could have a chat after dinner.' I flicked the kettle on, and found two mugs. 'If you're not too tired.'

'Come and chat now,' said Ruby on a sigh. 'I've had enough of crunching numbers.'

I joined her at the table with a feeling of trepidation. 'Numbers?' I saw she'd been using a giant calculator that she must have borrowed from Bob, and there were lots of little biro-scribbled figures on a notepad.

'I had a burst of energy earlier,' she said, glancing at the cluttered kitchen. Her eyes widened, as if she'd just noticed the mess. 'After I'd finished baking, I thought I'd make a start on some of the paperwork that's piled up.' She cast me a shamefaced look, and I tried to hide a guilty look, hoping she wouldn't guess I'd already gone through it. 'I know I've taken my eye off the ball, and it's not fair to expect Jane to do everything, and I realise that you can't stay forever' – my stomach lurched – 'but I'm starting to wish that I'd stayed in bed.'

'Oh?' I said carefully, smoothing a hand over my hair. The warm weather was making it frizz more than usual. I was embarrassed that Tom had seen me looking so ungroomed, and annoyed that I even cared. 'Is there a problem?'

'I've hardly any money left.' Ruby tip-tapped her pen on the edge of the table. 'I'm behind on the rent and some bills.'

'Ah,' I said, attempting a look of surprise.

'How much did you take today?'

I tried not to glance at the half-empty money belt on the sofa.

'Not a lot,' I said, adding swiftly, 'I think people are more interested in the beach in this weather.'

'At this rate, I won't have a business to go back to.' She cast her gaze down, her voice dropping to a whisper, as if the reality had just hit home. 'I'm useless.'

'No, you're not.' My hand shot out to cover hers. 'You're going through a rough patch, that's all, but things are going to get better.'

Air gushed from her nostrils. 'How?'

The Hudson Grange wedding. 'I could pay your bills,' I said, wondering why I hadn't thought of it before. 'I've got some money put by.'

'Absolutely not.' Ruby drew herself up like a puff adder and threw her pen down. 'I won't have any niece of mine bailing me out. I'd feel like an even bigger failure, thank you very much.'

'It was just an idea,' I said quickly, wondering if I could do it without her noticing.

'And don't think I won't notice if you try,' she warned. 'I know what you're thinking.'

'You do?'

'Well, no, I'm not psychic, but I can guess.'

I released a sigh. 'There is the wedding at Hudson Grange.'

She gave me a look. 'The job I told you to cancel?'

'Y-e-e-es,' I said. 'Except, I didn't.'

Ruby narrowed her eyes. 'Go on,' she said, but I could tell she wasn't annoyed.

'It turns out they're happy to pay above the odds for the short notice.'

Her chin rose. 'More than two thousand?'

'Three and a half,' I said, unable to help a smile breaking out as her eyes grew large. 'It should tide you over for a bit.'

Ruby slapped her palms on the table, making the papers – and me – jump. 'Well, in that case, I'd better read the email you were going on about, and start thinking about what to order.' Pushing her chair back she rose, more animated than I'd seen her to date. 'Where's my laptop?'

'I put it back on charge.'

'Let's get it open, then.'

Having set the wheels in motion, I now wanted to backtrack. Not only would I have to see Megan again, I hadn't told Ruby I was competing for the job with a big-name London florist.

'Shall we have dinner first?' I made to get up, but Ruby placed her hands on my shoulders and gently pressed me down.

'I'll do it.' She kissed the top of my head. 'I'm so glad you're here, Carrie,' she said, her grip tightening. 'I reckon I'd still be in that bed if it wasn't for you.'

Moved, I lifted my hand to cover hers and twisted round to face her. I was overcome with shame that, just an hour ago, I'd been planning to leave her to it. 'I haven't really done much,' I said.

She shook her head. 'Telling you about Donny has helped. I feel…' she made a floaty gesture with her fingers, 'lighter. And you've reminded me that I still have a business to run,' she said. 'I'm never going to meet my son, or my granddaughter, which means I'll never really be happy' – she held up a hand as I tried to speak – 'but I can still work, and that has to mean something.' Her eyes glazed with tears. 'If a miracle happens, and Donny changes his mind one day and comes looking, he'll see that I wasn't a completely terrible person.' She wiped the back of her hand across her cheeks. 'I want to make my son proud.'

✿

'How could I leave, after that?' I said later, to Jasmine. We were FaceTiming on our phones, because I couldn't get to sleep. This was partly because I was still digesting a man-sized portion of chicken casserole and mashed potatoes, a doorstop wedge of lemon cake, and half a Danish pastry, and partly because I was dreading having to face Megan and Tom. Together. At Hudson Grange.

'Why didn't you tell her Bridezilla wants you to compete with another florist?' Jasmine demanded, her delicate face filling the screen. With her cloud of Barbie-blonde hair and doll-like features she looked nothing like most people's idea of a science teacher, and didn't behave like one either, outside work. She believed people's body clocks were set to the time they were born, so was at her best around 2 a.m. and thrived on very little sleep.

'Because I'd already made it sound like a done deal.' Feeling a waft of warmth from the open window, I flung my duvet off. 'She looked so relieved in the end I couldn't bring myself to tell her it might not happen.'

'Well, you'll just have to make sure you produce a masterpiece of a floral arrangement, so Bridezilla can't say no.'

'That's a laugh, I wouldn't know where to start.'

Jasmine's head bobbed down, and I could see from the fairy lights and rose-patterned wallpaper that she was in her room, which overlooked the back garden. I'd have given anything to be in my bedroom at that moment, traffic roaring past, wondering whether Jasmine was going to bring a man home, and whether I should put my earplugs in just in case.

'What are you doing?' I said, when her head reappeared. Her mascara was a black mass beneath her eyes and her lipstick was smudged. A horrible thought struck. 'Have you got someone there?'

'Just a little man,' she said, in a theatrical whisper, shifting her phone so I could see a male body, face down on the bed beside her as though he'd been shot. His top half was naked, but at least he still had his jeans on.

'He conked out as soon as he lay down,' Jasmine said, swinging the phone back to her. 'It's all that plastering.'

I frowned. 'My plasterer?' I said.

She pressed a finger to her chin and made a naughty-girl face. 'M*a-a-a-y*be.'

'Jasmine!'

'You said I should keep an eye on things here,' she said, fluttering her spiky eyelashes. She was wearing the brilliant-blue contact lenses that made her look like a robot. 'He's just so fit, I couldn't help myself.'

'For god's sake don't wear him out, Jas, or he'll never get the job done.'

She giggled. 'Have you bumped into your ex yet?'

'He wasn't an ex, we were friends,' I protested, wondering why I bothered with the pretence. Everyone but Tom knew I'd been madly in love with him.

'Yes, I have,' I said, and quickly brought her up to speed.

'Christ,' she said when I'd finished. 'So, Bridezilla is your ex-best friend, and she's marrying the man you were in love with.' She frowned 'We'd better find you a date for this cosy foursome she's planning.'

'That's totally not the point, Jas.'

'What was that noise?' She pushed her face to the screen. 'Did you just trump?'

'It was Ruby,' I said, stifling a giggle. It sounded as if she was making balloon animals in her room. 'She can't stop.'

Probably because she'd polished off seven Rice Krispie cakes after dinner, while jotting down ideas after reading Megan's email. I'd pretended to watch TV, hot with guilt that I hadn't told her the full story. 'Anyway, I've more important things to think about than men.'

'Shame, because I've already put you on My Single Friend.' Jasmine sounded inordinately pleased with herself.

'*No-o-o-o.*' I groaned.

'Oh, yes. Your password is carrieD123, with a capital D.'

'Oh, Jas, you know I'm not into dating websites.' I thrashed my head from side to side for effect. 'Dating websites are full of perverts.'

'Have you met them all?'

'I don't need to.'

'You can be matched with someone in your area,' she said. 'There's probably a lot less choice in Shipley, so men will be falling over themselves to take you out.'

'Thanks, I think.' I remembered the boyfriend I'd invented. 'I don't suppose there are any war correspondents in Shipley?'

'Sorry?'

'Nothing,' I said. 'Did you write a profile too?'

'Of course, but don't worry, I'm always sensible on social media, even on someone else's behalf.'

Her teaching job prohibited her from writing anything salacious, which was probably just as well, considering her fantasy was to lick Nutella off Hugh Jackman's abs.

Her face took on a concentrated look that I recognised from when she was marking homework. 'What are you doing?'

'Mmm, don't stop, babe,' rasped a male voice. 'That's so good. Oh, yes, keep going, that's ama-a-a-azing.'

Jasmine dropped me a wink.

'Are you?...'

She nodded. 'I'm massaging his—'

'Don't say it!' I covered my eyes.

'—shoulder,' she said and gave a headmistressy tut. 'You've got a dirty mind, Carrie Dashwood.'

'I know what you're like.' I risked a glimpse through my fingers. 'Tell him good night from me.'

I ended the call and fretted for a while about the state of my kitchen, which I'd barely given a thought since being at Ruby's. Then, determined to empty my mind and get a good night's sleep, I pressed the relaxation app on my phone, and settled on a soothing waterfall sound.

Ten minutes later, I had to get up for a wee.

Chapter 16

Calum had set up the stall by the time I arrived the next morning, and was sitting in the van, eating a bacon roll.

'Sorry,' I panted. I hated being late, but I'd had a restless night, filled with bad dreams and heartburn, and had slept through my alarm. 'Has Jools been?' I said, recovering my breath as I peeked into the back of the van.

Calum wiped grease off his chin with a paper napkin. 'Not yet,' he said. 'Maybe she's stuck in traffic.'

Hmmm. According to Jane, the delivery was never late.

'There's not much stock left,' I said, loath to mention that most of it had been stolen. When Calum had returned the day before, he'd made admiring comments about my sales prowess, and I couldn't bring myself to disabuse him.

'You could call our neighbour,' he said, licking his fingers. 'She's got loads of flowers in her garden, and she could fetch some from ours too.' He reached into the glove compartment for a pen and a piece of paper, and scribbled down a number. 'Give her a ring if the delivery doesn't turn up, which I'm sure it will.'

'Thanks,' I said as he left, smiling when he blew a kiss at a strutting seagull.

I looked up and down the stretch of road, but there was no sign of the little white Fiat I'd taken for granted would be there, just a delivery van outside the souvenir shop.

Alarmed by the sight of the empty buckets, I flipped through the order book, found a delivery note, and rang the number at the top.

'All Seasons Nursery,' snapped a gravel-voiced woman, as if I'd interrupted her doing something vital. 'It's because we 'aven't been paid, love,' she said, once I'd explained who I was and why I was calling. 'We sent a final reminder and our terms are clearly stated.'

My heart dive-bombed. 'I'm sorry.'

'Me too.' Her voice warmed up. 'Your aunt's a good customer normally, love, but we're running a business here.'

'I'll pay by credit card,' I said, and gave her my details. There was no need for Ruby to know.

'Too late for today's delivery,' the woman said, cheerful now. 'Jools will be back tomorrow, yeah?'

'Thank you.'

Ringing off, I examined the sparse selection of remaining flowers, and peered into the buckets, as if by magic something might be growing. Perhaps I could rearrange what was left – two stems per bucket – but I might as well stick up a sign saying: *Nothing to see here, jog on.*

Would it be ethical to fill up with supermarket bouquets? But there wasn't a supermarket close by, and I could hardly leave the stall to go and find one.

I briefly considered calling Ruby. Perhaps she'd be galvanised into action – but then again, the reverse might be true. Although she'd seemed more positive the night before, planning the flowers for Megan's wedding, her mood was still fragile after facing the state of her finances. This might send her into a fresh decline.

'Excuse me, could I leave these with you?' I looked up to see a young woman, holding out a yellow-and-white-striped paper bag. 'They're for Ruby,' she added, her gaze enquiring beneath a blunt-cut fringe. 'She hasn't been in for her toffee whirls.'

'I'm Carrie, her niece,' I said. 'She's taking a little break.'

'That sounds nice.' She smiled in a friendly way. 'I'm Marnie Appleton,' she said, pressing a hand to her chest. 'I run the sweet shop near the end of the parade.'

'Oh!' I took the proffered bag and peered inside. A deliciously buttery aroma escaped, but after last night's feast I couldn't face eating yet. 'You won an award,' I said, recalling what Mr Flannery had told me.

'Well, it was more for the sweet shop than me,' she said, with a self-deprecating shrug. 'Ruby would probably have won if she'd entered, because she's here every day, whatever the weather. At least I've a roof and four walls to protect me in winter.'

'It's nice of you to say so.' I dimly wondered whether Ruby would be back on the stall before winter.

'Actually, there's another reason I'm here.' Marnie glanced at the few flowers that were left. 'I'd like to place an order.'

'Great,' I said, moving across to the workbench. 'Let me get the book.'

'No Jane?' Marnie tucked a flyaway strand of chestnut hair behind her ear. 'She's usually here first thing.'

'She's on a break too,' I said, squashing an unwelcome image of Jane trussed up in a corset with a riding crop, chasing her husband around a hotel room.

'It's a lot of work for one person,' said Marnie, seeming concerned. 'Have you done anything like this before?'

'No, but it's fine. It's just that some flowers were stolen yesterday, and—'

'Oh my god, I saw some in a wheelie bin round the back of the shop,' she said, her brow crinkling. 'I wondered where they'd come from.'

I brightened. 'Should I go and get them?'

'I wouldn't bother.' She shook her head. 'Even if they're still there now, they won't be fresh. I expect it was Biff, or one of his dozy mates from college, doing things for dares.' Her tone suggested she'd been on the receiving end before. 'They never learn, but I suppose they're bored. I could have a word, if you like.'

I looked past her, taking in the sweep of golden beach and the ancient pier jutting into the sea. We'd rarely visited this area when growing up, preferring the more obvious attractions of Weymouth, but although Shipley had a lovely, old-world charm, there probably wasn't much for teenagers to do.

'Thanks, but don't worry,' I said, opening the order book. 'I'll put it down to experience. Now, what can we do for you?'

'It's a christening for a friend's baby, at the beginning of September,' she said. 'I offered to organise some flowers for the church.'

'I didn't think people still got their babies christened.'

'Beth's very old-fashioned.' Marnie gave a conspiratorial smile. 'She's thirty-two going on seventy.'

I took down the details, glad to have a booking I could tell Ruby about. 'Bunty's an unusual name for a baby,' I said. 'I like it.'

Marnie grinned. 'Alex, my boyfriend, is campaigning for us to bring back more old names when we start a family,' she confided. 'Roger, Beverley, Nigel, that kind of thing.'

'My parents are Judith and Ken,' I said, getting into it. 'You never hear of babies named Kenneth these days.'

'Exactly.' Marnie's eyes danced. 'Anyway, I'd better get back to the shop or Aggie, that's my assistant, will be...' She pursed her lips. 'Actually,' she said, smiling, 'she'd probably manage perfectly well without me.'

As she left, with a suggestion that I pop into the sweet shop some time, I slipped the toffees into my bag, then took out my phone and rang the number Calum had given me.

'Doris Day. How may I help you?'

My heart slipped. Resisting the urge to hang up, I said, 'It's Carrie here—'

'Oh, Carrie, I hoped you'd change your mind.' She sounded delighted. 'I was thinking about it last night, while I was babysitting Erica. I'm sure Ruby's son is angry at your aunt, and doesn't want to upset his adopted family, but if they could sit down together and talk it out, I think it would enhance both their lives.' She took a breath. 'I know I'm oversimplifying, but sometimes the simplest solutions are the best.'

I silently counted to five. 'I wasn't calling about that,' I said, good manners preventing me from telling her to mind her own business. That, and the fact that I needed her help. 'I was calling because our supplier didn't turn up and I've almost run out of flowers, and one of your neighbours, Calum, said—'

'Oh, Calum!' Doris cut in, seeming unfazed that she'd got the wrong end of the stick. 'He's such a lovely boy, he's a credit to his parents. He offered to cut my grass the other day, but I told him I'm as capable of gardening now as I was in my thirties, though my husband usually did it then.' She paused. 'Did I mention that Roger's dead? It's a blessing in a way, because he would never have accepted his son being married to another man.'

'I'm sorry,' I said, not sure what I was apologising for – the fact that her husband was dead, or had been homophobic. 'The thing is, Calum said you had some lovely flowers in your garden that you could bring down, and some from their garden too. I know Jane wouldn't mind,' I said hastily. 'I would come and get them myself, but I'm on my own at the stall.'

'Ooh, yes, I saw Jane and Dennis throwing bags in their car the other day. Not that I was being nosey,' she said, as if I'd passed judgement. 'I was outside, dabbing some Brasso on my knockers.' An involuntary snort escaped from me. 'I know, door knockers must seem old-fashioned,' she said, misunderstanding. 'But Roger insisted we have them, front and back, a lion's head, and one shaped like a trowel, because he did love his gardening.'

I was starting to feel slightly hysterical. Time was marching on, and if Doris was unwilling or unable to supply me with flowers, I might have to close the stall until tomorrow.

'I'll pay you,' I said, recklessly. 'For the flowers, I mean.'

'Don't be so ridiculous!' She sounded scandalised, as if I'd proposed a drugs deal. 'It will be a favour to your aunt,' she said. 'Give me half an hour.'

While I waited, I rearranged the few flowers left, so they looked marginally less tragic, then double-checked there were no orders for that day, and that the phone was working, should anyone wish to call, then I ran into Cooper's to grab a coffee, figuring there was nothing left worth stealing at the stall.

Once back, I settled myself on an upturned bucket to check there were no further emails from Megan, relieved when I saw that there weren't. On impulse, I googled her name, but there were too many Megan Fords, the most prolific being a feminist comedian. I furtively typed in Tom's name, but the only reference that appeared – apart from his veterinary surgery – was on his father's Wikipedia page, under 'family' beside all Mr Hudson's business achievements.

The sun warmed my arms as I clicked on the 'Hudson's Country Hotels' website, and scrolled through photos of extravagant grey-stone buildings in picturesque settings, with lavishly landscaped gardens. More photos revealed plush bedrooms with mullioned windows and balconies, and elegant dining rooms, where 'locally sourced food' was cooked by award-winning chefs. They looked a lot less flashy than I'd expected – quite classy, in fact – but it was clearly not the kind of industry Tom would be happy working in, and it was just a pity his father wouldn't accept that.

I finished my coffee and moved into the shade as my neck began to burn, and taking *The A–Z of Flowers and their Meanings* out of my bag, memorised a couple more: lisanthus *(gratitude and charisma)* and gardenia *(purity and sweetness).*

A family passed by, two young children carrying fishing nets on bamboo sticks, and the hot-and-bothered-looking dad paused to ask, 'Do you know where we can catch crabs?'

I could only imagine what Jasmine would make of that. 'There's a harbour on the other side of the bay,' I said, putting my book away. 'I think there are rock pools there.'

'You think?' He scowled. 'Don't you live around here?'

They'd gone before I could think of a pithy retort like, 'No. Actually, I don't.' On second thoughts, maybe it was just as well.

Idly, I picked up my phone and logged on to My Single Friend, using the password that Jasmine had given me. Maybe it would do me good to meet someone who wasn't a friend or colleague of Jasmine's, or someone I worked with. *Or Tom.* Still reeling from my intense reaction,

I determinedly scrolled through several matches in the area. Jack, aged twenty-nine, Toby, thirty-three, and Chas, thirty-nine.

I clicked on Toby, after reading his short profile, which basically said he was a painter. He sounded less of a cliché than Jack, who claimed to love staying in watching films, and taking long walks on the beach 'but not at the same time', while Chas was 'divorced and looking to play', which didn't appeal one bit.

Also, Toby looked quite nice in his photo – a bit like Greg Rutherford, who I'd taken a shine to during the Olympics, and his subsequent stint on *Strictly Come Dancing*. He was gazing slightly to the left – Toby, not Greg Rutherford – looking slightly embarrassed, whereas Chas had posted a mirror-selfie, lifting his top to reveal a clutch of muscles, and Jack was posed with a sweater draped round his shoulders, as if heading to the golf course.

I tried to think of a witty opener, before typing *Hi!* and hitting 'send'. Jasmine was brilliant at first-liners, but I couldn't pull them off.

Too late, I looked at the profile she'd written for me.

Sleeping Beauty looking for Prince Charming to wake her up. Failing that, a man with nice teeth will do. Must like Game of Thrones.

In the profile picture I looked unusually seductive, my hair tumbling forward and my eyes half closed, the dressing gown I was wearing gaping around the boobs. In fact, I'd been full of cold and was dozing on the sofa in front of *Gogglebox* when Jasmine snapped the picture on her phone.

'For god's sake,' I murmured, trying to work out how to delete it. It would be more realistic to use my driving licence photo, despite Jasmine protesting it made me look like an accountant.

'But I am,' I'd said.

'Exactly.'

A shadow fell over my phone, and I looked up to see Doris marshalling buckets of flowers with Mary Poppins style efficiency.

I blinked and stood up. 'How long have you been here?' I said.

'Not long.' She picked up the watering can and trickled some water into the nearest bucket like a pro. 'Shall I write out some labels?' she said when she'd finished, tugging off her gardening gloves and twitching a crease out of her smart, cream trousers. 'You might not know what some of these are called.'

'I don't know what *any* of them are called, but they're gorgeous.' I took snapshots with my eyes, while she chalked their names onto wooden markers. The deep orange centres were already attracting bees, as well as admiring glances from people wandering past. 'They smell so good,' I said, fingers tracing the silky petals of a pale pink flower with a beetroot-coloured middle.

'Those are mine,' Doris said proudly. 'Oriental poppies.' She pointed to a bucket of deep purple flowers. 'Those are from Jane's garden.'

The smell was like the best perfume, and I was blindsided by a memory; the scent of dew on Sweet Williams in my grandparents' garden in Bridport. I hadn't realised until that moment that I'd been carrying it with me for years. 'These are better than anything from the wholesalers,' I said, disloyally. 'I *have* to pay you.'

'I've already said no.' Doris plucked a pair of secateurs from her canvas bag and trimmed a couple of stray leaves. 'You can let me do you a favour instead.'

Chapter 17

I should have known there was no such thing as a free lunch – or free flowers.

'What kind of favour?'

Doris reached inside her bag and drew out a folded piece of paper.

'What's this?'

'It might be an address.'

I narrowed my eyes. 'It's either an address or it's not.'

She patted her hair as if checking it was still there. 'It's an address,' she conceded. 'For Ruby's son.'

I wasn't sure I'd ever gasped before, but it was the only way to describe the sound that escaped me. 'How—?'

'I saw the baby wristband, and the letter, when I was cleaning Ruby's bedroom, after you'd left the other morning. I'd already overheard her say his name was Peter Robson.'

'Doris, that's…' *immoral, outrageous, a diabolical invasion of privacy.*

The words were plugged in my throat, but before I could get them out, she said, 'I think your aunt wanted us – *you* – to find them.'

I stared. Could she be right? Ruby hadn't made much effort to put the letter and photo away in the first place, and she'd known I was coming to stay.

'This is emotional blackmail,' I managed, as a group of women clustered round the stall, cooing over the flowers as if they were newborn babies.

'We're celebrating a hundred years of the Women's Institute,' said one, with a horsey smile. 'Wish we'd asked you to do the flowers for our chapter's celebration dinner, instead of that over-priced place in Weymouth.'

'Next time,' I said, realising too late we'd all be dead by then. 'Are you a member of the Women's Institute?' I asked Doris, once the WI women had crossed to the ice-cream van. I was determined to ignore the crackle of paper I'd stuffed into my pocket.

'Certainly not, I'm a maverick.' Doris tugged a lacy handkerchief from the breast pocket of her blouse. 'I don't belong to groups,' she said, bending to brush pollen off her gleaming court shoes. 'Especially not groups of women, with their hormones.' Straightening, she gave me an arch look. 'Stop trying to change the subject,' she said. 'I might have found out where he lives, with a little help from my friend, but the rest is up to you.'

'But Ruby said there was nothing anyone could do.'

'Talk is cheap.' Doris slipped her handkerchief into her bag. 'Your aunt is clearly in crisis and needs your help.'

'Not if it isn't in someone else's best interest,' I said. 'Her son doesn't want anything to do with her, he said so in his letter. He threatened her with a restraining order.'

'That was a long time ago, and there could have been any number of reasons why, back then.'

'So why hasn't he got in touch since?'

'You can ask him that yourself,' she said firmly. 'That's the favour you can do. Not for me, for your aunt.'

I sidestepped a woman dragging her shopping trolley through the flower stall as if it was invisible. 'But I'm already helping,' I pointed out. 'And say I did go and talk to him, and he got angry, it could make everything worse.' Ruby's words from the night before flashed through my head; her assertion that she'd never be happy, but still wanted to make her son proud. *Didn't she deserve a second chance?*

Maybe if I talked to Peter I could at least put her case forward, and if he slammed the door in my face it wouldn't matter, as Ruby would never know. Of course, it would be better if he changed his mind and came to see her of his own accord, but that might never happen. And what if he did have a change of heart, but it was too late and Ruby had died – probably of a broken heart? He'd be filled with regret that his daughter had never met her grandmother. He might even have had more children…

Normally, I shut down my imagination if it threatened to run riot, but suddenly it was rampaging all over the place. I could practically see Peter on his knees at Ruby's graveside, tears dripping off his nose.

'If I'd wanted to take it further I could have found him myself,' I said churlishly. 'There's such a thing as the Internet, you know.'

'You've enough on your plate,' said Doris. 'It was no trouble to ask—'

'Your friend…'

'Ellen Partridge.'

'How come she knew where to look?'

Doris's eyes flicked this way and that. 'She prefers to operate under the wire, so it's best not to ask too many questions,' she said in hushed tones, inclining her head to indicate that walls had ears – even though there weren't any walls.

'Fine,' I snapped, my resistance slackening. I fished the piece of paper from my pocket and read the address. 'It's not that far from here,' I said, as if Doris didn't know. 'Only an hour.'

'Maybe he didn't want to be too far away after all.' Doris looked pleased by this assumption.

'Why does this matter to you?'

She dipped her hand in her bag then popped a sweet in her mouth. 'Pineapple cube?'

I shook my head, knowing she was playing for time.

She rattled the sweet around her teeth then seemed to make up her mind. 'When my Roger died, he and Eric were estranged.' The words came out stiffly, as if they needed oiling. 'I was forty when Eric was born, his father five years older. It was a different generation, and he couldn't accept that Eric wasn't like other boys. When Eric "came out",' she made quotation marks with her fingers, 'Roger disowned him.' She shook her head, eyes filled with sadness. 'I loved my Roger, but he was a stubborn old goat,' she said. 'I know he thought the world of Eric, but never got a chance to tell him before he died.' She swallowed hard and her eyes watered. 'Went down whole,' she gasped, blinking tears away. 'Anyway,' she said when she'd recovered. 'I don't like the thought of Ruby's boy not knowing his biological mother, no matter what the circumstances.'

I tried to formulate a response, but Doris was already walking away with tidy strides, her gardening gloves poking out of her bag.

'Bollocks,' I said loudly, attracting a glance from the elderly man I'd seen eating an ice-cream on a bench the day before. As if on cue, he pulled a violin from a shabby case and tucked it under his chin, then played a melancholy tune that would have made a perfect soundtrack to my conversation with Doris.

Passers-by began throwing coins in his open case and a couple paused to listen, arms entwined around each other's waists. A breeze tugged the hem of the young woman's white sarong, and for a tortured second I imagined they were Tom and Megan.

A feeling of envy persisted when they approached the stall and the young man bought a single rose to tuck behind her ear. It was the 'Hollywood' couple who lived opposite Ruby, as photogenic close up as I'd imagined they'd be. They finally moved away, fingers laced, smiling into each other's eyes. I couldn't help hoping they'd trip up.

I took out my bottle of water and took a reviving drink, Doris's words cantering around in my head, and jumped when my phone buzzed in my pocket.

I took it out to see that Toby had replied. *Hi.*

It seemed neither of us were budding Poet Laureates.

So, you're a painter? Very imaginative.

Yes, I am, for my sins.

I tried to recall some types of art. *Impressionist or realist?*

There was a bit of a pause, then, *I'm rubbish at impressions and I like to think I'm a glass-half-full kind of person.*

I smiled. At least he had a sense of humour.

I can be a bit abstract myself.

Interesting. Maybe we can go for a drink and discuss this further?

It all seemed so quick and slick, but I supposed that was the point.

Okay, when?

How about tomorrow night? We could meet at The Anchor in Shipley at 7.30 p.m.

I'll see you there, then. I fumbled to add a smiley emoticon, and accidentally sent a poo with eyes.

I've been told I sometimes talk shite, but never that quickly!!

I went hot all over.

Sorry, I pressed the wrong one.

Thought so ☺

I hastily typed *I'll see you tomorrow* and logged off before I could show myself up even more.

Chapter 18

Back at the flat there were no delicious cooking smells, and no sign of Ruby in the living room. Guessing she'd returned to her bed, I removed my money belt and counted out the day's takings. Not bad, thanks to Doris and Jane's flowers, which had practically sold out.

I'd brought back a fresh posy of lemon and lilac freesias *(friendship and trust)* and replaced the wilting ones in the vase on the table.

Glancing through the window, I saw that the sun had dipped, throwing the street into shadow. The Hollywood couple were back from their stroll and appeared to be dancing, their heads close together, as they glided around the room.

Did they ever argue? I wondered.

Did Tom and Megan ever argue? Why was it so hard to picture them married, when at his party they'd looked so perfect together?

A noise from the spare room – my bedroom – made my head whip round.

'Ruby?'

'In here!'

She was on her knees on the swirly carpet, her dressing gown billowing around her, surrounded by open boxes and blocks of foam, with a glinting knife in her hand.

'I didn't realise the time,' she said, blinking at me through the gloom.

'Ruby, what are you doing?' Almost stumbling in my haste, I hurried over and grabbed the knife off her. 'Why have you got this?'

She tried to swipe it back, but I held it out of her reach.

'It's one of my tools,' she said. 'I had an idea for a table arrangement, and got a bit carried away going through these boxes.' Catching my expression, her eyes softened. 'I wasn't planning to top myself, if that's what you were thinking.'

'Of course not,' I lied, my heart tripping over. 'I just didn't want you to cut yourself.' I glanced up. 'The light's terrible in here.'

'True,' she said, accepting my words at face value. She glanced around, as if seeing the state of the room for the first time. 'I'm sorry I didn't make an effort to clear it out for you.' She grimaced. 'Your parents would have a fit if they could see it.'

'It's fine,' I said. 'You need somewhere to store your work things.'

'I always meant to move them to Jane's.' She shifted onto her bottom and stretched her legs out, her robe falling apart to reveal surprisingly hairy shins. 'She's got more room at hers, but I've somehow never got around to it. That's how rubbish I am.'

'Of *course* you're not rubbish,' I said, wishing I hadn't jumped to the wrong conclusion. Already the brightness I'd seen in her face when I came in was leaching away. 'What sort of arrangement were you thinking of making?' I looked at a box spilling flowers that looked real. 'Silk?' I said, picking up a snow-white rose.

'They were for a winter wedding that was called off at the last minute.'

'Does that happen often?'

'I've only done one so far, so I don't really know.'

'Jane showed me the photos,' I said, kneeling opposite, trying to beam positive thoughts into her head. 'They looked lovely.'

Ruby shrugged, staring at her hands lying limply in her lap. 'It was easy really, everything traditional.'

'Is it normal to use artificial flowers?'

She jerked a shoulder. 'They can be more expensive, but at least they last forever.'

'Good point,' I said.

Ruby flexed her fingers. 'The bride was allergic to real ones.'

'Ah.'

'And at least you can use flowers that aren't in season.'

'But they wouldn't smell of anything.'

'You spray them with scent.'

'Of course.'

My bright façade faltered as conversation ground to a halt. I reached up and clicked the lamp on, feeling slightly entombed in the tiny room. 'What were you thinking of making just now?' I gestured with the knife I was still holding. 'I'd love to see you in action.'

Ruby heaved a deep sigh, as if I'd asked her to compose a sonata, and shuffled her hands through her hair. 'I can't really be bothered,' she said.

I was seized with panic, remembering I had to take a flower arrangement to Hudson Grange, to impress Megan with. Perhaps I could persuade Ruby to make up something using her silk flowers, and I wouldn't need to attempt something with whatever was left on the stall tomorrow – especially as I had no idea where to start.

'What else is in here?' I dragged the box closer and pushed my hand inside, expecting to find more flowers. Instead, my fingers brushed something stiff, and digging deeper I tugged out a pair of floral puppies, made up of white carnations. They were nestled together in a wicker basket, paws dangling over the edge, dressed as a bride and groom with swivelly eyes and plastic noses. The groom-pup had on a top hat, and the bride was sporting a veil.

'This is… amazing,' I said, though in truth I was undecided. Was it cute, or tacky? I supposed it was a matter of taste.

'I made it for the wedding that never was,' said Ruby, eyeing the pups with mild interest, as if she'd forgotten about them. 'I made a swan too, for the bride's table at the reception, but it wasn't very good.' She picked some fluff from her dressing gown sleeve. 'It looked more like a turkey.'

'It's so clever,' I said, checking for imperfections. 'I've never seen anything like it.' I doubted I'd choose it for my own wedding, but there was no doubting the skill involved. And if Megan was impressed that Jay Simmons had designed a bouquet in the shape of a handbag, it was probably right up her street. 'Can I keep it?'

Ruby jolted upright. 'Whatever for?' she said, but there was something proud about the tilt of her chin, and her lips had formed an involuntary smile.

'It's inspiring,' I said, knowing I should just come clean and tell her I was planning to take it to Hudson Grange, but I couldn't risk her refusing when I had nothing else to show. 'I wouldn't mind having a go at something like this myself.'

'Oh.' Seeming nonplussed, Ruby poked half-heartedly among the flowers scattered around. 'You could start with a heart shape, I suppose.'

Unwilling to expose my ineptitude, I scrambled to my feet. 'Maybe it's getting a bit late now.' I placed the flower-pups and craft knife on the end of my bed, and held out my hands to Ruby to help her up. 'What shall we have for dinner?'

Neither of us felt like cooking, so we worked our way through several slabs of cake in front of the television. All the time, I was aware of Peter's address still tucked in my pocket. My thigh felt hot, as if it was burning me, and I wondered what Ruby would think if she knew it was there.

A couple of times I opened my mouth to broach the topic, but she'd settled her gaze on a wildlife programme, where a leopard was savaging a deer, and in the white light from the television, her face was unusually relaxed.

I couldn't risk making her cry again.

I wondered whether Peter was on social media, or had an email address where I could contact him. It might be better to approach in writing first. Or was that cowardly? Face to face would have more impact if I was going to plead Ruby's case. I imagined him shutting the door on my foot, and nearly choked on my cake.

Swilling some tea, it occurred to me that I was hiding too much from Ruby. Should I ask her to come with me to see Megan on Sunday? But even as the thought crept in, I knew it was me Megan wanted to see, and if Ruby turned up she'd probably change her mind, regardless of how stunning the flower arrangement was.

And I couldn't deny a part of me was morbidly curious. Perhaps seeing Megan again would somehow make her marriage to Tom seem real. If I saw them together I might even be convinced they were meant to be together, and the weird, niggly feeling I had would go away.

And if it didn't? Either way, I had to accept they were getting married, and that if Tom wasn't marrying Megan it could be someone else one day.

'What are you thinking about?' Ruby's words were a welcome intrusion.

'I was wondering how you cope on the stall in winter,' I said, wishing I could confide in her. I had a feeling she would give good advice, but it wasn't fair to burden her when she was already low. 'It must get freezing out there.'

'You get used to it,' she said, ripping open a packet of crisps with her teeth. 'We just wrap up more warmly, or sit in the van, and if the weather's really bad we don't open.'

'Doesn't Jane mind working all weathers?'

'Jane's a tough old bird,' she said affectionately, palming crisps into her mouth. 'She loves the job.'

'Is she happily married?'

Ruby looked mildly surprised. 'As far as I know,' she said, after swallowing. 'Why do you ask?'

'Oh, no reason.' I looked into my mug of tea, wondering how close they really were. It seemed they were both hiding things from each other.

'Ooh, I've got some toffees for you,' I said, suddenly remembering. Reaching down for my bag, I pulled them out and handed them over.

Ruby retrieved one, and studied it as though it was an experimental drug. 'She makes them herself, you know.'

'She seemed lovely.'

Ruby finally slotted the toffee in her mouth. 'So, any men on the horizon for you?' she said, cheek bulging.

'Actually, I've a date tomorrow evening.' I was half hoping she'd disapprove, and I could stay in. 'I don't have to go, though,' I prompted. 'We could watch a film together, and I could make us a salad.'

'Salad?' She looked vaguely disturbed, as if I'd suggested frying our own kidneys.

'Something a bit more, you know, healthy.' I was still bloated from all the carbohydrates I'd ingested.

'Salads don't fill me up,' she said, swiping another toffee from the bag. 'And I don't need babysitting, so you go on your date, love, have a nice time.' Her brow pinched. 'Where did you meet him?'

'Oh, through a dating app called My Single Friend,' I said, fiddling with the piping on the arm of the sofa.

'Whatever happened to being chatted up in a pub?'

I smiled. 'Too old-fashioned, I suppose.'

She gave a slow nod as she slid the toffee between her lips. 'Are your mum and dad still happy?' It was my turn to look surprised. 'At their wedding, they seemed genuinely in love, but it's been what…' She did a mental calculation. 'Nearly thirty-five years.'

I nodded. 'Impressive, I know.' I thought for a moment. 'They have their moments, but, yes, they do still love each other.'

'That's good.' Ruby smiled, a little sadly. 'It would have been nice to see more of them over the years.'

'Dad said you couldn't wait to get away from Dorchester.' I was careful not to sound accusing. 'Though I don't think he thought you'd end up in Hong Kong for so long.'

'They could have come over to visit, but they had the business. And you girls, of course.'

'What was Henry like?'

'Kind,' she said, with a trace of sadness. 'He was a godsend, actually. He was older than me, and had never wanted children. He had money, and had just been offered a job at a big bank in Hong Kong when I met him. He was just what I needed.'

'Did he know about Donny – I mean Peter?'

She gave a quick shake of her head. 'I told you, no one knows.'

'I'm sure Dad would understand if you talked to him,' I ventured, but Ruby didn't answer. She chewed her toffee with a slightly wild-eyed look that told me not to pursue it, so I turned my attention back to the television, where a three-toed sloth was swimming through a lagoon.

'It's as if she's got her own take on the past, and won't consider it any other way,' I said later to Jasmine, via FaceTime.

'It's obvious why,' she said, in her soft, Scottish lilt. 'She knows she can't change the decisions she made then, so there's no point torturing herself about what might have happened if she'd handled things differently.'

'I suppose so.' I nested the duvet around my head, despite the heat – even with the window cracked open, it was still muggy – and thought about Tom, and how I could have handled things better ten years ago. How, if I'd told him how I felt, or had stood up to Megan, or hadn't run, things might have turned out differently.

'What's going on there?' I said. I could hardly comprehend that a week ago I'd been juggling my search for a job with frantic phone calls to the house insurers, who seemed hell-bent on wriggling out of paying for my ruined kitchen.

'Not much,' said Jasmine, rubbing her eyes, leaving black make-up smears underneath. She yawned, which always made me smile, because she looked like an angry kitten. 'I fell off my bike this morning, and the plaster in the kitchen is taking forever to dry.'

'Are you OK?' I said, alarmed.

She looked around and spoke to someone off-camera. 'That's our neighbour, Vinnie,' she said, moving her phone so I could see a pair of tanned, muscular calves. 'He drove me to A & E because I thought my ankle was fractured, but it wasn't, so I invited him round for a drink.'

I shook my head. 'What about whatsisname, the plasterer?'

She looked blank for a moment. 'Oh, him.' She pulled a face. 'I decided to put things back on a professional footing after I spoke to you the other night, but he hasn't taken it too well.'

'Oh, Jas.'

'It's fine,' she said, waving a half-full wine glass. 'He emptied a tin of paint on the drive but I've cleaned it up, and his brother's replaced him on the job.'

After she'd rung off, I lay for a while, mentally wandering through my narrow, end-of-terrace house; up the carpeted staircase, into the glossy-tiled bathroom, which Jasmine had filled with bottles and lotions, into my bland bedroom with its built-in cupboards and tidy surfaces, back to the living room, where Jasmine did her marking at the beech-wood dining table, and where I discovered her straddling a boyfriend on the leather sofa one evening.

She'd asked more than once if she could buy the house, should I ever decide to sell up, and it was true that it sometimes felt more like hers than mine. I'd never really put my imprint on it, the way Jasmine had with her bedroom, turning it into somewhere that felt like home (with a slutty edge), yet I'd been so proud the day I moved in; I'd had a real sense of achievement.

Upon moving – I'd refused to think of it as running away – to Manchester, I'd immediately set some goals:

1. *Stop thinking about Tom and Megan.* (Not as easy as it sounded, at least for the first few weeks, when I drove Sarah mad going over and over what had happened.)

2. *Get a job.* Which hadn't proved too difficult once I'd thrown myself into it. I'd never been afraid of hard work, and what I lacked in experience, I'd made up for in enthusiasm, and a willingness to make tea for everyone, until a vending machine was installed.

3. *Move out of Sarah and Phil's.* Which wasn't so much a goal as a necessity. I loved my sister and brother-in-law – had drawn up a budget for their wedding, and squeezed into an unflat-

tering bridesmaid's dress on their big day – but proximity brought out Sarah's bossy side, so when Carly, a girl at Cars 4 U, asked if I'd be interested in flat-sharing, I'd jumped at the opportunity. It had worked well enough, until she left to go travelling with her boyfriend, but my fourth goal had been to buy my own house, and surprisingly it hadn't been that hard. Property wasn't as expensive in the north, and I didn't go out much before I met Jasmine, preferring box sets and books in the evenings to partying. Plus, I'd always been good at saving.

But once I'd moved in, and the excitement wore off, there'd been a sense of something missing. A man, according to Sarah and Mum, who kept insisting I had to let down my guard, even though I hadn't realised it was up.

Admittedly, relationships had been a bit thin on the ground.

After Carly moved out, I'd shared the flat with a curly-haired cartoonist called Sam, who'd worked in the coffee shop near the office, but it had only lasted a few months. When I got sick of supporting him, and asked him to leave, he drew a mean caricature of me, with ginormous bosoms and squinty eyes, and left it pinned to the fridge.

My guard probably was up, after that. There'd been many dates, but none had come to anything.

Lying in Ruby's spare room, with its unfamiliar outlines, I suddenly felt adrift.

I don't belong anywhere.

To stem a rising tide of panic, I fiddled with my relaxation app, until I found the sound of gentle rain on a window, and my final thought before drifting off was that I had nothing to wear for my date the following evening.

Chapter 19

Normally on a Saturday, I'd have a lie-in, before going for a walk in the park at the end of our road. If Jasmine was at a loose end, we'd go somewhere for coffee, and I'd usually have a wander round the library, picking out some good books. In the afternoon, I might pop round to Sarah's and play with the twins, or squeeze in a visit to Mum and Dad's.

But Jane had made it clear that Saturday was the stall's busiest day, so by eight o'clock I was knee-deep in flowers, eating cake for breakfast. I'd stuffed some banana loaf in my bag before leaving the flat, along with some cheese straws, pressed on me by Bob at the foot of the stairs.

'I was wondering if Ruby might come out for a spin later,' he'd said, fingering the small gold medallion nestling in his chest hair, as though it could somehow transmit a message to her.

'You can ask her yourself, if you can get her up.'

Conscious that we kept alluding to Ruby in either a state of undress or prone in bed I'd hurried past, cheeks burning.

It was another sultry day, the sun blazing from a cloudless sky, and in a fit of spontaneity I'd cut some jeans into shorts, and teamed them with a plain white top that hopefully didn't scream 'boardroom meeting'.

The trouble was, I'd accidentally cut one leg shorter than the other, and had to keep tugging at the fraying edge. I also had a suspicion my buttocks might be visible if I bent over, and I'd failed to bring any suitable footwear from home. I was wearing the bright orange trainers last worn at my wall-climbing sessions, and they didn't really go.

After putting the stall up, Calum had gone for a breakfast fry-up at Cooper's Café, so I sat on a pallet and finished my cake before biting into a cheese straw. At this rate, I'd be half a stone heavier by the time I left Shipley.

The sun was pleasantly warm on my arms and bare legs, and as I looked across at the sea, my muscles softened. I thought I'd adjusted well to city life, but being back in Dorset was like pulling on a favourite T-shirt. The sounds of the square behind me, and the hypnotic rhythm of waves was reassuring, and my panic from the night before receded like a bad dream.

Also, it was rather nice not having a boss breathing down my neck, or having to listen to his politically incorrect jokes, or comfort the receptionist, Gemma, who often cried because her boyfriend preferred playing Grand Theft Auto to hanging out with her.

Maybe I could freelance, I pondered – get away from that office environment, which could be as cliquey as school had been.

A pair of seagulls paraded past, aggressively eyeing my third cheese straw, and I dropped half of it in fright. They began fighting over it, so I grabbed my bag and retreated to the safety of the van. Maybe an office environment wasn't so bad after all. At least there weren't any seagulls in Manchester.

The work phone on the seat beside me started ringing, as though I'd set it off.

'Is that Carrie?'

'Jane! Hi, how are you?'

'Knackered,' she said, in a satisfied way that made my ears tighten. 'I can hardly walk this morning.'

'Too much information, Jane!' I made my voice jovial, so she wouldn't think I was judging her – even though I was.

'Ooh, you dirty minx,' she chortled. 'I can hardly walk, because I tripped on the way into the hotel and sprained my ankle.'

'Oh, no, I am sorry,' I said, insides clenched with embarrassment. 'I didn't mean to imply—'

'Mind you, it didn't stop us indulging, if you get my drift.' I did. 'Dennis even wore the grey tie I bought him, and let me rip his shirt off, so the buttons went everywhere, just like in the film.' Jane sounded awestruck. 'I've promised I'll sew them back on, when we get home.' A wave of laughter built, and I had to bite my lip. 'He's got quite into the whole Christian Grey thing,' she went on, warming up. 'He's even booked us a ride in a helicopter.'

'That's nice.' I prayed she meant 'ride' in the literal sense.

'He'll need a bit of persuading to use the butt plug though,' she said, thoughtfully. 'He thought it was a chess piece.'

I tried to turn a giggle into a cough, and ended up nearly choking. 'Everything's fine here,' I said, in strangled tones. 'In case you were wondering.'

'That's why I was phoning,' she said, surprised. 'How's your aunt?'

'Much better,' I said, wiping my eyes. 'I think she's looking forward to the wedding, she's been going through the order.'

'Oh, wonderful!' Jane sounded so thrilled, I forgave her over-sharing. 'Well, I'll let you go. I've a husband here, beckoning me into the shower.'

As she cut the call off, I noticed the swell of people in the square, and found myself searching for Tom, then reminded myself he probably didn't work weekends and was spending the day with Megan.

Don't think about Tom.

The seagulls were still circling, so I switched on the radio in the van and pulsed my shoulders to a Kings of Leon song, which seemed to loosen my thoughts.

I'd hidden Peter's address in my purse, and wondered whether to drive out to his house tomorrow, after I'd paraded the flower-pups for Megan's approval. No warning, no Internet searching – just do it. For Ruby. And to get Doris off my back. Now the address was in my possession, it seemed wrong to go back to Manchester without at least trying. What was the worst that could happen?

I decided not to think about that.

My mind jack-knifed straight back to Tom, and the day he'd asked me to test him on one of his veterinary exam papers, which was about 'small companion animals', and instead of 'right stifle (genual) joint' I'd said 'genital' in relation to swelling. He'd laughed for ages and said he would think of that in the exam, and I'd made a point of mispronouncing all the difficult words after that, enjoying his reaction. He'd started giving silly answers, like, 'I'd dress the chihuahua in a dinner jacket, and send him on a world cruise,' until we were both clutching our sides.

I felt close to tears suddenly, and it was a relief to see Calum returning, patting his belly with a satisfied grin on his face.

'I've just spoken to your mum,' I said, banishing memories of Tom as I climbed out of the van.

Calum glanced at my exposed thighs and away again, colour staining his cheeks, and I wished I hadn't hacked at my jeans. 'Did she tell you they're staying for another week?' he asked my trainers.

'WHAT?'

He reeled back, as if he'd had a glimpse of evil. 'I spoke to her last night and she said she'd call you.'

'It must have slipped her mind.' *While she was describing her sexual odyssey.* 'Sorry I shouted,' I added, feeling bad.

He gave an awkward grin. 'They're having a really good time,' he said. 'Mum reckons she's never seen Dad so relaxed.'

Now *my* cheeks were aflame, as a mental picture of Jane in skimpy pants sprang into my head. 'I'm sure they deserve their holiday,' I said, hastily brushing crumbs off my top before the seagulls dived in for dessert.

'They definitely went prepared, like.' Calum folded himself into the van, which he'd asked to borrow for a few hours. 'It's one of them activity holidays,' he said sticking his head through the open window. 'I heard Mum saying to a friend she was planning to wear Dad out, and I know she'd ordered all this lubricating stuff off the internet for blisters.'

I risked a look at his guileless face and realised he was being serious.

'Enjoy the rest of your day,' I said, keen to bring this line of conversation to an end. He'd told me he was taking his girlfriend shopping in Bristol. 'I'll see you later.'

As he drove off, I felt a twinge of guilt that he had to come back to take down the stall, but he didn't seem to mind, and I reflected that his girlfriend was lucky to have him.

'I'll take a bunch of these for the missus, love.' The booming voice belonged to a man with Victorian muttonchops, wearing a loose white shirt. 'It's her birthday today and I forgot until I came out for a newspaper.' He'd tucked the paper under his arm and was digging in his pocket for change. I took the bunch of lilies and made a cone with brown paper, making an effort for his obviously long-suffering wife.

'Hey, what did the old flower say to the young flower?' he said.

'Sorry?' I looked up from tearing off a strip of Sellotape.

'It's a joke,' he said, his face full of mischief.

My stomach shrivelled. I hated it when people told jokes, from years of Dad getting the punchlines wrong. 'I don't know,' I said. 'What *did* the old flower say to the young flower?'

'What's up, bud?' He bellowed with laughter. 'Da-bum-CHING,' he said, doing the actions.

'That's a good one.' I reorganised my face into a grin.

'Plenty more where that came from,' he said, as I passed him his flowers and took his money. 'What do you call a sunflower—?'

'Excuse me,' I said, holding up a finger as I tugged my phone from the pocket of my too-short shorts and pressed it to my ear. 'I have to take this,' I said, making apologetic eyes. He shrugged and wandered off, the bunch of flowers incongruous in his meaty paw.

As I ended my pretend call and lowered the phone, I saw a message from Jasmine with a photo of the kitchen attached. A man was bent over, attaching a piece of skirting board, an inch of bum-crack on show.

Somewhere to keep our tea-towels? she'd written.

Gross. I replied. *Got a date tonight, by the way.*

Whoa! she typed back. *Better dust the cobwebs off your lady parts.*

Ha-di-ha. I'll call you later.

As if on cue, a message pinged in from Toby.

Are you still on for tonight?

I am if you are.

I cringed. Being flirty didn't suit me, despite Megan's efforts to teach me back in the day. She'd made it an art form: an upward sweep of her eyelashes and a sultry glance was all it had taken. Failing that, a hand on the arm and a breathless, 'Oh my god, you're so *funny*,' usually did the trick.

Trying to emulate her in front of my mirror I'd looked like I was suffering a series of nervous twitches, and my 'breathless' voice sounded asthmatic.

I am Toby replied, adding a smiley face.

I plundered my brain for a witty painting reference.

I hope you won't give me the brush off. Too desperate. *Joke!* I added.

He replied right away. *If I do, you can call a CONSTABLE*

I wondered if we'd end up talking in art puns when we met, and whether I should google some ideas, just in case.

I'll remember to bring some MONET! I typed, quickly adding *See you later* ☺ aware of a woman in a wide-brimmed sun hat hovering by the dahlias.

As I served her, shoving in some white heather for luck, and trying to stay interested while she told me a story about a relative who once grew a sunflower so tall he had to put scaffolding around it, I thought I glimpsed Tom near the beach.

My heart flew into my throat, but when I looked again it was just a man who looked a bit like him, eating chips from a plastic carton.

Once the customer had gone, I sat on an upturned bucket for a while, with Ruby's *A–Z of Flowers and their Meanings* to calm myself down. Daisy: *innocence and purity*, gerbera: *cheerfulness…*

Checking that the seagulls were bothering someone else, I took out another cheese straw and ate it quickly.

❀

Six hours later I was fighting the urge to be sick, and not just because I'd eaten six more cheese straws by the time Calum returned.

I'd just showered and washed my hair, and was draped in a towel, hunting through my bags for something to wear that didn't scream 'business lunch' or 'another business lunch', wondering when my wardrobe had become so… *businessy*. Probably when I was promoted to head of accounts and started modelling myself on Alicia from *The Good Wife*, without the budget.

I had plenty of municipal-looking shirts, skirts and trousers, and jackets with nipped- in waists, in my cupboards at home, and couldn't understand why I'd brought a couple to Shipley with me 'just in case'. In case of what? An impromptu invitation to a town-planning meeting?

'Look,' I said to Jasmine, passing my phone across the array of clothes I'd spread out.

'God, that room's a state,' she said. 'I can barely see the bed.'

'Never mind the room.' I propped my phone on top of a pile of boxes, and held up a dark grey top for inspection. 'Why haven't I got any colour in my clothes? It's the middle of summer.'

Jasmine pushed her face closer to the screen. 'Because you're worried you'll make yourself stand out,' she said, as if it was obvious.

'Not that old chestnut.' She was right though. I'd worn a slinky emerald dress to the firm's Christmas do one year, prompting my boss to ask who'd invited Joan from *Mad Men*, and the ensuing attention had sent me scuttling back to my neutral palette.

'I suppose I could wear the shorts I wore to work.' I plucked them off the floor.

'Dear god.' Jasmine dramatically clutched her throat. 'You actually showed your thighs in a public place in broad daylight?'

'Yes, and they're really sunburnt.' I peeked inside my towel at my glowing flesh. 'I'm not used to being outside all day, and I didn't bring my sun cream.'

Jasmine pointed behind me. 'What about that?'

Turning, I spotted a silky, rose-patterned kimono hanging on the back of the door.

'That's one of Ruby's dressing gowns.' I moved over to touch the material, which felt deliciously cool between my fingers. 'I can't wear this.'

'Why not?' Jasmine gave a kittenish twitch of her nose. 'Once it's on it'll look like a summery dress,' she said. 'Just put a proper belt round it, and for god's sake don't wear your brogues. Or your trainers.' She did a few star jumps, her hair bouncing. 'And take some condoms, just in case.'

'I don't have any condoms,' I said, prissily. 'I'm not planning to sleep with him.'

'I should hope not.' She was twerking now, buttocks jiggling in her silky PJ bottoms. 'Sleeping's the last thing you should be planning.'

I tutted. 'You know how I feel about *indulging* on a first date.'

She gave a squeal of laughter. 'You're so adorable.' She dropped into a lunge. 'When was the last time you had S.E.X?' she said, spelling it out.

'You know when.' I adjusted my towel, which kept slipping. 'It was with that carpenter guy, Shaun, who worked in the building next to Cars 4 U.'

'The one who took you to see *Alvin and the Chipmunks?*'

'It was meant to be quirky,' I said, turning to the mirror on the wall by the door and patting my eye-bags with the pads of my fingers. 'He was actually really nice.'

'Wasn't he obsessed with volcanoes?'

'Not in a swivel-eyed way,' I said. 'It was educational. The word volcano is from the Roman name Vulcan. Which is also a planet in *Star Trek*.'

'Fascinating. So why did you stop seeing him?'

'Oh, Jas, you know why,' I said. 'He smelt wrong.'

'Another of your excellent excuses.'

'It wasn't an excuse, I…' I glanced at my phone screen. 'Jas, what are you doing?'

She'd jutted one knee low down and thrown her arms wide, as though balancing on a tight-rope. 'I'm exercising,' she said.

'Why?'

The doorbell shrilled. 'That'll be Vinnie.' She straightened and spruced her hair with her fingers. 'He's taking me out to dinner.'

'He's keen.'

'Obviously.' She gave a 'why wouldn't he be?' grin. 'Listen, I'd better let him in and get changed,' she said. 'Have fun tonight, Carrie, and if it goes tits up remember there are plenty more—'

'— fish in the sea. I know.'

'I was going to say, "fit men online".'

'Whatever.'

'You go, girlfriend.' She snapped her fingers to and fro. 'Ciao.'

I'd barely rung off when Mum called, despite it being almost bedtime in Kazakhstan.

'I'm getting ready to go out,' I said, wedging my phone between my shoulder and ear, while I eased some underwear on, glad she couldn't see me. Mum's mobile was an old model and she didn't understand FaceTime. 'Everything OK?'

'Just checking in,' she said. 'Your dad's constipated because of the change of water.'

'Too much information, Mum.' At least it wasn't sexual, thank god.

'How's your aunt?'

'OK,' I said, warily. 'A bit better, I think.'

There was a thoughtful pause. 'Have you seen anyone you know over there?'

I froze. 'Like who?'

A sigh gusted down the line. 'I was just thinking of you being in Dorset and I realised I sometimes miss it,' she said. 'Your dad and I were hiking the Charyn Canyon this morning, which is nice, but basically a bunch of rocks, and it struck me how lucky we were to live on the Jurassic Coast.' She sounded nostalgic. 'I think we used to take it for granted,' she said. 'We even stopped going for walks once you and Sarah were teenagers. Do you remember our walks? Sarah nearly pushed you off a cliff once, but your dad managed to grab you by your hood.'

'How could I forget?' I said, drily. 'We always argued on those walks.'

'I'm just being silly.' She sniffed. 'I think I'm missing the twins.'

'You've only been gone a few days.'

'We might come and visit Ruby once we're back,' she said. 'She is family, after all.'

My eyes popped. She *must* be feeling homesick. 'She'd like that,' I said. 'There's a lot about her you don't know.' Understatement of the year.

'I'm glad you're getting on.'

I looked at the time. 'Sorry, Mum, I've got to go.'

'Ooh, another of your dates?'

I'd got into the habit of making a funny story out of my dating disasters, and my family had grown to enjoy them. I sometimes thought they'd be disappointed if I ever settled down.

'I'll look forward to hearing about it,' she said. 'Now, I suppose I'd better go and get your dad into bed.'

'Have fun.'

'You too.'

Dropping my phone, I slipped Ruby's silky robe on over my underwear, then removed the belt from my work trousers and looped it around my waist. The effect was quite stylish. The hem of the robe fell just below my knees, and although the colour of my shins was more rare beef than butterscotch, it made a change from mashed potato.

There was just enough cleavage on show, but I would have to be careful about leaning forward in case the robe came adrift.

I twisted my hair up, pulling a few strands forward, and brushed on mascara and lip balm, and some bronzing powder on the apples of my cheeks.

'You look gorgeous,' Ruby said, as I stepped into the living room and did a little twirl. She'd been surprisingly enthusiastic about my date, insisting I help myself to her Jo Malone shower gel.

Her forehead scrunched. 'Is that my dressing gown?'

'Do you mind?' I said, anxiously. 'Does it look like a dressing gown?'

'No, I don't, and definitely not on you.' She pushed herself off the sofa. 'What about shoes?'

I glanced at my feet, which were bare. 'I can't believe I forgot to bring sandals,' I said. 'I figured I could buy some flip-flops once I was here, but I haven't got round to it.'

Her face brightened. 'What size are you?'

'Five and a half.'

'I've got just the thing,' she said.

As she bustled to the cupboard on the landing I resigned myself to wearing my trainers. I was trying to think of a funny story I could tell Toby to explain them, when Ruby returned with some surprisingly classy wedges in the sort of nude shade favoured by the Duchess of Cambridge.

'They go with anything,' she said, dropping to one knee and slipping the shoe on my foot like Prince Charming.

'They're lovely.' I twisted to admire the effect. 'Shame about my toenails.'

'Hang on.' Ruby sprang to her feet again, and fetched some tulip-pink varnish from her bedroom. 'This should do the trick.'

Down on both knees, she proceeded to paint my nails. There was definitely a Cinderella vibe going on.

'There,' she said, standing up with a smile. 'Now you look perfect.' She smoothed a tendril of hair off my cheek, and, on impulse, I gathered her up in a hug. She smelt of salt-and-vinegar crisps and warm skin.

'Sure you don't want to come?' I said, into her hair. 'You could give Bob a call and ask him to meet us there.'

'I think he's still upset that I refused to go out with him this afternoon.' She pulled away, sadness rolling in like mist. 'It doesn't seem fair to get too close with all my baggage,' she said, plucking a hair off my sleeve.

'I don't think he'll mind if he really likes you.'

'Oh, I forgot to say that Jane called me to say she and Dennis are extending their break.' She blinked at me. 'Are you sure you don't mind staying until after that wedding? I'm going to need some help.'

'Of course I don't,' I said, managing to keep my smile intact.

Seeming satisfied, she headed back to the sofa, and the table she'd piled with snacks and fizzy drinks for an evening in front of the television.

'You have a lovely time,' she said, pulling her dressing gown tight as though suddenly chilly, before picking up the remote control.

It was clear from her middle-distance stare that her mind had drifted elsewhere, and as I located my purse and let myself out I made my mind up.

Tomorrow, I was going to visit the address tucked into my bag and talk to Peter myself.

Chapter 20

I arrived at The Anchor five minutes early, limping as if I'd walked across hot coals. My feet felt on fire, and I regretted my decision not to drive the short distance from Ruby's.

Dropping in a chair at a table outside the pub, I bent to inspect the damage. No blood, thank goodness, just a pair of angry blisters on my heels.

As I eased down the shoe straps my robe fell open, revealing my balconette bra. I hastily adjusted it and tightened my belt, already hot and bothered. My hair was slipping its moorings, and the skin on my lower legs had a boiled appearance.

I hauled my bag onto my lap and pulled out my phone, half hoping Toby had cancelled, but there was only a WhatsApp photo from Sarah, of the twins, dressed as *Star Wars* characters for a party. Seeing their puffy-cheeked smiles, a wave of homesickness rolled over me. I'd probably be looking after them now, so Sarah and Phil could have a night off. The twins liked me to read *Harry Potter* because I 'did it properly', not like Mummy and Daddy, who 'miss bits out and think we don't notice'.

I replied with a smiley face and a cheery 'kiss them good night from me' and opened another two photographs, this time from Mum. In one, she and Dad were in front of a bridge, only the tops of their heads visible, and in the other, Dad was pinching his thumb and forefinger so it looked like he was holding the sun.

Playing silly buggers! Mum had written.

Smiling, I glanced up. The Anchor overlooked the harbour, where colourful fishing boats were bobbing on the water, burnished by the lowering sun. Most of the outside tables were busy already, and the sound of laughter and chatter mingled with clinking glasses and cutlery from inside. A mild breeze ruffled the hem of my robe, carrying the smell of the sea and a hint of cod.

On impulse, I googled some art stuff, and tried to memorise a few names before putting my phone away.

Should I wait for Toby to find me, or go and order a drink?

What if he didn't turn up?

All the reasons I hated blind dates flooded into my head: the awkward exchanges and crushing disappointment when you realised you had nothing in common; the resolve, by dessert, to stay single forever.

At home, Jasmine and I had a system where she would ring after half an hour, and if things were going badly I would say, 'Oh my god, are you OK?' shooting my date a look of alarm, and Jasmine would put on a surprisingly good Russian accent and say, 'Carrie, you haff to come at whonce, I am havink a catastrophe here, I haff set my hair alight with candle and need the lift to hospital,' or some variation. Trying not to laugh I'd make my apologies and leave, certain my date would know I was lying, but too relieved to care. It was better than going to the toilets and doing a runner, which happened to me once. I'd watched, bemused, as my date legged it across the restaurant car park and leapt into his Aston Martin, leaving me to pay the bill.

A hand landed on my shoulder and I screamed.

'Oh god, I'm so sorry.'

Swivelling round, I watched a Greg Rutherford lookalike backing away, hands in the air as if worried I might pull a gun.

'You scared me,' I said, trying to laugh, but it came out as a panicked gargle.

'Sorry, I'm sorry,' he repeated, his local accent strong. 'I shouldn't have crept up on you like that.'

'No, no, it's fine, I was miles away.' Heart pumping like a piston, I registered that he was better looking than his profile picture; strong-jawed, with red hair cut close at the sides, and styled in a quiff on top. His eyes were round and grey, like rain-washed pebbles, currently wide with alarm.

I stood up and held out a hand, keen to reassure him. 'I'm Carrie,' I said, mindful of my own profile photo, which looked nothing like me – apart from the fact I'd been wearing a dressing gown then too.

Lurching forward, he shook my hand, relief brightening his features.

'Toby Denton.' There was a scattering of freckles across his cheeks, giving him a friendly schoolboy look, but his vintage jeans hugged manly thighs, and beneath the sleeve of his tight, white T-shirt, a serpent tattoo curled around his bicep.

'Good to meet you,' I said. His handshake was the right side of firm, his palm slightly clammy with nerves – or perhaps it was mine.

'I'm really sorry I frightened you.' He briefly tightened his grip before letting go. 'I'm an idiot.'

'Don't worry about it,' I said, nudging my hair into place. 'I'm a bit jumpy lately.'

'OK.' His smile was wide and a little shy, his front teeth slightly crooked. The sight of them was oddly heartening.

'Shall we go in?' I said.

Seeming as relieved as I was that the ice was broken, he raised an imaginary sword. 'To the pub!' he said, the ensuing blush clashing with his hair.

Smiling, I led the way inside, trying not to hobble in Ruby's shoes.

'I'll have a full-fat Coke,' I said as he hovered, one eyebrow raised in enquiry. 'I'll grab us a seat.' Casting around for somewhere to sit, I spotted a secluded booth by the window and slid into the leather seat, relieved to take the weight off my throbbing feet.

I took a moment to adjust my robe and shoes, and place my bag on the floor, before Greg returned with two tall glasses rattling with ice cubes.

'So,' I said, as he settled opposite, racking my brains to remember his profile description. 'You're a painter.'

He nodded, and took a sip of his drink. 'That is correct, ma'am.'

'What do you paint?'

He cast his eyes upwards. 'Houses mostly, but other buildings too,' he said. 'I did the sweet shop along the parade last year, and a church a few months ago. That was interesting.'

'I bet,' I said, rummaging around my limited knowledge. 'So, you chronicle real life, a bit like Lowry, or' – I tried to think of an artist who painted buildings – 'wasn't there an Italian chap?' I wanted to say Cornetto, but knew it wasn't right. 'Cannellini.' Was that a bean?

'I'm not an artist,' he said with a half-laugh. 'I'm a painter and decorator.'

'Ah. Right. Sorry about that.' Cheeks prickling with heat, I picked up my glass, took a large gulp, and swallowed an ice-cube whole.

'I suppose it's a bit of a come-down if you were expecting Banksy,' Toby said, interpreting my stunned silence and watering eyes as disappointment.

'Not at all,' I croaked, blinking away tears and flapping a hand at my throat.

Realising what had happened, he half rose from his seat. 'Shall I thump you on the back?'

'Not on a first date,' I managed, as the ice cube slid down my windpipe. 'You must have wondered what I was on about in my texts.'

'I kind of guessed you'd got the wrong idea.' Toby smiled and sank back down. 'You're not the first, to be honest.'

I noticed a spot of yellow paint on his temple. 'Have you been working today?'

He nodded. 'My boss, Harry, keeps us busy,' he said. 'He and his wife had a baby girl a few months ago, and he's so besotted he keeps knocking off early to go home.'

'Us?' I raised my voice over a babble of voices as a group settled into the booth behind ours. 'Is it a big company?'

'Not really.' His gaze fell to the table, and he traced a pattern on the surface with his finger.

Silence bloomed, the easiness suddenly gone.

A waiter passed, carrying a tray piled with plates of spaghetti. 'Should we have something to eat?' I said, though I wasn't really hungry.

'If you'd like to.' He looked up, eyes politely expectant.

'I'm happy to have something if you're hungry.'

'Likewise.'

We stared at each other and smiled, and the atmosphere relaxed again.

'I'm sorry,' he said. 'It's so long since I've been on a date, I've no idea how they work.'

'I've been on quite a few,' I said, 'and this one's already better than those.'

As the tips of his ears reddened, I realised it was true. Probably because he wasn't a serial dater, he had a refreshing air of being himself, rather than out to impress.

'I should be honest, though,' he said, spinning his glass on the table. My stomach tightened. *Here we go.*

'I've never seen *Game of Thrones*,' he said, solemnly.

An involuntary laugh escaped. 'There's no hope for us, then. I'm a massive fan. What about *The Walking Dead*?'

But he'd hunched forward now, forearms on the table, and I realised that the real confession was coming. 'I have a wife, Em, she's the one I work with, we work together, with Harry,' he said in a rush. 'We've not been separated long.'

I let his words settle in. They weren't that surprising, really. Most of the men I'd met in the past had been newly separated, as if they couldn't bear being alone. It was just a question of how much baggage they were carrying.

'Go on.'

He studied his fingers. They were nice; long and square-tipped with clean nails. 'We were hoping to start a family, but it wasn't happening,' he said. 'It... caused problems.' From the way he said it, I guessed it was an understatement. 'We decided that we needed some time apart.'

Not sure how I felt about that, I said, 'So you're not looking for anything serious?'

'I don't know.' He held my gaze. 'I thought it best to be upfront, in case your biological clock was ticking.' He said it as if my clock was a precious thing, and there was something admirable about his openness.

'It isn't,' I said, smiling. 'I've a niece and nephew I love to bits, but I'm not ready for children yet.'

Having got that out of the way, Toby visibly relaxed and we chatted for a while. I gave him the bare bones of why I was in Shipley, and he told me Ruby's stall was such a part of the landscape he didn't really notice it any more.

'I'd love to visit Manchester, for the music scene,' he said.

'I don't know what it's like these days,' I admitted. 'There hasn't been an Oasis or Joy Division for a while.' I had a sudden flashback to Megan and me in my bedroom, miming dramatically to 'Love Will Tear Us Apart', after I let her listen to my album.

As if I'd conjured her up, I thought I heard her laugh.

'Didn't the lead singer kill himself?' Toby was saying, as my pulse sky-rocketed.

There it was again, from the booth behind us.

'Weren't The Smiths from Manchester too?' Toby continued, widening his shoulders and sitting back. 'Morrissey was a bit of a misery, too. I prefer something more upbeat, if I'm honest, like Olly Murs.' He grinned. 'I'm joking,' he said. 'Actually, I'm not.'

I raised a smile, but I'd tuned in to Megan's voice now, which seemed to have risen high above everyone else's.

'This time next month I'll be back from my honeymoon, as Lady of the Manor.' Her tone was self-mocking yet smug.

'And then you'll be dropping the sprog.' Her friend's accent spoke of boarding schools and ski slopes, and I guessed it was one of her old friends from school. 'I still can't see you as a mother, Megs.'

'None of us can,' said a voice with a hint of New York, and I vaguely recalled an American cousin Megan had looked up to. 'I remember when you played with your dolls you carried them upside down, and jammed their heads between your knees to change a diaper.'

Gales of laughter followed.

'Hope you're taking your folic acid.'

'With my blueberry smoothie every morning!'

'I expect she'll get a nanny as soon as it's walking,' said another female voice, brisk and gravelly.

'Of course!' cried Megan. 'I want to take a back seat for a while, once Tom's running the company, and make my mark on the house, maybe throw some parties once my father-in-law retires. He's going travelling, so I'll be able to do what I want.'

I wondered if Tom knew of her plans. And how was a baby going to fit in?

'Make sure you go straight back on the Pill,' said the gravel-voiced friend. 'You don't want to be knocking out babies every year.'

My stomach knotted. It was hard to imagine Tom as part of this group, being friendly with their partners or husbands. But then, I didn't really know him anymore.

'Everything OK?' Toby's voice startled me and my hand shot out, knocking my glass over and sending brown liquid cascading across the table.

'I'm so sorry,' I said, reaching down to grab a tissue from my bag. I stood up and attempted to staunch the flow, and Toby rose and accepted a napkin from the circulating waiter.

'Don't worry,' he said, dabbing at his thighs. 'Could have happened to anyone.'

'Carrie?' Megan's face appeared round the edge of the booth, eyes sparkling. 'I *thought* I recognised your voice.'

That was all I needed; an audience for my humiliation.

'Hi,' I mumbled, scrunching the soggy tissue in my hand and pasting on a smile. 'Fancy seeing you.'

'Twice in as many days, after all this time!' She got up and came over, looking stunning in a simple navy-and-white striped T-shirt dress that complemented her tan and showcased her lollipop-stick legs. I couldn't help firing a glance at her midriff, but there wasn't as much as a curve.

Eyes roving over my outfit, she did a comedy double-take. 'Oh my god, Carrie, are you wearing your dressing gown?' she hooted.

Looking down, I clasped the edges across my blushing cleavage, like a Victorian maid. 'It's vintage,' I said, risking a glance at Toby, gratified to see he was checking his phone and not looking at Megan at all.

'Well, you've definitely got the figure to carry it off,' she said, in the generous tone people used when they were flattering those less fortunate than themselves. 'I always envied you your boobies.'

She reached out and gave them a jiggle, and one of her cronies, peeking over to watch, brayed, 'Wait until you've breast-fed, Megs, you'll be tucking yours in your knickers!' She had bouncy, golden curls more suited to an eighties beauty queen. 'Better stock up on Spanx!'

Megan ignored her, switching her attention to Toby.

'You must be the war correspondent,' she said, deploying her most devastating smile. *Oh. Shit.* 'I thought he wasn't due yet?' She addressed the last bit to me, without taking her eyes off Toby, who was glancing behind him as if Megan must be addressing someone else.

Shit, shit, shit.

'Cooper, isn't it?' Her words dropped into the dumbstruck silence as she stuck her hand out. 'I'm Megan.'

Toby dutifully took her fingers and gave them a tweak. 'Nice to meet you,' he said, giving me a befuddled look over her shoulder. I pulled a pleading face I hoped said, '*Please* go with it.'

'We were at school together,' I said to him, brightly. 'I told Megan you were coming next week because you were in...'

'Budapest,' Megan supplied, which was just as well as I'd completely forgotten where my fictitious boyfriend was supposed to be working. 'You were doing something terribly important,' she said, 'but I'm glad you're here. You can both have dinner with Tom and me one evening, how about that?'

She passed a beaming smile between us, then slid an arm around my waist. It was like being squeezed by an anaconda, and I knew I wasn't imagining the wave of animosity coming off her. 'It's good to catch up with one of my oldest friends,' she said, wrinkling her nose. 'It's *so* nice to be back in touch.'

She tightened her arm ever so slightly, and my robe pulled apart at the edges. I tried to wriggle away but she held on, smiling brightly at Toby, who was starting to look like he wished he'd stayed at home.

'Tom is so thrilled you've found The One,' she went on, her nails digging into my flesh. 'We were talking about you earlier.'

'That's nice.' My face felt in danger of shattering from the effort of smiling, while Toby gestured with his eyes that my underwear was on display.

'I'll check our diary and let you know.' Just when I thought I couldn't bear it a moment longer one of her friends called, 'Come on, Megs, our food is here,' and finally her arm fell away.

I took a stumbling step towards Toby, as if I was a hostage being released to a negotiator, and he put out a hand to steady me.

'Ooh, don't forget, eleven o'clock tomorrow,' she said, pinching my elbow as she passed. 'I can't *wait* to see what you've done.' She fluttered a wave at Toby. ''Bye, Cooper.' She flicked her glossy hair. 'You've a diamond there, look after her.'

She wafted back to her friends and said something I didn't catch, which made them roar with laughter. I rearranged my clothing, mentally preparing my goodbye to Toby, when he said quietly, 'I'll go and get us a proper drink, and you can tell me what that was about.'

Chapter 21

'You were in late last night.' Ruby peered at me through the permanent twilight of her room, her eye mask round her forehead like a bandana.

'Sorry.' Head pounding, I placed a mug of tea beside her. 'I hope I didn't disturb you.' I cringed, remembering that, at one point, singing had occurred.

'I wasn't asleep.' Ruby shuffled upright, worrying her hair with her fingertips. 'I was watching a horror movie.' She nodded at the small television set perched on top of her chest of drawers. 'Talking of horror, you did quite the version of *Delilah*.' Her mouth twitched. 'Must have scared the neighbours.'

I winced. 'Sorry about that.' When I drank too much – a rarity – I tended to warble Tom Jones classics, which was odd, considering I could barely remember the lyrics when I was sober. Jasmine had recorded me once, but I'd made her delete it.

'Did you have a nice time?'

'I think so,' I said, turning to open the curtains, wincing again as a shard of sunlight struck my eyes. My head felt heavy, as if someone had filled it with cement while I was sleeping. 'He was nice.'

'Nice enough to see again?'

'I don't know.' I dropped onto the side of her bed, sending particles of dust whirling into the air. My stomach rolled queasily. 'I'm not really looking for a relationship.'

'So why go out with him?'

Because I invented a boyfriend more interesting than anyone I've met in real life, and Tom's marrying Megan, and I haven't had a proper relationship in ages, and I'm never going to be with Tom because he's marrying Megan, oh, and they're having a baby, and I'm almost thirty—

'Carrie?'

I jumped. 'It was my friend's idea, really,' I said, rubbing my eyes with my knuckles. I'd forgotten to remove my mascara and my fingers came away black. I'd also fallen asleep in the robe I'd gone out in, but at least that didn't look out of place. 'She's always trying to set me up. I think she thought there'd be a better class of man in Dorset.'

Ruby smiled over her mug. 'Maybe she's right,' she said. 'Although it wouldn't be very convenient to meet someone here if you're going back to Manchester.'

'True.' Her words gave me a jolt. Was it possible I was starting to think of Shipley as home? Ridiculous. I'd only been here a week.

'What's his name?' Ruby sipped her tea.

'Toby.' I tried to recall how we'd left things the night before. We'd sat outside the pub with our drinks for a while, away from Megan and her friends, and I'd told him all about her and Tom, and the boyfriend I'd invented on the spur of the moment – which made him laugh, a nice deep rumble – and how Megan was considering letting Ruby do her wedding flowers, depending on the outcome of my flower sample.

'Not even at her mum's house, I have to go to Hudson bloody Grange so she can show off,' I'd grumbled. 'And I'm competing with a criminal florist who designs flowers like handbags for slebs, and charges an absolute fortune.' I was slurring a little after my second – or was it third? – glass of wine, my words falling over themselves.

As daylight had faded from the sky, and the fairy lights outside the pub had come on, reflections twinkling in the harbour, we'd carried on chatting, though I couldn't recall the exact details. Toby had mentioned his wife, Em, a few times, and their boss's baby, Bunty – surely the same Bunty that Ruby would be doing the christening flowers for? – which had deepened their longing for a child of their own.

I remembered he hadn't seemed particularly drunk when he offered to walk me back to Ruby's. He'd given me a piggyback some of the way as my feet had swollen up, pretending to stagger beneath my weight – at least, I thought he was pretending – and I kicked my shoes off and stumbled the rest in bare feet, clutching Toby's firmly muscled arm.

When we arrived at the back of the bakery I'd prodded his bicep, and now I cringed at the memory of me saying, 'Woof, woof!'

In the glow of the light by the door he'd looked vaguely self-conscious, and when I had launched into *Delilah* he'd patted my shoulder awkwardly and suggested I drink a glass of water before going to bed.

'Care to join me?' I'd said, with an appalling attempt at coquettishness, hooking a finger over the neck of his T-shirt and pouting my lips for a kiss. He gently but firmly unpeeled my finger, and while I struggled for an art-related pun to sum up the evening, had beaten me to it by saying, 'Hope you don't feel too *sketchy* in the morning,' and gently cuffed my arm.

'At least he was a gentleman,' Ruby said, when I imparted this last bit of information, recounting how he'd helped me unlock the door and walked away backwards, watching until I was inside. 'Some blokes would have taken advantage.'

'I'm not the sort to be taken advantage of, even when I'm drunk,' I huffed.

Her mouth turned down. 'I wish I'd had some of your self-control when I was young.' Her hand moved down, and I saw she'd been looking at old photos. 'Maybe I wouldn't have got myself into trouble.'

'That's me and Sarah,' I said, picking up a school photo of us in uniform, our hair in bunches, Sarah giving me the side-eye. Three years older, she'd got to the age where being lumped with her little sister, wasn't cool. 'I'd just got my second teeth and wanted my little ones back, that's why I'm not smiling.'

'Your dad sent me it.' Ruby's smile returned. 'I've got plenty more.'

'Look how happy Mum and Dad are.' I picked up a wedding photo of them, Mum in a half-lift, her tulle wedding dress rucked up at the back. She had her hands on Dad's shoulders, and was laughing with her head thrown back.

'He almost dropped her,' Ruby recalled, fondly. 'That dress was surprisingly heavy.'

'Is that Donny, I mean Peter's, father?' I picked up a picture of a young man and studied it closely. 'He looks nice.'

'Of course it's not.' She knitted her eyebrows. 'It's your grandfather.'

'Oh, yes, of course it is,' I said, noticing the resemblance around the mouth. 'I haven't seen many pictures of him when he was young.'

'I do miss him, you know, in spite of everything.' She took the photo from me and put it face-down on the bed. 'Donny, I mean Peter, looks a lot like him.'

It was as if now she'd told me about her son, she couldn't quite stop herself from mentioning his name. 'He's nothing like his father,' she added. 'Not in looks, anyway.'

'What's this?' I picked up a square envelope, which was blank, feeling notepaper inside.

'It's a letter I wrote for Donny, explaining why I gave him up,' she said, face tensing. 'I was going to give it to him when we met, but didn't get the chance.'

Her wistful tone strengthened my wilting resolve to visit Peter, and I remembered with a lurch that I had to be at Hudson Grange in less than an hour.

'You've got a day off,' Ruby said, writhing back down in the bed, and while she was smoothing the duvet around her, I slipped the envelope into my jeans pocket. 'Why don't you make the most of the weather and go to the beach?'

'Maybe.' I rose, pain stabbing at my temples. 'What are you going to do with yourself?' It seemed wrong to leave her in bed. 'Maybe we could both go out later. We can have a picnic at Lulworth Cove, or a wander around the castle. I haven't been for years.'

'Maybe before you go home, but not today,' she said, turning her back to me. 'Go and get some fresh air, love, and I'll cook us some dinner for when you get back.'

Feeling dismissed, I headed back to my room and opened the curtains. Sunshine flooded in, spotlighting the flower-pups, which had slid to the floor in the night. I picked them up and set them down on the bed.

'I'm relying on you two,' I said sternly. 'You'd better not let me down.'

Groom-pup's top hat was wonky, and bride-pup's veil had tilted over her eyes. I straightened both with a sigh and looked at my phone.

There was a message from Toby.

I enjoyed last night. I feel like visiting Budapest now. And becoming a war correspondent.

I smiled. *Best stick to painting. Less chance of being shot at.*

I nearly was, once. Story for another date? As friends?

My smile froze. *Was my singing that bad??*

God, no, it was great, you could easily win The Voice!! I like you, but I just don't think I'm ready for a relationship yet.

I analysed my feelings – not easy with a throbbing headache – and decided my heart wasn't exactly broken. My pride was dented, but at least he wasn't going to lead me on. He was a man who knew himself well, and I liked that.

I liked him.

Carrie?

Sounds good. I typed quickly. *You give great piggybacks!*

It's my favourite form of exercise ☺ *Hey, if you ever need Cooper again, I'm available!*

'You're too kind, sir ☺

Good luck with your presentation this morning.

I'll need it ☹

You'll smash it! x

My mouth was smiling again. Being put in the potential friend-zone wasn't the worst experience I'd ever had.

Wrenching my hair into a ponytail, I took myself for a shower.

Twenty minutes later, after swallowing a couple of painkillers and a slice of lemon cake, I was on my way to Hudson Grange with the flower-pups and the wedding portfolio in a canvas bag in the footwell of my car.

Despite only visiting Moreton once before I'd somehow remembered the way, as though the journey had scored itself on my brain. The view flashed by in a sun-dappled blur of green and blue, the car engine protesting from lack of use. The battery had required a jump-start, and it was lucky that Bob had been at the bakery, whipping up a batch of loaves – though I suspected he was secretly hoping to talk to Ruby – and could attach my jump-leads to the engine of his van.

As I drew closer, it felt as if an inferno had ignited in my stomach, and I began to wish I hadn't succumbed to the slice of lemon cake. To distract my brain, I tuned into a local radio station and tried to concentrate on a heated discussion about Brexit, but I couldn't stop thinking about Tom and Megan.

Would Tom be happy living at Hudson Grange after he was married? I couldn't imagine it, when he'd been so keen to leave at eighteen. And could Megan really persuade him to stop being a vet? I imagined that she and Mr Hudson made a formidable team, and the fact that Megan had won Tom back after a ten-year absence was testament to her determination.

Or was I doing him a disservice? He wasn't a puppet; at least he hadn't been. He'd stood up to his father for years, and escaped Megan's clutches once. Surely the fact they were about to marry and become parents must mean he truly loved her. I couldn't imagine Tom getting married to please anyone but himself.

I'd always avoided looking fully at the truth, like turning away from a bright light that would hurt my eyes, but it was inescapable.

Tom loved Megan. He'd never loved me, and never would.

I switched off the radio, my eyes brimming with tears, and realised I was already in Moreton. It looked perfect in the buttery sunlight; a row of thatch-roofed cottages on one side, and a glittering strip of river visible through trees on the other.

Blinking furiously, I crossed a narrow bridge and followed the road up a winding hill until I rounded a corner and came across the arched, stone entrance to Hudson Grange. Driving slowly up the gravelled driveway, I took in the view of the house as it drew closer.

It looked much the same as I remembered, from its grey-stone exterior, chimneys, and cockerel weathervane, to the oak front door and sweeping acre of garden. There was a sporty red hatchback outside that I guessed was Megan's, alongside a sleek black car with chrome bumpers. Next to that was a dusty Land Rover.

Tom's?

Heart kicking, I switched off the engine and rubbed my eyes, trying to ease the ache still clamped across my brow. When I looked up, Megan was approaching, a dagger of sunlight falling across her face.

Resisting the urge to slam the car into reverse, I retrieved the canvas bag.

Breathe in, breathe out.

'Don't let me down,' I whispered to the flower-pups, fumbling the door open.

They didn't reply.

Chapter 22

'I'm so glad you're here,' said Megan, folding me into a tight embrace, seeming not to notice how stiff I was. 'Tom has to go into work, so it'll just be me.'

My heart flew into my throat as he came out of the house, closely followed by Hovis. Megan released me and let out a squeal as the dog jumped up at me, tail whipping back and forth.

'Get down,' she snapped, swiping at his head.

'He's fine,' I said, as Hovis flinched away.

'He doesn't mean any harm,' Tom said behind her, a mild rebuke in his voice. 'Hi, Carrie.'

'Hi.' I daren't look directly at him, scared my feelings were stamped all over my face, but couldn't miss the look of suppressed annoyance he flashed at Megan.

Seeming not to notice, she said, 'Try not to be too long, babe,' before sweeping back into the house – just as she had ten years earlier. I followed without looking back, wondering whether Tom was remembering that night too.

With a grand-hostess air, Megan led the way through the high-ceilinged hallway, past a bright, book-lined dining room, and a kitchen with a marbled island, where a uniformed housekeeper was washing crystal wine glasses.

It was unsettling being back in the place where my plan had backfired so spectacularly all that time ago, and I wished I'd put my foot down and insisted we meet somewhere neutral.

I couldn't clearly remember the interior of the house, but as I glanced back at the wide stairway the past came rushing back, and I half expected Mr Hudson to materialise, and look at me like something the cat had deposited.

Not that they had a cat.

'Can we do this outside?' I said, but Megan was too far ahead, so I had to hurry after her, into a spacious, sunlit room, where a couple of Chesterfield sofas faced each other across a Persian rug. There was a smell of freshly brewing coffee coming from a silver pot on the coffee table, next to a pile of *Country Life* magazines, and a tall vase of mop-headed flowers I recognised as hydrangeas (*gratitude* – or, negatively, *frigidity and heartlessness*).

A grand piano dominated the opposite end of the room, with thick-framed family photos jostling for space on top. It was like being on the set of *Downton Abbey.*

I looked for signs of Tom, but the photos were too far away, and there was nothing else to suggest he'd set foot in the stately room recently.

'This is Jay Simmons,' said Megan, waving her hand at a man perched on the edge of the sofa, facing away from me.

My spirits plunged as I edged forward. He must have turned up early with the intention of clearing the air between them, and looked like he might have succeeded.

'Jay, Carrie Dashwood.'

With a face like thunder he nodded at me and muttered, 'Hi.'

I nodded back, taking him in. He was bald, his head a perfect, light brown egg shape, and he was all in black – thick, black-rimmed glasses, V-neck T-shirt revealing a swirl of dark hair, skinny jeans with turn-ups, and pointy shoes – and was gripping his coffee cup as though he was throttling it.

In comparison, Megan looked cheer-leader bright in a white cotton dress and sliders, her hair swishing like black satin around her shoulders.

I nervously tugged my scoop-neck top over the waistband of my candy-pink jeans, wishing I'd tied back my hair, which was extra bouncy, and that I hadn't worn red lipstick.

It seemed pathetic that I'd been secretly hoping to impress Tom, by showing him how capable and in control I was. I would have to make do with Megan. I didn't want her feeding back to him that I'd fluffed it.

'So, you're my competition,' Jay said, setting his cup down, his smooth face set in a close-lipped smile. His charcoal eyes were magnified through his rectangular lenses, and not remotely friendly.

'I prefer to call it pitching for a job.' It was my best professional voice – apart from a tiny quaver at the end.

Jay leaned back and spread his legs, flinging one arm across the back of the sofa. It was a gesture presumably intended to intimidate, spoilt by the fact that his flies were undone.

'I don't think I've too much to worry about,' he said, in a thespy way. 'Been in the business too long, sweetheart.'

'You haven't seen what I've got yet.' I indicated the vase of flowers on the table, which looked like they'd been plonked in. 'Even I could have done that.'

He followed my gaze. 'Those?' He pointed at them, as if to make absolutely sure. 'You think I brought *those*?'

He and Megan looked at each other and burst into showy laughter, any animosity there'd been between them, gone.

'I did those, silly, they're from the garden,' Megan said, shimmying over to pat my arm, her engagement ring flashing like a warning. 'Now, would you like some coffee before we take a look at Jay's arrangement?'

'Not for me, thanks,' I said, scanning the room. If Jay's arrangement wasn't here, where was it?

'Flowers have to be kept cool in this weather or they droop,' Jay said, dripping scorn, bringing his foot onto the opposite knee. 'Isn't that the first rule of being a florist?'

'I wouldn't know,' I bit back. 'My aunt's the florist, not me. I'm here to represent her, as Megan agreed she could supply the flowers for her wedding.'

'Oh, did she now?' Jay tossed Megan a sniper-like look that brought her hurrying to his side.

'Provisionally,' she said, smoothing the air with her hands. 'The thing is, Carrie, I owe Jay, for dropping him without waiting to hear the outcome of his arrest.' She gave a pantomime shrug. 'My bad.'

And my fault for calling him in the first place.

'I understand that,' I said, attempting to soften my tone, reminding myself that Ruby needed this job. 'But you promised to look at both our arrangements before deciding.'

'True.' Megan glanced at my bag. 'It's in there?' Her eyebrows sprang up. 'Yours wasn't in a bag,' she said to Jay, and I couldn't make out if she was being genuinely accusing, or pretending to be.

'It certainly wasn't,' he replied, in a similar tone, rubbing a hand around his jaw. Shuffling forwards, he steepled his fingers. 'Let's have a shufty then.'

He exchanged a look with Megan as I stepped up to the coffee table, and my pulse accelerated as I put down the bag and reached inside. In the absence of any perfume, which I rarely wore, I'd blasted the flower-pups with Dove antiperspirant. It had a strong floral scent that attacked my nostrils as I lifted the pups out and placed them next to the coffee pot.

'Obviously, this is just a sample,' I said, fighting an urge to sneeze. I retrieved the portfolio and held it out. 'I know you didn't have time to look the other day, but I've brought it so you can see what else…' My words petered out.

The hush was so total I could hear my stomach gurgle.

I looked from Megan to Jay, both staring at the flower-pups with identical expressions, though I couldn't determine what they were.

Sounds leached into the room: the housekeeper warbling the chorus of 'Mamma Mia'; the drone of a lawnmower through the open window; the creak of floorboards overhead.

Suddenly Jay jerked forward, knocking the table with his foot, and I jumped as a spoon clattered to the surface.

'May I?' His voice had a rather muffled quality as he reached out a bony hand to the pups.

'No!' I stepped forward, palm up like a traffic warden. 'It's very delicate,' I said, not wanting him to discover that the flowers weren't real. 'It's just for show,' I clarified, as he hovered his hand in the air. 'I don't want it to get damaged.'

Megan had dropped to her knees and was eye-to-eye with groom-pup. He looked particularly appealing in his black top hat, and although bride-pup's eyes were a bit skew-whiff I was sure it wouldn't be a deal-breaker. The overall effect was what counted, and they couldn't have looked more weddingy.

'It smells *really* strong,' she said, with the same peculiar timbre to her voice; as if she'd got biscuit crumbs stuck in her throat and was trying not to choke. 'What kind of flowers are they?'

'Mostly carnations,' I said. 'But if you'd like something similar we could use white roses, and they don't even have to be white—'

A sound erupted, like someone squeezing a duck.

I shot a glance at Jay. He was doubled over, cradling his head as though in terrible pain, and his shoulders were vibrating.

'What's wrong with him?' I said to Megan.

She'd rocked forward onto her hands, her head hanging down between her arms, and as I watched her bucking, like a cat retching up a fur-ball, I realised what was happening.

They weren't just laughing, they were almost paralysed by hilarity, unable to move out of their contorted positions.

'Oh. My. God,' Megan managed at last, pushing herself up and swiping the backs of her hands across her face. Her cheeks were magenta, smeared with eye make-up, and Jay looked like he'd been weeping.

'I don't see what's so funny.' I was stiff with shame and embarrassment. 'My aunt worked hard on that, and it shows how skilled she is.'

'Oh, Carrie, you're so sweet,' said Megan, husky-voiced from laughing. 'I can't believe you seriously thought something like this would do.' She gave a strangled splutter. 'I mean, they're not even real flowers.'

'I thought you liked themed designs.' I hated that they were laughing at Ruby. I remembered the look of shy pride on her face, and the absorbed expression she'd worn before I disturbed her as she was rummaging through her boxes. 'You sounded impressed by Jay's handbag flowers.'

'Hardly in the same league,' Jay squawked. 'I mean, *Jesus WEPT*!'

'He would if he saw *that*!'

They creased up again.

'This is just to show you what Ruby can do,' I pressed on, determined to have my say. 'Obviously, we'll use real flowers on the day.'

'Oh dear,' Jay said softly, dashing his fingertips beneath his eyes, removing all trace of amusement. 'You'd better come with me, and I'll show you how it should be done.'

Megan sprang to her feet and straightened her dress, her face twisting once more as she caught sight of the pups.

'I haven't laughed like that for years,' she said, reaching to give my frozen fingers a squeeze. 'I'd forgotten how funny you were, Bagsy.'

I was glad Tom wasn't there to witness my loss of face, as Megan picked up the flower-pups and cuddled them under her arm.

'They can come with us,' she said, sharing another look of amusement with Jay.

If they weren't best buddies before, they were now; at my expense.

Chapter 23

Jay practically pranced from the room, with Megan by his side, and I followed them, face burning, into the kitchen, which was now empty and spotlessly clean. Ruby's whole flat would have fitted inside it.

I thought briefly of the messy kitchen in the house Tom had shared with his fellow vets, the surfaces scattered with coffee cups, cereal packets and takeaway leaflets, and could see why he'd felt more at home there.

'Here we are!' Jay flung wide the doors of a walk-in larder, and flounced inside.

It was several degrees cooler than the rest of the house, and lined with packets of fancy pasta, jars of preserves and expensive looking olive oils.

One shelf had been cleared to showcase Jay's floral arrangement, and as I clapped eyes on it I tried not to groan out loud. Far from the over-the-top affair I'd been expecting – a life-size replica of Madonna perhaps, made entirely of daisies – I was looking at an understated bouquet in subtle shades of sapphire-blue and ivory, bound with a silky sash that had been secured with a diamanté pin – the only remotely flashy aspect.

It was perfect in its simplicity, and, judging by his self-satisfied smirk, Jay knew it.

'I've gone for a preppy seaside theme, with peonies, ranunculus, nigella, delphiniums and cerinthe.' He reeled off the names of the flowers as though they were his children. 'It was obvious the moment I met her, that Megan has exquisite taste,' he went on, flashing an obsequious smile that revealed a gold tooth. 'I knew it was going to be a case of less is more.' He stabbed me with his gaze, before lifting the bouquet as carefully as if it were a baby bird and holding it against Megan's hair. 'Suits her colouring, don't you think, and brings out those amazing eyes.'

I'd like to bring out your eyes, I thought.

'It's superb,' Megan gushed, angling her head and fluttering her eyelashes at me. 'I could have matching posies on the tables at the reception.'

Jay whipped out a smart-phone and took a couple of snaps, and Megan played up, pouting flirtily, waggling the wedding-pups for the camera, and making little whining noises in her throat.

She looked like a Disney princess, with a bitchy vibe.

'Let me take a couple of you holding the bouquet in the kitchen, where the lighting's better,' said Jay. 'I can put some pictures on my website, darling. You're going to be a stunning bride.'

'You should see my dress,' she said, sliding me a look. 'Tom's going to be blown away.'

'I hope he hasn't seen you in it, darling, you know it's bad luck.'

'Of course not.' She widened her eyes at the thought. 'Ooh, and I want rose petals scattered behind me as I walk down the aisle.' She twirled around with the bouquet, the wedding-pups discarded on the worktop, and pointed through the window at the grounds, where presumably the ceremony was to take place. 'There'll be a pergola at the end, where Tom and I will exchange our vows' – she cast me a little look as if to check I was listening – 'and actually, if you could entwine some white roses around the pergola, that would be super-duper.'

'Not a problemo,' said Jay, sucking up to her like mad. I might as well have been invisible. 'Leave it to me, sweetheart.'

Anger rising like one of Bob's loaves, I snatched up the pups and said loudly, 'So I'll tell my aunt it's a "no" then, shall I?'

'No to what?' said a voice behind me, and I whipped around to see Mr Hudson in the doorway.

My breath caught in my throat.

At first glance, Michael Hudson looked barely changed from the last time I'd seen him. He was wearing a salmon-pink shirt and immaculately pressed beige trousers, his brown shoes as shiny as conkers. On a second glance, I noticed white streaks running through his hair, and a bruised look in his brown eyes, which I guessed was to do with his wife's death.

He entered the kitchen and put the plate he'd been carrying into the sink, before turning to me, eyebrows lifted in polite enquiry.

'I was pitching to do the flowers for the wedding,' I said, refusing to be intimidated as I snatched up Ruby's arrangements. It was blindingly obvious that, compared to Jay's, they were completely unsuitable.

'Do I know you?' He leaned against the counter, his forehead rippling. 'That red hair,' he mused. 'You look familiar.'

'We knew each other at school.' Megan handed her bouquet to Jay, and moved over to slip her arm through Mr Hudson's. 'She introduced me to Tom at his twenty-first, before she moved away and lost touch.' She gave me a glowing smile that I felt was more for Mr Hudson's benefit than mine.

'Ah, yes,' he said. 'You were Tom's friend…'

'Carrie,' I said flatly. I wanted to leave and never come back. I wasn't looking forward to telling Ruby there was no booking after all, but hopefully she would find it in her heart to forgive me.

'Carrie, of course, I remember.' Mr Hudson rubbed his chin while he studied me with narrowed eyes. 'Tom talked about you to his mother.'

Megan stiffened.

'I knew him when he was at veterinary college,' I said. It felt like a massive betrayal of how I'd really felt, but I could hardly blurt out that I'd been in love with him.

'You were crying the night of the party.' His gaze narrowed further. 'I saw you on the stairs.'

I was surprised he'd remembered. I could feel the laser-beam of Megan's eyes.

'I'd had too much to drink,' I said, dropping my gaze to my feet. They were still sore from the night before, even in the comfy sandals I'd found in Ruby's cupboard. 'Anyway, I'd better get going.'

'Your aunt's a florist?'

I lifted my head. 'Ruby's Blooms,' I said. 'She has a stall near the beach in Shipley.'

He gave a fleeting smile that transformed his face, and I saw a resemblance to Tom that wrenched at my heart. 'I tried to buy some buildings along the parade there a long time ago, but the sweet-shop owner put up quite a fight.' He sounded as if he admired the owner's gumption. 'I don't remember your aunt's stall.'

'It's been there quite a few years now,' I said, not sure why I was bothering when he was just being polite.

'She made those dogs,' Megan butted in, eyes flicking to Jay and away, and I turned to see him smiling behind his hand.

'Cute,' said Mr Hudson, eyeing my aunt's puppies with an inscrutable expression. 'Tell her to go ahead.'

'What?' snapped Megan, before I could open my mouth.

He looked at her for the first time.

'Fiona liked to support local businesses,' he said, in a way that suggested Megan ought to have known. 'My wife,' he said to me. 'No offence,' he added to Jay, who was giving me daggers.

'And that's amazing,' said Megan, recovering quickly and giving me a charitable smile. 'But Carrie's aunt runs a stall, which means she's essentially a market trader.' Her eyes shot to the pups. 'I mean, the arrangements are *lovely*, but a little bit amateurish compared to what Jay can offer, and this is my *wedding*.'

'I'll pay for the flowers,' Mr Hudson said.

'But…' began Megan, then clamped her mouth shut, perhaps sensing he wasn't to be persuaded otherwise. When her eyes met mine they were like ice picks. 'Fine!' she said, her voice strained. 'I was going to suggest she did the flowers for the reception, anyway.'

'Were you?' Jay's voice could have frozen jelly.

'Yes, I was,' Megan said, with such conviction I nearly believed her. 'I did kind of promise, after all.'

As he passed, Mr Hudson patted my shoulder. 'Tell your aunt to send her invoice to me,' he said. 'Now, would you like me to show you out?'

Chapter 24

I grabbed my bag and portfolio, my face hotter than a nuclear reactor, and thanked Mr Hudson before rushing out of the house.

After throwing myself in my car, I sat for a moment and wondered what had just happened. I glanced through the windscreen, half expecting someone to emerge, and sure enough Megan appeared as though I'd magicked her up. She trotted daintily across the gravel, a protective hand on her abdomen, as if to remind me she was pregnant.

Prepared for the inevitable onslaught, I lowered the window, only to find her eyes smiling into mine.

'Sorry about that,' she said, miming a look of goggle-eyed confusion. 'I'm sure Michael knew that Tom would be cross if I let Jay do the flowers, and that's why he stepped in, but I thought it only fair to give Jay a shot.' She pouted her bottom lip. 'I'm sure you understand.'

Not really.

'Anyway,' she said, not waiting for a reply, tossing her hair like a pony. 'I meant to say, keep Tuesday evening free.' It took all my self-control not to recoil when she reached in and squeezed my shoulder. 'There's a new seafood place in Shipley called Off the Hook,' she said. 'Tom and I could meet you and Cooper there at seven thirty?'

Cooper? Oh god, she meant Toby.

I was about to make an excuse when it hit me that I'd done nothing so far to convince either Megan or Tom that I was fine with them getting married. I couldn't bear that Megan's lasting impression might be of a Miss Havisham type, hankering after a man who'd never loved her, and begrudging her once-best-friend the wedding of her dreams.

'Sounds good,' I said, jabbing the key in the ignition, and deciding not to react to anything that had happened inside the house. 'I'll check with Cooper and let you know.' *Providing Toby hasn't come to his senses and blocked my number.*

'No hard feelings?' She dipped her head and looked at me through her spiky eyelashes, almost as if she wanted me to challenge her.

'No hard feelings.' My smile was so taut my cheekbones were in danger of snapping. 'Speak soon.'

'I hope so.' She straightened as Jay came out and called her name. In a patch of gloom from the overhanging roof, he was cast into ghoulish shadow, and looked as if he'd like to run somebody over. Probably me.

'Got a bit of making up to do there.' She gave a comedy eye-roll and a final, dazzling smile, before backing away with a wave. I didn't doubt her ability to win him over. She'd clearly been honing her skills for the past ten years.

'Oh my god, Jay, your flies are undone!' she squealed.

He looked down, hands shooting to his crotch.

I waited until she'd steered him round the side of the house, their voices mingling hotly, before swinging the car around, and heading back down the drive.

The engine began to cough like an old man.

'Oh, no, not now,' I pleaded. 'Just get me back to Shipley.'

As if it had heard and was willing to try, the car inched forward until we'd passed through the archway, where the engine promptly cut out.

No, no, no, no, no. Forehead itching with sweat, I turned the key and revved until the engine started again, then pressed my foot hard on the accelerator, shooting forward several metres. Just a bit further and we'd be on the hill back down to the village, where the momentum would give the engine the boost it needed.

'Come on,' I urged, picking up speed, just as Tom's Land Rover came tearing around the corner.

'Shit!' I swung the steering wheel wildly to the left, taking the car up a grassy verge where it collided with the trunk of an oak tree. As I jolted forward, there was a sound of crumpling metal, and a bang as the airbag inflated and whacked me in the face.

'AARRGGHH!'

In the rear-view mirror, the Land Rover braked and slewed to a halt, and the driver's door flew open. I dropped my face onto the airbag and made a whimpering sound, and nearly hit the roof when a set of knuckles rapped urgently on the window.

Twisting my head, I saw Tom peering in.

'Get out,' he was shouting, pointing to the front of the car, and when I peered past the airbag, I noticed a plume of smoke curling from under the bonnet.

'Oh, bumbags.' I unsnapped my seat belt and shoved the door open, bashing Tom in the knees.

'OW!' He crunched over, grimacing in pain.

'Sorry.'

'No, no, I'm the one who should be sorry,' he said through his teeth, as I staggered out. 'Are you OK?' His hand flew out to steady me, and I jolted away.

'I'm fine.'

He looked at me closely, a furrow between his eyebrows. 'Your cheeks are a bit red.'

'Nothing new there,' I said tartly. Resisting the moonlike pull of his eyes, I fidgeted with my clothes, which felt bonded to my body. My hair was drooping forward like tangled wool, and my headache was worse than ever. 'I'm fine.' I flexed my shoulders. 'Which is more than I can say for my car.'

We turned at the same time and took in the damage, which wasn't as bad as I'd feared – just a crumpled bumper.

'It needs a new battery.'

'It's completely my fault,' said Tom at the same time, pressing the heel of his hand to his forehead. He looked so achingly familiar, in faded blue jeans and a navy T-shirt, the sun picking out golden highlights in his hair, that I had to look away. 'I took the corner way too fast. I was hoping to see you before you left.'

'You were?' I kept my eyes fixed ahead and fought to control my breathing.

'The flowers,' he said, ruefully. 'Megan wanted me back, to help choose between you and that idiot Simmons. I wouldn't have gone in the first place, but there was a whippet with chronic diarrhoea.'

The flowers. Obviously. Why else would he be hurrying back?

'Sounds nasty,' I said.

'Apparently, it had eaten a packet of butter.'

I sneaked a look and saw he was watching me, concern etched on his face.

'Not that I know much about flowers,' he said. 'I'm assuming she decided to go with you in the end?'

I managed a nod. 'My aunt,' I corrected. No point telling him I suspected Megan's only intention had been to flaunt their relationship, and to humiliate me in front of him. 'Your father had the final say.'

His eyebrows lifted. 'I didn't think he'd still be here,' he said, glancing over his shoulder, as if his dad might be racing down the drive.

'He was… *nice* to me,' I said.

'Good.' He rubbed his palm over a sprinkling of stubble round his jaw. 'He's mellowed a bit since Mum died.'

My brain hummed with questions, but they were too emotive. 'Where's Hovis?' I peered at the wonky Land Rover, expecting to see his whiskery face at the window.

'I left him at the cottage, at the surgery,' Tom said, and shook his head as if mentally reprimanding himself. 'Megan's allergic to his fur, so I tend not to bring him too often.'

I remembered how she'd swiped at Hovis earlier, and guessed it was more than his fur she was allergic to.

'Are you sure you're OK?'

I nodded, and a loaded silence fell, broken by the warbling of a blackbird in the oak tree. It was probably wondering why there was a car attached to it.

'I suppose we'd better swap insurance details,' I said. 'I don't know how I'm going to get the car back to Shipley.' My eyes brimmed with tears, and I turned away so that Tom couldn't see. 'I was supposed to be going somewhere this afternoon.' It suddenly felt imperative that I made the effort to talk to Peter. I'd imagined returning to the flat and telling Ruby that not only had I secured her the wedding booking (which she'd thought was secure, anyway), I'd found out where her son was and had arranged a joyful reunion.

Of the two, I knew which she'd be happiest about. I'd be able to go home with the knowledge that I'd done something valuable with my time in Shipley. It wouldn't matter so much that my past had been raked up and shoved in front of my eyes; my stay would have been worthwhile.

'I'll sort out getting your car towed and pay for any repairs, so you don't lose your no-claims bonus,' Tom said, his voice becoming businesslike. 'Maybe you could call your boyfriend?'

Boyfriend? Oh, bloody Toby again. Or should I say, Cooper. I was starting to feel haunted by the man, and I'd only met him once. Toby that is. I reminded myself that Cooper didn't exist.

'Megan mentioned bumping into you both last night.'

Of course she did.

'He's working today,' I said quickly. It was far too presumptuous to ask Toby for this kind of favour – especially since I was already planning to invite him to what would probably be the most awkward meal of the century, on Tuesday evening.

'Working?' Tom's eyebrows lowered. 'Isn't he a—'

'War correspondent, yes,' I snapped, regretting it when Tom's face closed up. 'He's catching up on some paperwork at my aunt's place, and anyway, he hasn't got his car.'

'Oh?'

'He, um, came up on the train.'

'Up?'

I wished I could transport myself to a distant cloud. 'From London,' I said. 'He wanted a break from driving, he did a lot of it in…' *Where, where, where?* 'the… war zones.' Oh god, was I making a mockery of genuine war correspondents, out in god-only-knew-where, in genuine danger?

Tendrils of hair were stuck to my face and neck and the sun was so hot I was beginning to feel faint.

'Look, let me give you a lift to wherever you want to go.' Tom ran a hand through his own hair so it stood up at a weird angle. 'It's the least I can do.'

'Oh, no, I couldn't,' I said, stomach pitching like a trawler. 'I'll take a taxi.' As I reached into the car for my bag and keys, the wedding-pups peeped up at me from the canvas bag on the front seat. I felt oddly guilty as I slammed the door on their pitiful faces and locked it. 'Do you have the number of a cab firm?'

'Don't be silly.' Tom was striding purposefully to his car, jangling his keys in his hand. 'I insist.'

'But what about…' I daren't say Megan's name in case it conjured her up, but he interpreted my pause.

'She thinks I'm working anyway,' he said over his shoulder.

'Well, listen, just drop me back in Shipley.' I trotted after him. I would have to work out a way to go and see Peter another day – or perhaps one evening, after I'd finished on the stall.

'Just tell me where you were going, and I'll take you there.' Tom had pulled open the passenger door and gestured for me to climb in. 'I won't take no for an answer.'

'But it's quite a drive and I don't know how long I'll be.'

'It doesn't matter.' He paused, one hand on the open door as he studied my simmering face. 'I'll wait for as long as it takes.'

Chapter 25

'Sorry about the smell,' Tom said, lowering the windows. 'I had a hen with an infected eye in here yesterday.'

'It's fine,' I said, feeling shy as I examined the interior. It looked like an extension of his surgery, with a cat basket on the back seat, beside a box of latex gloves, and a brightly coloured felt garment that looked like a coat for a dog. There were several collars, and a couple of dog leads strewn around, and an opened packet of worming tablets on the floor. Tom bent to pick it up, and lobbed it into the glove compartment, his wrist brushing my knee.

I jerked away, my face tight with heat.

'So where are we going?' he said, seeming not to notice. He switched on the satnav, and although I knew the address off by heart, I burrowed the piece of paper out of my bag and studied Doris's sloping handwriting.

'It's 21 Orchard Road, Christchurch, Bournemouth.' I read out the postcode in an Australian accent and cringed. 'Sorry.'

He smiled as he keyed it in, and I was overcome by an urge to stroke the faint dark hairs on his arm. It reminded me of the time I'd turned up early for a Sunday morning dog-walk and caught him coming out of the shower in a skimpy towel. Clapping eyes on his wiry chest and trail of fuzzy hair below his belly-button, had fired an urge to hurl myself at him.

Panic bubbled up. How was I supposed to act normally for an entire journey? What could we talk about that wouldn't be inflammatory? Apart from his visit to the stall the other day, we hadn't been alone together for ten years.

Did he still like science fiction films, and going for long walks to 'burn off energy'? It was hard to envisage him doing either with Megan. She'd only liked films starring Brad Pitt, and used to make her mother drive her to school, despite only living a five-minute walk away.

As we set off, at a more sedate pace than Tom had been driving earlier, I dug out my phone and busied myself scrolling for new messages, even though looking down made me feel queasy.

There was a text from Sarah that made me smile: *Chloe just asked why ladies have beards on their front bottoms, and Jack said it's because they're called 'furginas'!!!! Would have been funnier if Phil's mum wasn't here* ☹

I sent back a salvo of smiley faces and a love heart, then tried to discreetly WhatsApp Jasmine *I'm in a car with tom* but hit the wrong keys. It came out as *iminent a vase with tin.*

Did you sit on your phone??? she replied.

Feeling too sick to try again, I chucked my phone in my bag and twisted my head to the window, letting the air brush my overheated cheeks.

'So, who is it you're going to see?' Tom said, as we drove through Moreton village and headed for the A351. 'Sounded important.'

I turned to look at him, just as he turned to face me. Our eyes clashed, and blood surged to my face. 'It's a long story,' I said, switching my gaze to the road ahead.

'We've plenty of time.' He spoke lightly, but I sensed his curiosity. 'Is it something to do with your aunt?'

I thought about it. He was never going to meet Ruby, and I'd be back in Manchester soon. Would it matter if I told him?

I expelled a long breath. 'It's my aunt's long-lost son,' I said, the knot in my chest unravelling. 'She gave him up for adoption when he was a baby, and now she'd like to get to know him.'

He flashed me a look of frowning surprise. 'And she's sending you as... What? Some sort of mediator?'

'Not exactly.' I looked at my knees, pressed primly together. 'She doesn't know I'm going.'

Tom slowed the car at a set of traffic lights, and pulled a yellow-and-white stripy bag from the doorwell. 'Have a humbug,' he said, taking one and passing the bag to me. 'Then you can tell me the whole story, if you want to.'

By the time I'd finished, I'd crunched through another humbug, my headache had eased, and I'd kicked off my sandals and tucked my feet beneath me. Tom had listened carefully, nodding occasionally, and had only spoken twice: once to ask if it was possible my dad knew, but wasn't comfortable talking about it, to which I replied no, I was certain he didn't, and second to ask if I'd thought about what I was going to say when I got there.

'Not really,' I admitted. 'It was a spur-of-the-moment decision. I was going to play it by ear.'

'Not like you, Dashwood.'

My stomach dipped. It was what he'd called me sometimes. 'I know,' I said, stuffing another humbug in my mouth to hide my confusion. 'I'm normally very organised, but since coming to Shipley and finding out Ruby's secret' – *and that you and Megan are not only getting married, but expecting a baby* – 'all that's gone out of the window.'

'I think you're acting instinctively,' he said, turning the car as the satnav directed us away from the coast and down a sun-dappled road, where an elderly couple were strolling arm in arm, with a tiny long-haired dog that looked like a wig on a lead.

'Maybe I am.' I'd never thought of myself that way, but liked the sound of it. Or was instinctive bad, in the way being impulsive could be perceived as behaving recklessly?

'Like when you stopped to rescue Hovis and brought him to the surgery.' Tom flashed his wide-lipped smile, apparently unaware of the effect it had on my pulse rate.

'Anyone would have done the same.'

'I doubt it,' he said, resting a hand on the gear stick. 'Most people would have driven past, or not noticed.'

My neck and shoulders softened as I basked in his apparent approval.

Behave, I chided myself. He was being nice to an old acquaintance that was all. One he'd run off the road in his car half an hour ago. *Driving back to see you.*

NO!

I imagined the word as a big red cross, to stop my thoughts diving in directions they shouldn't.

Think of Megan, I told myself. Think of the child she's carrying, and the wedding that's going to take place, less than a week from now.

Actually, I didn't want to think of Megan.

'Was going to Manchester an instinctive move?'

The car windscreen seemed to warp in and out. 'Mmmhmm,' I managed, sucking hard on my humbug. 'I don't think tho.'

'I phoned your parents' house once, you know.'

My head whipped round. 'You did?'

He nodded. 'After I moved to Scotland. Your mum said you were with someone.' *What?* When?

'Sam?'

I stared at him, numbly. 'I was,' I said, at length. *Why* hadn't Mum told me? 'For a few months, anyway.'

He gave a crooked little smile. 'You're a pretty close bunch, aren't you, you and your family?'

Feeling squeezed out of shape, I said, 'I suppose I take them for granted.' *Well done, Carrie.* His mum was dead, and his dad had never supported his career choice. As parents went, I should be cherishing mine.

'It must be nice to have them close by.'

He called my parents' house from Scotland. He'd found their number and called to ask after me. 'Mum and Dad are very hands-on with Sarah's twins,' I said, half wishing he hadn't told me. 'But Phil's parents live close by, so it can get a bit competitive.'

I gathered from the tilt of his head he was interested, and, desperate to escape my knotty thoughts, found myself recounting stories about the twins, which segued into tales from Cars 4 U, and then I was talking about Jasmine.

'We're really different, but hit it off when she came to look at my spare room,' I said.

'Is this the one from Scotland?'

I nodded, pleased he'd remembered. 'She brought a family pack of Doritos and a bottle of wine, and said she wouldn't look round the house until we'd made each other laugh. Which immediately made me laugh.'

He cast me a glance, a smile touching his eyes. 'What did you do?'

'My impression of Dot Cotton from *EastEnders*,' I said, feeling my cheeks glow.

'The one that sounds like the queen?' He grinned. 'I remember you doing it for me.'

I remembered too. It was after a bracing coastal walk to Corfe Castle, when we were sitting on a rocky crag, Hovis sending up barks to the wheeling seagulls. Tom had asked if I had any hidden talents, and confessed he could tap dance after having lessons as a child. I'd told him I liked doing impressions, and launched into my Dot Cotton without thinking.

'Your Majesty, I'm in awe,' he'd said, touching an imaginary forelock.

I'd assumed he was joking.

'It does not sound like the queen!' I said to him now, swiping his arm. 'Jasmine thought it was Margaret Thatcher.'

'I rest my case.' He flashed me a look of warm amusement that made my heart flip over. 'You need to widen your repertoire.'

'Take the next turning on your right and you have reached your destination.' The robotic voice of the satnav was like an ice cube down my back. As Tom steered the car down Orchard Road we fell silent.

It was an attractive street, quiet and tree-lined, with red-brick houses set behind hedges, most of them sporting neat front lawns and window boxes brimming with flowers. There was a smell of barbecue smoke in the air, and shrieks of childish laughter floated through the car windows. I felt suddenly guilty. Here I was, planning to gatecrash a family Sunday, which was almost certain to result in me being turned away – if not threatened with the police.

I considered asking Tom to turn the car around.

'You're sure about this?' he said, slowing the car to a crawl to read the house numbers, eventually stopping outside number 21.

'I don't know.' Nerve ends twanging, I peered past him. There was a leafy birch tree blocking my view, but adjoining the house was a garage with the door up, revealing a car inside.

'They're home,' I said, digging my nails into my palms. 'But what if I'm making a big mistake?'

'It's not too late to change your mind.' Tom turned the engine off and sat back. 'Nobody will ever know.'

I looked at his profile; his strong, straight nose, and the way the sunlight created a golden fuzz around his hair. 'What would you do?'

A knot of tension rippled along his jawline. 'I'd talk to him,' he admitted, turning slightly to face me. 'It's not like he doesn't know about Ruby, and it might be different talking to someone who knows her, but isn't her, if you see what I mean.' I did. 'Less emotional.'

'Maybe.' I wound a strand of hair around my finger and pulled, the resulting sting sharpening my resolve. 'I suppose the worst he can do is tell me to clear off.'

'Exactly.' He lightly touched my knee, and this time I didn't flinch. 'If anyone can talk him round, it's you,' he said.

I tried to smile, but my mouth wouldn't respond.

'Would you like me to come in with you?'

I realised I would like it – more than anything – because having Tom beside me just felt right, and it was this realisation that had me snapping my seat belt off and fumbling with the door.

'I'll be fine,' I said, willing the emotion to retreat. 'But thanks.'

He cast me a businesslike nod. 'I'll be here if you need me.'

'I'll try not to be too long.' I pushed my feet back into my sandals and snatched up my bag before clambering out of the car.

The heat was oppressive and perspiration broke out on my temples. I ran my hands over my hair and clothes, and blew out a breath. 'You can do this,' I said out loud, startling a ginger cat, which shot through the hedge. 'Come on, Carrie.'

I pushed open the gate and headed for the front door, my senses assailed by the scent of herbs from a shrub bordering the path. My legs felt numb from sitting in the car, and to anyone glancing through the window I probably looked a bit tipsy.

I tried to rehearse a few opening lines, but couldn't get beyond, 'Hi, I'm Carrie,' which even a tongue-tied parrot could have managed.

Taking a shaky breath, I raised my hand and knocked on the blue-painted door before I could change my mind and race back to the car.

I resisted the urge to look back, to see if Tom was watching. The fact he was there felt both surreal yet somehow predestined, and I still couldn't get out of my mind that he'd tried to contact me from Scotland, and I hadn't known. Did that mean he hadn't been thinking about Megan, after all?

I glanced at the window to my right, in time to see the curtain twitch, as if someone had just moved away.

Maybe Donny didn't like visitors at the weekend. Not Donny, I reminded myself. *Peter.*

I chewed my knuckle, and decided I would knock once more before trying the back of the house, when I heard movement inside.

I felt a throb at the base of my neck and my mouth dried up. I straightened my shoulders, and arranged my face in what I hoped was a friendly expression as a door chain clattered on the other side of the door, and a couple of bolts were slid back.

They were certainly security conscious.

As the door began to open, I said, 'Hi, I'm Carrie Dashwood,' hoping I didn't sound like a local councillor canvassing votes. 'I'm so sorry to bother you…' My words trailed off as I was met by a girl with a thick blonde fringe swept across her forehead, and a lollipop jammed in her mouth.

She looked around fourteen, skinny and not very tall, but upright. She was wearing a blue vest top with long white shorts, but it was her bright blue eyes that made the breath stick in my throat. It was like looking at a young version of Ruby, and I knew without a doubt that the girl was her granddaughter.

Chapter 26

'Who's there?' called a voice from inside the house, and before I could gather my scattered thoughts a man came into view.

My first impression was how ordinary he looked: medium height, sandy hair, light-coloured eyes, and wearing the sort of weekend uniform beloved of dads everywhere; cream cargo shorts and an open-necked checked shirt.

I couldn't detect any immediate resemblance to Ruby.

'She's called Carrie something,' the girl said, pulling the lollipop out of her mouth, leaving a bluish tinge around her lips. 'I like your hair.' She gave it a critical look. 'I wish mine was ginger.'

'Th-thanks,' I stuttered, hand fluttering up self-consciously.

'Can you go and watch your brother, Kate?' the man said. 'He keeps dive-bombing the paddling pool.'

Another grandchild! I imagined telling Ruby, pictured her look of open-mouthed joy, and the thought of it kept me pinned to the doorstep.

'Where's Mum?' The girl – Kate – was eyeing my bag with interest, as if she'd like to grab it off me and have a good root through. She'd be disappointed. I wasn't the type to lug my life around in it, which is why it was so small.

'She's still painting the back bedroom,' the man said, ruffling her hair. 'Now, go!'

Kate rolled her eyes, but ducked obediently under her father's arm and retreated into the hallway.

The man stepped forward, a look of polite interest on his even features. His feet were bare and white, as though unused to daylight, and he smelt very faintly of chlorine. 'How can I help you?' he said.

I desperately searched for prompts to start a conversation, and spotted the next-door neighbour sprinkling her roses. 'Could I trouble you for a glass of water?' I said, hoping he might invite me in. 'It's really hot out here.'

'Is that why you knocked on our door?' A slice of annoyance lodged between his brows. 'You should carry water with you in this weather.'

'Oh, I forgot,' I said, wrong-footed. 'Silly of me.'

He rubbed his forehead. 'You can't go around knocking on doors, asking strangers for a drink of water.'

'I don't,' I said, wishing I hadn't. Now he was hacked off with me, and I hadn't even told him the real reason I was there. 'Look, it doesn't matter about the water.'

'It's not that I begrudge anyone a drink, it just seems odd that's all.' He glanced over my shoulder and narrowed his greyish eyes. 'Is that your car?'

'What?' I turned. The top of the Land Rover was just visible above the hedge. 'It's my... husband's, actually.' *Oh hell.*

The frown deepened. 'Your husband sent you to this *exact* address, to ask for a glass of water?' His eyes were slits of suspicion as he took a step back. 'It's a scam, isn't it?' he said, reaching for the door handle. 'I invite you into the kitchen where you try to *charm* me,' he gave a little snort, as though the idea was ludicrous, 'and while we're in there, your so-called husband slips upstairs and steals our stuff.'

'*What?*' He'd obviously been watching too many crime-busting shows. I shot out a hand to stop him closing the door. 'Look, forget about the water,' I said. 'That's not why I'm really here, though I am quite thirsty, actually.'

'So, you lied?' His tone was openly hostile.

'Not *lied,* exactly.'

'What do you call it then, when you say something that isn't true?'

Bloody hell. 'Look, Donny, I shouldn't have tried to get in your house under false pretences, even though I could really use a drink right now, but…'

He'd gone as stiff as a waxwork. 'What did you just call me?'

Shit. 'I–I mean, Peter… Mr Robson.'

'She sent you, didn't she?' *Shit.* This couldn't have gone worse if Ruby had rocked up in person. 'Who *are* you?' he barked. 'Some sort of private detective?' I instantly thought of Doris. This was all her doing. 'Tell her the answer's the same as the last time she tried to wangle her way into my life. I'm NOT INTERESTED.'

The door began to swing shut. 'I'm actually Ruby's niece,' I burst out. 'Your cousin, actually.' I wished I could stop saying 'actually'. 'She hasn't sent me, actually, I came of my own accord, because I know how desperately she wants to meet you, and her grandchildren, and if you could just give her—'

The door crashed shut, and there was the sound of bolts being fired across.

Bending, I thrust open the letterbox and peered through, in time to see his calves scissoring away.

'Please, give her a chance to tell her side of the story,' I shouted. 'She loves you and thinks about you all the time. She gets depressed every year on the anniversary of your adoption.'

'Serves her right for giving me away!'

I dropped to my knees on the doorstep and pushed my face closer. 'She doesn't think she deserves a second chance, but I do.'

I squinted down the hallway. There was an open door at the other end, a beam of sunlight spilling across oak floorboards.

'Peter?'

'I'm calling the police!' he yelled.

Bugger. 'She lives on Main Street in Shipley, above the bakery, if you change your mind,' I yelled back, in desperation. 'Or you can find me at her flower stall in the square, if you want to talk.' I fumbled out the envelope containing Ruby's letter and shoved it through the letterbox. As it fluttered from my fingers, a set of thickly lashed eyes appeared in front of mine.

'I'm Jen, Pete's wife,' said a low-pitched voice. 'When your aunt came before it was a bad time. Pete's adoptive mum had just died, his father was ill, and he was very angry.'

'Ruby didn't know,' I said, thinking that if you could judge someone purely by their eyes, Jen was a lovely person. 'She doesn't want to cause any more upset,' I blundered on. 'To be honest, she's accepted she'll never get to meet him, but I hate seeing her like this.'

The eyes – brown with green flecks – blinked a couple of times. 'I've tried talking to him,' she said, apologetically. 'He can be very stubborn.'

'Come away from that door!' Peter roared.

Jen's eyes widened. 'Go,' she urged. 'He really will call the police.'

I snatched my fingers away, and the letterbox snapped shut.

I knelt for a moment, fighting a wave of dizziness, and when I stood up and turned to leave, Tom was there.

'Come on.' He placed a hand on my elbow, and as he steered me back to the car I noticed the next-door neighbour was only pretending to water her roses, the hosepipe spraying her garden gnomes as she goggled over the fence.

'I really need a drink,' I said.

Tom handed me a litre bottle of water, which I suspected he kept in the car for overheated dogs, and I glugged half of it down before slumping into the passenger seat. I snagged the seat belt as I tried to pull it across my body, and tears leapt to my eyes.

'Let me.' Tom leaned over and fastened it for me, and I longed to fall against him and cry my eyes out. 'I take it that didn't go according to plan.'

I shook my head, not trusting myself to speak.

'Well, at least you tried,' he said, with unbearable gentleness.

We didn't speak again on the way back to Shipley. I tried to push thoughts of Peter and his family from my mind, but they were already lodged there. They were real, actual, living people, and I'd ruined their day. I imagined the scene I'd left behind – Peter dialling the police, his wife trying to placate him, their children frightened of the crazy woman who'd been shouting through their letterbox.

He would hate Ruby even more now. He might even come and confront her, and not in a good way. Then Ruby would hate me. I should never have come. And yet… he was Ruby's family, whether he liked it or not, and Kate was her granddaughter. And there was a grandson too.

It must be killing Ruby, knowing the family was there, but unreachable – like exhibits behind glass. Not even that. You could go and look at exhibits, but if Ruby tried she would mostly likely be arrested.

It was harder than ever to accept she had to live with it, but I couldn't see how there was anything more I could do.

The car stopped and my eyes flew open.

'You nodded off,' Tom said. 'I think you needed a nap.'

My throat felt raw. 'Was I snoring?'

'Only a tiny bit.'

He was joking, but I couldn't raise a smile. I glanced at the dashboard and saw with a start that it was nearly four o'clock. 'Where are we?' We were parked in a sun-drenched courtyard, outside a whitewashed building with an uneven, red-tiled roof.

'At my place. The surgery,' he clarified, fiddling with his keys. 'I thought you might want to freshen up before I take you back to your aunt's.' He paused. 'I can make some coffee, and call the recovery people to pick up your car.'

I knew I should refuse; insist he drop me at Ruby's right away. It suddenly felt like we'd shared something significant, and the air between us was littered with unsaid words. I shouldn't be on my own with him. What if Megan stopped by?

'OK,' I said. I stepped out of the car and stretched. The air was like warm silk on my arms, and the sky was the colour of bluebells (*everlasting love*).

Tom let us in through a side door that opened into a small, oak-beamed kitchen with a flagstone floor. Hovis gave a woof and leapt off a bow-legged armchair, and I bent to fuss him, enveloped by a sense of coming home.

'The living area's separate from the surgery,' Tom was saying, throwing his keys on a well-scrubbed table with an empty fruit bowl in the middle. 'There aren't any syringes lying around or sick guinea pigs in the house.'

'It doesn't matter if there are,' I said, realising he was trying to put me at ease. Even so, he seemed nervous as he moved around, fumbling a fresh filter into a shiny coffee machine and spilling beans on the counter. 'Real coffee?' I teased. 'Makes a change from that Co-op stuff you used to drink.'

'I still like it,' he protested. 'Megan bought me this, she prefers the proper stuff.'

Jealousy flickered. 'Does she come here often?' I wondered if he'd mentioned her to remind me they were getting married – as if I needed reminding.

'Hardly ever.' It came out abruptly.

I thought about her fur allergy, then remembered Megan saying that she sometimes stayed over, and she and Tom cuddled up in the bed in the attic room. Perhaps he'd just been trying to spare my feelings. But if that was the case, he must think I cared that he and Megan were together.

'I think he needs to go out,' I said, as Hovis raised a hopeful muzzle to the door.

'He probably needs a wee. You can let him go, he won't run off.'

I opened the door, and Hovis shot into the courtyard with a little yip, his nose snuffling the ground.

I turned back, and discreetly looked around. It was good to see Tom in context again, and the place looked a lot like the house he'd once shared; washing by the machine, books on the worktops, empty mugs, some veterinary books on a shelf – and my photo of Hovis on the windowsill. I wondered if Megan had noticed; whether she even knew it had come from me. I longed to open cupboards and drawers, and have a good poke through, but instead I said, 'Megan's invited us for a meal on Tuesday evening.'

'Sorry?' He was rinsing a mug at the sink, swishing water around, his back radiating tension. 'Invited who, where?'

'Me and Tob— Cooper, to Off the Hook with you and Megan.'

Tom put down the mug with exaggerated care. He reached for a tea towel and roughly dried his hands before turning to look at me. 'Do you want to go?'

My ribs tightened. 'Do you?'

Irritation scudded over his face. 'Maybe you and Megan should go on your own. You can talk about wedding stuff.'

'I don't want to talk about wedding stuff.' I bit my lip. I hadn't meant it to come out so sharply. 'I mean, there are other things to talk about besides weddings.'

'Is Cooper interested in weddings?'

'Sorry?'

'Why does he want to have dinner with people he's never met? Doesn't he want you to himself while he's in Shipley?'

I couldn't make out his tone. 'He, erm... I...' I scratched my nose. 'He's not the possessive sort.' My mouth felt twitchy with nerves, and to my horror, I heard myself say, 'Actually, we've only been on a couple of dates.'

Tom's forehead creased. 'According to Megan, he's The One.' He did capital letters with his voice.

'I might have given her that impression.'

His eyes were twin question marks. 'Why?'

'To shut her up, I suppose.' I wanted to melt with embarrassment.

'So, he's *not* The One?'

Hovis let out a noisy yawn, as though he'd heard enough.

'Not really,' I muttered.

Tom folded his arms. 'I'm getting the impression you don't really like Megan.' He sounded more curious than angry.

A shaft of sunshine beamed through the window, and highlighted the planes of his face. He looked incredibly handsome.

'So, what if I don't?' I was suddenly sick of pretending. It had been a long and confusing day, and although I had no one to blame but myself for messing things up with Peter (I couldn't really pin it on Doris) I felt deflated with exhaustion. I wanted to take to my bed with a plate of custard creams and stay there for at least six months. My bed, in my house, in Manchester.

'You know that night?' he said, out of the blue. 'My twenty-first.'

My chest clenched. 'What about it?'

'I'd been hoping...' he tipped his head back, as if searching the edges of the ceiling for the right words. 'I was going to ask you out, properly, I mean.' His head came down and his eyes latched onto mine. 'I had... *feelings* for you, Carrie, but I didn't know if you felt the same way.' *What?* 'I was worried if I said something it might scare you off and spoil our friendship, but when you turned up, and I saw you in that dress...' he shook his head, with a look of bemusement. 'I wanted to kiss you there and then.'

My head felt hot and heavy. I tried to speak, but when I opened my mouth, all that came out was a sigh.

'And then you introduced me to Megan and she kind of took over, and suddenly you were leaving, and saying Megan was perfect for me, and that you were going to see your sister...'

'I had feelings for you too.' My heart was leapfrogging about, and when Hovis brushed past my legs, I almost screamed. 'I didn't want to bring Megan that night, but she was desperate to see the house.'

He stared, his eyes like magnets. 'She told me *you* were desperate to see the house.'

'You know I wasn't bothered about where you came from.'

'It was a touchy subject,' he said, looking wretched. 'Girls before... they always wanted to see the house. See what my family was worth.'

'I saw you kissing her.' The words burst out, and he flinched as though I'd punched him.

'*She* kissed *me*,' he said, with conviction. 'I didn't plan it, I promise.'

'Well, whatever she told you after I'd gone, wasn't true.' I was almost panting now in my haste to get the words out. 'When I saw you together you looked so right, I convinced myself you'd never see me as girlfriend material, and after that kiss, the only way I could cope was to leave.'

'Run away, you mean?'

'OK, run away.' I could hardly deny it.

'Christ almighty.' He pushed his hands through his hair. 'So, if Megan hadn't been there that night, we might have got together?'

My vision blurred through a haze of tears. 'Maybe,' I whispered. 'It was what I wanted, more than anything.'

As the words left my lips, I wanted to snatch them back. It was too late for this. Ten years too late.

'Carrie…'

'She's having your baby,' I said, wiping my fingers across my lashes. 'You're getting married next week.'

'The pregnancy wasn't planned.' The words sound ripped from him. 'I'm sorry?'

'We spent the night together, a couple of months after Mum died.' His face was pale and tense. 'It sounds pathetic,' he said, 'but Megan had helped a lot while she was ill, and my mother really liked her. She kept saying how lovely it would be if Megan and I got together, and Megan was always around, even after Mum died, because she works for my father. I think I started to see her through their eyes.' I held my breath, while Tom's words kept pouring out. 'One night, she suggested a drink, and – cliché alert – one thing led to another.' He shook his head, as if trying to order his thoughts. 'It's no excuse, Carrie, but I hadn't had a relationship for ages' – my heart did a treacherous somersault – 'and she said she'd always loved me, but I felt terrible afterwards, like I'd led her on, because although I appreciated everything she'd done for Mum, I knew I wasn't in love with her.'

I was having trouble taking it in. I might have invented a boyfriend, but Megan had made up a whole relationship, based on a one-night stand. *Except that it wasn't…*

'You slept with her before.' My voice sounded raw.

'What?' His gaze refocused. 'Who told you that?'

'She did. She called me the day after your party.'

He shook his head. 'She slept in one of the spare rooms. Not with me, I can promise you that,' he said grimly. 'After you left, and she told me you couldn't wait to leave Dorset, I got drunk and ended up sleeping in the stables.'

'That's not the impression she gave.'

'Maybe you misunderstood?'

'No.' I'd never been more certain. 'Even if it didn't happen, she wanted me to believe that it had.'

'And you didn't think to call me?'

'Tom, I tried, but it kept going to voicemail.'

He looked ill. 'I lost my phone at the party,' he said. 'At least, I thought I had.' He blinked. 'Megan brought it round to the house a few days later.'

We stared at each other, as the scale of it all sank in.

'I should have called *you*,' he gave an agonised grimace, 'but after what you said about Megan being perfect for me, and that was why you'd brought her to the party…' he paused, and rubbed the back of his neck. 'It was stupid male pride, I suppose. I told myself I didn't know you as well as I thought, that you were young, and I had to let you go.' His voice had a muffled quality. 'I honestly can't believe this.'

'I suppose it's a compliment really.' I could hardly get the words past the tightness in my throat. 'She obviously saw me as a threat, and must love you a lot to have said all those things.'

'I don't know.' He picked up a tin of dog food and put it down again. 'I sometimes get the feeling it's not so much me as my family name she wants.'

'Or just to be part of a family.'

He looked pensive. 'Maybe. She's not close to her mother, and her father's pretty useless.'

'And now she's pregnant.'

He rubbed his face with both hands. 'She told me after we… that she hadn't taken her Pill, and when she said she'd missed a period…' his words trailed off. 'I can't… I don't *want* to let them down.' He sounded distraught. 'She said she couldn't go through with the pregnancy if we didn't get married. She doesn't want to be a single parent.'

My stomach turned over.

'But wouldn't it better to be a happy single parent than a miserable married one?' I could hardly believe I was suggesting their child would be better off without him. 'Actually, scrap that,' I said, holding my hands up. 'I would probably like you a lot less if you were the sort of man to run out on his pregnant fiancée.' I was lying, but hopefully he couldn't tell.

'Christ, what a mess.' He released a shaky breath. 'I'm so sorry, Carrie, for… everything.'

'It's not your fault,' I said, though it sort of was, and as if he was thinking the same thing, he gave a tight little smile that ripped at my heart.

'You were probably better off without me.'

'That's not for you to decide.'

We looked at each other for a long moment, the air between us heavy with all the things we couldn't say, and I thought how much I wanted to touch him – to take away the anguish in his eyes.

'Tom, could I have a word?'

We turned to see Mr Hudson peering round the door, his eyebrows disappearing into his hairline. For a second I thought I was hallucinating, and Tom appeared similarly frozen.

'Sorry,' Mr Hudson said, holding up a hand. 'I didn't mean to interrupt.'

As I jerked backwards, I bashed my ankle on Hovis's chair, and he fired off a torrent of barks. Mr Hudson looked from the dog, to Tom, to me, and back to Tom. He seemed in the grip of an emotion he couldn't express, his jaw working.

'Dad...' Tom began.

'I'll call you.' His father's tone was difficult to interpret, and before either of us could speak he'd vanished, leaving behind a waft of expensive cologne.

'Do you think he'll tell Megan I was here?' I said, heart hammering.

Tom closed his eyes briefly. 'We weren't doing anything wrong.' He sounded resigned. 'Don't worry, I'll deal with it.'

Reality seeped back in. 'I should go.'

'Carrie.' He reached for my fingers. 'I wish I knew what to say.'

'I think we've said it all.' I stared at him, miserably. 'Would you mind driving me home?'

Chapter 27

Tom dropped me off after a tense, wordless journey, and I suggested we forget about everything we'd discussed.

'I don't think I can,' he said, with such sadness in his voice that my heart seemed to twist out of shape. 'I don't love her.'

'Maybe your feelings will grow.' I looked at him squarely, determined not to waver. 'Whatever her faults, Megan definitely loves you, and more importantly, she's having your child.' I knew I was contradicting what I'd said earlier, but I couldn't be the person who broke up a family before it had even begun.

When he tried to speak again I held up a hand, knowing if he said anything else I would come undone. 'You have to give it a chance, or I'll never forgive myself.'

He looked at his hands. 'I know.'

'I'll be going back to Manchester soon, so let's carry on as normal until then. Please, Tom.'

I wanted so badly to hurl myself at him and never let go that I didn't wait for his reply. I jumped out of the car, slammed the door without saying goodbye, and ran up to the flat.

'I was getting worried about you.'

Ruby was in the kitchen, smearing a chunk of cheese with peanut butter.

'I'm sorry,' I said dully. 'I ended up going for a drive and my car broke down. I lost track of time.' I edged past her to the sink and washed my hands.

'Your car broke down?' Ruby put the piece of cheese on a plate. 'Why didn't you call?'

'What could you have done?' I hadn't meant to sound accusing, but guilt about going to see Peter was eating away at me, and trying to get my head around my conversation with Tom was playing havoc with my nerves. 'You don't even have your own transport.'

Ruby pulled her chin in. 'No, but it would have stopped me worrying and I could have called Calum...'

'It's not fair to rely on him all the time,' I said, drying my hands on the tea towel.

'I was going to say' – Ruby nudged me with her hip – 'I could have called Calum to tell him I was coming to get the van, and picked you up myself.'

It was so difficult to envisage Ruby anywhere but in front of me, swaddled in a dressing gown, I could only blink at her. 'I didn't realise you could drive.'

'Oh, Carrie,' she said on a deep sigh. 'I know I haven't presented myself in the best light so far, but I'm normally quite good in a crisis.' She arched an eyebrow. 'Like I said, it's been good for me having you here.' She screwed the lid back on the jar of peanut butter. 'It's given me a reason to cook again for a start.' She nodded at the worktop, where a batch of scones was cooling on a wire rack. 'I was going to make us a crab linguine for dinner,' she added, and I noticed she'd spread the ingredients out, and placed a shallow pan on the hob. 'I was waiting for you to come home.'

It was the word *home* that did it. 'Oh, Ruby,' I said, and burst into sobs.

'Carrie, what on earth is it?' Placing a solid arm around my waist, she steered me to the sofa and pressed me down. Settling beside me she took both my hands in hers. 'Talk to me, sweetheart.'

'I… I…' I sobbed, incoherently. I couldn't remember the last time I'd cried properly. It felt like several years' worth of tears were sluicing down my face. I couldn't tell her about going to see Peter, or that she had another grandchild – I just couldn't. I would have to pray that Peter wouldn't take things any further, and that nothing bad would come of it.

Instead, I told her about Tom.

'My darling, I had no idea you even knew the Hudsons,' she said when I'd finished, and it wasn't without irony that I accepted a tissue from her, and blew my nose. 'No wonder you seemed a bit funny about me doing the flowers for his wedding.' I hadn't mentioned the other major player in the sorry saga – Megan, the ex-best-friend.

'It came as a bit of a shock, that's all.'

'I can always change my mind,' Ruby said, as I scrubbed away another spurt of tears. 'About doing the flowers, I mean. I don't need the business that badly.'

'Yes, you do, and it's fine, really.' I dredged up a watery smile. 'I have it from the horse's mouth that Mr Hudson really wants you to do them.'

Her eyebrows shifted. 'He does?' She looked quietly pleased, and my stomach tightened. The wedding *had* to go ahead, if only so Ruby could get her business back on track, and pay her bills. 'But are you *sure* it's what you both want? It sounds to me like this Tom was in love with you, and still is.'

Her words provoked a thrill that died as fast as it flared. I'd have given a lot to have heard it once, but it hardly mattered now. 'He wants to be a good dad, and that means marrying the mother of his child,' I said. It came out a bit snarly from all the crying, and Ruby pursed her lips.

'Well, that's noble of him, I suppose.' She sounded unsure, and it struck me that this was the first time I'd seen her concerned about something apart from her own situation. It was a shame it had to involve me and my stupid heartbreak.

Not heartbreak, I rebuked myself. It was an unexpected blip that was all. I'd got over Tom before and I'd do it again, just as soon as I was back in Manchester.

'Will you still be up to helping me with the flowers?' She gave my arm a squeeze before standing up. 'There might not be time to do everything on my own before Jane gets back.'

If only Jane hadn't planned a pervy holiday, none of this would have happened.

'I'm positive. I am a fully grown adult,' I sniffed. 'Could I please have a scone with strawberry jam, to keep me going until dinner?'

She beamed at me, her first proper beam, and the sight of it lightened my mood ever so slightly. 'Of course you can,' she said. 'And after dinner, we can make a flower animal together. Anything you like.'

'So, tell me all about it.'

I flumped on my bed and positioned my phone against the wall, so I could still see Jasmine while I plumped up my sleep-flattened pillow. She was wearing pyjamas with dachshunds on them, and her hair was all mussed up.

'About what?' I said, not really in the mood for talking any more.

'The history of Shipley and its residents,' she said, flipping her eyes up. 'Your date with Toby, of course.'

'Oh, him.' I flopped my head on the still-flat pillow and pulled my knees into a foetal position. Not easy, when I'd eaten enough to stretch my stomach to its limits. 'It was OK.' I sighed.

Jasmine grimaced. 'That bad, eh?'

I thought for a moment. 'Actually, he was really nice,' I amended, remembering the art puns, his athletic good looks, and him piggy-backing me to Ruby's. It felt like light years ago. 'But he's still in love with his wife, and just wants us to be friends.'

'Can't you wow him with your personality, hen, show him you're worth ten of her.' Jasmine exaggerated her Scottish accent for effect.

'Honestly, I don't mind.' I twisted a length of hair around my finger. It felt limp from all the sweating I'd done, but I couldn't face washing it. 'It wasn't meant to be.'

'You can always pick another.' She clutched her heart, dramatically. 'The man of your dreams is out there somewhere, you just haven't met him yet.'

I couldn't face going over my conversation with Tom, so told her about my visit to Hudson Grange.

'She sounds like a right rocket, as we say in Scotland,' Jasmine said, when I got to the bit about Megan and Jay laughing themselves silly at the wedding-pups.

'What does that mean?'

'She's a shitehawk.'

'Hmm,' I said. 'That does sort of sum her up.'

Jasmine paused in the act of pouring boiling water onto a Pot Noodle and looked at her phone screen. 'Are you OK?'

Tears swelled again, and I hoped she couldn't see.

'I saw Tom today, that's all,' I managed. 'But, I'm fine.' I rolled onto my back so that the tears ran into my ears. 'How was your dinner with Vinnie?'

'Good,' she said, taking my cue. 'We went dancing afterwards, I mean proper dancing.' She jabbed her hips from side to side and snaked her arms around, her pyjama top riding up. 'He knows this bar and took me for a lesson.'

'Sounds amazing,' I said.

She did a spin and tripped over. 'Oops. I think I sprained a buttock, but it was fun.'

'Looking forward to your holiday?'

'Can't wait.' She stirred the noodles with a flourish, and took a second Pot Noodle from the cupboard that she'd assigned herself after moving in; one which had escaped the water damage. 'You will be back by then, won't you?' Before I could answer, she dived over and picked up her phone. 'I meant to ask, what colour do you want the kitchen wall painted?' She swung the screen over a colour chart on the worktop and I gave it a desultory glance.

'Oh, I don't know,' I said. 'You pick something.'

Her eyes filled the screen, zigzagging with astonishment. 'Are you insane?'

'Possibly.'

'You really want me to choose? Me?' She stabbed herself with her finger. 'Can I pick an actual colour that's not beige, beige or light beige?'

'Yep.'

Her eyebrows dived together. 'But when you finally gave me permission to paint my room purple, you wouldn't come in because you said it made you feel scared.'

If I hadn't been at Ruby's, I'd have been all over that paint chart, picking a colour that was fresh and neutral, much like the colour that had been there before the water pipe burst – magnolia, perhaps, or linen. But at that moment I couldn't think of anything that mattered less. 'Honestly, Jas, I don't care.'

'Care?'

'Mind,' I said, covering my face with my arm. 'I don't mind.'

'Right, well I'm going to go, if you're sure you're OK,' Jasmine said.
'I promised Vinnie I'd make him a gourmet supper...'

'He's there?' My head shot round.

She waggled one of the Pot Noodles. 'Keeping my bed warm, not
that he needs to, it's been roasting here today.'

'Jas, you're unbelievable.'

'I know.' She dipped a curtsy, then frowned.

'What is it?'

She was squinting past me, pretending to adjust a pair of spectacles.
'What, in the name of Peter Andre, is that yellow beauty?'

I looked to where she was pointing with a pretend-shaky finger and
laughter fizzled up. 'Me and Ruby had a flower-arranging session after
dinner,' I said. 'They're not real.'

'You don't say.'

'Can you tell what it is?'

'It looks like...' she tipped her head, and pretended to think. 'Is it
a one-eyed donkey?'

I picked up my pillow and pretended to lob it. 'Duck,' I said, and
she did. 'No! I mean, it's a duck.'

I was still chuckling as I undressed for bed and set my alarm.

Thank God for Jasmine, I thought, lying on top of the duvet in the
stuffy room, my wonky flower-duck beside me.

Unlike Megan, she was everything a friend was supposed to be.

Chapter 28

It was almost a relief to be back at work on Monday morning, after my rollercoaster weekend.

It was another hot day, sunshine rippling across the square, over the beach to the sea, where a pair of hopeful surfers were paddling their boards in the shallows.

I stood in the shade of the flower stall and tried to stay focused, listening politely while Calum told me that a Sunday picnic with his girlfriend had ended in A & E, when she was stung by a wasp and her leg swelled to twice its size. I even managed a horrified laugh when Jools, the delivery lady, told her own insect horror story, involving being bitten by a spider that she swore had eyes and winked at her.

But as I fetched some water from the standpipe and watered the flowers and plants, then scrubbed the buckets and swept up petals, I kept glancing around, expecting a visit from a furious Mr Hudson, or for Megan to appear, having heard about my visit to Tom's cottage. Or for Peter to show up with a uniformed officer, or Tom to come down, to at least let me know what was happening with my car.

Seeing Tom was what I wanted most and least. I would have to steel myself to turn him away, regardless of the dream I'd had, of us locked in a passionate embrace on top of a fluffy cloud, while my family looked on in smiling approval, salsa music playing in the background.

I'd woken, tangled in my duvet, to the sound of my phone alarm thrumming out a beat of bongos and maracas.

In the event, only Doris turned up, bringing fresh flowers from her garden.

'It seems a shame that I'm the only one to benefit from them,' she said, freeing up a couple of buckets and cramming them with tall lilies, and a confection of tissue-pink roses, their scent gathering strength in the heat.

'Better put those in the shade,' I said, shifting the bucket beneath the canopy, and onto a pallet close to the workbench.

Doris gave a brisk nod. 'You're learning.'

'You know I'll never be a florist,' I said rather bad-temperedly. 'Flowers are fine, but I'm much more comfortable with numbers.'

Doris's head bobbed an eager endorsement. 'Nothing wrong with that,' she said. 'The world has enough people doing flouncy things.' Her expression grew haughty. 'I enjoyed being married to an officer of the law, but I didn't want to become one.'

'What *did* you do, Doris?' I was hoping to delay her bringing up the one topic I was dreading.

She opened her handbag, which was parakeet-green to match her A-line skirt, and provided an eye-catching contrast to the meringue whiteness of her blouse. In comparison, I looked like a faded photo in my beige T-shirt and jeans.

'I was a secretary at a furniture company, before Roger and I got married,' she said, tugging out her gardening gloves. 'A very classy one too.'

I could easily see her with a shorthand pad in her hand. 'But you gave it up?' I said, as she got busy at the wheelbarrow, pinching dead leaves off the plants.

'My boss liked spanking ladies' bottoms.' She picked up the watering can and tipped it over the soil. 'It was before political correctness came in.'

'Blimey, that's… awful.' I thought of my mild-mannered boss at Cars 4 U. The only bodywork he'd been interested in was of the vehicular variety. So much so, his wife had filed for divorce.

'I was more than happy to give up my job and become a good housewife and mother.'

'Good for you.' I meant it, but she looked offended.

'I'll have you know I became a leading member of our local Neighbourhood Watch scheme, which Roger set up after a spate of robberies on Maple Hill in the eighties.'

'Sounds fascinating.' I meant that too, but it came out sounding droll.

Doris stopped fiddling with the wheelbarrow and gave me a hard stare. 'Any luck with you-know-who?'

My shoulders tensed. 'Shall I get us a drink?' I glanced at Cooper's Café, the tables outside all taken by visitors baring various parts of their bodies to the sun.

'No, thank you,' Doris said. 'I had a red blossom tea and a birdseed muffin before I came out.'

'Birdseed?'

'I had some left over,' she said, bafflingly. 'So?'

I checked for customers, disappointed to see there weren't any. Better get it over with. 'OK, I went to see Donny, or should I say Peter, and it didn't go at all well.'

Doris's mouth turned down. 'Well, that's a pity. I thought if anyone could get through to him it would be you.'

I remembered Tom saying the same thing, and didn't know whether I should be flattered, or upset that I didn't possess whatever qualities they'd bestowed. 'Why?'

'Because you're family.'

'Oh. Well, he doesn't want anything to do with Ruby.' I was gripped by a sudden sense of unfairness. 'He won't even give her a chance.'

Doris tutted. 'Is there anyone else you could appeal to?'

'His wife said she'd try to talk to him, but he seemed so angry I can't imagine him going for it.'

'What a bugger.' Doris tugged her gloves off and rammed them back in her bag. 'It seems such a waste to have all that bad feeling when we'll all be dead one day.'

It was a bit dramatic, but I guessed she was thinking about her husband, turning his back on their son. 'I suppose not everyone can have their happy ending.' I thought of Tom, and a lump formed in my throat. 'To be honest, I've probably made everything worse.'

Doris's features settled. 'You'll have given him food for thought,' she said resolutely. 'He might come around yet.'

I somehow doubted it. 'Thanks, anyway,' I said, still not sure whether I should be tearing a strip off her for interfering.

'At least we tried.' She patted her bob a bit too vigorously, as if pressing down her disappointment. 'Will you tell your aunt?'

'Definitely not.'

'Then I shan't either.'

A moment of silent understanding passed between us.

'Thank you for the flowers,' I said.

She inclined her head, then spun on her sensible heel and tip-tapped across the square to the newsagent's, just as my pocket vibrated.

It was the work phone. I pulled it out, praying it was only a booking and not Megan.

'Carrie?'

It was Megan.

I'd have expected her to confront me face to face, but maybe she was too upset by whatever Mr Hudson had told her.

'Hello,' I said, with a surprising absence of panic. Maybe discovering she'd misled me about spending the night with Tom had blitzed my guilt about spending an afternoon with him. 'What do you want?'

'Ooh, steady!' she tittered, not sounding remotely upset. 'Just letting you know I've booked a table at Off the Hook for tomorrow at seven, so I hope you and Cooper can come.'

For a second, I wondered whether I'd misheard. 'A table?'

'A square thing with legs.' She paused for me to appreciate her wit. 'The meal? You and Cooper, me and Tom – if I can drag him away from work, that is. He keeps stalling. The seafood restaurant?' Her voice rose. 'Oh, do say you'll come, Carrie, I'm dying for us to get together.'

'I forgot to check if it was OK.' My mind was racing. I couldn't believe Mr Hudson hadn't mentioned me being at the cottage, then reminded myself that Tom and I had only been talking, not making passionate love on the kitchen table. *More's the pity.*

'Carrie?'

I jumped. 'Sorry?'

'Tuesday night?' A note of irritation had crept in.

I thought for a moment. It was unlikely Tom would come to the meal, but if I turned down the invitation it might look odd – as if we were trying to avoid each other's company. Easier to accept, and leave it to Megan to cancel when Tom refused. Then I could spend the evening with Toby to take my mind off things. 'Fine,' I said, a bit too forcefully. 'We'll see you there.'

'Great! I'll order a bottle of champers and we can make a night of it!'

'Should you be drinking?' I said, without thinking.

'I meant for everyone else, not me.' As she rang off, with a cheery, 'Ciao for now!' a terrible thought snuck into my head. *What if Megan wasn't pregnant?*

She could be faking it, knowing Tom would stand by her. If she wasn't pregnant, they'd have no reason to be together! It was hard to believe that a woman in the twenty-first century would go to those lengths, but what if she had?

My heart raced, making it hard to concentrate as I laid out a selection of flowers on the workbench for a customer, snipping them to size, before gathering the stems and tying them with blue ribbon.

As soon as she'd gone, I whipped out my phone and called Sarah.

'How far along were you before you started to show?'

'Started to show what?' she said. 'Chloe get out!' There was a scrabbling sound, and my niece started grizzling in the background. 'She's bored, and keeps getting in the tumble drier,' Sarah said, sounding frazzled. 'I'll be glad when the school holidays are over.'

'Aren't you going to Portugal next week?'

'Yes, thank god,' she said. 'Give the kids a beach and some sea and they'll be in heaven.'

'You could have come here,' I said. 'It's lovely.'

'Bit of a busman's holiday, considering we grew up in Dorset.'

'But wouldn't it be nice for the children to see some of the places we used to go to?'

'They don't take much in at this age, apart from where the nearest ice-cream van is, but maybe one day,' she conceded. 'Funnily enough,

Mum's been saying the same thing. I think she's missing Dorchester.'
Chloe's grizzle became a roar, and I heard Jack tell her to stop being a
stinky noisy-knickers.

'Sorry,' said Sarah, 'what was it you wanted me to show you?'

'Don't worry, it wasn't important.' I felt suddenly silly. As if Megan
would fake a pregnancy. She was a lot of things, but not stupid. She
would know she couldn't keep it up, beyond a certain point. *The point
where she and Tom were married.*

I was thinking in clichéd film-plot terms. 'You need to get a grip,'
I said.

'I'm doing my best.' Sarah sounded hurt, and I realised I was still
on the phone. 'You wait until you're a mum.'

'Oh, no, I didn't mean you…'

But she'd already hung up. *I was talking out loud to myself. Love you
xx* I texted, knowing she'd have forgotten it in the next ten minutes.

'Did you get to see your vet?'

Startled, I turned to see the woman that Jane had introduced me
to about a century ago. Celia, I remembered. Without her Labrador
today. 'Sorry?'

'You asked for directions?' She tucked her walking stick under her
arm and picked up a pot of peppery-scented pink and white phlox. 'I'll
take this, please,' she said, pulling a sequinned purse from the pocket
of her tribal-print jumpsuit.

'Yes, I saw him, thanks. My car broke down and he gave me a lift.'
Talk about putting a unique spin on events.

'He's marrying that awful woman who works for his father, according to Paddy.' She lifted the visor of her baseball hat and gave me a
direct look. 'Paddy, my boyfriend,' she said. 'He's a groundsman at
Hudson Grange.'

'You mean Megan?'

Celia nodded. 'My daughter, Laura, and her partner, Mario, have bought a wine cellar in Langham, and this Megan swanned in, scouting sites for a new type of boutique hotel her boss is interested in.' She said 'boutique' as though it was a swear word. 'She offered them *half* what the place is worth.'

'Really?' I said. I wondered if Tom knew.

'When they said no, she got a bit nasty.' Her expression suggested she didn't know what the world was coming to. 'Lord only knows what he sees in her.'

'Well, that's their business.' I took the money for the plant. 'He's a grown man, I'm sure he knows what he's doing.'

Celia made a harrumphing sound, as she dropped the plant in her Adidas rucksack and zipped it up. 'Doris said you had a crush on him once.'

What? 'How... how on earth would she know that?' I stammered.

Celia's eyes grew round. 'Doris Day moves in mysterious ways.' She twirled her stick like a magic wand, almost cracking a passer-by over the head. 'And since when do men know what's going on under their noses?'

She had a point, I thought, watching her stride towards the parade, the sun bouncing off her silver trainers.

Mr Hudson hadn't noticed how far he'd pushed Tom until he'd left home, and Tom hadn't had a clue about my real feelings, though I must have been giving off signals. And then there was Peter/Donny, blinded by hurt to the fact that he had a whole other family who would love to get to know him.

'Bloody men,' I said, plucking a foil-wrapped scone out of my bag, attracting the attention of a lurking seagull. 'Why should I be the one to enlighten them?'

Then I remembered Tom saying he'd had feelings for me, and my stomach bunched up in a knot. *How had I not noticed that?*

I pulled out my mobile and rang Toby. 'You know you offered to be Cooper if I needed you again?' I said. 'Would you mind being my date tomorrow night?'

Chapter 29

My car was parked in its usual slot behind the bakery after work the following evening, the flower-pups in the canvas bag on the front seat.

'A chap said to tell you it's sorted and paid for, and here are your keys,' Bob said, coming out with them hanging from his finger.

'What sort of bloke?'

'A mechanic type, in overalls.'

Not Tom then. 'No other message?'

Bob pursed his lips as though trying to work out what I wanted him to say. 'Nope,' he said. 'Sorry.'

To my relief, the car started first time, with a gentle purring sound.

'Are you sure you don't mind driving?' said Toby, putting the flower-pups on the back seat and adjusting the passenger seat to accommodate his long legs. He'd explained that his wife was using their car that night, to go to a support group – though he didn't say what type of support. 'I'm happy to pay for a cab.'

'You're doing me a favour, remember?' I said. 'And, anyway, it's not far.'

'I can direct you there,' he said. 'Em and me did the paintwork at Off the Hook.'

'Nice food?'

'I don't know, it hadn't opened then,' he said. 'To be honest, it's a bit out of my price range.'

'Don't worry, tonight's on me.'

'We can split the bill,' he said.

'Show me the *Monet*!' We spoke at the same time and then chuckled with embarrassment.

Toby looked over his shoulder. 'Who are your creepy friends?' he said.

I glanced in the rear-view mirror, where I could see the flower-pups peeping out of the bag. Bride-pup had lost an eye, and groom-pup's nose was missing. They both looked thoroughly fed up.

'They're my lucky mascots.' Though harbingers of doom would have been more appropriate, considering everything that had happened since taking them from Ruby's.

'Each to their own,' Toby said with a grin.

It felt odd having a virtual stranger in my car, but my nerves were outweighed by a feeling of dread about the evening ahead. I'd fully expected Megan to cancel, but as she hadn't called, I'd had to assume she and Tom were going to be there.

The day had passed in a haze of anxiety. I'd kept on glancing at my phone, before remembering that neither Tom nor Megan had my mobile number. Then I kept checking the work phone for messages, and making sure it was working. At one point I almost rang Tom, but after I'd pleaded with him to carry on as normal, it didn't seem fair to ask him to ask Megan to call off the meal, especially as I'd agreed to go. With any luck, he'd have an animal emergency at the last minute and wouldn't be able to attend.

'You look nice.' Toby said it as he would to a sister – or a friend.

'Thanks.' I was glad I didn't look like the dowdy flower-seller Megan probably had me pegged for.

Calum had finished work early, and when he turned up at the stall I'd asked him to hold the fort, while I zipped into a clothes shop called Sassy Lassie on Main Street. After picking out some knee-length denim shorts, a few stripy tops in nautical colours, and a pair of espadrilles, my eyes had alighted on a knee-grazing, sleeveless dress with a crossover neckline, in a flattering shade of blue. Unwilling to leave it to chance, I'd tugged it over my head in the tiny changing room, liking the way it gathered at the waist, and flared over my hips. It even complemented my hair, and once I'd straightened it – watched over by Ruby, who approved of me going out with 'that nice young man who walked you home' – and covered my sunburnt nose with foundation, darkened my eyelids a smoky-grey, and stuffed my feet into another pair of shoes from Ruby's collection, I barely recognised myself.

'You don't look so bad yourself,' I said, grating the gears as Toby indicated I turn right at the junction and drive along the seafront.

In truth, I'd barely noticed, but a surreptitious glance confirmed he'd scrubbed up nicely, in light-coloured trousers and a muscle-hugging shirt a shade lighter than his copper hair. He smelt good too; like cinnamon and leaves.

'So how do you want to play this evening?' He rubbed his hands on his thighs. 'Do you want to make her jealous?'

'Oh, I don't think so,' I said. The idea of Megan being jealous of me was laughable. 'Maybe we should play it by ear.'

'And if they ask about my work?'

'Just say you're having a break and would rather not talk about it.' I'd looked up 'a day in the life of a war correspondent' on my phone earlier, but logged off when I saw the words 'government convoy' and 'shot in the head', feeling guilty.

'I googled "a day in the life of a war correspondent" earlier,' Toby said, with a bashful grin. 'Just in case.'

I gave a wry smile. 'I should have picked something less... *dangerous.*'

'Like painter and decorator?'

I caught his eye. 'Exactly.'

His gaze was understanding. 'I get that you were trying to impress her.'

'Pathetic, when you put it like that.'

'We've all done it,' he said. 'When I first met Em, I pretended to like the same music she did, even though I'd never heard of Charanga.'

'Charanga?'

'It's Cuban dance music, apparently.'

'Oh god.' I snorted with laughter.

'It turned out she was winding me up,' he said. 'She really liked the Sugababes.'

I couldn't help noticing how animated he was when talking about his wife – which boded well for them getting back together at some point.

'It's here,' he said, almost too late, and I was honked at by the car behind us as I veered wildly into a space at the side of the road. 'Sorry about that.'

The restaurant was only a stone's throw from the sandy beach, and flanked by dunes and a boatyard. It had floor-length windows, and a terrace overlooking the sea, where several diners were admiring the view.

'Nice,' I said, wishing the journey had been longer. Now we'd arrived I immediately wanted to leave.

'Come on, it'll be fine,' said Toby, flicking my arm. 'We'll show that Megan how fantastic you are, and that Tom bloke what he's missing, and then you never have to see them again.'

'Except when I help my aunt deliver their wedding flowers.'

'Maybe she could find someone else to help with that.'

'You make it all sound so reasonable.'

'Well, it doesn't have to be complicated.'

He got out and came round to the driver's door, while I primped my hair in the mirror. My eyes looked too bright and my cheeks were marshmallow pink. I practised smiling, and saying, 'Hi, you guys, it's great to see you,' but it didn't sound like the sort of thing I'd say.

'Ma'am,' Toby said, and as I stepped out into the balmy evening and took his proffered arm, I found myself wishing he really *was* my boyfriend.

'I don't think they're here yet.' I glanced around for the Land Rover, or Megan's sports car. I couldn't see either, but still dragged my feet as we approached the restaurant, as if we were visiting a maximum-security prison.

As we stepped into the spice-scented entrance I spotted Megan at a table by the window, and realised she must have watched us walk up to the entrance.

Toby had seen her too. 'Keep smiling,' he murmured, as Megan lifted her chin imperiously.

'Over here, Rick,' she called. 'They're with me.'

A man with a lobster-patterned apron tied around his waist hurried over, and shepherded us across the gleaming floor to her table, which was covered with a white linen cloth, and set with silver cutlery. The wine glasses alone looked like they'd cost more than the entire contents of my kitchen.

'I'll fetch some menus,' murmured Rick.

Classical music bubbled above the muted buzz of conversation, adding to the aura of sophistication, and Megan rose like royalty greeting her subjects. 'I'm so glad you could come!'

She looked unusually demure in a simple, crocheted tunic dress the colour of clotted cream, which made her eyes look extra vivid. Her hair was fastened in a sleek ponytail, swept forward over one shoulder, and her feet were caged in strappy gold high heels.

'You look amazing!' she said to me, gripping me in a subtly perfumed embrace, her peach-tinted lips almost brushing my cheek.

'So, do you!' My hands listlessly patted her back. I could feel her shoulder blades, like fins, but when I stepped back I noticed a gentle curve at the front of her dress, and was flooded with guilt. She was obviously pregnant. What had I been thinking?

'You've already met T... Cooper,' I said, jerking my eyes up to her glowing face.

'I certainly have.' Rocking back, she enveloped him in a flirtatious gaze that made him blush fiercely. 'I must admit, I thought a war correspondent would look more' – she pinched her chin, and gave an exaggerated pout – '*grizzled*,' she concluded. 'Isn't that a fantastic word?' She looked from Toby to me, her face wreathed in delight, but I had the impression she didn't believe he was a war correspondent, and probably wasn't buying that he was my boyfriend either.

'He's moving away from that now,' I said, slipping my hand into Toby's and giving him what I hoped was an adoring look. 'Which is why he was in...' Oh hell, where was it again?

'Budapest,' Toby chipped in, returning my look with such an ardent one, he almost went cross-eyed. 'It was getting too much, being on the front line. No sleep, being shot at, terrible pay.' He gave a convincing shudder, having clearly read more than I had about what the job entailed. 'Plus, I missed this lovely lady, and wanted to spend more time with her.' He placed a strong arm around my shoulders. 'She's the most important thing in the world,' he said, and placing a finger under my chin, he tilted my face and placed his lips on mine.

'More important than reporting from a war zone?'

I unclamped my lips from Toby's – as kisses went it wasn't bad, but it didn't set off any fireworks – and saw an uncertain look cross Megan's face.

I gave Toby's hand a squeeze. 'Could you pour me a small drink... darling?' I said, as a waiter hurried over with a gigantic bottle of champagne in a silver bucket, not dissimilar to the sort we filled with flowers at the stall. 'I just need to...' I glanced around for a sign to the toilets, surreptitiously looking for Tom.

'Oh, the ladies is over there, through the door at the end and turn left,' said Megan. 'Don't worry about Cooper, I'll keep him entertained.'

Slipping back into playful mode with disorientating speed, she gave him a saucy wink, and gestured for him to sit at the linen-covered table.

Toby threw me a look that was less adoring boyfriend, and more death-row-victim-hoping-for-a-last-minute-reprieve, but I'd reached the pinnacle of my acting skills and needed a moment to regroup.

'Won't be long... sweetie.' I aimed a kiss at his cheek, noticing a sheen of perspiration on his upper lip. His theatrical abilities had clearly peaked, too.

'Hurry back,' he said, fervently. 'I'll miss you.'

Feeling bad for him, and not daring to look at Megan, I shot off, a little arthritic in Ruby's cork-heeled wedges, and as I pushed through the door and turned left, I cannoned straight into Tom, coming through a side entrance.

Chapter 30

'Carrie!' he shot out an arm to steady me, alarm spreading over his face. 'Where are you going?'

'Where are *you* going?' I fired back, heart catapulting into my throat. 'I didn't think you were coming.' He looked good, in dark jeans and an olive-green shirt, and I fought an animal instinct to nestle against him.

'I wanted to see you,' he said, with heart-wrenching honesty. His hand was still on my arm, sparking a frenzy of butterflies in my stomach. Through the window, the blue horizon of sea and sky stretched behind him, and I wished we were in a boat on the ocean, just the two of us, with no more misunderstandings – and no Megan.

Pierced by remorse at wishing her away I said, 'We're supposed to be carrying on as normal.'

'Why are you here then?' he challenged. 'This isn't exactly normal.'

'Because Megan invited me, and I thought it might look odd if we both said no.'

He shook his head, and I noticed fresh dark crescents underneath his eyes. 'Carrie, we need to talk—'

'Thanks for getting my car back to me. How much do I owe you?'

His hand dropped. 'I told you, I'd sort it out. Carrie, look at me.'

'Did your father say anything, about me being at the cottage?' I said, before my resistance melted.

'He spoke to me, but not about that.' His features grew serious, as though trying to decipher a riddle. 'He started talking about wanting me to be happy, and how in love he'd been with Mum.' He pushed closer, as a chattering group of people flowed into the restaurant. 'Then he apologised for not being a good father.'

'Wow,' I said. 'I wonder what brought that on.'

Tom's eyebrows shifted. 'I don't know, but he sounded genuine.'

'Well, that's something.' I touched his sleeve. 'It sounds like he wants to mend bridges.'

He glanced at my fingers, and I let my hand fall away.

'Oh, there you are!'

We wheeled around, as guilty as if we'd been caught snogging against the brick wall, to see Megan approaching, a bright smile fixed to her face.

'Hi, sexy.' She kissed Tom hard on the mouth, bringing an unwelcome flashback of the last time I'd seen them kiss at his twenty-first – only this time, Tom's arms were stiff by his side.

Seeming not to notice, she gave me a shark-eyed look. 'Cooper's getting restless,' she said pointedly, draping her arm around Tom's waist and leaning her head on his shoulder. 'He's on his third glass of champagne, and starting to get a bit maudlin.'

'Cooper?' Tom looked like he'd forgotten about my so-called boyfriend. 'God, Carrie, I'm sorry,' he said, looking crushed. 'I shouldn't have kept you talking here—'

'It's fine,' I cut in, my face hotter than the sun. 'Let's go and order some food.'

The thought of eating made my stomach cramp, but I was overcome with a masochistic need to see the evening through, and to exit with some dignity intact. I followed Megan and Tom to the table, the straps of Ruby's shoes re-opening my blisters.

'Sorry,' I mouthed to Toby, who was tracking my return with a stagey, love-struck smile. 'There you are, sweetheart, light of my life.' He put down his glass and half rose, but his knees were wedged under the table and he ended up in a half squat. 'Come here, buttercup.' He tugged me onto the chair beside him and hooked his arm round my neck. 'I've missed you, baby-cakes.' He began nibbling my ear with the fervour of a rabbit with a lettuce leaf. 'You smell scrumptious.'

Ignoring Tom's curious gaze, I smiled inanely and grabbed a menu.

'Aren't they cute?' drawled Megan, as Tom sat opposite Toby.

'Tom Hudson,' he said, extending a hand, and Toby let go of me to pump it firmly.

'Good to meet you, sir.'

'It's just Tom.' His eyes twitched to mine and away again, and I briefly wished I hadn't told him I'd exaggerated my relationship with Cooper for Megan's sake. *Except he's not Cooper. And we're not in a relationship.*

'Cooper's been telling me how much he adores you,' Megan gushed, smoothing her dress against the backs of her thighs as she took her seat. 'He was saying you can't wait to start a family.'

As her hand went to her stomach, a pained expression flew across Toby's face, and I knew she was lying. He'd broken up with his wife because they couldn't conceive; he wouldn't have said something like that, even in character.

'Maybe one day,' I managed, reaching to give his knee an apologetic squeeze. My glance strayed to Tom, who was staring at his phone as if willing it to transform into a time machine and spirit him away.

'Give me that.' Megan swept it off him and into a black patent bag which she plonked at her feet. 'It's rude to have phones at the table.'

'I'm on call,' he said, a muscle leaping in his jaw. 'You know Carl's on holiday this week, and Beatrice has a cold.'

Megan made a face. 'If you came to HCH, you wouldn't need to worry about absent vets.' Her deliberately casual tone suggested it was a well-worn argument. 'You could set your own timetable.'

It was unsettling, seeing them sitting together. They definitely weren't coming across like an about-to-be-married couple, despite Megan's attempts to create an aura of intimacy, touching Tom's hand, and angling her body towards him.

'Let's not do this,' Tom said a touch wearily, folding and unfolding his napkin. 'You know I love what I do.'

'What about you, Cooper?' She rested her arms on the table. 'Would you rather root around an animal's anal glands, or oversee a bunch of lovely hotels where' – she held up her palm as Tom started to speak – 'there's already a team of amazing staff, thanks to *moi*' – she fluttered her eyelashes – 'and all you have to do is visit them to make sure things are running smoothly, go on lovely trips, and look for locations in which to build another lovely hotel?' She made a balancing-the-scales motion with her hands. 'Not a difficult choice, is it?'

'There's a bit more to it than that,' Tom said, twisting his watch around his wrist. 'I get a lot of satisfaction from being a vet.'

Toby's head looked a bit loose on his shoulders, and as he adopted an expression of deep concentration I realised he was totally sozzled. 'What was the question?' he said to Megan.

There was a momentary pause, and everyone studied their menu.

'So, what were you doing in Budapest?' Tom asked Toby, clearly keen to steer the topic away from the hotel business, not noticing the way Megan's lips pinched together.

Seeing me watching, she bent them into a facsimile of an interested smile.

'What do most people do in Budapest?' Toby leaned back, yawned and scratched his armpit. 'No, really,' he said, squinting at Tom. 'What DO people do in Budapest?' He snorted. 'Budapest! It sounds weird when you keep saying it.'

Megan sniggered. 'Someone's a little bit tiddly.'

'Are you ready to order?' We turned as one to see a baby-faced waiter poised with a notepad and pen. 'I can recommend the crab chowder.'

'I've never had lobster thermidor, so I'll go for that,' Toby said, flinging his menu back on the table.

I chose the first thing I'd looked at, which was something to do with prawns, Megan ordered the chowder, and Tom said he'd have whatever the special of the day was. Grilled sea bass, according to Baby-face.

Megan picked up a fresh champagne bottle and hovered it over Tom's glass.

'Water for me,' he said. 'I've an early start in the morning.'

Smile undimmed, she diverted the bottle to mine. 'I'm driving,' I said.

'You can have one,' she insisted. Her voice was light, almost playful.

After she'd filled my glass to the brim I knocked it back in one, shivering as the bubbles fizzed down to my stomach. How was I going to get through the meal when the evening was a big fat lie? Nothing felt quite right, like an out-of-tune cello in an orchestra.

Toby and I weren't a couple.

Tom was only marrying Megan because she was carrying his child.

Megan's reason for inviting me out was to showcase her amazing life, and to toy with me. Just as she'd done when we were teenagers, only I hadn't seen it then.

Suddenly, I'd had enough.

'I expect you're planning to get a nanny when you've had the baby,' I said. 'Isn't that what you were saying to your friends the other night?'

A flush ran over her face. 'It was a joke,' she said, in a 'don't you know what one is?' tone. 'Although I don't see anything wrong with having a nanny.' Her eyes were on maximum power. 'It's the twenty-first century, women can go back to work when they've had children.'

'But aren't you planning to give up working once you've persuaded Tom to run the company, after his father retires, so you can play at being lady of the manor?' I affected an upper-class voice, like the one she'd used at The Anchor. 'I'm going to throw *amaaazing* dinner parties, and invite magazines to photograph me being *gorgeous*.' Okay, maybe she hadn't quite said that in so many words.

Her face had blanched. 'You jealous little—'

'My father's retiring?' said Tom, giving Megan a puzzled look. 'He didn't say anything to me.'

'Why would he, when you barely talk to him?' The dazzling smile she switched on was so at odds with her tone that Tom blinked a couple of times.

'But—'

'I wouldn't want my child raised by a nanny,' said Toby in a doom-laden voice. His eyes were glazed with tears. 'Shit, I want a baby *so* much.'

I gave his forearm a little squeeze, alarmed by how different he was from our date at The Anchor. But he hadn't had much to drink then, and champagne clearly wasn't his friend. 'There's plenty of time to think about that.'

He nodded and sniffed. 'Sorry my little fruit-bat,' he said, scrabbling for my fingers. 'I'm a bit 'motional tonight.'

'Clearly,' said Megan, her colour returning to normal now the spotlight had shifted off her.

'You don't look at all pregnant,' Toby said loudly, just as the rousing piano concerto that had been playing in the background ceased.

Several people craned their necks to look.

'Well, I can assure you I am.' Megan had flicked from annoyance to mild amusement now, glancing from Toby to me as though we were exasperating toddlers.

'She looks pregnant from where I'm sitting,' said a woman with cobweb-thin blonde hair. Her over-mascaraed eyes were fixed on my stomach.

This seemed to delight Megan. She raised one finely threaded eyebrow at me, her lips curving into a smirk. 'Do you remember our last day at Bedworth, when I lent you that Topshop skirt and Alana Morris thought you were pregnant, because it bunched up a bit at the front?'

'Megan,' Tom said, a warning note in his voice. 'That's not funny.'

'Ooh, get you, sticking up for her!' Her amusement was undercut with spite.

'Why's everyone talking 'bout babies?' Toby pinched the bridge of his nose. 'S'not fair, when I can't get pregnant.'

Megan turned a spurt of laughter into a cough as fresh music started up, and everyone returned to their food. The sun was sinking, spreading a warm glow across the diners, but the atmosphere at our table was frosty.

'How far along are you exactly?' I heard myself say to Megan, and felt the weight of Tom's gaze on me. I wasn't even sure why I'd asked, and in the peachy light, saw that her face had tensed.

'It's funny you should ask.' Her eyes blazed into mine.

'Oh?'

Bending down, she jabbed her hand inside her bag and produced a square of paper. 'I went for a scan this morning,' she said. 'It was meant to be a surprise for Tom later, because I knew he couldn't make it.'

'I didn't know about it,' he said, taking the piece of paper. He studied it, and his expression flooded with pleasure. It was like seeing the sun come out, or a fire blaze into life, and I briefly closed my eyes because it hurt to look at it.

'It's very early, less than three months,' Megan said, watching his face. 'Due next February.'

'Do you know if it's a boy or a girl?' He sounded a little bit choked, and I knew I'd lost him again – not that I'd ever had him.

'I want it to be a surprise, don't you?' She plucked the picture from his fingers and passed it to me, a satisfied smile creasing the edges of her eyes, and as I looked at the ghostly image – reminiscent of Sarah's scan photo of her twins – I realised I'd badly misjudged her.

Worse than that, regardless of whether Tom loved Megan, finally seeing their baby as an actual human being was bound to cement their bond – a bond that would never be broken.

'Congratulations,' I mumbled, feeling sick to my stomach as I handed the photo back after Toby waved it away, looking devastated. 'I'm sorry if I forced your hand.'

'Don't worry.' She gave a quick, efficient smile that didn't reach her eyes this time. 'I know this must be hard to take, if you and Cooper are trying for a baby.'

'God's sake,' he muttered.

'Maybe we should call it a night.' Tom looked suddenly shattered and couldn't – or wouldn't – meet my eye.

'Fine with me,' Megan simpered. 'Let's have an early night.' She touched his hand, then dipped to her bag once more and took out her purse. 'I'll go and tell the chef, and settle up,' she said. 'Give him a little extra for his trouble.'

None of us spoke as she strode towards the kitchen, and we were sitting in the same position like mannequins when she returned.

'Come on, then!'

Tom rose, like an automaton, and gave me an unreadable look before following her out of the restaurant.

'How did I do?' said Toby, propping his chin on his hand. 'Do you think they bought it?' His eyes had such a teary brightness, I felt charged with sorrow.

'You did fine,' I said, a headache starting to squeeze behind my eyes. 'Let's go.'

I slipped my bag onto my shoulder and stood up.

'Let's have a li'l dance,' said Toby, his voice damp with boozy sentiment as he lurched to his feet. 'C'mere, babe.' He grabbed my waist, twirled me clumsily, then bent me backwards to the horrified amusement of the diners.

'Toby, stop it,' I said in a strangled voice.

He obediently let go, and I crash-landed on my back.

A collective gasp went up.

'Oh, no, sorry.' Toby swayed above me, his face crumpling into concern. 'She's not even my real girlfriend,' he announced to the restaurant at large, then burped.

'I'm OK, I'm fine,' I said, in a lively way, as if lying on the floor had been my intention all along. As I sat up I spotted a piece of paper under the chair where Megan's bag had been. The baby-scan picture must have come out with her purse, and despite everything it didn't feel right to leave it there. Reaching over, I swiped it up and folded it into my bag, then held out my hands so Toby could haul me up.

'Sorry, love of my life,' he said, trying to cuddle me to him.

I wriggled away. 'It's fine, you can stop now, they've gone.'

'Thanks for your custom,' someone said sarcastically, as we hotfooted it to the door without looking back. 'Come back soon. Not.'

At the car, Toby paused, and gave me a befuddled look.

'That meal didn't fill me up at all,' he said plaintively. 'I'm absolutely starving.'

Chapter 31

Lashing rain and a howling gale would have suited my mood the next morning, but as usual it was sunny and clear. By the time the stall was up and running, and the flower delivery checked in, it looked like being another flawless day.

'Shame to be working,' Calum observed, finishing his coffee and the last mouthful of a bacon roll. 'You OK?' he said, as I slumped on a pallet and checked my phone for the twentieth time.

'I made a bit of a fool of myself last night.' Talk about a gross understatement. I itched with embarrassment, recalling Tom's face when I gave away that his dad was retiring, and Megan's viperous expression as she produced her baby-scan photo.

'Too much laughing juice?' Calum waggled an imaginary pint glass.

'Probably not enough,' I said grimly, shooing away a persistent seagull, intent on scavenging every last crumb that Calum had dropped. 'I'm expecting a backlash.'

'That bad, eh?'

'It's this place,' I said, as Calum paraded around the stall with a rose between his nose and upper lip. 'I was practically normal in Manchester, but being in Shipley has made me crazy.'

'Maybe the Shipley version is the real you.' He replaced the rose in its bucket and sneezed dramatically. 'Anyway, Mum'll be back next week and then you can leave.'

As he strode in the direction of work, followed by two hopeful seagulls, I stared at my phone once more, as if it was a crystal ball that might reveal what Tom and Megan were doing.

When it rang, I dropped it in fright.

'Everything OK, Mum?' I said, once I'd retrieved it. 'Bit early, isn't it?'

'We're five hours ahead over here.' She sounded breathless, and I imagined her haring along. 'We like to get out before lunch to go walking, and—'

'Have an authentic experience?'

'That's getting old now, Carrie,' she said. 'How are things there?'

Hmmm, let me see, I thought. *I've been to see Ruby's son, who was adopted at birth, the one you and Dad don't know about, met her granddaughter, Kate, and probably ruined the rest of that family's summer. Oh, and you remember Tom Hudson, the reason I left Dorset? Well, it turns out he's still with Megan, and they're getting married in three days, and expecting a baby.*

'I'm keeping the flower stall going, and Ruby's a bit better,' I said. 'Mum, why didn't you tell me Tom phoned, back then?' I'd been trying not to dwell on it, knowing 'what-ifs' could drive a person mad, but it kept circling my mind. 'You could have at least mentioned it.'

'Tom?' Mum sounded thrown. 'It was ages ago, love, and why would I have told you?'

'Er, because I might have wanted to hear from him.'

'But you'd moved on and were living with that cartoon chap,' she said reasonably. 'There was no point stirring things up.'

I wanted to stay mad at her, but I couldn't. She'd only done what she thought was best at the time.

'How did you find out?' Mum's voice grew suspicious. 'Have you seen him?'

'We might have bumped into each other.'

'Oh, Carrie…'

'It's fine,' I fibbed. 'He's getting married at the weekend.' I didn't say who to.

'And you're okay with that?'

Not remotely.

I made a noise I hoped passed muster, and asked how the holiday was going.

'Good, but I've had enough now.' She paused to catch her breath. 'Kenneth, will you please slow down!' she yelled. 'I thought we'd drive down on Friday, after we get back,' she said in her normal voice. 'We might even stay the weekend, if Ruby doesn't mind.'

'Oh.' It was the last thing I'd expected her to say. 'I'm not sure there'll be anywhere for you to sleep.'

'You could always go back to Manchester.'

'Ruby's spare bed isn't big enough for two.'

'Well, one of us could sleep on the sofa.' She paused, as if waiting for an outpouring of gratitude. 'Look, Carrie, it was mean of us to ask you to put your life on hold to take care of your aunt,' she said. 'And to be honest, it'll be nice to see Dorset again.'

'What does Dad think?'

'It was his idea too,' she said, and I wondered how that worked. Telepathy? 'Family's important in Kazakh life, and they place great value on living together.' She'd morphed into a guide-book tone. 'It's got your dad thinking he'd like to get to know his sister a bit better.'

Oh dear. 'Right,' I said.

'We could even stay longer and help with the flower stall until Ruby's back on her feet.' Mum was on a roll, my mention of Tom forgotten. 'It's not as if we don't know how to run a business; we did it for plenty of years.'

I tried to work out what I was feeling. Relieved, that I might be able to wriggle out of helping with the wedding on Saturday? Knowing Mum, she'd be only too keen to muck in, but did I want her to?

'Bloody hell,' I said, rubbing my forehead, as if the action might repair my thoughts.

'What is it, what's wrong?'

I realised I'd sworn out loud. 'Oh, some flowers have died,' I said quickly.

'What, just like that?'

'They're old ones.' I didn't give her time to respond. 'Give my love to Dad, and I'll tell Ruby you're coming on Friday.'

'I'll assume it's OK if I don't hear from you,' she said. 'And you should make sure the flowers are fresh when they're delivered, Carrie.'

As we said our goodbyes a woman approached, eyes darting over the buckets. 'Do you have anything like this?' She showed me a photo on her phone of a jug full of what looked like Doris's lilies. 'My sister bought them here, and they looked so lovely I thought I'd get some too.' She glanced around, face falling. 'Have they sold out already?'

'I can give my supplier a call, if you'd like to pop back later.'

'OK.' The woman smiled. 'I'm having a dinner party tonight and they'll look lovely on the table.'

Doris sounded pleased to hear from me. 'I'll be there in half an hour,' she promised, and sure enough she appeared as I was wrapping a bunch of white carnations in lieu of a wreath, for a man on his way to a funeral.

'You should really send people to mine and let them pick their own,' she said, decanting an armful of lilies into a bucket I'd got ready, and a couple of dozen more roses into another. I wondered if her garden regenerated overnight, like something from *Dr Who*.

'That's not a bad idea.'

'It's a terrible idea,' she said, as if I'd suggested it. 'I don't want a load of strangers in my garden, planting their big feet all over my borders.'

'O-*kay.*'

'So, have you got everything you need for this wedding on Saturday?'

I couldn't remember even mentioning it to her. 'Ruby's going to order the flowers to be delivered to her flat,' I said, having remembered to speak to Jools about it earlier. 'We'll probably have to go to Hudson Grange on Friday to dress the doobrey—'

'Doobrey?'

'The archway, pergola thingy, and drop off the table arrangements…' My words trailed off as I remembered that this time next week, Megan would be Mrs Hudson – unless she decided to keep her surname, though I doubted she'd pass up the opportunity to be officially recognised as part of a hotel dynasty.

'Shame you went away and let her get her claws in,' Doris said, tartly.

'How did you even *know*?'

She gave a careless shrug. 'His mother knew Ellen Partridge back in the day, and she mentioned a young woman called Carrie, who her Tom thought the world of.'

I remembered Mr Hudson saying that Tom had mentioned me to his mother. Not that it had done me any good. 'There's too much gossiping around here.'

Doris crossed to the workbench and flicked through the order book as if she worked there. 'It's not in my nature to gossip,' she said, with a perfectly straight face. 'I'm just telling you what I heard.'

'Well, it's all too late now,' I said.

'Don't you be so sure.'

'What do you mean?' I was as keen for her answer as if she was the Dalai Lama.

'I mean, if something's meant to be it'll be, and if it isn't it won't.'

I couldn't help feeling let down. 'Thanks for those pearls of wisdom.'

'It's not over till the fat lady sings,' she said, with a knowing nod as she slammed the order book shut. 'Or, as Roger used to say, till the bugger gets caught and I can give him a good kicking and lock him up.' I wondered what sort of police officer her husband had been.

'I'm afraid it *is* well and truly over.'

'And I think someone wants to talk to you.' As she looked past me my heart seized.

Tom.

But it wasn't Tom. It was Toby, in paint-spattered overalls, looking sheepish.

'I behaved like a babbling baboon,' he said, ducking under the canopy out of the glare of the sun.

'That's a bit strong.'

'I can't believe I got plastered.' He scrabbled a hand through his hair. 'I'm just on my way to a job, but wanted to apologise if I let you down last night.'

'You've nothing to be sorry for.' I decided to gloss over him directing me to the house he'd shared with his wife, because he'd forgotten he was staying at his parents', then trying to get me to come in, and share a plate of chicken risotto because he was hungry.

Ruby had laughed when I got in and told her, making a funny story out of it like I usually did for my family. *Another of Carrie's disastrous dates.*

'He was getting his own back for you singing to him last time, but I'm sure he'll make it up to you next time,' she'd chuckled, before heading to bed with a book called *The Dragonslayer's Nephew*, and it was so nice to see her with something besides food or a tear-drenched tissue in her hand, I didn't bother to mention there wouldn't be a next time.

'I'm the one who's sorry, for putting you through it,' I said to Toby.

'To be honest, I can't remember that much.' He winced. 'I'd barely eaten all day, and the champagne went straight to my head.'

'I didn't notice,' I deadpanned.

'She's not a nice woman, is she?' he said, even though Megan had been relatively pleasant to him. 'Shame she's pregnant, because I reckon he's not that into her.'

I thought of the look on Tom's face when he saw the scan photo, and my stomach contracted. 'Babies can bring people together, so I'm sure they'll work it out.' I flinched. 'Toby, I'm sorry. I keep forgetting why your marriage broke up.'

'It's fine.' He gave a sad little smile that tugged at my heartstrings. 'I think I'm going to try and give things another go with Em.'

'I'm glad,' I said, meaning it.

He smiled properly. 'I don't think I'll ever find anyone I like as much as her – no offence – and even if we can't have kids I want to be with her.'

'Well, I hope she feels the same,' I said. 'Good luck.'

'Same to you.' He stooped to kiss my cheek. 'I'm glad you get the *picture*.' He paused. 'A little art joke.'

'Ah. Good one.'

He gently flicked my hair before walking away, and was soon swallowed up by a coach-load of tourists embarking by the square.

I turned, half expecting to see Doris avidly watching and taking notes, but saw a small queue of customers instead.

'Oh god, I'm sorry,' I said, and managed to sell a good quantity of everything, including the lilies to the lady having a dinner party. It seemed half of Shipley were buying flowers for relatives' birthdays, or plants to put in their hanging baskets, and, in one case, six yellow roses to say sorry for 'being a bastard' to a well-meaning neighbour.

By mid-afternoon, the beach was packed with bodies baking in the sun, and splashing in and out of the sea, while the square was almost empty.

I'd almost stopped expecting to hear from Megan, when a glance at the work phone revealed a voice message that turned out to be from her.

'Hey, Carrie, if you're there, just wanted to say no hard feelings about last night.' Her voice was husky, as if she'd just climbed out of bed. 'Call back when you can, I need to talk flower arrangements.'

Heart thumping I called right back, refusing to dwell on the thought of her and Tom cosied up together, discussing my outburst the night before, and Tom reaching the conclusion that it was probably safer to stay with the devil he knew.

She picked up right away, as if she'd been waiting for my call.

'It's Carrie,' I said, aiming to keep my voice on an even keel. 'What is it you wanted to know?'

'What the hell you thought you were playing at last night?'

I should have known. 'I'm sorry,' I began stiffly, but she interrupted with a whoop of laughter.

'Just kidding, it's fine,' she said. 'In fact, Tom and I talked for ages when we got back and are closer than ever.' I heard the tinkle of a spoon on a china cup. 'I was just saying to my girl-crew,' there were hollers in the background, 'he's finally coming around to the idea of leaving his practice in the hands of a manager, so he can be around more when the baby's born.'

'But why should he give up doing something he loves?' I couldn't help the words shooting out, and could have kicked myself for giving her more ammunition.

'Maybe he loves me more than his job, Carrie, imagine that.' Her voice was rich with satisfaction, and an image of a beautiful, silky cat toying with a mouse sprang up. 'Being the mother of his child has made him appreciate me in a whole new light.'

Someone in the background said something I couldn't catch. 'Oh, yes,' she said. 'I wanted to check where your aunt is getting my flowers from, for the wedding.' It was as if she couldn't stop saying the word 'wedding'. Or maybe that was all I could hear.

'Why do you need to know?' There was a disbelieving rumble of voices. 'Have you got me on speaker-phone?'

'Just proving to the girls what I'm up against,' she said, and for a second she dropped the pretence of being nice. 'They can't believe I ever used to hang out with someone like you.'

They're not the only ones, I didn't say. I wasn't about to give her the satisfaction of knowing she'd got to me – though she probably knew. 'She's using All Seasons, her regular supplier,' I said, as calmly as my thrashing pulse would allow. 'And a couple of locals who specialise in hand-raised flowers.'

'Hand-raised,' tittered one of her cronies.

'Shouldn't it be home-grown?'

'Holy crap, they'll be covered in soil, Meg. Are you sure you don't want me to call my florist?'

'You'd better make sure they're real, and there won't be any fake flower piglets, and tell her—'

The last voice was cut off, and Megan's dulcet tones poured into my ear. 'All Seasons sounds good,' she said. 'So, I guess I'll see you on Friday.'

I thought she added 'or not', just as the line went dead. Maybe she was planning to stay out of my way from now on. I sincerely hoped so.

My head was pounding, and I desperately needed a drink. I was debating nipping to the newsagent's for a bottle of water, when someone tapped me on the shoulder.

'Carrie?'

I swung round, and for a moment was blinded by the sun, and couldn't see who the female voice belonged to. Then my vision cleared, and I found myself staring at a pair of sapphire-blue eyes. My heart gave a leap of shock. 'What are you doing here?'

'You said you'd be at the flower stall,' said Kate Robson, thumbs hooked through the straps of her quilted rucksack. 'I want to meet my grandmother.'

Chapter 32

In shock, I glanced behind Kate in case Peter was hovering out of sight. 'Are you with your dad?'

She shook her head, her sideways fringe fluttering in a light breeze. 'My parents don't know I'm here,' she said.

A flicker of hope, that something good was about to come out of the last few days, fizzled out. 'You shouldn't be here alone.'

She shrugged off her rucksack and dropped it at her feet. 'Dad wouldn't have let me come if I'd told him.'

'Where does he think you are?' The last thing I needed was a missing teenager on my hands, especially one belonging to a man who had every reason to hate me.

'I said I was going to the beach with my friends.' She was dressed in floral shorts, and under her loose-fitting top I could see what looked like the top half of a turquoise swimming costume.

'Aren't you a bit young to be out on your own?' I said, which was rich considering Sarah and I had spent most of our summer holidays out of sight of our parents – though the furthest I'd tended to stray was the grassy hollow at the bottom of our garden, with a book.

'I'm nearly fifteen.' She said it kindly. 'I am allowed out without my parents if I promise to answer my phone when they call.'

'How did you get here?' I fretted, already feeling responsible for her well-being.

'I got the bus,' she said, as if it was obvious. 'It took, like, two hours because it went through all these villages, and this old lady couldn't get her walking frame on, so the driver threatened to drive off and everyone got angry and we said we'd call the police if he did.' She was animated, as if she'd been on an adventure, and reinforced the image by plucking a complicated-looking water bottle out of her bag, as if on an expedition.

'So, this is my grandmother's stall?' she said, after taking several gulps with her head thrown back. She looked around her as if noticing the flowers for the first time. 'It's nice.'

Hearing her say 'grandmother' was strange, yet that's exactly what Ruby was.

'You look a lot like her.' The words flew out without permission. 'When she was younger, I mean. And, yes, this is her stall.'

'Cool,' she said. 'And you're my first cousin once removed.' Her gaze swept over the shorts, stripy top, and espadrilles I'd bought from Sassy Lassie, but I was conscious of looking as sweaty as I had when I turned up on her doorstep. Hardly the image of a responsible woman. 'I looked it up.' She gave an impish grin. 'It's really exciting, don't you think?'

Her enthusiasm was infectious, but I punched my hands onto my hips and tried to look stern. 'You really should call your parents, and tell them where you are.'

She shrugged, fiddling with the catch on her water bottle. 'Look, I heard what you said through the letterbox, and I read the letter you left my dad—'

'You shouldn't have done that.' I wouldn't have dared, if it had been me, but then I couldn't imagine something like that ever happening in our household. The only thrilling mail Sarah and I ever had, were cards with money in on our birthdays, from Auntie Barbara in Wales.

'I know, but I got to it first and after I'd read it I gave it to Dad, and told him to man up and see what she had to say.'

I tried to get my head around this image. 'And did he?'

She nodded. 'Mum said there are two sides to every story, and he should get over himself and stop acting like a brat, because that's not how he'd been brought up.'

'Wow,' was all I could think to say. 'That's harsh.'

'She thinks deep down he wants to meet her, but he feels really guilty about betraying Nanna. That was his adoptive mum.' Kate moved to the workbench and riffled through the tray of ribbon spools. 'She was a nice lady,' she said, pulling out a leaf-green length of satin and wrapping it around her wrist. 'But I expect Ruby's nice too.'

'She is.' I felt a bit choked. How had someone so young got to be so sensible? 'So, you already knew about her?'

'We talk about everything,' Kate said matter-of-factly. 'My mum says keeping secrets can make you sick, so it's best to share them and then they're not secrets any more.'

'Your mum sounds brilliant.' I thought of Ruby going into a decline every year, isolated by guilt and sorrow. 'She should be a psychologist.'

'She is.' Kate picked up a spray of purple freesias and ran them under her nose. 'Do you think my grandmother would let me work here at weekends?'

Her hopeful gaze was suddenly childlike, and I remembered she was only fourteen. At that age, my main concern had been getting good grades at school. 'Kate, don't you think your dad should meet her first?'

'Why?' She replaced the freesias and dusted her hands together. 'I can see what she's like and report back. Tell him how nice she is.'

'I don't think he'd like that.'

'I can go on my own, if you're busy.' She reached for her bag, her fringe falling over her face. 'I've got the address, and I know it's not far from here. Google maps.'

'No,' I said sharply. 'You can't just barge in, it'll be too much for her.'

'But I know she'll want to meet me.'

'Of course she will, but not without warning.'

'I don't see why,' she said reasonably. 'It's good to be spontaneous.' Maybe having a psychologist parent wasn't a good thing, after all.

'Look,' I said. 'Wait until I've finished here, and I'll walk you back to the bus stop.'

'It's there.' She pointed, and I swivelled to see a blue-and-white double-decker, pulling away from the kerb on the beach side of the road. 'And I'm not going until I've seen her.'

'Go and talk with your parents first, and I'll tell Ruby you want to meet her and organise it properly.'

Kate hoisted her rucksack onto her shoulder. 'I'd prefer to do it today, as I've come all this way,' she said politely. 'I think we've all wasted enough time, don't you?'

I couldn't really argue with that, but felt compelled to try. 'The shock might be too much.'

'Well, you go in first and tell her, and I'll wait outside.'

I was starting to see she had a stubborn streak, just like Ruby's. 'And if I say no?'

'I'll shout through the letterbox,' she said, way too drily for someone so young. It struck me how much more grown up she seemed than Megan, who was twice her age.

'Fine,' I said, caving in. I'd done nothing but act on impulse since arriving in Shipley, and maybe this time the result would be a positive one. 'Give me half an hour to pack up the stall.'

By the time I'd finished, with her help, to a soundtrack of questions about my family, about Ruby's likes and dislikes, and whether Ruby would mind Kate taking some photos on her iPhone, my head was spinning and Calum had arrived to take over.

If he was puzzled that I'd acquired a helper he didn't comment, and as he drove off with a cheery, 'Laters!' I reluctantly led the way up Main Street to the bakery.

'She lives here?' Kate looked delighted, shielding her eyes to peer through the gleaming window. 'I love bread,' she said. 'I have it with every meal.'

Something else in common with her grandmother.

'It's round the back,' I said. The door was propped open to let out the heat, and anxiety rippled through my chest as I stepped inside.

'Can I look in there?' Kate stuck her head into the kitchen. 'Wow, look at the size of that oven.'

'Maybe another time,' I said. 'Are you coming?'

''Course I am.' She followed me up the stairs. 'Do I have a grand-father too?'

'No,' I said, forgetting to sugar-coat my words. 'She never married.'

Kate fell silent as we reached the landing, clutching the straps of her rucksack.

'Are you sure about this?' I took out my key, hand shaking slightly. 'It's not too late to back out.'

'I'm sure.' She straightened her shoulders; a gesture that was oddly moving. It was a shame her father hadn't embraced the situation with the same equanimity, but it was probably easier when you were a generation removed, and didn't have abandonment issues.

I sucked in a breath. The occasion seemed to demand more than the sound of seagulls fighting by the skylight window – soaring violins perhaps, and a camera crew to capture the moment.

'Wait here until I invite you in, OK?' Kate pushed her fringe aside and nodded. 'Will you be alright?'

'Just do it,' she said, smiling to take out the sting. 'It's cool.'

It was anything but cool in the flat. As I closed the door gently on Kate's calm but eager face, I was hit by a wall of heat. The windows were shut, trapping the warmth of the day, and the tumble dryer was on. So was the oven. Closer inspection revealed a tray on the side, filled with chopped peppers, onions and courgettes, and there were two chicken breasts on a plate, covered with cling film. Ruby must have got distracted while preparing dinner.

She was probably in the bath, which was no bad thing as she was about to meet her granddaughter for the first time. Better to be damp but clean, than grubby in her old blue dressing gown.

Her laptop was open on the table, beside a notepad covered in doodled flowers. It looked like she'd placed the order for the wedding flowers, and my heart stuttered at the thought. Thanks to Kate turning up, I hadn't thought about Tom or Megan for at least an hour.

Pushing them aside I crossed to the bathroom, but the door was ajar and I could see Ruby wasn't inside.

Her bedroom door was shut. She must have gone back to bed. Had something happened? I hovered, my hand on the handle. What if introducing her to Kate was a really bad idea? She might be upset that Peter hadn't come, but surely would see that Kate – apart from being the sort of girl anyone would love as a granddaughter – could be a bridge to her son.

Mind made up, conscious Kate was waiting and probably worrying, I was about to knock when I heard noises: soft female laughter and the rumble of a man's voice.

'What the…?' I flung the door wide and was greeted by the sight of Bob the baker's hairy buttocks, before Ruby flung the duvet over him. 'Aunt Ruby, what's going on?'

'Carrie, my god, what's the time?' She shot up and looked wildly around, as if to make sure she was where she thought she was, before pulling her pillow around to cover her nakedness. 'I was going to cook dinner,' she said, shaking her head, 'but Bob popped in and we got talking and…' She lowered her lashes, modestly. 'One thing led to another.'

'So I see.' I kept my eyes on her rosy face, pretending not to notice Bob easing his boxers on under the duvet.

'I took your advice, Carrie, and told him everything,' she said, as if she couldn't quite believe it was true. 'He's been brilliant.'

'Clearly.'

Bob reared up like a grizzly bear, flattened his hair with his hands and cleared his throat. 'So sorry you had to see that.' He sounded genuinely upset. 'I wouldn't want you to think I've taken advantage of your aunt. I came up with some milk and some finger rolls, and—'

'It's not that,' I interrupted, edging further into the room. At least the window was open, a faint breeze stirring the curtain, dispelling any lingering trace of their… intimacy. Any other day, I'd have been delighted for Ruby, but of all the times to succumb to Bob's charms, this had to be the worst. 'You've got a visitor.'

'A visitor?' It was as if I'd spoken in tongues. 'What sort of visitor?'

'Someone you'll want to see.' I stumbled across to the cupboard and started rifling through her clothes. 'Here, put this on.' I flung a flower-patterned, wraparound dress down on the bed.

'I don't know if it'll fit me,' she said, fingering the fabric. 'I'll just put my dressing gown on.'

'No!' I picked up the dress and thrust it at her. 'It's stretchy, it'll be fine.'

She exchanged a look with Bob, who swung his legs out of bed and into his trousers. 'I'll leave you to it,' he said softly, buttoning up his shirt. He leaned over to place a tender kiss on her forehead. 'Speak soon.'

'Sorry, Bob,' I said, panic building. Kate would be wondering what was taking so long. 'It's just that this is important.'

'Don't worry.' He raised his hand in a sort of wave. 'I'll be around if you need me.'

As he left, Ruby said, 'Carrie, who is this person?'

She'd finally caught my urgency and was out of bed, mummified in a sheet. 'It's not your mum and dad, is it?' She actually sounded as if she'd be pleased to see them.

'No, but funnily enough they're coming to visit on Friday.' I turned my back so she could get some clothes on, and snatched a brush off the dressing table. While she adjusted the dress around her bosom, tutting about it being tight, I dragged the brush through her hair.

'Ouch, Carrie, stop that, and tell me who it is.' She grabbed the brush and lobbed it on the bed. 'Is it Mr Hudson, about the wedding? I've ordered the flowers, they'll be here—'

'It's not Mr Hudson.' I bent down, and attempted to push a pair of red mules on her feet.

'I can manage,' she said, doing it herself. 'My feet are a bit swollen – Carrie, what are you… *hmmmpphh*?'

'It's just a bit of lipstick.' I smeared some across her cheek as she twisted her head.

'Now look what you've done.' She ducked her head to look in her dressing-table mirror. 'I look like Coco the bloody clown.'

As she scrubbed at her cheek with a tissue, I sank down on the bed. 'I'm sorry, Ruby, I just want you to make a good impression.'

She lowered her hand and turned to me. A look inched over her face that could only be described as terrified hope with an edge of excitement. 'Oh, Carrie, tell me it's true. Is it… she dropped next to me and gripped my knee. 'Is it… is it my Donny?'

'Peter,' I said automatically and shook my head. 'Sorry, Ruby, it's not him—'

'Then who the fifty pence is it?' she cried, finally losing patience. 'Is this person in my flat?'

'Yes,' called a high voice from the living room. 'I'm here, Grandma.'

Ruby's jaw dropped. She clapped her hands to her cheeks, her shining eyes like marbles. 'Grandma?' It came out in a jagged whisper. 'Did I hear that right?'

I nodded, biting my lip. Bob must have let Kate in.

'Oh, my darling girl.' Ruby's face collapsed with emotion. She reached for my hands and squeezed them, two fat teardrops spilling down her cheeks. 'What have you been up to?'

'She's called Kate, she's fourteen, and she's the spitting image of you when you were her age.' I released a hand to wipe my own damp cheeks. 'Now go, for god's sake.'

But Ruby was through the door already, and the cry she gave was one of such unadulterated joy that my eyes couldn't stop leaking tears as I followed her through, in time to see her granddaughter fall into her open arms.

Chapter 33

'I think I should drive you home now, before your parents get worried,' I said eventually, feeling like a party-pooper. It had been an emotional rollercoaster, cramming our whole lives into an hour, sustained by Bob's milk and finger rolls, and we were all feeling drained.

Kate had wanted to know every detail of Ruby's life, and she'd happily obliged, trying to hold back tears when she spoke about giving up Peter, unable to stop them falling when Kate mentioned she had a little brother, Samuel.

'I don't want to leave,' Kate said now, hugging Ruby's arm as they sat together on the sofa. Ruby looked so overcome that I knew her life had changed irrevocably, and I felt a brief swell of happiness for her.

'You can come back, once you've cleared it with your parents,' she said gently, though it was obvious she'd have been happy for Kate to move in.

'Can I take some pictures?' Kate hoicked out her phone and attached a selfie-stick, and took several of herself with Ruby, looking radiant, and a couple with me in, too, and my smile was wider than I'd have expected after the last twenty-four hours.

'Shall I come in with you?' I said an hour later, parking opposite Kate's house. The last thing I wanted was to get out and face Peter, but I was worried about Kate going in alone, and what might happen when she revealed where she'd really been. She still looked lit up, and had barely stopped talking all the way back. It was obvious from her pink-cheeked excitement there was something up, and her parents were bound to ask.

'You don't need to, I'll be fine,' she said. 'I'm going to tell them straight away.'

'But what if they're angry with you?'

'Mum won't be,' she said ruminatively. 'Dad will probably go ape, but he'll soon calm down, and I can guarantee by tomorrow he'll want to know everything.'

It seemed like a lot for her to deal with. 'But what if he doesn't?'

She shrugged, seeming invincible. 'I know my dad,' she said, with enviable confidence. 'It'll be fine, I promise.'

I reminded myself she'd had fourteen years more experience of dealing with him than I had, and I would have to trust her. 'If he wants to talk to me about anything, you have my number,' I said. She waggled her phone. God only knew what her father would make of the photos she'd taken. 'Maybe you shouldn't show your dad the pictures yet.'

She looked at me from under her fringe. 'When he sees how happy we are, he won't be able to resist.'

'He might ban you from ever seeing her again.'

She gave this a second's thought. 'He's not going to lock me in my room,' she said, though I had a feeling he'd wish he had once he knew. 'I don't think there's anything he *can* do, really, and Ruby's completely cool, so it's not like I'm in danger or anything.'

There was clearly no dissuading her, and I gave up trying. 'Shall I wait here for a while, in case he wants to come and shout at me?'

She smiled. 'No need, cuz.' The term prompted an answering smile. Already I wanted to introduce her to my parents and Sarah. I knew they'd love her, once they'd got over the massive shock.

She planted a kiss on my cheek and scrambled out of the car. 'I'll be in touch,' she said, as if I'd been interviewed for a job.

'Good luck.'

I watched her march to the front door, put her key in the lock and disappear inside.

It was gone seven, and there was a light on in the house, even though the evening was still bright. I was tempted to creep up and peer through the window to check for scenes of disruption, but forced myself to start the car.

It seemed unwise to let a fourteen-year-old girl convince me things would be fine, but as I pulled away I realised I believed in Kate.

It was a shame that belief didn't extend to other areas of my life.

As I drove past the sign for Shipley, I was tempted to divert to the surgery to see if Tom was there, but what could I say if he was?

He hadn't been in touch since our aborted meal at the restaurant, and if Megan was right and they'd talked into the night, it meant he'd come to terms with them getting married.

It wasn't that I thought he was in love with her suddenly, but if he'd decided to make a go of things for the baby's sake, perhaps hoping his feelings for Megan might grow in the process, who was I to persuade him to change his mind again?

Although he'd confessed to having feelings for me in the past (I could barely get my head around that) it didn't mean they still existed. Despite his frustration about what might have been, he hadn't shown any desire to turn the clock back.

No, it was best to stay away from him, until I could leave Shipley for good.

I parked along the parade and walked in the shadow of the buildings, past the sweet shop, before crossing over to the beach, which was empty apart from some paddling teenagers, and two families embroiled in a heated sandcastle-building competition.

The sun was setting, staining the sky orange and making a silhouette of the pier. I tried to empty my mind of everything but the view, but it was no good. Mixed up with my bittersweet feelings about Ruby and Kate was a sadness deeper than any I'd felt before; that I'd missed out on what I was certain was my only shot at love.

'Bollocks,' said Sarah, as I made my way back to the car. I'd called her on impulse, hoping her common sense would rub off and restore my sense of order. 'There isn't just one man for every girl, you know. It's impossible to meet all our perfect matches, so we settle for the one that ticks the right boxes at the time.' She paused. 'Although, obviously, you *have* met more possible matches than most.'

'Ha ha.' And she didn't even know about Toby.

'Only you never give them a chance, because you're always comparing them to Tom, but now he's definitely out of bounds you can try a bit harder in future.'

'Maybe,' I said, too weary to argue. 'How are the twins?'

'Having a sleepover at Phil's sister's,' she said. 'We're meant to be having a date night, but we're both so knackered we're having an early night instead.'

As I slumped through the door at Ruby's, I found her on her hands and knees in the living room, a bucket of soapy water at her side, scrubbing at a stain on the carpet with a nailbrush. Little Mix was blasting from a music channel on the television.

She looked up as I came in, her face mottled with colour. 'Was she OK?'

'She was fine,' I shouted. 'What are you doing?'

'I can't settle, so I've put together an album of photos for Kate' – she gestured at an old-fashioned album on the table – 'then I found some dye in the bathroom and sorted out my hair' – she pointed to her retouched roots – 'and then I thought I'd get cleaning.' Her voice was buoyant. 'I haven't felt this good in I don't know how long.'

Crossing to the TV to turn it down, I spotted the Hollywood couple in the window opposite, having an argument. She was jabbing the air near his nose with her finger, and his arms were spread wide in a gesture of defence.

Upset, I turned to see Ruby advancing, and before I could move she'd grabbed me in a soapy hug. 'I still can't believe you went to see him, but I'm so glad you did. Thank you from the bottom of my heart.' She rocked me in her arms until I could hardly breathe.

'You're welcome,' I gasped, when she finally released me, and summoned a smile. She looked reborn, a sparkle in her eyes, her hair bright and fluffy, whereas mine felt drab and lifeless. 'I had a bit of help from Doris,' I admitted.

'Oh, that woman.' Ruby waved the nailbrush, which was dripping suds on the carpet, but I had the feeling not only that she didn't mind, but she'd wanted it to happen. Maybe Doris had been right, and Ruby had been crying out for help all along.

'You know this doesn't mean Peter will automatically want to meet you,' I cautioned. I was sure in her mind she'd already leapt ahead to a happy reunion, but to my surprise she nodded.

'I know.' She dropped the nailbrush back in the bucket with a splosh. 'I've had a long time to get used to the idea of my son not being in my life,' she said evenly. 'I think I might be able to handle it now.'

I was gripped by a horrible thought. 'But what if Kate decides not to come back?' Ruby would be plunged back into depression, but worse than before.

'My darling Carrie.' She took my face tenderly between her wet hands. 'Just knowing that lovely girl exists in the world, because I gave birth to her father, makes me happier than I've any right to be.' An expression of wonder illuminated her face. 'It's enough. I mean it,' she insisted, perhaps seeing doubt in my eyes. 'Now, why don't we have a drink to celebrate? There's some wine in the fridge.'

'Actually, Ruby, I think I'll have an early night.'

She scoured my face, eyes thinning. 'Are you OK?'

'Just tired,' I said. I couldn't bear to deflate her moment of joy by mentioning Tom, and anyway it was true. I'd experienced more emotion in the last two days than I had for years, and was craving sleep. I was even planning which app I would use to relax me – forest sounds, including the crackling of a campfire.

Once in bed, it sent me quickly into a coma-like sleep, but I dreamt I was camping and a bear kept scratching at the tent, and when I unzipped it Megan was there, her teeth bared in a razor-sharp smile.

I woke with a start, clawing at the air, and scrabbled for my phone. Peering bleary-eyed at the screen, I saw it was almost 6.30 a.m. Disabling the alarm, I tumbled out of bed and into the bathroom, and my nerve-endings sat up in fright when I entered the kitchen and saw Ruby. She was dressed in a loose white tunic top, baggy purple trousers and sandals, and had a money belt strapped round her middle.

'Bob popped up with some fresh milk,' she said, with the same tone of optimism from the evening before. 'I was going to bring you a cup of tea in bed.' She swished and dunked a tea-bag in a mug, smiling over her shoulder. 'I thought you could have a lie-in.'

'I have to get to the stall,' I said, aware of my bed-hair and pillow-creased face.

'Sweetheart, I thought it was time to ease myself back into work.'

'What?' I stared at her, jolted awake. It was unusual enough to see her upright at this time of the day, fully clothed. The idea of her leaving the flat and working at the stall was too much. I had to run her through a new filter and adjust my settings.

'Come down later, if you like. It'll be nice, the two of us there together.'

'Ruby, are you sure you're ready?'

She dipped her chin. 'I've been feeling sorry for myself, I'm not ill.'

'It sort of *was* an illness.'

'Ye-e-es,' she acknowledged. 'Maybe. But thanks to you I was feeling better even before last night. I'd never have been brave enough to talk to Bob, otherwise.' Her colour rose, no doubt reacting to what else she'd been doing with Bob. 'The very least I can do is give you a few hours off, and I've managed on my own before.'

'If you're sure,' I said, doubtfully.

She finished her tea and jiggled her stomach with her hand. 'I'm not even hungry,' she said. 'I think it's all the excitement.'

I couldn't help smiling as she did a *Strictly*-style cha-cha-cha move, and kissed my cheek on her way out. 'Let me know if Kate calls,' was her parting shot.

It was odd being in the flat on my own. I doused some cornflakes in milk, cupped the bowl in one hand, grasped a spoon in the other, and wandered around while I ate.

I paused at the window and looked out. It was quiet, patches of pale sky visible above the rooftops, which were bathed in early sunshine.

Opposite, a door opened onto the pavement, and Hollywood man stepped out in form-hugging Lycra, Velcroing an iPod holder to his bicep. He checked a fitness band on his wrist, then set off backwards down the road, blowing kisses. I looked up to see his girlfriend craning out of the window, her tousled hair drifting in the breeze.

Glad they'd resolved their differences from the night before, I put my bowl in the sink and looked around. There was nothing to do, and I found myself thinking of the stall; wondering how Calum was, and whether Doris might pop by with more flowers.

It occurred to me that I might as well go and help, or I'd only end up thinking about Tom and feeling even more miserable. At this rate, I'd be the one in bed with Ruby trying to cheer me up.

I took a quick shower, flattened my hair, and dressed in my denim shorts and another new top. Digging around in my bag for my lip balm, I remembered the scan picture Megan had dropped at the restaurant, and took it out. It had got a bit crumpled, and was bigger than I remembered. When I turned it over and smoothed it out, I saw that it wasn't the baby photo; it was part of an email printout.

Before I could process my actions, I'd read the words on it.

I read them again, and a third time, wondering if I'd suffered a brain malfunction, then turned it over and over and read it again.

Feeling an earthquake in my chest, I prowled the flat a couple of times, then grabbed my phone and called Jasmine.

Chapter 34

'WHAT?' Jasmine's face was squashed up to the phone screen, her eyes big with shock.

'It wasn't *her* baby photo, it was her stepmother's,' I repeated, turning my phone and zooming in on the email printout, so Jasmine could get an idea of the words that had scored themselves on my brain.

Dear Megan,

We thought you'd like to see the latest scan photo. It's a boy!! We're so pleased after four girls, and I hope you understand why your father and I can't make the wedding, it's just too much at the moment, my blood pressure's sky-high. We hope you'll visit soon, perhaps after the baby's born. We'd love for you to meet your half-brother and sisters.

Love, Crystal x

Megan wouldn't want to visit. I remembered the way her mask had slipped when she told me her stepmother was pregnant 'again'. She'd never got over her father 'replacing' her with more girls, so the fact he was having the son he'd always wanted would hardly be a blessing in her eyes.

'She must have printed it out and cut the photo bit off, see?' I said to Jasmine, shaking the piece of paper. I was still having a hard time believing it.

'God, what a cow,' Jasmine breathed, as I brought her back into view. 'Who does that kind of thing?'

'I know, it's weird.' I dropped on Ruby's sofa like a chopped log. 'She's an attractive, intelligent woman, who could be running her own corporation—'

'Clearly, with those skills,' Jasmine cut in. 'Don't they say most top business people have a psychopathic nature?'

'Exactly!' I clutched at my hair. 'Yet she faked a pregnancy to win a man who doesn't love her, because she knows he's too decent not to marry her. I mean, who wants a man on those terms?'

'One with control issues, Daddy issues, and Christ knows what other issues, and the marriage could just be about money anyway,' said Jasmine. 'What are you gonna do?'

'I don't know.' My head was buzzing with the effort of absorbing it all. 'I still can't believe it,' I said, but it wasn't strictly true. I knew by now that Megan would do whatever it took to get whatever she wanted.

'You've got to tell Tom.'

'I shouldn't have to!' My voice was almost a wail. 'Megan should.'

'So, you should tell her.'

'You're right.' I stood up, adrenaline flowing through me. 'God, Jas, what a mess.'

'I bet you can't wait to come home, hen.'

For a second, I couldn't think where she meant. I looked at her, and noticed she was wearing a workman-like shirt with the sleeves rolled up, covered in red splotches.

'Jasmine, what have you done to my kitchen?' I peered behind her at the wall, eyes popping at the colour, which resembled freshly drawn blood.

'You said I could choose.' She ducked her head so I could see it more clearly. 'I thought some yellow tiles would be a nice contrast.'

It wouldn't, it would be hideous, but I didn't care. There were more important things than wall colours, and if things worked out I wouldn't be living there much longer anyway.

Wait. *What?*

Just because I now had proof that Megan was lying about being pregnant, it didn't mean I was going to end up living happily ever after in Shipley. I loved my Manchester life, and couldn't wait to get back. Tom would want to come too, and set up a vet's practice there; we'd buy a house together, or he could move in with me and Jasmine, though she was allergic to animals so that wouldn't work because of Hovis...

I reeled in my spiralling thoughts.

First things first.

I had to talk to Megan.

'It looks... nice,' I said to Jasmine, who'd positioned the phone so I could just see her eyebrows, which were dancing up and down. 'Really cheerful, in fact.'

'Carrie, seriously, if you go and see her, be careful.' Jasmine's face reappeared, looking concerned. 'She might go feral and lash out,' she added. 'Make sure you meet somewhere public, and get a tetanus jab just in case.'

'I don't think she's violent,' I said, but I wasn't so sure. At that point, I wouldn't have put anything past Megan.

After promising to update Jasmine later, I rang off and paced around the flat, while I tried to work out the best way to handle things, and when nothing clever sprang to mind, called Megan's mobile.

'Can you meet me in half an hour at Cooper's Café?' I said when she picked up. 'It's Carrie,' I added when she didn't speak, though I knew she knew it was me. 'We need to talk.'

'Oh, Carrie, if it's about the other night, I've already said it's fine.' She sounded bored. 'I'm rather busy today.'

'It is about that.' I didn't want to play my cards too soon, and give her time to think of a convincing reason why the printout didn't mean what I thought it meant. 'I need to see you in person to apologise, it's playing on my mind.' Blood rushed to my cheeks at the lie, and I was glad we weren't FaceTiming.

'I've a lot to do,' she said coolly, clearly loving that I was practically begging. 'I've a final dress fitting, and the wedding photographer's coming round this afternoon.'

'Please, Megan, it's important to me.'

I knew she wouldn't be able to resist playing the magnanimous friend, bestowing forgiveness on her silly old school pal, probably relieved that once it was over she'd never have to see me again. Though it wouldn't surprise me if she wangled a way of proving she and Tom were married, by offering to send me a photo of the wedding, or a slice of cake.

'Fine,' she said at last, making it clear she was doing me a massive favour. 'My fitting's not until one, so I suppose I could pop over, maybe even visit Tom at work and persuade him to come home early.' She lowered her voice seductively. 'Not that he'll need much persuading.'

I mimed jabbing her eyes out down the phone, but managed to keep my voice calm. 'I'll see you in half an hour then.'

Cooper's Café was busy when I arrived, and rather than hang about outside, and risk being spotted by Ruby, I slipped through the side door and ordered a coffee, then sat at a table by the window so I'd see Megan arrive.

I had a good view of the flower stall, and as I blew steam away from my coffee, I watched a smiling Ruby engage a passer-by in conversation. The woman responded, going on her way with a bunch of dahlias and a spider-plant, and it struck me how right Ruby looked, in her purple trousers, surrounded by flowers, against a backdrop of sand and sea. Toby's words about her being part of the landscape came back, and I could understand why the stall had endured, even if custom wasn't always as brisk as it might be.

Now she was back, she could throw herself into building up business to see her through the winter months; perhaps expand into doing deliveries, and even take on a driver.

My phone trilled, and as if we'd tuned into the same frequency it was All Seasons Nursery. 'I was just thinking about flowers,' I said, stupidly.

'Oh, were you now?'

It was the woman I'd spoken to before, and she sounded thoroughly fed up.

'Er, yes?'

'Well, so was I,' she said, in that same, hacked off way. 'I'm afraid I'm going to have to charge a twenty per cent cancellation fee.'

I started. 'Cancellation fee?'

'Are you 'avin' a laugh?'

'Sorry, *what?*'

'You do know the booking's been cancelled?' Her voice iced over. 'The bride rang to inform me' – she put on a la-di-da voice – 'that she'd decided to go with another florist; someone who understood her needs.'

I groaned. So, that's why Megan had called, wanting to know the name of Ruby's supplier. Of all the underhand, sneaky…

'She never told you?'

'No, she didn't.' Anger burnt in my chest. Megan had ditched Ruby to get back at me, probably in favour of Jay Simmons. I wondered what story she'd spun Mr Hudson to explain the switch. 'I'm so sorry,' I said, gritting my teeth.

'We'd already sourced them all, and have to cover the inconvenience, love, I'm sure you understand.' She'd grudgingly warmed up. 'I'm going to do a bill for your auntie, and thought I'd let you know.'

'I'll pay it,' I said, and once again read out my credit card details to her. She'd know them off by heart at this rate. 'And I really am very sorry.'

'Me too,' she said, wistfully. 'Not every day we get an order like that.'

I rang off, my fury with Megan tempered by guilt that this was somehow my fault. That I should never have come to Shipley in the first place.

But if I hadn't, Ruby might never have met her granddaughter…

'There you are!'

I jerked with shock, sloshing coffee on the table. 'Megan!' Where had she sprung from? 'I didn't see you come in,' I said, hating that she always caught me unawares.

'You were busy with your phone.' She placed her bag on the table and folded herself into the chair opposite. I wondered if she'd overheard my conversation.

Removing her floppy-brimmed hat and owl-like sunglasses, she glanced around with vague distaste, as though finding herself in a crack den. 'It's a shame to sit inside in this weather,' she said, 'but I'm staying out of the sun as I don't want even a hint of sunburn for the photos.'

'But surely vitamin D is good for the baby?' I wanted to see her reaction. I was still reeling from the news that she'd cancelled the flowers, and all I wanted now was for her to come clean.

'I'm sure it is,' she said loftily, 'but for the sake of a couple of days—'

'Drop the act, Megan. I know you're not pregnant.'

Her expression grew so tight, her skin looked stretched. 'Not this again.'

'You're not pregnant,' I repeated, sliding the printed email message across the table. 'But your stepmother is.'

Her eyes dipped down, hiding a flash of panic. 'Where did you get this?' She snatched it up and put it in her bag, and I realised my mistake.

'It fell out of your bag in the restaurant the other night.'

'Doesn't prove a thing,' she said, quickly reviving, though her face had turned the colour of a hard-boiled egg. 'Crystal is pregnant too, so what?'

'That picture you showed us didn't seem right.' I thought back. 'I've seen one before, when my sister was pregnant, and it was like a proper photograph.'

'So, my gynaecologist emailed it to me,' she snapped. 'For god's sake, Carrie, why are you being like this?'

'Why are *you*?' I shot back, and the woman at the table behind Megan lowered her Kindle to watch. 'How could you do this to Tom?' I said, bringing my voice down a couple of notches. 'You know he doesn't want to marry you, so why not let him go?'

'What, so you can have him?' Her eyes were like cold metal. 'I haven't worked my arse off to get where I am, for you to turn up and ruin it,' she said. 'Once we're married, and Tom's running the company, I'll make sure there are babies aplenty to keep him there.'

'And in the meantime?' I matched her tone, relieved that at least she'd dropped the pretence. 'When he realises there is no baby?'

'Women have miscarriages, don't they?'

Her words were like freezing water in my face. 'Megan!'

'What?' She fiddled with the straps on her bag, and I noticed a tremor in her hand. 'By the time the honeymoon's over I probably will be pregnant,' she said. 'It's a case of getting Tom in one place long enough for it to happen.'

'Why Tom?' I said, shaking my head. 'You could have anyone.'

'Believe it or not I care about him.' One fingernail drummed out a rhythm on the wood-topped table. 'And Michael has been more of a father to me than mine ever was.'

I stared at her for a moment, connections firing in my brain as I put it all together. I saw the fifteen-year-old Megan again, crying in the toilets because her father had left without her; sobbing again in my bedroom, because he'd had a baby – a girl – with his pretty, young wife.

'You want to be part of a family, and can't bear that Tom doesn't love you,' I said, almost feeling sorry for her.

'Oh, it was alright for you. Little brainbox, with your wonderful family, and boys thinking you were quirky and cute.' Her words were like needles.

'You were jealous? Of *me*?' I stared at her, dumbstruck.

'You had it all, didn't you?' she said. 'You're the one who could have had your pick.'

I remembered Ruby's words, about loving parental support being everything, and felt myself melting back to my teenage self, wanting to make Megan feel better about herself.

'Look, it's not too late to do the right thing.' I reached a hand across the table. 'You'll feel better if you do.'

Her face worked briefly, and she averted her gaze as if to settle her thoughts. 'Just leave me alone, Carrie.'

'Sorry?'

She shifted her eyes and gave me a mocking look. 'Go back to wherever you came from, and leave me alone.'

'Not until you've told Tom.' I withdrew my hand. 'If you don't tell him, I will.'

Slowly, she got to her feet, and rested her hands on the table, bringing her face close to mine. 'I'm getting married the day after tomorrow,' she said lightly. 'And if you go to Tom with your little tale, I'll tell him you're lying because you've always been jealous of me. And he will believe me, Bagsy, I can promise you that.' She straightened, and flattened her gauzy top across her belly. 'He's already felt the baby move.' She placed a hand on her tiny curve and turned to an imaginary Tom. 'Oh my god, did you feel it?' she cried, her face alight with fake happiness. 'That's a baby in there! Our child! Can you believe it?' She shot out a hand, grasping an invisible arm. 'You're going to be the most amazing daddy, I know it.'

A couple at one of the tables looked on in astonishment. The girl turned to her red-faced boyfriend, and he lifted his palms in a gesture of innocence.

'It's not mine,' he said, laughing nervously.

The woman with the Kindle came over. 'Congratulations, you look amazing,' she said to Megan. 'How far along are you?'

'Oh, it's early days yet,' Megan replied, as innocent as a choirgirl. 'I've a long way to go, but I feel great, not a hint of morning sickness.' As she relaxed into the role of expectant mum, I remembered again what an accomplished actress she was. She was wasted at HCH.

If only I'd taken a photo of the printout, or recorded our conversation on my phone, I might have had a leg to stand on, but I knew with sickening clarity that even if I managed to talk to Tom, without proof to back anything up she would twist it around, and make me the deluded liar.

Megan had won, again.

'Well, I'd better get going, lots to do,' she was saying, when I tuned back in, as much to me as the woman, who had been giving her tips for keeping stretch marks at bay. 'Good catching up with you.'

My throat was tight with tears. 'Did you ever like me, Megan?'

'Oh, Carrie.' For a split second she looked torn as she picked up her bag. 'I don't think I liked anyone much, after Daddy left home.'

Then she gave me a dazzling smile, slipped her sunglasses back on, and sashayed out of the café, her hair as sleek as a crow's wing in the sunshine.

I brushed away a tear. It was time for me to go, too.

Back to Manchester, where I would stay this time.

Chapter 35

As I stood up to leave, Kate texted.

All hell broke loose when I told Dad, he threatened to ground me for a year and call the police, talk about an overreaction! Mum talked him down and he's coming round... Coming round? My heart lurched. I hadn't expected that. Ruby would be over the... *to the idea of meeting Ruby! X*

Ah. Still, he was considering it, which was more progress than I'd imagined, and it was good to know Kate was OK.

Can't wait to see you both again, but Mum says not til Dad's met Ruby – if he wants to ☹ x

Sounds fair I replied. *Tell her to call me if she wants to talk, and keep me posted. Hope to see you soon xx* I felt a stab of guilt, knowing I'd be leaving soon, but maybe if things worked out, Kate could come to Manchester one day to visit.

Manchester. Despite everything, the thought wasn't as appealing as it had been just moments earlier. I was beginning to wonder if I was more rooted in Dorset than I'd realised – or was it because Tom lived in Shipley?

It didn't matter. I was going, regardless.

I decided not to tell Ruby that Peter was considering a visit, in case her hopes flew up in spite of what she'd said the night before. Instead,

I bought her some coffee and took it over, and told her Kate had been in touch and was fine.

Her face relaxed into a beam. 'I'm so glad,' she said, squeezing my fingers. 'I'd have hated her to get into trouble because of me.'

I put the coffee on the workbench and waited while she wrapped a bunch of creamy roses for a customer.

'Weren't they Doris's?' I said when Ruby bustled back, stuffing a ten pound note in her money belt.

'She came by with some first thing. They've been really popular, apparently.' I nodded. 'She's going to supply me in future, for a small fee. Ooh, and I told her about Kate,' she said, her face blooming with happiness. She seemed to have shed five years overnight. 'She got that Agatha Raisin look on her face and said, "So glad we could be of service."'

I managed a smile.

'She's an interfering old whatsit,' said Ruby, clasping me to her once more, as if all the feelings she'd suppressed for so long desperately needed an outlet. 'But in a good way, don't you think?'

'I do,' I said, gently disengaging. 'Ruby, I'm afraid there's bad news about the wedding flowers.' I told her that Megan had cancelled the order, though not the real reason behind it.

Ruby looked briefly affronted. 'It's a shame she didn't call and tell *me* she'd decided to go with this other florist,' she said. 'I'd have been perfectly capable of meeting her needs, if we'd discussed what they were in person.' But she didn't sound too upset, and I guessed that in light of meeting Kate – and the fact that a week ago she wouldn't have cared if the stall had gone up in flames – it wasn't that important.

'Ah well, there'll be other weddings, though not like that one,' she said, throwing a wave at Mr Flannery who was outside his shop, looking over. 'He fancies me,' she said behind her hand. 'Hasn't a cat in hell's chance.'

I pushed my hair off my face, feeling about a hundred. 'Can you manage if I go back to the flat for a bit?' The thought of interacting with people – even Ruby – was suddenly too much.

'What is it?' Her smile dimmed. 'Oh, Carrie, I was forgetting how hard it must be for you, with Tom getting married tomorrow—'

'I just feel a bit off-colour,' I cut in.

'Go.' She flapped her hands. 'Remember, I've been doing this for years.'

'Usually with Jane, and you've not been well.'

'Who's talking about me?'

We swung around to see Jane approaching, limping slightly (her sprained ankle, I hoped), in canvas shorts that revealed knees like turnips. Her face was a mask of delight as she took in the sight of Ruby.

'Look at you, you grumpy old cow!' She punched Ruby's upper arm with surprising force. 'I thought I'd better come back after all, to help with the wedding, but it looks like I'm not needed.'

'You're always needed, you daft old bat.' Ruby grabbed Jane in a headlock and ruffled her hair into an even bigger frizz. 'Not that there is a wedding any more.'

'What?' Jane broke free, her glasses at a crazy angle. She gave me a fierce glare. 'What did you say to put them off?'

'She didn't say anything, you dozy mare.' Ruby gave her a playful shove. 'They just couldn't bear the thought of you turning up in your wellies.'

Jane stuck her tongue out, and Ruby thumbed her nose back. They were like a pair of teenage boys, and it suddenly made perfect sense that they didn't discuss their personal lives in detail.

'How was your break?' I asked Jane, before she could ask me anything else about the cancelled flower booking.

'Not over, if you're sure you can manage without me until Monday.' She removed her glasses, peering blindly as she polished them on the hem of her baggy vest top. 'Let's just say, I haven't quite finished with Dennis.'

'I suppose you've got him putting up shelves, poor bugger,' Ruby said, shifting to attend to a customer, who'd gathered an armful of irises *(warmth and affection)* and gypsophila *(baby's breath)* and clearly didn't know what to do with them.

Jane replaced her glasses. 'I'll have him putting up something,' she said to me, eyes glinting.

'That doesn't even make sense.'

'He's lost five pounds, you know, and my thighs are like jelly. I think it's safe to say our marriage is back on track.'

'That's...' *gross* '... amazing,' I said queasily. 'And I really am sorry about the wedding.'

She scrunched up her face, then smiled. 'Listen, you got your aunt back,' she said kindly. 'That's all that really matters.'

Not if you don't get more money coming in, it isn't.

As she left with a backwards wave, my mind churned with all the things that were still undone, and when Ruby touched my arm, I jumped. 'Go on,' she said. 'I promise you, I'm fine now.' She looked suddenly traumatised. 'God, Carrie, I owe you so much. I don't deserve you. I've been the worst aunt in the world.'

'What? Don't be silly.' I leaned over to kiss her soft cheek. 'I think I just need a little lie-down, that's all.'

Her hand flew to her forehead. 'I'd ordered a load of jam jars for the table decorations,' she said. 'They might turn up this afternoon. I don't know what I'm going to do with them all.'

'I'll pay for them,' I said, wishing I'd thought to ask Megan for a deposit in the first place.

Ruby's eyebrows squashed together. 'You'll do no such thing,' she scolded. 'Now, away with you.'

I couldn't muster an argument, and left her there, feeling the weight of her worried eyes on my back as I headed up Main Street.

The light in the flat was different in the middle of the day, poking into the corners of the living room, picking out the odd cobweb Doris had missed on her purge.

I knew I should call Jasmine, or even start packing to go home. Instead I stared out of the window, hands cupping my elbows, feeling as insubstantial as a ghost.

Megan's face zoomed into my head, withered and contorted like a witch's mask. I wished Tom could have seen her at the café – heard the things she'd said.

I wandered into the bedroom and lay on the bed and, burying my head in the pillow, I cried until my eyes felt broken, before tumbling into a deep sleep.

It was still light when I woke, but the sun had moved, casting a rectangle of light on the opposite wall. I'd tunnelled under the duvet at some point and now threw it off, feeling sticky and hung over.

Ruby was in the kitchen, clattering crockery and softly singing 'Livin' on a Prayer'.

I must have slept all afternoon.

My bladder felt fit to burst, and I staggered to the bathroom like a drunk. After relieving myself, I splashed my face with cold water, recoiling from my reflection in the mirror. My hair had risen like a giant Yorkshire pudding, and my eyelids looked stitched together. I splashed on some more water in an effort to repair the damage, then straightened my bed-rumpled clothes and headed to the kitchen to tell Ruby I'd be leaving first thing tomorrow.

'There you are, sleepyhead.' She danced over to gather me in yet another heartfelt hug, her hand cupping my head. I'd never been cuddled so much, and it felt nice to sink into her. 'Feeling better?' she said.

Not really. 'A bit. I didn't mean to sleep so long.' Over her shoulder, I spotted a plate, heaped with golden, buttered toast, and a steaming pot of tea beside two mugs.

Pulling back, I saw she'd got changed into loose red trousers and a short-sleeved top patterned with embroidered roses. 'Sorry, I should have cooked dinner,' I said.

'Dinner?' Her eyes danced. 'It's breakfast time, sweetheart,' she said. 'You slept all night.'

'*What?*'

She gave a gurgling laugh at my shocked expression. 'You were dead to the world when I got home, and I couldn't bear to disturb you.' Her face coloured. 'Bob went and got fish and chips and we ate them in front of the telly, and I told him all about Kate.'

'I can't believe it.' *So much for leaving first thing.*

'I know,' she said. 'I've gone from keeping my past a secret, to telling anyone who'll listen. It feels liberating.' She pressed a palm to her cheek. 'I wish I'd done it years ago.'

'I meant, I can't believe I slept all night, but that's good,' I said.

'You must have needed it.' She patted my arm. 'Now, clear a space at the table and I'll bring your breakfast over.'

There was an open box of jam jars in the centre, nestled in a bed of straw.

'I didn't even hear the delivery man,' I said, still stunned that I'd slept so long. I didn't even feel refreshed.

'He left them outside the door.' Ruby picked up her things, and took a bite of toast. 'I'm off to the stall now,' she said. 'I'm looking forward to seeing your mum and dad later.' I'd forgotten they were coming. 'Are you sure you're OK?' She paused in the doorway, and I realised I'd taken out a jam jar and was staring into it, as if it held the answer to the meaning of life.

'I'm fine.' I forced a smile. 'Just imagining how pretty these would have looked filled with flowers.' *Great. Now I'd reminded myself about the wedding.*

'Maybe I'll do a display for the flower stall,' she said. 'Bring some down later, if you like.'

'OK.'

Once she'd left, I found my phone and saw a couple of messages. Mum and Dad were arriving late afternoon, and suggested I find a guest house for them to stay in. *So you don't have to go home right away xx*

They'd be lucky to get a room at this time of year. Ruby would no doubt offer them her bed, and I'd head back to Manchester once they arrived.

Jasmine had texted hundreds of question marks and I quickly replied, *Home tonight, will explain all then x*

Tease she responded, which meant she'd been waiting for a reply. She wouldn't normally be up this early if she wasn't teaching. *Vinnie's helping me tile the wall in the kitchen, decided to go for black.*

Black?

Joke!! Sticking with custard yellow.

She could coat the walls with custard, for all it mattered. I was still having difficulty imagining slotting back into my old life.

'You'll be fine when you get there,' I said aloud, and began folding my clothes into bags. I hadn't realised how at home I'd made myself,

finding a place for my things in the cluttered room, and as I returned
Ruby's wedges to her shoe cupboard, another layer of sadness settled
over me.

I had a quick tidy round, in anticipation of my parents' arrival,
and by midday the flat was spotless. There was nothing left to distract
me from thinking about the preparations that would be taking place
at Hudson Grange, for tomorrow's wedding. No doubt Jay Simmons
was swanning about, transforming the garden and house into a flowery
wonderland.

Bastard.

I pictured Tom, looking devastatingly handsome in a smoke-grey
suit and tie, watching Megan drift towards him in a lavishly embel-
lished wedding dress. Then I thought about Hovis, banished from the
ceremony because of Megan's allergy (if it even existed), whimpering
for his master.

I couldn't bear it.

I slammed out of the flat and headed to the square, past groups
of meandering tourists, and Mr Flannery loitering on the step of his
shop, to the stall.

Ruby was talking on the phone, a cluster of sweet peas in her hand.
'That was Mr Hudson,' she said by way of a greeting, putting the phone
down when she'd finished.

I tried not to betray the surge of feeling hearing his name provoked.
'What did he want?'

She gave a baffled shake of her head. 'Well, initially to apologise
for the flowers being cancelled, which he assured me wasn't his doing.'

'It wasn't,' I confirmed, heart pattering a little faster.

'He's offered to pay in full, and said he'll swing by later with a
cheque.'

Something inside me lifted a little. 'That's very decent of him.'

'Isn't it?' She brought the sweet peas to her nose and absently sniffed them. 'He also said he's planning to host a wedding fair at Hudson Grange next month, and asked if I'd liked to set up a stall there.'

'Wow, that's nice.' I wondered why he was phoning today, with all the preparations that must be going on.

'He sounds lovely,' she said, looking puzzled. 'Not at all like I'd imagined he would be, from what I've heard. Although Jane thinks he's marvellous.'

'I know.'

'Everything's looking up since you came here, Carrie.' Emotional again, she put down the flowers. Worried she was moving in for more hugging, knowing it would set me off crying if she did, I bent and rearranged some asters, accidentally dislodging a couple of petals.

'It sounded like he had his hands full,' Ruby said, as if she'd just remembered. 'He was having to phone round and tell people the wedding was off.'

I stood up so fast I got a head rush. 'What did you say?'

'Apparently, the wedding's off.' Her eyes grew large, as understanding dawned. 'Oh, Carrie, does this mean that Tom... that you and him?' She blinked. 'Carrie, what does it mean?'

'I don't know,' I said. I was breathing too fast and everything looked brighter, as if someone had injected me with a mood-altering substance. 'It might not mean anything.'

Ruby seized my hands. 'Then don't you think you should find out?'

Chapter 36

I ran to my car, Ruby's words ringing in my ears.

The wedding was off.

Questions clawed my brain. Had Megan developed a conscience and told Tom the truth? It seemed unlikely, considering her glittery-eyed vehemence the day before.

Which meant Tom had ended things. But why, when Megan had been at pains to tell me how close they'd grown after the night at the restaurant? What could have changed his mind so close to the big day?

And why hadn't I heard from him? Or was I being presumptuous, assuming events had anything to do with me?

Maybe he'd somehow found out that Megan wasn't pregnant. But how?

What if he was ill, or had been in an accident?

Unable to bear not knowing, even if I ended up making a fool of myself, I decided to drive over to the vet's to see if he was there.

'This is stupid,' I said to the flower-pups, eyeing me wonkily in the rear-view mirror as I headed to Nightingale Lane. 'He's probably not even working today, not when his wedding's been called off.' Bride-pup seemed to cock a sympathetic ear, but it was only the effect of me taking a corner too fast. 'Anyway, I'm probably the last person he wants to see.' Groom-pup appeared to concede I had a point. 'Thanks a lot,' I huffed. 'What would you know? You're made of flowers and they're not even real.' He seemed offended. 'OK, I'm sorry, that was uncalled for.'

This was madness. I was talking to an inanimate object on my way to see a man who probably wasn't in the mood for visitors, and I had no idea what I was going to say when I got there.

It reminded me of the night of Tom's twenty-first. I was even rehearsing opening lines in my head.

'Tom, I've just heard the news, I'm so sorry...'

'Aunt Ruby had a call from your father, and mentioned the wedding's been cancelled...'

'Tom, if you ever need to talk...'

Oh, sod it, I'd play it by ear when I got there.

I lowered the window, breathing in through my nose and out through my mouth to a count of eight, which is what Jasmine would have advised. It wouldn't do to burst in – *was I really planning to burst in?* – looking demented.

As I turned into Nightingale Lane and slowed outside the primary school, I spotted Tom's Land Rover in the small parking area at the vet's.

My heart-rate tripled.

I'd half expected him to be at Hudson Grange, appeasing his father and handling Megan, but I knew when things were tough he'd find solace at work.

I quickly checked my appearance in the mirror. My hair was bigger than I'd have liked and my eyes were slitty, and I was wearing the clothes I'd slept in, but there was nothing I could do about that.

'He won't notice,' I said to the flower-pups. 'Stop looking at me like that.'

I stepped out of the car and froze.

Megan had emerged from the vet's and was hurrying towards me.

Her head was down, her hair up in a bun, her eyes shielded by sunglasses. Her outfit looked thrown on – white sneakers with ripped white jeans, and a thin, blue, zip-up cardigan. She had a cardboard box tucked under one arm, her handbag over the other, and wasn't looking where she was going.

The temptation to dive into my car and hide was overwhelming, but she was almost in front of me, and sensing this would be my last opportunity to speak to her, I said, 'Hello, Megan.'

It was hardly a ground-breaking opener, but it had the effect of stopping her in her tracks. 'Oh, it's you.' She shimmied her bag onto her shoulder and took off her shades. Her gaze dug into me like barbed wire. 'Bad news travels fast.'

'I was just…' I gestured vaguely, heat flooding my cheeks as I realised how it looked.

'Rushing to console him?' Her mouth twisted in a smirk. 'He's in bits in there,' she said. 'I was just picking up some of my stuff.' She indicated the box under her arm. 'Some of the underwear he bought me for my birthday.'

I didn't respond. I knew she wasn't going to tell me what had happened, and I wasn't going to ask. Apart from anything, I didn't trust her to tell the truth.

'You're leaving Shipley?'

She elevated an eyebrow. 'Jay offered me a job a while back, not that it's any of your business. He's hoping to expand abroad,' she said, as though it was normal to be considering a career change when her cherished wedding plans had just gone up in smoke.

'Will you go?'

She slipped her sunglasses back on so I couldn't see her eyes – only my rumpled reflection. 'Why not?' she said, with an airiness that wasn't even forced.

'And what about Tom?'

She hunched a shoulder. 'You win some, you lose some,' she said, adjusting her bag. 'I gave it my best shot, it didn't work out, so...' Another shrug. 'Time to move on.'

I goggled, partly in awe at her ability to reshape her life in an instant, but mostly in horror at how little she appeared to care about what she'd done. Had it all been a game, but now the cards were on the table she was content to throw in her hand?

Or was it all an act?

'Maybe you should go to Canada and make peace with your father, and get to know your half-siblings.' I hadn't meant to say that. I'd intended to bring her to task for being a scheming bitch, and to tell her she deserved to be miserable for the next ten years. Clearly, my brain had other ideas, as I added, 'I don't think you'll ever be happy until you love yourself.'

Her smirk sagged.

A weighty silence swelled.

The sun beat down. Gentle birdsong in an overhanging tree competed with the distant chime of an ice-cream van. It seemed almost obscene that the day was so determinedly bright. Thunderbolts and zigzag lightning would have been more fitting.

'He doesn't want you, you know.' Megan's chin lifted, and I detected a tiny quiver in her lower lip. 'He blames you for bringing things to a head.'

As her words burrowed in, my heart shrank.

'Think about it,' she said, gaining ground. 'If he cared, wouldn't he have spoken to you by now?'

I stayed silent, not knowing what to say.

'I guess this is goodbye, then.' She was more cheerful now, as if sensing her barb had landed where it hurt. Raising her sunglasses, she looked at my hair as though it was crawling with lice. 'I hope I never set eyes on you again.'

I finally found some words, knowing they wouldn't be what she wanted to hear.

'Goodbye, Megan. I hope you find whatever it is you're looking for.'

Before she could retaliate, I got into my car and drove slowly down the road, watching her in the wing mirror. She grew smaller, and looked a little forlorn with her box and her bag, her bun tilting to one side, and despite everything, I felt a bit sorry for her.

Then she spun around and stalked to her car, which I'd failed to notice earlier, and threw her things inside.

I braked, holding my breath until she'd driven off, then reversed back to the vet's and parked alongside Tom's Land Rover.

'Can I help you?'

The receptionist was staring at her computer screen, the glare bouncing off her glasses so it looked like she had no eyes.

'Could I speak to Tom Hudson, please?'

'He's not working today.' She gave a bristle, like a tiger protecting its cub, and I guessed his confrontation with Megan hadn't gone unnoticed. 'You could speak to one of the other vets.'

'I don't have an animal,' I said, backing away, knocking into a woman who'd come in with a cat stuffed into a basket. It yowled, and tried to lash out at me, but only succeeded in bashing its paw on the wire.

'Now look what you've done.' The woman gave me a dirty look. 'There, there, Tabitha,' she soothed, as the cat bared her fangs. 'She's here for her check-up,' she added to the receptionist, and while they were engrossed I slipped out, and round the side of the building to the little courtyard.

Hovis was on his belly, chewing a rubber monkey, but jumped up when he saw me, wagging his tail.

'Hey there, boy.' I scratched him under his chin, and he rolled on his back and offered his tummy for rubbing. I crouched down and indulged him, feeling the roar of my heartbeat in my ears.

What if Tom didn't want to see me? He'd probably had enough for one day. For a lifetime.

I stood up, wiping my clammy palms on my shorts. He could always tell me to go, but I wanted – needed – to know he was OK.

I gave a light knock on the open door and stepped inside, letting my eyes adjust. The kitchen was empty, a mug by the sink, and an open tin of dog food by Hovis's bowl.

'Tom?'

I ducked through a low wooden door, into a small sunny hallway with a couple of open doors leading off it. 'Tom?'

I was surprised he couldn't hear the thud of my heart, and nearly jumped out of my skin when he appeared at the top of the narrow staircase.

'Carrie?' He ran halfway down and stopped, one hand on the banister, staring as if I was a phantom. 'What are you doing here?'

'I – I'm sorry,' I stuttered, clasping my fingers together to stop them shaking. 'The door was open, and I—'

'No, I mean in Shipley.' He jumped down the last few steps and stood in front of me, just like he had on the night of his twenty-first, only this time his hair was rumpled and he hadn't shaved.

'Where else would I be?' It was a poor attempt at levity, which I instantly regretted when his eyebrows knitted together.

'Megan said she spoke to you on Wednesday, and you told her you were going back to Manchester.'

My insides drooped. 'And you believed her, because she's such a pillar of honesty.'

'Carrie.' He took a step closer, and I smelt something lemony. His wrinkled T-shirt was damp, as if he'd had a quick shower and not dried himself properly. 'I went to your aunt's after surgery on Wednesday, to talk you, but your car wasn't there.' He reached out his hand then let it drop. 'I knocked, but there was no answer.'

I remembered driving Kate back to Christchurch and Ruby, over-excited in the flat, with music blasting out of the television.

'You could have come to the stall,' I said shakily.

'I did, the next morning, but your aunt was there…'

'Why didn't you talk to her?'

'She was so busy.' He combed his fingers through his hair. 'I suppose I took it as confirmation that you'd gone, but I know I should have double-checked.'

'It's OK.' I shook my head, hating how smudged and weary his eyes looked. 'It doesn't matter now.'

'You know the wedding's off?'

I nodded. 'Did she tell you she wasn't pregnant?' I tried not to feel like a schoolkid telling tales. 'It was her stepmother's baby photo.'

'She didn't have to,' he said, a tremor in his voice. 'I caught her stuffing her face with Mr Kipling's French Fancies.'

Random. 'Well, they are quite tasty—'

'She never eats cakes.' His voice sounded odd. 'She looked so guilty, I just knew.'

The penny dropped. 'She was doing it to look pregnant.'

His white-lipped silence said it all.

'Oh god, Tom, I'm so sorry.'

His eyes were glassy with tears. 'I suppose I'd got used to the idea.' His voice caught. 'How could she do that?'

I felt a wrench inside. 'I don't know,' I said. 'Maybe she wanted it to be true.'

'She didn't even sound that sorry when she admitted she'd lied.' A trace of anger entered his voice, and I guessed he'd been going over it all in his head. 'It was almost like she'd been playing a game where only she knew the rules, but once it was up...'

'She decided it was time to move on.'

'Exactly.' He rubbed his eyes with the heels of his hands. 'As soon as I told him, my father fired her,' he said heavily. 'It turned out he'd had his suspicions, and even before that he said she'd been getting too cut-throat, offering to buy properties for less than they were worth, even though he'd told her he doesn't operate like that anymore.' His breath came out in a jagged sigh. 'She'd bigged up her mother's royal connections, apparently. I think he'd been half expecting an introduction to the queen.'

'Oh, Tom, I don't know what to say.' My mind swirled. 'I suppose at least it's brought you and your father closer.'

'There is that.' A brief smile appeared. 'He offered to let everyone know the wedding was off, and I'm afraid I left him to it.' His mouth tightened again. 'Megan just came to tell me she was keeping the engagement ring, and to take back the coffee maker she bought me.'

So, that's what had been in the box. 'Charming.'

'I didn't really like it anyway.'

At last, something seemed to fall away from him, and as our eyes locked together my mind scrolled back to the night of Tom's twenty-first. It hadn't all been Megan's fault. Tom had had issues, trying to break free from his father, and I wasn't equipped to deal with it, or brave enough to hold out for what I wanted.

Maybe the timing hadn't been right for us then. Or later, when I was with Sam, and Tom was tending to horses up in Scotland.

He cleared his throat, seeming to refocus. 'How... how's Cooper?'

'Sorry?' It took a second for my brain to catch up. 'Oh, listen, I'm sorry about the other night.' My cheeks pulsated. 'He got drunk, and I behaved like an idiot.'

Tom's face had regained some colour. 'He seemed nice,' he said evenly.

'His real name's Toby.' I might as well come clean. 'He's a painter and decorator, and I doubt he's ever been to Budapest. Oh, and he's still in love with his wife.'

Tom seemed to digest this for a moment, his gaze soft. 'And how do you feel?'

My stomach squeezed with longing. 'How do you think?'

His gaze grew intense, and desire tore through me, so strong I was surprised I was still standing.

'Carrie.' His mouth twitched, as if words were fighting to get out. 'I just...'

He was *so* handsome. 'Go on.'

'It's just... if it was my twenty-first tonight, and you turned up in that gorgeous dress, with your smile, and that hair...' He paused, his eyes burning into mine. 'I can't imagine letting you go, and not telling you I loved you.'

'Loved?' It was obvious from the heat in his eyes what he was trying to say, but I wanted to hear it.

'That I *love* you.'

Joy fizzed through me, like a rocket going off. 'And you're not just rebounding from finding out about... because you might need some time to—'

'I'm not rebounding,' he said, looking more like his old self with every second that passed. 'If anything, I'm bouncing to where I want to be.'

I gave a blurt of laughter. 'That's terrible,' I said, giddy with happiness.

'I know, I'm sorry, but it's true.'

As I closed the gap between us, Hovis ran in and dropped his rubber monkey. His damp brown eyes darted hopefully between us.

'I think he wants a walk.'

'I think you're right.'

When I looked at him, I read in Tom's face all the memories we shared, which had bound us together through the years like the pages of a book, and I knew that this was where I was always supposed to end up.

As I straightened, I spotted a holdall standing by the front door. 'Were you going somewhere?'

'I was.' Tom reached for my hand and drew me gently to him. 'I was coming to Manchester to find you.'

My heart skipped. 'You were?'

He gave a solemn nod. 'Another five minutes and you'd have missed me.'

His face came closer, and finally his arms were around me and his lips were on mine, and our first kiss was everything I'd always dreamed it would be, despite my phone vibrating halfway through.

'Sounds like I'm not the only one who wants you.' Tom's voice was husky with longing and I gave him another, lingering kiss before reluctantly taking my phone out.

'Sorry,' I said, light-headed with bliss, 'but it might be my first cousin once removed.' I laughed at his puzzled look, amazed by how right it felt to be standing in his hallway, Hovis hovering by the door. 'I've so much to tell you,' I said.

The first text was from Mum. *We'll be at Ruby's by six, will you be there? Xx*

I quickly typed *Yes xx*

The second was from Kate. *Dad's agreed to meet Ruby, and promised not to go off on one. He's thinking next weekend if you can arrange it, and I thought while they talk me and you could hang out for a bit. Is that OK? Xxx*

I bit my lip. I was supposed to be going back to Manchester tonight. I was almost certain Tom would come too, if I asked him, and perhaps might even stay, but his home was in Shipley, and I suspected he loved living here.

And so did I.

Of course, I would have to return, to sort out the house; perhaps call Jasmine's bluff and ask her to buy it. And I needed to find a job, but there was bound to be someone in Shipley who needed help with their accounts. I could always ask Doris to keep her ear to the ground, and I was sure that Ruby wouldn't mind if I stayed with her a bit longer.

'What is it?' A furrow of anxiety appeared between Tom's brows. 'Is something wrong?'

I looked at him, my world shifting and rebalancing. 'Tom, do you want me to stay?'

He didn't hesitate. 'More than anything, if you want to.'

Joy bubbled through my veins. 'Yes, please.'

I typed, *Can't wait xxx* and hit 'send'.

'OK?' Tom's face had cleared.

'Couldn't be better.'

I knew we would talk about Megan again, while we came to terms with her lies, but for now it was just the two of us, striking out in a new direction.

Finally.

Our smiles were huge, and through the open doorway I spotted a jug of pink and blue flowers on the table in the living room; the asters I'd given Tom. *A talisman of love and a symbol of patience.*

'Shall we go for that walk now?' I said, holding out my hand. 'I think Hovis has waited long enough.'

A Letter from Karen

It's been wonderful to revisit Shipley, and to write Carrie and Tom's story, and I've loved researching how to run a flower stall – which isn't easy, it turns out! But where nicer to have a stall than opposite the beach, in summertime?

I have lovely memories of my grandfather growing flowers, particularly roses, carnations, and sweet peas, which smell so evocative, and enjoyed learning about their meanings and symbolism. I now find myself choosing flowers to suit an occasion.

I'm already looking forward to returning to Shipley for my next book, which has a lovely Christmassy theme. I hope you'll come back to find out what everyone's been up to, and to meet some new characters.

Writers like to know if they're getting it right, so if you enjoyed *The Beachside Flower Stall*, and feel like popping a review online, it would mean a lot. Just a line or two will do.

If you'd like to contact me with thoughts and feedback, I'd love to hear from you, or you can sign up to my email list below:

www.bookouture.com/karen-clarke/

www.writewritingwritten.blogspot.com

 karen.clarke.5682

karenclarke123

Acknowledgments

A lot of people are involved in making a book, and I would like to thank the award-winning Bookouture team for making it happen. Particular thanks to my wonderful editor, Abi, for her clever and insightful comments, to Anne for her seamless copy-editing, Emma for the gorgeous cover, and Kim Nash, for spreading the word.

Special thanks to flower sellers, Paula's Petals in Aylesbury, and Somora at Flower Love London for answering my questions. I've learnt a lot, but couldn't do what you ladies do – your days start far too early!

As ever, I owe my lovely readers a massive thank you, as well as the blogging community, whose reviews are a labour of love, and Amanda Brittany, for her tireless feedback and friendship.

And last, but never least, thank you to my family and friends for their constant encouragement, my children, Amy, Martin and Liam, for their unwavering support, and my husband Tim for everything – I couldn't do it without you.

Made in the USA
Columbia, SC
05 July 2018